WESTERN

Rugged men looking for love...

The Cowboy's Christmas Treasures
Jill Kemerer

Christmas On The Ranch
Jennifer Slattery

MILLS & BOON

THE COWBOY'S CHRISTMAS TREASURES
© 2024 by Ripple Effect Press, LLC
Philippine Copyright 2024
Australian Copyright 2024
New Zealand Copyright 2024

First Published 2024
First Australian Paperback Edition 2024
ISBN 978 1 038 93560 1

CHRISTMAS ON THE RANCH
© 2024 by Jennifer Slattery
Philippine Copyright 2024
Australian Copyright 2024
New Zealand Copyright 2024

First Published 2024
First Australian Paperback Edition 2024
ISBN 978 1 038 93560 1

MIX
Paper | Supporting
responsible forestry
FSC® C001695
www.fsc.org

Published by
Harlequin Mills & Boon
An imprint of Harlequin Enterprises (Australia) Pty Limited
(ABN 47 001 180 918), a subsidiary of HarperCollins
Publishers Australia Pty Limited
(ABN 36 009 913 517)
Level 19, 201 Elizabeth Street
SYDNEY NSW 2000 AUSTRALIA

Cover art used by arrangement with Harlequin Books S.A.. All rights reserved.

Printed and bound in Australia by McPherson's Printing Group

The Cowboy's Christmas Tresures

Jill Kemerer

MILLS & BOON

Jill Kemerer writes novels with love, humor and faith. Besides spoiling her mini dachshund and keeping up with her busy kids, Jill reads stacks of books, lives for her morning coffee and gushes over fluffy animals. She resides in Ohio with her husband and two children. Jill loves connecting with readers, so please visit her website, jillkemerer.com, or contact her at PO Box 2802, Whitehouse, OH 43571.

Books by Jill Kemerer

Wyoming Legacies

The Cowboy's Christmas Compromise
United by the Twins
Training the K-9 Companion
The Cowboy's Christmas Treasures

Wyoming Ranchers

The Prodigal's Holiday Hope
A Cowboy to Rely On
Guarding His Secret
The Mistletoe Favor
Depending on the Cowboy
The Cowboy's Little Secret

Visit the Author Profile page at millsandboon.com.au for more titles.

I can do all things through Christ
which strengtheneth me.
—*Philippians* 4:13

To my incredible husband, Scott.
You never complain about the stacks of books
I leave around the house. You put up with my
irrational fear of spiders. You accept the fact I
need a minimum of five bottles of half-and-half in
the fridge at any given moment, and I never worry
about my car because you're on top of it. I love you.
Merry Christmas!

CHAPTER ONE

"HE'S GOING TO make a good daddy." Brooke Dewitt unpacked empty jars next to her sister-in-law, Reagan Young, who was stirring wax in a warmer at the dining room table. Reagan had offered to help her make homemade candles for Christmas gifts, so Brooke had brought her almost-two-year-old identical twin daughters over to her brother's ranch. The twenty-minute drive from her house in downtown Jewel River, Wyoming, had been easy for mid-November, with no snow yet. Her brother, Marc, was currently in the living room giving Megan and Alice horsey rides. Their squeals and laughter melted her heart into a puddle.

She would do anything for her girls.

"I agree." Reagan rubbed her tiny baby bump. "Marc's going to be a great father."

"He's protective." Brooke hooked a finger around her low ponytail to bring it over her shoulder. "But fun, too."

"You're right about that." Reagan's light brown eyes twinkled. "He still worries about you, you know."

"I know. I don't mind." She spoke the truth. Marc had been more of a father figure to her than their own dad had been before he'd left when she was twelve and Marc was sixteen.

Brooke appreciated the sacrifices Marc and their mother had made over the years, especially the recent ones.

It was hard to believe it had been over eighteen months since Brooke had had the stroke. Being separated from her infant twins for four weeks had devastated her. Almost as much as when she'd found out her husband had died in a helicopter accident while on a training mission overseas. Ross had known she was pregnant, but he hadn't known she was carrying twins.

He'd never met his beautiful girls.

The twins would never have a daddy. She couldn't in good conscience dip her toes in the dating pool, not when she had no plans to get remarried. She wouldn't be having more children, either. The risk of a postpartum stroke was too high. They'd already lost their father. They couldn't lose their mommy, too.

"I still can't believe Ed had a heart attack." Reagan checked the temperature of the wax. Yesterday, local builder Ed McCaffrey had collapsed at his office in town. Brenda, his administrative assistant, had called 911 and performed CPR until the ambulance arrived. She'd likely saved his life.

"I feel so bad for him. It's horrible." A metallic taste developed in her mouth. She hoped he made a full recovery, and not just because he was remodeling her house. "I can't believe it, either."

"I mean, he's always been so full of life. And he's nice. He did an amazing job renovating my chocolate shop. And your mom's bakery."

"He's the best." Brooke couldn't trust herself to speak beyond that. She'd hired Ed's company, McCaffrey Construction, to renovate the three-bedroom home she'd bought this summer in downtown Jewel River. Ed hadn't flinched when she'd explained that she needed the house to be wheelchair accessible in case she had another stroke and ended up with a temporary or permanent disability. By now, most of the renovations had been completed. The halls and doorways had been widened, and vinyl plank flooring had been installed throughout.

But the gutted main bathroom needed tons of work, and the outdoor ramp leading to the back door hadn't been started. If she did have another stroke, she wanted to recover at home. She needed to be prepared for the worst-case scenario.

"When do you think Ed will be released from the hospital?"

Brooke shrugged. "Mom's been texting me with any updates she hears at the bakery, but no one seems to know much at this point."

"Do you think this will set back your renovations?"

"I don't know. Probably." She leaned forward to insert the wicks into the empty jars. "Hopefully, he has a backup plan for emergencies."

"I'm sure he does. And if it takes a few more weeks to finish your house, it takes a few more weeks. Everything will get done eventually." Reagan always knew the right thing to say. Her sister-in-law had a way of easing her mind without even trying.

But what if Ed didn't have a backup plan? Worse, what if he died?

Death was all too real in her world. She'd lost her husband over two years ago and had come close to losing her own life not long after the twins were born. She couldn't bear the thought of kind, capable Ed McCaffrey dying. Thanksgiving was only a week away. And then Christmas. What would it do to his son, Dean?

"The wax is the right temperature. Are you ready to add the fragrance?" Reagan selected a bottle marked Cinnamon and measured it into a small cup on a scale.

"Sure." Brooke rounded the table to stand next to her. "What do I do?"

"Pour this into the wax."

Brooke followed her directions, but it was difficult to concentrate with Ed's health on her mind. Reagan had her repeat the process with the vanilla fragrance.

"How do you feel about Dean staying with you guys?" Brooke asked as Reagan stirred.

"I'm glad." She checked the wax's temperature again. "No one should be alone during those first days following a crisis."

"True. Did he say how long he's staying?" While Dean McCaffrey and Marc had been best friends since elementary school, Brooke had never been close to him. She'd always liked Dean in a little sister type of way. Now that they were both grown-up, she'd noticed him in a mature woman type of way. And it unsettled her.

Dean had been a groomsman in Marc and Reagan's wedding this past spring, but Brooke's hands had been full as a bridesmaid and with the twins being flower girls. She hadn't spent much time with him. He'd been living in Texas for over a decade. He was more handsome now than she remembered. Quieter, too. More reserved. More intriguing.

"Marc seems to think he'll be here for a while," Reagan said. "Maybe Dean will take over your remodeling projects while Ed recovers."

"I can't imagine why he would. Although he does have the experience. He worked for his father all through high school."

"That's what Marc said. Don't worry, it will all work out." She called over her shoulder, "Hey, Marc, when do you think Dean will get here?"

A thumping sound, giggles and footsteps greeted them.

"Soon, I imagine." Marc carried Megan under one arm and Alice under the other. Their faces were red as they laughed and kicked.

"Unc Mawc, down!" Alice shouted.

"If I set you down, the tickle monster might get you." He grinned at Alice, then at Megan, who squealed.

He carefully set them on the floor, then bent and wiggled his fingers at them. They both took off running, screaming the whole way. Then he planted a kiss on Reagan's cheek and leaned over to take a whiff of the wax warmer.

"Smells like Mom's bakery. Are you sure these are candles and not her cinnamon buns?"

"That's what we're going for. Cinnamon Bun Surprise," Reagan said, snuggling into his side. She'd operated a successful candle business with her mother and sister for years before moving to Jewel River. Now she owned R. Mayer Chocolates, a gourmet chocolate store in town.

Brooke couldn't have picked a better bride for her brother. And while she loved that they were so affectionate, it always brought a pang to her chest. She'd had that kind of love once. And she wouldn't have it again.

"I'm surprised Dean isn't staying at his dad's house." Brooke craned her neck to check on the girls. As if on cue, they scampered back into the dining room. Each grabbed one of Marc's legs, pulling on his jeans to pick them up.

"Girls, leave Uncle Marc alone. He's played with you since we got here." She wiped her hands with a paper towel. "Come on. It's time to settle down. I'm putting on a Christmas movie for you."

The girls were infatuated with Christmas cartoons. She found the remote and helped the girls get settled on the couch. Then she unfolded a red-and-green-plaid throw blanket and tucked it over their legs.

"There. Cozy?" She bopped the tips of each of their noses with her index finger and gave them both a smile.

"Yes, Mama." They held their arms out for a hug. She hugged them and straightened. "I'm helping Auntie Reagan with the candles, so come get me if you need anything, okay?"

"Okay."

She returned to the dining room, keeping an eye on the twins as she took a seat. Both girls had their eyes glued to the screen. Reagan was placing metal clips on top of the jars to keep the wicks in place. "Ready to fill these?"

"Yep." Brooke followed her instructions and carefully filled each jar. Then she stepped back and admired their handiwork.

The candles looked great. In a day or two, after they'd cooled, she would apply the labels Reagan had printed for them. She couldn't wait to give them to her friends this Christmas.

"I told Dean he could stay here for as long as he wants." Marc rested his forearms on the table. "He mainly needs a place to stable Dusty."

"He's bringing his horse?" Brooke was taken aback. Why would he do that?

"He's dealing with a lot. He basically dropped everything to drive here."

What did "drop everything" mean? Before she could ask, a knock on the front door had them all turning their heads. Marc got up and hurried down the hallway.

"Looks like we finished just in time." Reagan turned off the wax warmer, while Brooke stood to pack away the other supplies. "I can drop these off after I close up tomorrow if you want."

Just one of the perks of buying the house in town. Reagan's chocolate shop, their mother's bakery and her mom's bungalow were within a few blocks of her house. Brooke had been grateful it had gone up for sale in the summer. She'd waited for the big renovations to be completed before moving out of her mom's place. Everyone told her to wait until all the projects were completed, but Brooke needed her independence.

She also needed to be able to recover from a medical emergency at home. With her girls.

The stroke had robbed her of her peace of mind. Every day she worried about having another one. If only the renovations were finished…

But she knew Reagan had spoken the truth earlier. The house would get finished at some point. Brooke would have to trust the Lord would provide what she needed.

The sound of the front door opening forced her thoughts back to where they belonged. On Dean. Poor guy was standing on the doorstep and probably terrified of losing his father. The man needed support and compassion. Her problems would have to wait.

As THE DOOR OPENED, Dean felt the first stirrings of hope since finding out his father—his larger-than-life dad—had collapsed from a heart attack. The light from inside the house glowed, and Marc didn't say a word, just pulled him in for a big hug.

Dean hadn't realized how much he'd needed that hug until Marc stepped back. "Come inside."

"I've got to take care of Dusty first." After getting Brenda's call yesterday, it was as if a switch inside him had flipped. It was time to make changes. He'd been living a shell of a life for over ten years.

Dean had immediately quit his job as a ranch hand. Then he'd packed his meager belongings, hitched his horse trailer to his truck, loaded Dusty in it and driven from Texas straight to the hospital in Casper. He'd called Marc on the way and had slumped in relief when Marc had insisted he stay with him and Reagan. Their ranch was forty minutes closer to the hospital than his dad's house on the other side of Jewel River.

That wasn't the main reason he wanted to stay with them, though. He had unfinished business at his childhood home. And he wasn't ready to deal with it.

"What else needs to be done?" Marc asked.

"Nothing."

"You know the way to the stables. I'll join you in a minute. Let me grab a coat."

Shivering as the cold air seeped through his unzipped jacket, Dean headed back to his truck. *Take care of Dusty. Then do the next thing. And the next.*

Before coming here, he'd stopped at the hospital. His father had been in the middle of a procedure, and the staff had advised Dean to come back in the morning.

His dad was probably hooked up to a million machines.

What was going to happen with McCaffrey Construction while he recovered? If he recovered…

Dean couldn't go there. Couldn't imagine the world without his dad in it.

The drive to the stables took all of two minutes. As his boots hit the gravel, the reality of what he was facing smacked him.

Dad might die. Even if he survived, Dean would likely be in town for a while. While he appreciated Marc and Reagan's hospitality, he didn't want to overstay his welcome. At some point, he'd have to move—temporarily—into Dad's place. The furniture and appliances had been updated, but everything else, except the basement, was the way he'd left it as a twenty-one-year-old college dropout.

He only had bad memories of that time in his life. He hadn't dealt with them, and he didn't want to. That was just one of the reasons he hadn't come back all that often during the past ten years.

As he stepped out of the truck, the reality of his situation overwhelmed him. *God, You aren't going to let him die, are You?*

During the long drive here, Dean had scrambled to remember every detail of the last time he'd been with his father. Their last phone conversation. The last text messages. Would there be any more? His father's health teetered on the edge.

Heart attack. Open heart surgery. Triple bypass. What did it all mean?

Icy blasts burrowed under his coat collar as a familiar sense of bleakness filled him. At least this time, he had friends to count on. He was older, wiser than the night ten years ago when his life had fallen apart.

Dean strode to the door of the stables. It slid open easily, and he switched on the lights before heading down the aisle in search of an empty stall. The scent of straw and dust and manure made him feel at home. Not surprising. It had taken a job on a ranch to save him from himself.

Within minutes, he'd led Dusty out of the trailer and gotten the horse settled into a stall. He was in the middle of filling a bucket with water when Marc strode his way.

"How are you holding up?"

"About as good as can be expected." He finished watering the horse, patted his neck one more time, then headed out of the barn with Marc. "I appreciate you and Reagan letting me crash here."

"Anytime. You're like my brother."

"You're the closest thing to a brother I have. It means a lot to me." Unlike Marc, Dean didn't have siblings. Didn't have a mother, either. She'd moved away after his parents divorced, disappearing from his life altogether.

"Stay as long as you need."

"I won't impose long. Just until I find out what's happening with Dad."

"You're not imposing." Marc put his hand on Dean's shoulder. "I want you around."

His throat grew thick with emotion. They piled into Dean's truck and drove back to the house.

The velvety black sky seemed to stretch forever as they walked to the house's side entry. Inside the mudroom, Dean took off his cowboy boots and hung his coat and Stetson on a hook on the wall. After washing up, he followed Marc into the kitchen. The place smelled like cinnamon. Overhead lights spread a cheerful glow as they passed the living room, where he caught a glimpse of two cute toddlers almost asleep on the couch. Brooke's girls. He recognized them from the wedding.

A Christmas tune played from a cartoon on TV. Christmas—another thing he couldn't bear to think about at the moment. Up ahead in the dining room, Brooke and Reagan stood side by side with matching sympathetic expressions.

Reagan was the first to step forward. She gave him a brief hug. "I'm so sorry, Dean."

Then Brooke approached, and he forgot how to breathe.

She'd captivated him at the wedding. How could anyone ignore her beauty? Her shiny black hair was tied back and pulled over her shoulder, and she looked up at him through enormous dark blue eyes. She had a casual style, and her figure could only be described as curvy.

As far as he could tell, she was perfect in every way.

She embraced him, and he wanted to sink into her arms for eternity. But, like all things, the hug ended too soon.

A bunch of jars took up one side of the dining table. Candles, he guessed. The cinnamon aroma grew stronger as he sat down.

"I'll put on a pot of decaf." Reagan flitted across the room toward the kitchen. "Marc, could you help me?"

He nodded and left Dean alone with Brooke, who pulled out a chair across from him at the table.

"It's a lot to take in, isn't it?" Her big eyes shimmered with compassion.

"Yeah, it is." He wiped his hand down his cheek as exhaustion took over. He'd been driving all day with only a few stops for gas and fast food.

"One minute everything's fine, and the next?" Her right shoulder lifted in a shrug. She tossed her head to the side as if to say, *What do you do?*

"Your dad has a heart attack followed by triple bypass surgery," he finished for her.

She reached over and covered his hand with hers. Her touch eased his tension. "How is he?"

"I'm not sure. He was having a procedure when I left the hospital. They wouldn't let me see him. Told me to come back in the morning."

"If you want to go back and stay there, Marc will take care of your horse." Her long eyelashes fluttered as she blinked.

Should he go back? Was that expected? He was too tired to even think straight.

"But you should probably stay here and get some sleep," she said. "Try not to worry. He's in good hands."

"How can you be sure?"

"I spent a week at the same hospital when I had my stroke. The staff knows what to do." How could she speak so calmly about it? He still couldn't wrap his brain around the fact she'd had a stroke. Brooke was so vibrant. "In the meantime, we're here for you. Whatever you need."

"Thank you." As he stared into her enormous eyes, it hit him again how much they'd both changed in the past ten years. He'd never been close to Brooke. She'd always seemed so much younger than him and Marc. She didn't anymore. "I have to ask, though. What have I ever done for you? Why would you offer to help me?"

She averted her gaze as if she wasn't sure how to answer. "Because your father means a lot to this town, and you're my brother's best friend. I understand how tough times rip your world apart like a tornado."

And there it was.

Reality.

His father did mean a lot to Jewel River. Ed McCaffrey was the guy everyone called to have their homes built, businesses refurbished, kitchens remodeled. His dad was reliable, dependable, and he excelled at everything he touched.

Basically, he was everything Dean was not. An alarming thought came to him. Would the town expect Dean to fill in at McCaffrey Construction while his dad recovered?

Those shoes were too big to fill. Always had been.

Marc returned and pulled out a chair to take a seat. "We've got you in the spare bedroom upstairs."

Reagan followed and sat, too. "I'm glad you're staying with us, Dean."

"Thank you. I appreciate it." He'd liked Reagan from the second he'd met her. She didn't have a mean bone in her body.

"I'll be out of your hair soon. But it's tricky because I don't have anywhere else to keep Dusty."

"You're not in our hair," Marc said. "You and Dusty can stay with us for as long as you want. I wish you weren't back under these circumstances, but it sure is good to see you."

Two beeps brought Reagan to her feet. Brooke followed her to the kitchen, and Dean watched them until they disappeared from view.

The emotions he'd been stuffing down since getting Brenda's call bubbled to the surface. He wasn't sure how much longer he could avoid the fear. What he needed was some time to himself.

"I'm pretty tired." He spoke the truth. He also knew he'd be awake for hours.

"Let's get you settled. Then you can have a couple of Mom's leftover doughnuts and some decaf. It will do you good."

"I can't argue with that." And he wouldn't, even if he could.

Dean forced himself to his feet and went outside to get his bags from the truck. Minutes later, he followed Marc upstairs to the guest room. Rubbed his temples with the span of one hand.

"Come down when you're ready." Marc clapped him on the shoulder and left the room.

Ready? He didn't think he'd ever be ready. The scene in the dining room had been what he'd been avoiding for a decade. A home. A life. A family. Things he couldn't—wouldn't—have.

If only he hadn't been such a hothead at twenty-one. He'd left town in a rush with get-rich-quick plans and the wrong people along for the ride. Within a year, the situation had unraveled, and one night had changed everything. He'd lost his job, his girlfriend and his self-respect.

That was why he'd started over as a ranch hand in northern Texas. And closed himself off to everything else.

"Dean, do you take cream or sugar?" Reagan yelled from the staircase.

He tilted his head back and gazed at the ceiling. They'd welcomed him into their home. Were fine with him and his horse being here indefinitely. He couldn't stay up here and avoid them, no matter how much he wanted to.

"Cream, please!" He tightened his jaw. Having to socialize with his well-meaning friends wasn't easy. He'd been a loner for ten long years. And now he had a feeling he was going to be thrust into the community, whether he wanted to be or not.

It was time to face facts. If Dad recovered, he *would* expect Dean to step in and manage the current projects. And if he didn't recover?

Dean would have to finish what he could and cancel anything that hadn't been started.

He didn't belong in Jewel River. Didn't know where he did belong, either, but it wasn't here.

In the next month or two, Dean would start over. Somewhere new. Somewhere that didn't tempt him to believe he could have the kind of life guys his age had.

He'd gotten off easy the last time his world had tipped over. His anger hadn't caused any permanent damage. But that was a blessing—and he couldn't risk a repeat.

CHAPTER TWO

"YOU JUST ASKED me that, Mom." Brooke propped her cell phone between her ear and her shoulder as she opened the door to the community center on Tuesday evening. She'd dropped off the twins at her mother's house a few minutes ago. "Okay, I'll try to find out. I'm walking in now. Love you."

Her leg was bothering her today. She hadn't slept well, and the damaged muscles weren't happy about it. Most of the time, no one was able to tell she'd had a stroke. On days like this, though, her limp made it obvious to the world that something wasn't quite right.

She ended the call with her mom, tossed the phone in her purse and gingerly made her way to the tables shoved together to form a U. Marc had saved her a seat. She was pleasantly surprised at how bright the newly renovated space appeared. The walls still had the smell of fresh paint. A decorated Christmas tree stood in the corner, and imitation evergreen garlands had been strung throughout the room. Red bows tied everything together.

How she loved Christmas. Her favorite time of the year. And this year, she wanted to enjoy it again.

"I haven't been here since it reopened."

"Looks good, doesn't it?" Marc helped her out of her coat.

"Yes, it does. By the way, Mom wants me to ask you—for the seventeenth time, I might add—if you made sure Dean was joining us for Thanksgiving." She slung her coat over the back of the folding chair, then took a seat.

Dean had been staying at Marc's ranch since Friday. While Brooke wanted him to spend Thanksgiving with them, she knew he might have plans to keep his dad company at the hospital. And shouldn't Mom be badgering Marc about it instead of her?

Mom's phone call was precisely the reason she'd moved into her new house *before* the renovations were complete. Her micromanaging ways made Brooke want to tear her hair out. Anne Young had firm ideas on how things should be done. And Brooke was finding her own way through single parenthood.

She and her mom got along best when they lived apart.

Marc groaned. "How many times can she remind me? She knows I asked him on Sunday and again yesterday. The only reason I haven't mentioned it today is because I haven't seen him. He's been at the hospital."

"How's Ed doing?" Dean had been visiting his father every day, but yesterday was the first day Ed had spoken. Apparently, he'd been heavily sedated in the ICU all weekend. She hoped things would start to get more normal for both of them.

"I didn't ask. I'm trying to give Dean space. I'll try to find out later when I get home."

Christy Moulten tapped Brooke on the shoulder. "Howdy, neighbor. It's good to see you here."

"Hi, Christy." Brooke rose slightly to give her a quick hug, then sat back down. "I love the wreath you put out. It's gorgeous. I'm still pinching myself that we're neighbors."

"Technically, you live four houses apart." Marc lifted his index finger. Smarty pants.

"We're neighbors." Brooke waved him off and turned back to Christy. She loved the woman. Christy had recently turned sixty-five, and her sons, Cade and Ty, had thrown her a big birthday party. Her Pomeranian, Tulip—a therapy dog for the nursing home—had worn a tiny party hat. The twins were obsessed with the little fluff ball.

"I wish you'd brought those babies. They get cuter by the minute."

"They're with Mom tonight. I hope she doesn't go overboard with the sugar."

Christy chuckled. "She does own a bakery. And she *is* a grandma. It's inevitable. I hope Cade and Mackenzie want children right away. The wedding will be here before we know it."

"I can't wait."

"Any news on when your bathroom will be finished?" Christy stopped by regularly, mainly to spoil the twins, and she knew all about Brooke's remodeling woes.

"No. That's kind of why I'm here tonight." Kind of? It was the only reason. Not knowing what was going to happen to her unfinished bathroom and the nonexistent ramp had been tying her in knots for the past couple of days.

Not many people truly understood why she wanted the house completely accessible for wheelchairs. Why would they? They hadn't been stuck in a hospital, barely able to move one side of their body for a week. They hadn't spent three weeks in a long-term rehab facility working tirelessly to regain their strength so they could go home to their babies.

They hadn't had their life put on hold for a month as they worried they might never recover.

And they had no comprehension of how terrifying it was that she could have another stroke at any moment. Stroke victims automatically had a higher chance of having another one. Her neurologist and Dr. South, her general practitioner here in town, had urged her to be aware of the symptoms and to manage her risk factors.

She knew the symptoms. Had memorized the risk factors. What no one told her, though, was percentages, and all her internet searches yielded no concrete numbers. How high of a chance were they talking about? Fifty percent? Seventy-five?

Her bathroom and ramp needed to be finished.

This morning she'd called Brenda, Ed's administrative assistant, for an update on what was happening with her bathroom. The news wasn't good. The subcontractors' hands were tied moving forward on the existing projects. If the materials had already been delivered, they would do the work. For everything else? They were waiting for the green light from Ed. When Brooke had asked Brenda who else could give them the green light, she hadn't gotten an answer.

Henry Zane, the building inspector, was attending the Jewel River Legacy Club meeting tonight and might have more information.

"I guess I'd better get to my seat." With a wave, Christy hustled over to her chair.

Erica Cambridge took her spot at the podium, and everyone grew quiet. Brooke had never been to one of these meetings before. She'd never had a reason to attend. Now she was curious to see what they were all about.

Clem Buckley, the steely-eyed rancher who absolutely terrified her, called everyone to rise while he led them in the Pledge of Allegiance and the Lord's Prayer.

"Welcome, everyone," Erica said as they got settled. "I know you're all busy getting ready for Thanksgiving, so I'll try to keep this as brief as possible."

She went through old business, and Cade, Clem and Marc gave updates on their committees. As the meeting wore on, Brooke wished someone would bring up the fact that McCaffrey Construction was on hold at the moment. Should she mention it? Or should she corner Henry after the meeting? She had no clue how these things worked.

"Erica?" Angela Zane, Henry's wife, held up her hand.

"Yes?" Was Brooke imagining it, or did Erica's face look pinched?

"Joey and Lindsey put together a short film for the Christmas festival. Will there be someone at the Winston a day or two ahead of time, so he can get it set up to play on a loop?"

"Yes, Dalton and I will be on hand with the volunteers the day before. I have to ask, though, is the film appropriate for children? Not too…intense? I seem to recall you mentioning, and I quote, 'extreme reindeer games where only the tough survive.'"

"Oh, no, hon. Joey scrapped that idea. This one is for the kiddos. He assured me it's a winner for every age."

Clem shook his head. "He's going to terrify the babies. I haven't seen a film of his yet that didn't involve blowing up buildings or people running for their lives."

"Clem does have a point." Erica held out her hands, palms up. "We'll need to preview it before showing it at the festival."

Angela's thumbs traveled over her phone screen. "I've got it right here. If I send it to you, can we watch it now?"

Erica hesitated. "Su-u-re."

Dalton, Erica's husband, stood and pulled down the screen at the front of the room while Erica wheeled over the audio-visual equipment.

As much as Brooke enjoyed Joey's films, she hoped this wouldn't take long. She needed answers, not a full Christmas movie.

Soon, the lights dimmed, and the movie began to play. A fireplace with a crackling fire appeared. Then a fluffy orange cat wearing an elf hat walked past it and let out a meow. A yellow Lab with felt reindeer antlers came into view, and he too walked past the fire. Then a butterscotch-colored Angora rabbit with a red Mrs. Claus cape tied around its neck hopped past. The camera zoomed to the window, where snow fell against a night sky, then returned to the fireplace, where all three animals were lying in a row on a rug in front of the fire. The words Merry Christmas danced across the screen. And then it was over.

Her girls were going to love it. They couldn't get enough of dogs, cats or bunnies. Very cute.

"Well, I'll be." Clem shook his head in wonder. "He did it. He actually made a film with no explosions."

"I think we should have a show of hands to approve this." Erica gazed around the room. "Who's in favor?"

Everyone raised their hands.

"Great. This is going to be a terrific addition to the festival." Angela beamed.

Erica was about to wrap up the meeting when Patrick Howard, the owner of the future service dog training center, stood. "This might not be the place to ask, but do any of you know what's happening with McCaffrey Construction while Ed's recovering?"

Relief blew through Brooke. Finally.

Henry Zane cleared his throat. "Construction can continue on the current projects, but his subcontractors don't have the supplies they need for all of them. Since Ed supervises everything himself, no one is certain what's going on. When he gets back, he'll sort it out."

"Is he expected back soon?" Patrick asked.

"Unlikely. I spoke with Dean earlier, and there's a good possibility Ed will be in Casper for at least a few more weeks."

"My dogs will be arriving in mid-January," Patrick said. "I don't know that I can wait too long."

Brooke thrust her hand in the air. "Could someone else act as supervisor in his place?"

Henry rubbed his chin and frowned. "Depends on if they're employed by McCaffrey Construction and what role in the company they already have. If he's authorized someone, then yes. I don't know if he has, though."

Brooke chewed on that information. Surely Ed had authorized someone else to handle the business in case of something like this. From all appearances, though, it wasn't likely. Now what was she supposed to do?

The meeting wrapped up, and she and Marc stood to leave.

"I'll talk to Dean about what's going on with his dad's business." Marc helped her into her coat.

"I was thinking of doing the same, but I feel selfish. He's already going through a lot. His dad's business should be the last thing on his mind."

"Acting as supervisor might give him something to focus on."

"Supervisor? Dean? But he hasn't been involved with McCaffrey Construction in ten years. I don't see that happening."

"You never know." Marc shrugged.

"Henry said he'd need to be an employee and authorized to work on behalf of the company. Or did I understand that wrong?"

"You got it right. I have a feeling that won't be an issue. Ed's always wanted Dean to join the company." Marc gestured for her to head to the door. "When Dean's not at the hospital, all he does is ride Dusty around the ranch. If he's going to be in Jewel River for a while, he might welcome the distraction. He's got the experience. Worked for his dad all through high school until he moved to Texas."

"Yeah, but it's a lot to ask..." They emerged outside in the parking lot, where cold air and a star-filled sky greeted them.

"He quit everything, Brooke." Marc matched her slower pace. "Packed up his truck, quit his job. He has no immediate plans."

"How did he manage to do that?" The picture of Dean that Marc painted seemed bleak. There must not have been much keeping him in Texas.

"I don't know. But something changed him a decade ago. He's never told me what happened. But he hasn't been the same since."

"If you think him taking over as supervisor will help him through this, I'm all for it."

They shared a smile as she settled into the driver's seat of her minivan.

"It can't hurt to ask," he said.

"All he can say is no."

"Maybe *you* should ask him."

"Why me?" She blanched at the thought.

"Because you actually have a house with unfinished projects. It might motivate him to say yes."

She buckled her seat belt and looked up at him. "I don't know."

"All he can say is no, right?" he mimicked her.

She sighed. "I'll think about it."

"You can ask him at Thanksgiving. I'll make sure he's there." Then he shut the door and waved before turning away to find his truck.

Thanksgiving was two days away. Why did she feel like she'd walked right into that one?

TUESDAY NIGHT, WHILE Marc was in town for a meeting, Dean stood on the walkway of his father's house and stared at the front door. The home he'd grown up in. The one he couldn't bring himself to enter.

He spun the key ring around his finger. Again. And again.

His conversation with his father at the hospital earlier still gnawed at him. Dad had finally been able to talk coherently. Too bad the conversation had gone to one of the few places Dean wanted to avoid.

His father had asked him point-blank to oversee the current projects for McCaffrey Construction. Dean had almost said no. He'd wanted to say no. Instead, he'd changed the subject.

He felt like a loser. Like a greedy jerk.

His dad had never abandoned his dream of wanting Dean to eventually take over the company. He'd also never listened when Dean explained he wasn't the man for the job.

Yet his dad clearly thought otherwise. Why else would he have kept Dean on the employee roster? And listed him as second-in-command? And kept his name on all the bank accounts? Dean hadn't even known about all that until this afternoon.

Why did his father still give him the benefit of the doubt? He didn't deserve it.

Back when he'd been twenty-one and an expert on everything, Dean and his dad had gotten into the worst fight of their lives. He had just dropped out of the construction management undergrad program to work for his girlfriend Lia's father in Dallas. His roommate, Colin, had gone along for the ride. They'd both received huge sign-on bonuses to work on commercial building sites.

To say Dean's father had been upset was putting it lightly. Dad had ranted about him having a perfectly good job in construction right here. He was supposed to work in Jewel River and join him in the family business. Why would he want to move to a big city and work for some girl's father when he could work for his own?

Dean had yelled that he wanted to make real money. His dad had scornfully called it a fool's errand. They'd argued at the top of their lungs for over an hour. And his father had said the words that had been seared on his brain: "One of these days, you're going to hurt someone with that temper."

To which Dean had replied, "Yeah, well, I got it from you."

He'd stuffed some of his belongings into a bag and left. Six months later, he and Lia had gone to a bar with Colin, and before closing time, he'd excused himself to use the restroom. When he returned, he'd found Lia and Colin kissing. Furious, he'd marched out of there with her on his heels. He'd told Lia to call for a ride, but she'd buckled herself into the passenger seat and refused to get out.

All the way to her apartment, they'd shouted at each other. He could still feel the pressure of the accelerator under his foot as he pressed it harder. They kept going faster, faster...

And then the scream.

The crash.

The eerie quiet when all he could hear was the hiss of air releasing from a mangled valve. The realization that both he and Lia had somehow made it out alive had brought a relief so intense, he'd barely been able to breathe.

The police had given him a citation for reckless driving. Her father had fired him the next day.

Dean's life had turned upside down. Not knowing what to do but adamant he wasn't going back to his dad to hear *I told you so*, Dean had packed his things and found a job as a ranch hand in rural Texas. It was where he'd been ever since.

And here he was, transfixed by the house he'd grown up in, pushing away the same things he'd pushed away after the accident.

Regret. Shame. The desire for respect.

Dean placed his foot on the first porch step, then brought it right back.

He'd been home many times over the past decade. He and his father had patched up their differences and kept things civil by not mentioning him working for McCaffrey Construction. In fact, they skirted any talk about construction in general.

But that wasn't what was keeping Dean from entering the house right now. No, the issue of him working for his dad wasn't why he couldn't quite bring himself to climb the porch steps.

The basement was the problem.

For years, his dad had asked him to help him clean out the basement. Some of the boxes held childhood mementos, toys and papers. Other boxes weren't his, though. Several were his mother's. And there were a few items of hers he didn't want to see again. One in particular.

He'd stolen it from her before she'd left town for good.

Anything he found down there would only remind him how far he'd fallen short of his dreams. And he didn't need any more reminders at this point in his life.

Snow began to fall. Big flakes—showy ones—danced

down. Made him think of snowball fights and sledding with his friends.

Dean let out a frustrated breath. His father didn't ask much of him. The man wanted him to join McCaffrey Construction and clean out the basement. Dean had no intention of joining the company, and he still couldn't handle tackling the basement.

Man, he was pathetic.

The snow chilled the exposed skin of his face and neck. He stared at the massive one-story home with shadowy tall pines behind it. *Nope*. Couldn't do it. Couldn't march up those steps and face the empty house. Without his father inside, it wasn't a home.

But maybe he *could* fill in as supervisor for his dad while he recovered.

There were only a handful of projects that needed to be finished. Patrick Howard's service dog training center was almost complete. Dan Bagley's pole barn would take about a week to wrap up. And then there was Brooke's house. A master bathroom and a ramp out back. A few weeks' worth of work if everything had already been ordered and delivered. And knowing his father, it had been. The man was as efficient as he was proficient. He gave everything his absolute best, and he'd taught Dean to do the same.

He strode back to his truck and started the engine. Now what? He'd been avoiding Marc and Reagan by doing what he always did—riding his horse and checking cattle. It was how he'd kept his distance from just about everyone for a decade.

Maybe it was time to change that, too.

Ty Moulten's ranch wasn't far away. He'd always been easy to be around, and he wasn't the type to smother him with sympathy. It just wasn't Ty's way.

Fifteen minutes later, Dean knocked on the front door of the ranch house.

"Dean." Ty's face broke into a smile. "Come in. Didn't expect to see you here."

A blast of warmth hit him as he entered the foyer. The sparsely decorated living room had hardwood floors, white walls and brown leather furniture. He instantly felt at home.

"Are you hungry? I was just getting around to eating. Had to find a cow that wandered off. I've got venison stew simmering. You're welcome to have some."

For the first time in a week, he realized he was, in fact, hungry. "Sounds great."

He took off his coat and followed Ty to the eat-in kitchen, where Ty rummaged through cupboards and drawers for bowls and silverware. Soon, they were both blowing on spoons full of stew.

"This is good. Spicy."

"I add a pinch of cayenne." Ty met his gaze and grinned. "It's better that way."

How long had it been since he'd hung out with Ty? Thirteen, fourteen years? They'd grown apart while Dean was away at college. Dean *had* flown up for Zoey's funeral, but that was five or six years ago.

For the most part, Dean hadn't kept up with his old friends. Except for Marc. They always got together for at least a few hours when Dean came to town.

"It's tough, huh?" Ty asked with a compassionate glance.

"The meat?" He glanced at the stew.

"No, your dad having a heart attack."

Dean shoveled in another bite and nodded.

"What are the doctors saying?"

"Not much. They think he'll be in the hospital for a few weeks."

"I'm glad he survived. Ed's a good guy."

"He is." That was one point Dean had never questioned. His father *was* a good guy.

"When my dad died, my entire world shifted. Pete Moulten. My hero. Could do no wrong. Dead? Seemed impossible."

"That about sums up how I feel about my father."

Ty reached for the pepper shaker. "What have you been doing? I mean, here in town?"

"Riding my horse around Marc's ranch, mostly."

"It helps. Riding around my ranch keeps the pain away. I've got more miles on my horses than I do my truck. It's the only thing I had after Zoey died."

It was the only thing Dean had after the night of the accident, too. He completely understood.

"Now it's more of a habit, I guess." Ty took a drink of water. "I miss her. Miss what we were supposed to have. My dad's death was different. He had a full life. I miss him, but not like I do her."

"You loved her."

Ty had a faraway look in his eyes. "She was my whole life. And then she was gone."

At least he'd had the love of his life. Dean hadn't allowed himself to get close to any woman after Lia. Hadn't really allowed himself to get close to anyone. He couldn't say he'd even gotten that close to her, either.

Brooke's sympathetic blue eyes came to mind.

No. No way he was getting close to Brooke. He couldn't bear to fall for her and have her see what he hid from everyone—what the accident had taken from him.

What no one knew, including his father, was that the accident had fundamentally changed him. He hadn't been able to drive with a passenger in his vehicle since the crash. On the few occasions he'd tried, he'd had a full-blown panic attack.

What could he possibly offer a woman if he couldn't even drive her anywhere? If he couldn't be certain he wouldn't snap and cause another accident?

He couldn't. And he wouldn't waste a minute thinking he

could have a woman like Brooke. She needed a man she could depend on. He'd never be that man.

He'd make the best of his time in Jewel River. Try to figure out what could be done for McCaffrey Construction's unfinished projects. Maybe even attempt to go through some of the boxes in Dad's basement. But as soon as his father was home and back to work, Dean was leaving town. Starting over somewhere else. Alone.

CHAPTER THREE

"I BROUGHT PIES. Two pumpkin, two apple and one pecan." Carrying a stack of plastic pie containers, Brooke's mom bustled into the kitchen of Marc's house.

"How many do you think we're going to eat? We don't need a pie per person." Brooke flashed a smile as she finished wiping Megan's hands, then tossed the wet paper towel into the trash. Marc and Reagan had offered to host Thanksgiving this year, so she'd arrived early to help cook. Reagan was busy making a tablescape—whatever that was—in the dining room, and Marc was doing ranch chores. Brooke reached for the pies her mom carried. "Here, let me."

"They'll all get eaten eventually. Thanks, honey. I'll go get the other ones." Mom kissed Brooke's cheek. "Happy Thanksgiving. You look beautiful."

"Thank you, Mom." Her mother didn't toss around compliments like confetti, so she would tuck this one away to savor later.

Alice and Megan charged toward their grandma.

"Oh, I see you!" She opened her arms wide and pulled them in for hugs. Then she kissed the tops of their heads. "My sweet girls."

"Gwammy!" They bounced in excitement, arms in the air as she straightened.

"Grammy's got to bring in the other pies. I'll be right back." She turned to leave, but paused. "Is Dean here yet?"

"Marc expects him soon."

"Good." She disappeared from view.

Despite Marc's insistence that Brooke be the one to broach the subject of Dean possibly supervising the projects for McCaffrey Construction, she'd decided she wasn't going to do it. Dean might be drifting in a sea of uncertainty, but despite what Marc thought, asking him to renovate her bathroom and build her a ramp was selfish. What he needed was for his father to heal and return home, not extra work.

"Girls, I need you to get out of the kitchen." Brooke guided them out. "This oven's hot. Go get your babies, okay?"

"Babies!" Alice yelled, clapping her hands and running on chubby legs to the living room.

Megan wrapped her arms around Brooke's calf and looked up at her with a pouty face. "Up, Mama."

"In a bit, Meggie. I have to check on the turkey."

Her bottom lip plumped out. Brooke leaned over and pretended to munch on her neck. "Gobble, gobble, gobble."

She giggled and ran off to join her sister.

Brooke shook her head, smiling to herself. Their personalities were shining through more and more as each day passed. It was hard to believe they'd be two in January. She'd have to ask Reagan for tips on throwing them a party. Her sister-in-law, whom she considered one of her best friends, was the most creative person she had ever met.

The mudroom door let out a creak. Brooke gave the potatoes a stir, then quickly peeked at the turkey so she could help her mom carry in the rest of the desserts. Hopefully, she'd also brought her highly anticipated corn casserole.

"Look who I found in the driveway." Her mom practically pushed Dean into the kitchen. "You thought you could sneak away on your horse, didn't you? Not today, mister. We have too much good food, and you have to help us make a dent in it."

He held the corn casserole in his hands. Phew.

"Sorry she forced you in here." Brooke took the dish from him. "Mom's mission in life is to make sure everyone is fed."

Her mother shot her a fake glare and brushed by carrying the other pies, a plastic bag dangling from her arm. "Don't apologize for me. I know what cowboys are all about. They retreat to the barn, lose track of time, and the next thing you know, supper's cold and everyone's cranky."

She cruised out of the room, and Brooke bit the corner of her bottom lip to keep from laughing.

"It's okay if you need to check on Dusty," she said. "I'll cover for you."

"No, that's okay. I'll stay." His hands dropped to his sides. "I fed and watered him this morning."

Dean had made an effort to look nice. His scruff had been trimmed, and he wore a button-down shirt with jeans. She, too, had taken extra care with her appearance. She had on her favorite stretchy jeans and a red sweater. Her hair was actually holding the curls she'd coaxed earlier with her curling iron, and she'd applied lipstick, blush and eyeliner.

"How's your dad doing?" She pointed to the counter behind him. "Would you toss me those oven mitts?"

"He's better." He handed them to her.

"How much better? Do the doctors have a plan? I feel bad that he's stuck there on Thanksgiving."

"I do, too. When I left him earlier, he was falling asleep. I told him I'd come up again tonight. Your mom already insists she's packing him a full meal. I don't think his nurses will be pleased, but I don't know how to say no to her."

"Mom's formidable. No one can say no to her." She opened the oven door and popped the casserole into the oven. "Did anyone say when he'd be released?"

Dean sighed, which made her think maybe she shouldn't be prying.

"He'll leave the hospital on Saturday."

That sounded promising. Maybe Ed would be back to work soon. Her goal of having the house completely renovated by Christmas *could* still happen.

"But they're sending him to a rehab center to build up his strength."

Her hope collapsed—not for her house or renovation dreams, but for Ed. And for Dean.

"I'm sorry. What rehab center is he going to?" He named the same one she'd been transferred to last year. "They're good. You don't have to worry about how he'll be treated. I spent three weeks there after my stroke."

He blinked twice as a wrinkle formed between his eyebrows. "Why did you have to stay for so long?"

"My left side was weak. At first, I couldn't lift my arm or move my leg at all. I had to do physical and occupational therapy every day for hours. The staff helped me regain my strength. It's amazing how much I took for granted before the stroke—basic things, like walking up a step or holding my babies. I'm grateful God spared me from permanent paralysis."

This time, at least. Who knew what the future held?

"I wish He would have spared you from having the stroke in the first place."

"Same here." She reached around him to open a drawer. He smelled good, like woodsy aftershave. After finding the can opener, she used the crook of her arm to slide several canned goods her way. "I'm doing everything I can to live my best life and keep moving forward."

"Your best life. I like the sound of that." He leaned against the counter and watched her open green beans, then dump them into a colander in the sink. "What's changed?"

"I'm mindful of my health. I keep a running list of doctor's orders in my head at all times." She lowered her voice to mimic the doctor. "Don't let yourself get too tired. Drink a lot of water. Rest often. Eat a balanced, healthy diet. Be aware of the signs of stroke."

His frown deepened. "You mean you could have another one?"

Growing serious, she nodded and kept her gaze on the colander as she shook it.

"I'm at an increased risk. I'll always be." She reached up for a baking dish. After greasing it, she stirred together all the ingredients for the green bean casserole. "I hope to never be a patient at the rehab center again. If I didn't have the girls, it wouldn't be such a big deal, but being separated from them?" She shook her head in defiance. "No. Not going through that again."

"Happy Thanksgiving!" Marc's deep voice bellowed from the mudroom. Then he entered the kitchen and grinned at Dean. "You made it."

"I'm here."

"Let me get cleaned up, and we can find out what the ladies need help with."

"Marc?" Mom called from the other room.

"Yes, Mother?"

"This leaf is stuck. The pegs aren't lining up correctly."

"Think you can help them with it?" Marc asked Dean.

"Yeah, go get changed. I've got it."

Marc hurried away, and Dean pointed his thumb to the dining room. "I'll go see if I can help."

Brooke nodded. Had she overshared? It wasn't like she went around giving everyone her sob story. The people in Jewel River already knew it. News and gossip traveled fast in these parts. So why had she confided in him?

His dad is in the same rehab center you spent so much time in. It's normal to open up about your own experience there. Don't beat yourself up. It's not a secret.

Dean deserved a relaxing Thanksgiving. From this point

on, she wouldn't mention anything that would remind him his dad had a long road to recovery ahead.

Just how long of a road would it be, though? She wished she'd asked.

"Brooke?" her mom yelled.

"What?"

"How long until the turkey is done?"

"We should be ready to eat in about an hour."

"Good. That will give us time to fill out our thankful leaves."

She rotated the corn casserole and jammed the green bean casserole next to it. It just fit. Then she washed her hands and went to check on the twins. She found them in the dining room. Reagan held Alice on her hip, and Dean was crouching with his hand outstretched to take Megan's stuffed dog. Meggie giggled as he brought it to his chest.

"This is a good puppy, isn't it?" His brown eyes crinkled in the corners. He cradled the dog, and Megan clapped her hands, clearly delighted. "What's the puppy's name?"

"Booboo." Megan turned away to grab a small blanket. "Cold."

"Booboo's cold?" He wrapped the puppy in the blanket. "We'd better warm him up. That's better."

Brooke hung back in the archway as unexpected emotions rose. She'd watched Marc with the girls since the day they were born. He treated them like any proud uncle would.

But Dean...he reminded her of Ross. Which, in turn, tightened a vise around her chest. The girls didn't have a father. If Ross had lived, they'd have one who loved them dearly. But he hadn't lived.

Her babies were facing a lifetime with no daddy. Was she making the right choice by refusing to even consider dating again?

While Dean had wished God had spared her from having the stroke, she personally wished God had spared her from losing Ross. For months now, she'd found herself forgetting things about him she'd clung to so tightly after his death. The way he smiled. His goofy laugh. Looking at a photo on her phone wasn't the same.

Her memories of Ross were fading more rapidly each day. How long would it be until she forgot him altogether?

She bunched her hands into fists.

Don't think about it. Don't dwell on the past. Enjoy this moment.

She'd been giving herself the same advice for well over a year, but sometimes it was hard.

The sound of water boiling over made her rush back to the kitchen. The potatoes were overflowing. She turned down the burner and mopped up the spill bubbling around the pot as best as she could.

"Here, let me." Dean had followed her. He took the dish towel from her hand and dabbed at the spills. "Don't want you to burn yourself."

"Thanks." His presence, or maybe his thoughtfulness, made her tummy swirl. It certainly wasn't hunger causing it. She'd been snacking all day.

"Your girls are cute." He stepped back, still holding the dish towel.

"Thank you." She wholeheartedly agreed. They were adorable, and yes, she knew she was biased. "Here, I'll take that." She took the cloth from him and hung it over the dishwasher handle to dry.

"I wish my dad was home." Dean blew out a melancholy breath.

"I wish he was, too."

"He didn't even qualify for outpatient care. I pushed for it, but apparently, Jewel River is too far from treatment centers for it to be feasible. The rehab center you were in—the one Dad's going to—you said it's good. Do you think he'll make a full recovery there?"

The change in subject startled her, but as she looked into his worried eyes, she was thankful he'd asked.

"Yes, I do believe he'll recover there. He's made it this far—the heart attack, triple bypass surgery. He's strong. He just needs a reason to work hard. I was motivated by the thought of returning home to my girls. They were babies, only three months old, when I had my stroke. To be separated from them for even a day was painful, and I was in Casper for a full month."

"Who took care of them?"

"Reagan and Marc, mostly. Mom stayed with me the first week when I was in the hospital. When I transferred to the rehab center, she visited most afternoons and helped out with the twins at night. I hadn't even met Reagan when she offered to help babysit. To think she would do that—sacrifice so much time to take care of a stranger's babies—I'll forever be in her debt."

The sound of voices made her turn.

"Do you have a gravy recipe in your family?" Mom was asking Reagan as they entered the kitchen. "It's one thing I've never mastered."

"My dad told me he adds some of the starchy potato water to the turkey drippings. Beyond that, I'm clueless."

"Potato water. Hmm…"

Brooke met Dean's gaze, and they both chuckled.

"What's so funny?" her mom asked, smiling.

"You and your gravy secrets."

"Laugh all you want, but it's not going to distract me from the fact you both need to fill out your thankful leaves." Mom thrust a stack of leaves cut out of construction paper at Brooke. "Pens are in the junk drawer. We'll be reading them out loud during supper."

Dean leaned close and whispered, "What's a thankful leaf?"

"You write something you're grateful for on it. Then we take turns sharing. If you don't want to—"

"No, no. I'll do it."

She looked into his eyes, and for the first time since she'd seen him since Friday, she saw signs of life. He appeared younger, more optimistic.

What a handsome man. And nice. Plus, the patience he'd shown Megan? He was good with kids.

With more force than necessary, she yanked open the junk drawer, found two pens and handed him one. She shouldn't be thinking along those lines. Shouldn't be noticing Dean as anything but Marc's best friend.

Truth be told, she wanted to be Dean's friend, too.

Just friends, though. If they spent too much time together, her heart would zoom way past friendship. She'd better play it safe. She had plenty to be thankful for. Letting her lonely side push her into wanting more—on Thanksgiving, no less— would only lead to trouble.

THIS WAS WHAT he'd been missing. A big family meal with a chandelier twinkling above the dining table, empty dessert plates holding crumbs, good conversation, the occasional burst of laughter and blessings scrawled on paper leaves. Dean's thankful leaf had been easy to fill out. Dad was alive.

He couldn't stop staring at Brooke sitting across from him. One of the twins had fallen asleep on her lap. The other was sleeping on Reagan's lap.

The decision he'd made this morning had been the right one. When he'd stopped by the hospital earlier, his father had spelled out what still needed to be addressed on the construction projects. At first, Dean had mentally pulled away. But as he'd watched his father struggling to remember where the materials for Patrick Howard's kennel room were and what installer had agreed to lay the tile for Brooke's bathroom, Dean had realized how important it was that the work get finished.

McCaffrey Construction was Ed's life's work. And Dean knew that if his father didn't have to worry about the projects being left unfinished, he'd be able to fully focus on his recovery. The doctors wanted to keep Ed's stress to a minimum.

So he'd patted Dad's hand and said, "Leave everything to me. I'll handle it."

The tightness in his dad's face had instantly released. Of course, a minute later, he'd commanded Dean to take notes. Dean had diligently typed everything into his phone as his father barked orders. He figured he'd call Brenda tomorrow for more information, even though it was a long holiday weekend.

"More coffee, Dean?" Anne smiled as she approached with the coffeepot. She seemed to be around the same age as his dad. An attractive woman who got things done. And a first-class baker. Those pies had been delicious.

"Sure, why not?" He thanked her after she poured. Brooke tilted her head and watched him with a thoughtful expression. What was she thinking? Why was she looking at him like that?

Beautiful *and* kind. No wonder he couldn't stop staring at her. He'd thought about her many times since Marc and Reagan's wedding and too often to count since rolling into town last Friday.

A blast of warmth heated his core, and he had a sudden urge to excuse himself to the stables and saddle up Dusty.

"I think the game's about to start." Marc pushed away from the table. "I'll turn it on."

"Ugh." Brooke pretended to gag. "Do we have to watch football?"

"I can't believe you're saying that." Marc looked stricken. "Of course we're watching football. It's Thanksgiving. We eat turkey. We count our blessings. And we watch the Cowboys."

"Watch them lose, you mean." Anne pretended to brush off one of her shoulders.

"Oh, I see we're starting the smack talk early, Mom." Marc followed Anne out of the room as they argued about the upcoming game.

"I'm going to run the dishwasher." Reagan handed the twin she was holding to Dean. "Do you mind holding Megan?"

"Um, sure." He opened his arms to take the child. As her warm body, heavy with sleep, nestled into his chest, he stilled. He'd held plenty of small animals. Calves, dogs, injured fawns, you name it. But a tiny human? Practically a baby?

He hadn't held one of those before. And he found that he liked it.

"I can put them in their cribs to nap if you don't want to hold her," Brooke said.

"No, I don't mind." This was the perfect time to bring up her renovation. But he hadn't thought through other logistics. Like the fact he was going to be in Jewel River through the holidays and maybe longer. He'd need to move out of Marc's spare bedroom and into Dad's house.

A shiver rippled down his back at the thought. All those boxes in the basement sitting there, waiting for him to sort through them. And now he wouldn't have an excuse to avoid them.

"I know my dad was still working on your house when he had the heart attack," Dean said. "I'm sure you must be wondering what's happening with the renovations."

Her cheeks flushed, and she gave a slight nod. "It's crossed my mind. But Ed's health is all that matters. My house can wait."

Her unselfish attitude bolstered his confidence. He was doing the right thing.

"This might sound out there, but Dad has always kept me on as an employee. Although I haven't worked for him in over ten years, he named me second-in-command. I have the authority to act in his place."

Her eyelashes blinked wide, and her pretty blue eyes glistened with hope.

"He's going to be in the rehab center for about a month.

Could be longer. This morning I told him I'd supervise the current projects."

"Really? That's great!" She let out a dreamy sigh. "My goal was to have all the renovations done by Christmas."

"I'll do my best to make that happen."

"And after they're done?" A crinkle appeared above the bridge of her nose.

"What do you mean?"

"What will you do then?"

"When Dad's ready to come back to work, I'll be moving on."

"Where will you go?"

Good question. If he didn't have a sleeping toddler on his lap, he'd stand. Pace. Instead, he stretched his head side to side to work out the kinks in his neck.

"I don't know yet. Did Marc tell you I quit my job?"

"He did."

"I'm not sure what my future holds. Can't think that far ahead right now. I'll handle Dad's business and try my best to deal with all the junk in the basement, and—"

"What do you mean? What junk in the basement?"

Why had he mentioned it? He should have kept his mouth shut.

"Dad's been bugging me for years to help him clean out the basement. A lot of the boxes are mine, but I know there's other stuff down there, too. I told him to rent a dumpster and toss it all, but he's worried there are things down there I'll want."

"I can help you with it. If you want help, that is."

The idea immediately tempted him. Having Brooke there would make the process less stressful.

But then she'd see all his silly childhood keepsakes. She might unbox the things his mother had left behind before she'd moved out for good.

So what? Maybe he *was* ready to tackle the boxes in the

basement. He'd get it over with, and it wouldn't hang over his head anymore.

"How long do you think it will take you to finish my house?" Brooke asked.

"I don't know. I'll have to come over and see for myself. I'm calling Brenda tomorrow to go over all the projects that are still unfinished."

"Stop by anytime. In fact, why don't you come over on Saturday? I could use an extra set of hands to set up my Christmas tree, and I hate asking Marc for help with everything, especially now that Reagan's pregnant."

Helping this beautiful woman set up a Christmas tree should be a hard no. And yet he couldn't stop himself from agreeing. "Okay. Would morning work? Or I can stop by later."

"Morning would be great."

One thing his father had mentioned about her house renovation kept nagging at him.

"I know you said you could have another stroke. Is that why you're making everything wheelchair accessible?"

She nodded.

"Do the doctors think you'll have one soon?"

"I could have one at any time, or I could live the rest of my life without having another stroke. I'm being proactive. I spent weeks in the rehab center. Like your father, outpatient care wasn't an option for me." She smoothed the baby's hair as she slept. "I want to be prepared for whatever happens, including the possibility of needing a wheelchair."

He took a sip of coffee as more questions piled up. A remodeling job of her scope didn't come cheap. How could she afford it all?

"My husband was raised by his older uncle. When the man died, Ross inherited his entire estate." She stared off toward the window. Had she read his mind? "After Ross died, it all went to me. Until recently, I didn't appreciate what it meant to have those funds available. In my mind, the best way to use the money is to get my affairs in order, starting with my house. We never know what a new day might bring."

He couldn't argue with that. Still, it seemed like overkill to remodel an entire home for an emergency that might never happen.

Brooke folded the paper napkin next to her dessert plate. "Let me know when you want to start going through the basement. I have a lot of people willing to help me with the twins. And I'm good at organizing."

It would be dumb to agree to spend more time with her. He liked her too much already. He should turn down her offer, but he needed moral support. "I could use the help."

Her radiant face flared heat up his neck. He definitely should have said no.

"Looks like I'll be staying in town for a while," he said. "I'll move my stuff over to Dad's place tomorrow."

"You can't stay there. It's too far away. It tacks on an extra forty minutes to get to the hospital. Are you sure you won't stay here?"

"I've taken advantage of Marc's hospitality long enough."

Her eyebrows drew together. "You should consider moving into Reagan's house in town. It's furnished and empty at the moment. Her renter didn't renew the lease. It's close to Ed's office. And it's only a few blocks from my house."

Only a few blocks away from Brooke? He liked the sound of that.

"I'll bunk at Dad's for now." He'd have to leave Dusty here, though. His father didn't have a barn for a horse.

"You could board Dusty at Moulten Stables. It's all of two minutes from Reagan's place. That way you could ride him whenever you felt like it."

Two minutes away from Dusty? Maybe he should stay in Reagan's house. He'd pay rent, of course. It would be convenient and give him privacy. Save him from being alone in his childhood home, surrounded by memories he'd rather avoid.

"Moulten Stables? Does Ty own it?"

"Cade. He opened the horse boarding business in September. It's right outside town." Brooke cuddled the child closer. "When Reagan comes back in, I'll mention it to her."

"Mention what?" Reagan appeared with another pie, which she set on the table. Dean couldn't eat another bite, yet his mouth watered just looking at it.

"The possibility of Dean staying at your house in town. He's going to supervise the projects for McCaffrey Construction until Ed is cleared to come back to work."

"You are? That's wonderful. You're helping so many people." Reagan appeared to be on the verge of tears even though she was smiling. "Please stay in my house. I'll go grab the keys. It's clean and ready whenever you want to go over there. But don't get the wrong impression—I'm not trying to get you out of here. You're welcome to stay as long as you want."

Dean glanced from Brooke to Reagan and back to Brooke. That was resolved quickly.

"Looks like I'm moving into town tomorrow. Thank you."

"We'll have to set up two Christmas trees," Brooke said. "One for you, and one for me."

He didn't bother telling her he always skipped Christmas decorating. His cabin in Texas had been smaller than a matchbox, and he hadn't had much Christmas spirit in years, anyhow.

Something told him this Christmas was going to be different, though. And his heartbeat quickened at the thought. All because of the beautiful single mom sitting across from him.

CHAPTER FOUR

UNDER NO CIRCUMSTANCES could he consider moving to Jewel River permanently. Mainly because Dean had never told his father about the accident and what it had done to him. He didn't deserve to be a partner at McCaffrey Construction.

Moving here would leave him exposed. It wouldn't take long for people to catch on to the fact he never drove with anyone in his vehicle. They'd want to know why.

He couldn't share his reasons. Too embarrassing. Wished he could strike that night—that entire year—from his memory altogether.

As he drove down Center Street on Friday morning, he took in the town's Christmas decorations. Wreaths hung from the front doors of the local businesses. Garland had been wrapped around the lampposts and topped with red bows. Large planters held small pine trees wound with white twinkle lights. He'd driven through Jewel River at Christmas a few times since moving to Texas, but he'd never really noticed how much effort the residents put into making it inviting, like a scene out of a holiday movie.

Dean glanced at the rearview mirror to check the horse trailer. Still there. Same as it had been every time he'd checked since loading Dusty in it at Marc's ranch. He'd called Cade

Moulten earlier about renting a stall at Moulten Stables. Cade had instructed him to bring the horse over whenever was convenient—and now was the time.

While Marc and Reagan had been kind and welcoming, he was used to living alone. He needed space. Lots of space. And quiet.

Still, he appreciated how his living arrangements had fallen into place due to the generosity of his friends.

God, I'm humbled at how You've looked out for me. Thank You.

Last night, Reagan had handed him the key to her house and texted him the address. Not because she wanted him to leave. She understood, without him having to go into details, that he needed privacy.

He'd unload his stuff there after getting Dusty settled. At some point this weekend, he should probably drive out to his dad's place and actually enter his childhood home. And tomorrow morning, he'd pay Brooke a visit. Anticipation made him smile as he thought about finishing her remodeling projects. They were the easy part. Clearing out Dad's basement was the hard part. It meant he had to go down there and tackle the mess. With her help, of course.

Maybe that was the real reason his internal warning system was waving red flags about Jewel River.

Brooke.

Finishing her house. Cleaning out the basement together. Helping her put up a tree for Christmas.

All of the above appealed to him. But he couldn't go and do something stupid like get close to her. She didn't know his secrets. And he didn't plan on sharing them.

Before long, Dean pulled into Moulten Stables. He parked in front of the barn. Out on the gravel, he studied the structure. What a beauty. He made his way inside and followed the signs pointing to the office. A tall, muscular man stepped out from an empty stall. He wore jeans, a sweatshirt and an unzipped coat. Held a pitchfork.

"Trent?" Dean hadn't seen his old classmate since high school graduation.

"Dean." Trent's face broke into a wide grin. He propped the pitchfork against the wall and held out his hand, which Dean shook. Trent was taller than him, and he had short, tousled brown hair, a day's worth of scruff and an open smile. "Good to see you. Cade mentioned you'd be stopping by. I'm the manager here. Moved back in late August."

"I thought you were living down south."

"I was. When Cade called this summer, it must have been God's timing. I was ready for a new adventure. I heard about your dad. Hope he's doing better."

"He is. They're getting ready to move him to a rehab center in Casper. He'll be there for a month or so."

"You're sticking around here while he recovers?" Trent angled his chin and watched him thoughtfully.

"I am." He didn't want to get into details about why he quit his job. At some point, he'd have to figure out what he was going to do with his life. Today wasn't that day. It could wait until after Dad returned home. "Cade mentioned you had a couple of stalls available."

"We sure do. Why don't you put your horse in the paddock out back? Then I'll take you around."

Dean followed his directions. The crisp air refreshed him, and Dusty seemed to enjoy it, too. The horse snorted and tossed his mane when Dean led him into the paddock. About a dozen horses grazed in the adjacent pasture. He spent extra time with Dusty before returning to the barn.

"Ready?" Trent gestured to the aisle. Dean strolled next to him as he listed all the features and answered his questions. Then they checked out the open stalls, and Dean selected the one he wanted for Dusty.

"You've got some impressive horseflesh out in the pasture," Dean said. "I can see why you'd want to manage this place."

"Like I said, I was ready to move on, and I'm happy with my decision." Back in the office, Trent nodded for him to take a seat across from him at the desk. He slid a packet of forms his way. "Exceptional horses. Top-notch facility. We have riding trails leading to the wooded part of the property. You can explore them whenever you want. I just need you to sign these forms and put down a deposit."

Dean skimmed the forms before signing them. Then he opened his wallet and handed Trent his debit card. "I'll check out the trails soon, but I have other stuff to take care of today."

"I know you've got a lot going on." Trent grew serious. "If you can't be here, I'll take care of your horse. Text me anytime."

"That would help me out a lot. His name is Dusty. I should be able to take care of him most days. There might be a time or two, though, when I can't. But I wouldn't want to pull you away from time with your family."

Trent laughed. "No family. Just me in that big old house across the road."

For whatever reason, the fact Trent was still single brightened his mood. With Cade engaged and Marc happily married, Dean had been getting a funny feeling, but with Ty and Trent still single, he could embrace his bachelor lifestyle without being embarrassed. He wasn't the only one without a partner.

Ty had a good reason, though. He'd lost Zoey. And Trent might be dating someone, or at least interested in dating someone. Hopefully not Brooke.

He wondered why he'd had that thought.

"I'd better get going." Dean rose. "Thanks again for everything. It's good to see you."

"We'll have to get together and watch some football or grab a burger." Trent accompanied him out of the office to the main door.

"Or both. Sounds good to me."

With his top priority taken care of, Dean drove to the address Reagan had texted him. As he climbed the porch steps, he noticed two large plastic bins and an artificial tree in a box near the door. The top bin had an envelope with his name. He slipped it into his coat pocket, then unlocked the door and stepped inside.

The cold interior did nothing to dampen the warm, inviting atmosphere. Hardwood floors ran throughout, and the living room had a fireplace and plenty of windows. He ambled through the kitchen, then continued to the bedrooms. The main bedroom had an attached bathroom. It reminded him of a cozy cottage. Muted neutral tones on the walls, in the furniture and in the decorations made it feel homey.

After turning up the thermostat, Dean went back outside. As he opened the tailgate to unload his belongings, he sized up the neighborhood. The street was lined with small bungalows similar to this one, and most of the porches were decked out with Christmas lights. He placed his bags in the driveway and slammed the tailgate shut. Taking two trips, he hauled everything to the main bedroom to deal with later.

Now what? Should he unpack his clothes? Buy a few groceries? Or crash on the couch for a while to clear his head?

He *could* head over to Brooke's a day early. *Don't even think about it.* Maybe he should drive to Casper. See how Dad was doing. Last night he'd smuggled in the leftovers Anne had packed.

Dad had been sleeping when he arrived, but he'd woken immediately. They'd talked for about an hour, with Dad sampling a few bites of everything, including the pie. Dean had given him a hug and told him not to worry. He'd assured his father he'd handle whatever came up at McCaffrey Construction until he came home.

The optimistic gleam in his father's eyes hadn't escaped

his notice. At some point, Dad would pressure him to stay, to join the business.

Dean didn't deserve it. Had never deserved it.

How could the man still have so much faith in him? After all the mistakes he'd made?

His father didn't know about his biggest mistake, though. The accident.

Dean wasn't in the mood to unpack. Rubbing his hands together, he remembered the envelope from the bins on the porch. He took it out of his pocket and read it. Erica Cambridge, Reagan's sister, had dropped off Christmas decorations in case he needed some.

He'd met Erica at Marc's wedding, and it didn't surprise him she would drop off decorations. The sisters clearly shared the generosity gene. He went to the porch and hauled the bins inside even though decorating for Christmas was the last thing on his mind.

Sighing, he thought of Brooke and her telling him that they should set up two trees—one at her place and one at his. Spending too much time with her would only make him want to stay. What kind of future could he possibly have here? He wasn't worthy of the kind of life people his age enjoyed. He'd had it all at twenty-one, and he'd blown it.

This cozy cottage was a temporary place to stay. Like Jewel River itself.

When his dad recovered, Dean would leave. Get back to the solitary life that suited him just fine.

BROOKE WIPED A warm washcloth over Megan's face Saturday morning. Had she gotten all the syrup from the pancakes? She gave her chin another wipe as Megan shook her head and cried out in protest. Alice banged her kiddie fork on the high chair tray next to her twin's. A few tiny bites of sausage Brooke had cut up earlier flew into the air and landed on the floor. Times like these made her long for a dog. It would make quick work of the messes on the floor after each meal.

"You're next, sister," Brooke muttered. She unstrapped Megan and set her on the floor, then turned to Alice. "Okay, let's get you cleaned up."

"No, no, no!" She threw the baby fork, narrowly missing Brooke's shoulder.

"That's enough of that, Alice. We do not throw our silverware." Brooke reached for the other warm washcloth she'd prepared. The twins were getting more outspoken and headstrong every day. Lately, she'd been overwhelmed and doubting her ability to raise them on her own.

Was she disciplining them enough? Too much?

Alice whined as Brooke wiped her face and hands. She cleaned her up as quickly as possible and set her down to join Megan. While the girls toddled off to the open-concept living room and dumped out a basket of toys, she wiped down their high chair trays and loaded the dishwasher.

She would not pressure Dean to rush her projects. Nor would she get her hopes up that they'd be done by Christmas. She'd simply be grateful he was willing to supervise the bathroom and ramp. But, oh, how she'd hoped everything would be done before Christmas.

When would he stop by? They'd agreed he'd come over this morning, but did that mean early? Late? She wished they had specified a time. At least she'd been able to shower and put on a little makeup before the girls woke. Now that they'd eaten, she needed to change them out of their pajamas. But first…coffee.

She reached for the cup she'd poured earlier, took a sip and frowned. *Blech.* Cold. She popped it into the microwave, leaning against the counter while it warmed.

Yesterday, while the twins napped, she'd gotten out all of her Christmas decorations from the detached garage. She hadn't attempted to wrestle the giant box with the tree inside, though.

It still sat on the shelf in the garage, where it would stay until Dean arrived.

Maybe he'd be too busy to help her set it up. Maybe he was having second thoughts about everything they'd discussed. What if he took one look at the gutted bathroom, shook his head and told her he hadn't realized it needed so much work? That he was sorry, but he couldn't do it?

And what about the ramp? Who knew how long that would take?

The microwave beeped, and she grabbed the mug, wincing as the hot steam singed her fingers. She set it on the counter. Looked like she wasn't having coffee first after all.

"Meggie, Alice, let's get dressed."

"No!" one of them yelled. Probably Alice. She tended to voice her opinion more readily.

Closing her eyes, Brooke said a silent prayer. *God, give me patience.* She hoped God didn't get tired of hearing from her, because she'd been saying that prayer an awful lot lately.

She went to the living room and picked up Alice, who began shouting and kicking as she carried her to the twins' bedroom.

"Stop kicking. You need to get out of your pajamas. We all get dressed. Every day. See? I'm wearing a sweater and jeans."

"No!" Alice twisted to avoid the changing table, but Brooke got her up there. She hummed a song and made quick work of changing her diaper and putting on tiny leggings and a matching sweater. Then she brushed her hair, kissed the top of her head and set her on the carpet.

She repeated the process with Megan, and by the time she returned to the kitchen, her coffee had grown cold once more. She sighed. Back into the microwave.

At least the girls were happy again. They were giggling and rolling around on the rug in the living room. She savored the sounds. Toddler giggles should be bottled.

Just as she was taking out the coffee mug from the microwave, the doorbell chimed.

Her heartbeat thumped in her chest. Dean.

After a quick sip—not too hot this time—she hurried to the
front door. At the sight of him standing there, she inwardly
swooned. He looked as handsome as ever in jeans, a sweatshirt
and an unzipped winter coat. He smiled, and the brooding air
that always seemed to surround him vanished.

"Come in." She held the door open and waited for him to
enter before closing it once more. "Want a cup of coffee?"

"I'd better not." His brown eyes shimmered with playfulness. "Already had two cups."

"Two barely get me started. I need a full pot."

"I get that. You have twins."

"True."

They shared a long, understanding—possibly even flirty—
glance. Brooke finally pried her gaze away. The pitter-patter
of little footsteps came closer. Soon, two sets of arms wrapped
around her legs.

"Hey, girls. How are you?" He crouched to their level, and
they hid behind her legs.

"I guess they're shy this morning." She pointed down the
hall. "Let's get out of the entryway. Come on. I'll take you to
my bathroom."

As soon as she began walking, the twins disengaged from
her legs and flanked Dean. They did a combination of walking and hopping down the hall on either side of him. Brooke
flipped on her bedroom light, then paused in the doorway of
the bathroom. Dean stood next to her. She was all too aware
of his presence, and the woodsy scent of his aftershave made
her want to lean in closer. Instead, she held herself rigid.

It had been ages since she'd been attracted to a man, and
clearly, she needed to nip whatever this was in the bud.

"As you can see, it needs a lot of work." *Please don't tell
me it's in worse shape than you expected.*

"It's in better shape than I expected." *Yes.* He stepped inside. The walls had been stripped of Sheetrock, and the wiring and plumbing were new. He touched the pipes sticking out of the walls and stared at the ceiling. "Plumbing is ready. Are the electrical outlets where you want them?"

"They are. The electrician installed a few extra, too."

"Good. I looked over the blueprints yesterday. Dad already ordered everything. It's sitting in the company's storage shed. On Monday morning, I'll call a crew about coming here to install the cement board for the shower and the Sheetrock for the walls. It will take several days to mud, sand and paint everything. Then we'll install the shower tray, tile, toilet, vanity, mirrors and lights."

"Did Ed tell you I want grab bars installed?"

"Yes, and I'll put in some blocking for additional strength."

"I'll need the ramp built out back, too."

"Show me where the ramp is going."

Brooke backed up, almost knocking over Alice. She bent to lift the girl and held out her other arm for Megan. Then she slowly straightened with a twin on each hip.

"Whoa. How'd you do that?" Dean's wide eyes made her chuckle.

"A lot of practice, right girls?" They snuggled closer with their cheeks on her shoulders and stared at Dean. "The dining area off the kitchen has a door leading to the backyard and driveway. There's a small porch with steps there currently." She carried the twins out of the bedroom with Dean right behind her. The girls shifted to watch him as she continued to the kitchen, stopping near the back door.

"Hmm...may I?" Dean gestured to the door handle. Brooke nodded. He stood on the porch and surveyed the area, then came back inside. "Looks like we'll have to tear out the porch and install new posts for the ramp. Before we can dig postholes, we'll need to have the utilities out here to mark where their lines are buried. Since it's almost December, I wouldn't be surprised if the weather will play a factor."

None of that sounded promising.

"As for the bathroom, I estimate it will take about three weeks."

"Only three weeks? That's wonderful." The bathroom would be finished in time for Christmas. She could start off the new year secure in the knowledge that the inside of the house was prepared for whatever came her way.

What if something bad came her way, though? She might be able to handle it in terms of being prepared at home, but what about mentally? Emotionally?

She needed the ramp. Needed the security it would give her. While she wanted to convince Dean how important it was that everything get finished—soon—she refrained. He was doing her a big favor. And he didn't owe her anything.

"I'll do my best to get the ramp done, too, Brooke."

Was she that transparent?

"I appreciate it. You're going through a lot, so if things take longer, I understand." She would try to be patient.

He stared at her with an expression she couldn't decipher. Heat blasted her cheeks. And she wished she still had the mug of coffee in her hands, for an excuse to look at anything besides him. A commercial from the television played "Jingle Bells."

The Christmas tree. She'd almost forgotten. "Any chance you're still willing to help me set up my Christmas tree?"

"Sure." He glanced around the space. "Where is it?"

"The box is in the garage. Bottom shelf. It's heavy, so if you don't want to—" A cold breeze alerted her he'd already gone outside and was down the porch steps. A few minutes later, he carried the large box inside.

"Follow me." Brooke crossed into the living room, not daring to look back as he hauled the box. He was one strong cowboy. It reminded her she'd been married to a strong soldier. If she had a type, both muscular men would fit it. She pointed to an empty spot near the corner, so it would be more out of the way. "Over there."

"You don't want it in front of the window?"

The large picture window overlooked the backyard. "Will it stick out too much? With the girls running everywhere, I don't know if it's wise."

"Good point." He set down the box and rubbed his chin. "The corner will work."

"What dat?" Megan pointed to the box. Alice stood next to her.

"It's our Christmas tree."

"Ooh, twee!" Alice clapped her hands.

"Mr. Dean is going to help us put it up, and then we'll decorate it later."

They turned to each other with their mouths in big Os.

"I think they like that idea." Dean grinned.

"I think you're right."

He moved the box to the corner and began unpacking it. Brooke had only used it once. It had been in storage for two years. She hoped the lights still worked.

Dean assembled the sections together in record time. When he plugged it in, all the lights worked.

"Ooh!" The girls gawked at it.

"I can fluff the branches later." Brooke dragged the empty box out of the way.

"We can get it done now," Dean said. "I don't mind helping."

She turned away at the sudden emotion his words brought up. His kindness kept poking at dormant things inside her. Things she believed she'd lost forever.

The desire to have a partner, to be able to rely on him for help—she wasn't certain she wanted those feelings back, because they only reminded her what she couldn't have. A husband, more children. Not with her health problems. She would not put a man through that stress, and she wouldn't put herself through another pregnancy. Her girls were too important to take that risk.

"No, that's okay." She forced a tight smile on her face. "You're busy."

"I'm not busy. Not today, at least."

She couldn't be ungracious. And it would be ungracious to turn him away. "Okay, but don't think I've forgotten about your dad's basement. When do you want to drive over there? We'll have to assess what we're dealing with."

"Oh, uh, I haven't thought about it. Been getting settled. I'll just meet you over there sometime."

"Let me know when, and I'll get someone to watch the girls."

"You don't have to—"

"You didn't have to take over my projects or set up my Christmas tree, either." She straightened her shoulders. "I want to help. I'm going to help."

He didn't meet her eyes, but he nodded.

It hit her then. Even if she allowed herself to dream of getting remarried—which she couldn't—Dean, or any guy really, might not be interested in her. A single mom with twin toddlers was a lot to take on.

"Are the decorations out in the garage, too?" he asked.

"No, they're in the laundry room."

"We passed it on the way to your bathroom, right?"

She nodded.

"I'll go get them."

"Okay, I'll fluff these branches while you do."

They'd decorate her tree. Maybe even decorate a tree at his house later. Then she'd help him with the basement and be thankful when her house was finished. After that, her time with Dean would end.

She'd be left with good memories, a functional house and her girls.

It would have to be enough.

CHAPTER FIVE

IF ONE MORE thing delayed him from getting started on Brooke's bathroom, he was going straight to the stables, loading Dusty in the trailer, driving out to Marc's ranch and checking cattle for the next three days. Dean had never fully grasped how stressful his dad's life as a builder could be. Almost nothing happened on time, and on the rare occasion it did, materials were missing or damaged, which delayed any progress he hoped to make.

The following Thursday morning, he parked in Brooke's driveway and took a minute to get his head on straight. All week he'd been trying to line up a crew to come out here. However, the time his dad had been in the hospital had put the subcontractors in a bind, and all but one had moved on to other projects. Patrick Howard's building needed that crew.

Looked like he was installing the cement board and sheetrock himself. The only construction projects he refused to do were electrical and plumbing. Too much could go wrong. At least Terry Burman had offered to help him with Brooke's bathroom.

On Monday, Dean had inspected all of the boxes his father had ordered for Brooke's bathroom. The shower tray was damaged, one of the boxes of tile was the wrong color, and the vanity had a chip in one of the doors. Dean had called the vendors. The new shower tray arrived yesterday, but the replacement tile wouldn't be here until late next week. A new vanity door should be arriving in ten to twelve days.

Dean opened the truck door and stepped outside. A cold wind blew. He remembered the old *ten to twelve days* from his late teens when he'd worked for his dad. He doubted they'd see the new vanity door for at least three weeks—a headache he'd deal with later.

It would be worth the headache to make Brooke happy, though. Every time he thought about her dark blue eyes and her sweet girls, something twisted inside him. He wanted to give her some peace of mind.

Decorating her Christmas tree on Saturday had made him feel even more comfortable with her than before. They'd talked about Christmas traditions and how neither had celebrated much over the past couple of years. When she'd offered to help him put his tree up, he'd shaken his head and told her he'd take care of it another time, that he was driving to Casper to see his dad.

He *had* gone to Casper, but that wasn't his reason for declining.

He liked Brooke. Too much.

Before he unloaded the materials from his truck, he checked his cell phone. Dad had left three messages concerning various projects. The man had moved into the rehab center on Monday and was slowly improving. The doctors still didn't think he'd be home until after the new year, though. They also warned it could be weeks after that before he'd be able to return to work.

Could he really act as Dad's surrogate for the next month or two?

Yeah, he could. He'd expected to feel out of his league, but his afternoon check-ins with Brenda energized him. Most of the remaining work on the schedule was on track to get finished.

As he unloaded the back of the truck, Terry pulled up and parked in the street.

"Howdy, Boss. Cold enough for ya?" Terry had recently turned sixty-four. Dean knew this because the man proudly announced it every time they spoke. On the shorter side with a protruding belly, Terry had a deep, bellowing laugh that erupted often and for no apparent reason. He seemed eager to be working with Dean, so that was good.

"Yeah, I hear it's about to get frigid." Dean wrapped his tool belt around his waist.

"Bah, this ain't nothing." A toolbox swung from his hand. "Ice storm of '84 made the North Pole look like the Bahamas. Never saw anything like it in my sixty-four years."

"I hope we don't see anything like it this winter."

"I wouldn't count on it..." Terry kept up a steady stream of chatter as they made their way up the driveway and porch steps. Brooke must have done more Christmas decorating. The porch posts were wrapped in red ribbon, two wooden reindeer with plaid bows flanked the welcome mat, and a cheery Christmas wreath hung from the door. Dean knocked, and within seconds, Brooke opened it.

"Brr, it's cold out there. Come in." Wearing a navy sweater and jeans, she rubbed her forearms. "Hi, Terry."

"Howdy, Brooke." He grinned, making a production of craning his neck. "Where are those two munchkins?"

As if on cue, Megan and Alice raced to the door.

"Dee!" One of the girls pointed up to Dean. He couldn't tell them apart. They weren't dressed the same, but everything else about them was identical. His heart gave a small tug at the fact that they were trying to say his name.

"Hey there." He bent, and to his surprise, one of the girls opened her arms for a hug. He obliged, and the other twin held her arms open. He hugged her, too.

"Alice and Megan, Mr. Dean and Mr. Terry are fixing Mommy's bathroom."

One of the twins turned to Terry, who pretended to find a coin behind her ear. She laughed and laughed.

The other twin stood in front of him and thrust a floppy puppy his way. Her big, twinkly eyes would melt iron. If she'd handed him a live porcupine, he would have taken it. "How's Booboo today?"

"Woof."

He pretended to pet it and handed it back to her. She hugged it tightly and swayed side to side.

"Do you need me to show you the way?" Brooke asked. Looking at her pretty face, he melted in a different way. Yes, he wanted her to show him the way. And he wouldn't mind if she stayed right by his side until the day was over. There was something about her that drew him to her.

"I think we can manage." He attempted a smile, but he was pretty sure his lips stuck to his teeth. "Come on, Terry, this way."

As they headed down the hall to her bedroom, the aromas of waffles, Christmas spices and the baby aisle at the grocery store mingled together. Music from the living room played children's songs. One of the twins let out a loud laugh, and the other joined her.

All of it was as foreign to him as a rocket ship to space. But it intrigued him just the same.

This bright, warm home with little children and their joyful sounds made him want to settle in and stay.

But he couldn't. He was here to finish a job—and that was it.

"Here we are." Dean entered Brooke's bathroom. Terry nodded as he stood next to him. "We're going to need to cut the cement board for the shower and the Sheetrock for the walls."

"Want me to set up the saw in the driveway?" Terry asked.

"That would be great. I'll measure everything. Oh, those two-by-fours in my truck? They're for blocking. We're adding a few grab bars in here."

"On it." Terry pivoted and left the room.

Dean took out the tape measure, a small notepad and a carpenter's pencil from his tool belt. He remembered the standard height to install a grab bar and handrail, but as he held the tape measure, he realized he needed the blueprint. He didn't know the heights to be accessible for people who used wheelchairs.

Striding down the hall, he tried not to catch a glimpse of Brooke or the girls. They made him long for things he didn't want to admit he'd purposely kept out of his life.

"Dean?" Brooke stood behind the long island and held a bag of cotton balls in one hand and a stack of paper plates in the other. Why? Who knew? He wasn't asking.

"Yes?" He gave the room quick once-over to see where the twins were—sitting at a child-size table.

"Why don't you have supper here, and we can head over to your dad's place later? Mom can watch the girls tonight. That way we can figure out what needs to be done in the basement."

He swallowed so hard his throat hurt.

"Uh…" Why couldn't he finish his sentence? The only thing she suggested that appealed to him was supper. That sounded right up his alley. The basement? Not so much.

She tilted her head and gave him a stern stare. "You said it needs to get done. Think about how happy your dad will be if he comes home to an organized basement. From what you told me, he's been wanting it done for a long time."

Dean stared at his feet. She spoke the truth. It *would* make his dad happy.

"It can be a Christmas gift for him." Her eyes had gone all sparkly again. "Supper is nothing fancy. Baked chicken and mashed potatoes."

Sounded good to him.

"We wouldn't have to actually go through any of the boxes tonight. We could just come up with a plan."

Maybe she was right.

"Okay. You talked me into it." He cleared his throat. "But we'll have to drive separately."

"Why?" She rounded the island, bending to place the paper plates on the table where the girls sat. Then she dumped cotton balls on the center of the table.

"Um, I may have to stay a while, and I know you've got to get back for the girls."

"Oh." She shrugged. "Okay. Do you think you'll be working here all day? Or do you have other jobs to go to? Supper will be ready around five."

"We'll be here for most of the day. We should be able to install the cement board and Sheetrock. We'll get a coat of mud on, too. It has to dry before we can sand it and put on another coat."

"Good. Oh, I forgot—feel free to use my garage. Marc warned me you'd need a spot with electricity. I can move my minivan into the driveway if you need me to."

"Thanks. I'll tell Terry."

She handed the girls glue sticks. "Are you ready to make snowmen?"

Dragging his gaze away, he forced himself down the short hallway to the front door.

Maybe the basement wouldn't be as bad as he thought. With Brooke there, the entire process might get finished in record time. At least she hadn't questioned him about driving separately.

A gust of wind blasted him as he stepped onto the porch. He shut the door behind him.

Do it for Dad. A Christmas gift, like Brooke said. Then the whole thing can be put behind you, and you won't have to feel guilty when you come to visit. It will be over. Done.

Visit? Where would he even be living next year? His future was murky. And he had a feeling it would be for a good, long while.

"DID YOU LOSE your key or something?" Brooke shivered next to Dean on the walkway leading to the steps of his father's house. The dark, overcast sky revealed zero stars, and the temperatures had been dropping all day. She wasn't sure why he was staring at the house with a strange look on his face, but she was too cold to wait around much longer. The sooner they got inside, the sooner she could get warm.

He shook his head as if he'd been lost in a memory. She understood that. She'd gotten lost in many memories in the weeks after Ross died. Maybe his dad's heart attack was still affecting him.

"Come on." She hurried up the steps and waved for him to join her.

His reluctance came through in each step, but he finally produced a key and unlocked the front door.

"See? That wasn't so hard." She playfully nudged him with her elbow and immediately regretted it. The man was all muscle…and stiff as a marble statue. Something about this house bothered him, but she didn't want to ask him about it. It had been difficult enough just getting him to join her tonight. That in itself had been a bit strange. Why had he insisted they drive separately?

She'd enjoyed catching up with him on Saturday while they'd decorated her tree. He was easy to talk to. His laid-back personality tempted her to share personal details with him that she tended to keep to herself.

Dean opened the door for her. Inside, she felt along the wall for a light switch. *Aha.* The overhead lights flashed on, revealing a comfortable—if dusty—living room with all the masculine details she would expect from a man like Ed. Hunting magazines on the end table, a huge television mounted to the wall and a pair of leather recliners near a big couch. Marc would feel right at home here.

"Should I slip off my shoes?" she asked.

"Don't bother. The basement's this way." He led her across

the room to an archway where a large eat-in kitchen had a funky smell. Dean skirted the U-shaped counter, checked the sink and half grimaced, half gagged. "I should have come sooner. The dishes in here are full of mold."

"Fill the sink with hot soapy water. We'll let them soak while we go downstairs."

"Good plan." The faucet sputtered before letting out a steady stream of water. While Dean opened a lower cupboard to find the dish detergent, Brooke discreetly checked out the place.

"This is where you grew up, huh?"

"Yeah." He squirted dish soap into the sink.

"Is it weird coming back? When I moved to Texas with Ross after we were married, I never expected to live in my childhood home again. Marc had been living on the ranch by himself—Mom had bought a place in town by then—but he brought me back after Ross's funeral. I remember that day so vividly. Most of the days before and after are a blur. I stepped inside the living room where I'd grown up, and three things hit me at once. The first was an overwhelming feeling of love. I'd been loved in that house by my mom and brother. The second was the fact my dad still wasn't there. And that made no sense at all. He'd left us when I was twelve, and I hadn't seen him since. Why any part of me expected him to be there, I'll never understand."

She hesitated. She hadn't told any of that to anyone, not even Gracie, her best friend.

"What was the third?" Dean shut off the faucet and wiped his hands on a dish towel, then tossed it on the counter before joining her.

"The third?" She paused a moment. "I realized I didn't belong there. Not anymore. I wasn't a kid. I was a grown woman with two babies on the way."

"What did you do?" His brown eyes watched her intently.

"I went upstairs and cried all night. Silently. I cried and cried as quiet as could be."

"I'm sorry, Brooke." The way he said her name made her think he would have taken away every last teardrop if he'd had the chance.

"Thank you. I didn't realize it at the time, but moving back home was the best thing that could have happened to me. I needed Marc and my mom. And later, Reagan."

"When did you move into your house in town?"

"A little over a month ago."

"I wouldn't have guessed. It's homey, decorated. You settled in quickly."

"Yeah, I was excited to have my own place again." She gave him a smile. "The day Marc moved me to his ranch? I couldn't see a future. It wasn't even possible for me to dream I'd be where I am now."

"Is that good or bad?"

"Mostly good."

"I'm glad." He ran his hand through his hair. "I'm relieved that I don't have to stay here, even temporarily. Reagan's house has been working out great."

"Why does staying here—even temporarily—bother you?"

"I don't know." One shoulder lifted as he looked beyond her. "I guess, like you, I'm not a kid. I'm a grown man."

"And sometimes houses hold memories and old expectations that we'd rather forget."

He nodded. A moment passed between them: an understanding, a connection.

"Let me grab my notepad and pen." She turned away and fished both from her purse. "Should we see what's downstairs?"

"Yeah."

"Don't sound so excited." She grinned, but he didn't return it, just pointed to the doorway ahead and to her left.

He flipped on the light switch. The carpeted stairs ended at a landing area, then turned and continued for three more steps. Dean reached the bottom and turned on the main lights.

A large, open room yawned before them, and Brooke took it all in. It was full of stuff.

"This is bad." Dean surveyed the space with his legs wide and hands on his hips. From her perspective, he looked like a warrior facing the enemy.

Maybe he was.

She tentatively joined him. Boxes, plastic totes and bins, bulging garbage bags and old furniture filled the space.

"Now I understand why you hesitated to come here. This is…" She didn't want to hurt his feelings or sound judgmental about Ed. It wasn't as if she didn't have several boxes in her garage she might never unpack. Who didn't have closets and attics full of things they needed to go through?

"Too much." He turned to her. "Too much to ask of you. I appreciate that you offered, but I don't expect you to—"

"It's fine," she said quickly. "We'll tackle it together. It looks worse than it is."

His face contorted as he stared at her. "I think you meant it couldn't get worse. There's so much crammed down here."

"And that's why organizing it will help your dad." She reassessed her initial reaction. Now that she'd had a moment to process it, she could see it more clearly. At least everything was contained in bins and bags and boxes. "How will we know what to get rid of, though? I'm sure some of this is special to him."

"There's a back storage area with shelves. He moved all of the important stuff there." He exhaled loudly as his stance softened. "All of this—" he extended his arms "—he wasn't sure what to do with."

"Then we can take care of everything in here without worrying if he'll miss it." She made sure to keep her tone upbeat. Dean was clearly overwhelmed and upset, and she wanted to make this as easy as possible on him. She took out her notepad and pen, then narrowed her eyes. "What do you think is in the garbage bags?"

"I don't know, and I don't want to find out."

"Mind if I take a peek?" She pointed her pen to the garbage bags on an old forest-green plush couch.

"Go for it."

The first garbage bag she came across had been tied with a knot, so she wiggled it loose and peered inside. "Old clothes. Men's. Probably your dad's."

"That's all?" He came over and looked inside.

"I'm not sure." Brooke pulled out old sweaters and jeans. "These are in good shape. The church's rummage sale would take them. Some of the church members store items throughout the year."

"Do you think Dad would be embarrassed to see other people around town wearing his old clothes?" Dean started untying the garbage bag next to hers.

"I'm not sure. Maybe. I guess you could ask him. Or Casper has several thrift shops where you could donate the clothes."

"That would probably be better. I'd ask, but I don't want him worrying about anything other than his recovery at the moment."

"Plus, it would ruin the surprise."

"Exactly." He wrestled the bag open. "This one has two old winter coats."

"See? This is already easier than you thought it would be."

He straightened and assessed the room. "Easier? Look around."

She chuckled. "We'll take it one bag, one box and one bin at a time. But first, let's get a general idea of what all is down here."

They opened the bins and unmarked boxes, and gathered odd items together. All the while, Brooke jotted notes. When they finished, they went upstairs. Dean zoomed straight to the sink and began scrubbing the dishes.

"Do you think we'll need a dumpster?" Brooke sat on a stool at the counter and tapped the end of the pen against the notepad as she reviewed her notes. "I wonder if anything down there is an antique? If it is, it should be sold."

"If we come across anything we aren't sure about, we'll put it along the wall and let Dad figure out what he wants to do when he comes home."

"Good plan. I like it." She jotted a list of supplies to bring next time—packing tape, more trash bags, sticky notes and permanent markers. "What about the boxes with the name Nancy?"

Brooke assumed they were his grandmother's. Her mom still had a few boxes of things that belonged to Grandma Dorothy. Mom had a hard time letting go, as did many people. Getting rid of Grandma's belongings was too painful, so they had stayed in the attic, unused for years.

"Nancy is my mom." Dean glanced up from where his forearms were buried in soap bubbles. "We can toss those boxes."

"After we go through them." Brooke wasn't tossing anything until she knew what was in it.

"She hasn't been back since I was a kid. She won't miss any of it."

"Still…" She didn't want to argue, but in this case, she needed to. "There might be other things in there, like important documents. Stuff gets stored in wrong boxes all the time."

His jaw clenched as he rinsed the final dish. Brooke tucked the notepad and pen back into her purse. From his body language, she'd guess he didn't agree with her, but he didn't want to argue about it, either.

"What day do you want to come back and dive into it all?" she asked.

"I don't know." He set the plate in a dish rack, wiped down the counters, hung the dishcloth over the sink divider and joined her. She stood, slinging her purse strap over her shoulder.

"The Christmas festival is Saturday, or I'd say we could start then," she said. "I suppose we could come over afterward."

"Christmas festival? Where's it at?" He nodded for her to head to the front door.

"Erica and Dalton Cambridge have been hosting it at the Winston for the past couple of years," she said on her way to the entry. "This year they're having a Living Nativity with real animals."

"I suppose you're going with your mom."

"No, she's working at the bakery to give her employees the day off."

"Reagan and Marc?" He turned out all the lights, except for the one above them, and reached for the front door handle.

"Reagan's busy with Christmas orders at R. Mayer Chocolates, and Marc's working around the ranch."

Dean paused and looked into her eyes. Her pulse quickened. This brooding, gorgeous man should be off-limits. But when he looked at her like that...

"Why don't I meet you at the Christmas festival?" he said.

"Really?" Her stomach twirled at the thought.

"Yeah. You'll have your hands full with the girls. I can help."

"You're offering to help me with Megan and Alice? At the Christmas festival?" She didn't mean to sound so incredulous.

"Sure." He shrugged. "Why not?"

Why not, indeed? "Okay, meet me there at ten."

"I will. Oh, Terry's sanding the first coat of mud at your place tomorrow afternoon. I won't be there—I'm meeting Henry Zane at Dan Bagley's pole barn tomorrow for the inspection. Then I'm driving to Casper to spend time with Dad."

"Your father will love that." Her spirits dipped at the knowledge that he wouldn't be around, though. She liked spending time with him. "And I hope Dan's barn passes inspection."

"Me, too." He opened the door. "Let's get out of here. It's been a long day."

She ducked her chin into her scarf and shuffled down the

steps to the driveway. Dean held open the driver's door of her minivan.

"See you Saturday." He bent and hitched his chin to her. "Be careful driving home."

After he closed her door, she let the vehicle warm up for a minute. The girls were going to love exploring the festival with Dean. She would, too.

She'd better not read more into it, though. Her future had a big question mark around it, and Dean deserved more out of life than what she could offer.

Maybe he was just being nice.

The thought should have brought relief, but it merely dampened her good mood. *Enough of that.* A boyfriend wasn't on her Christmas list. Not even a steady guy like Dean.

CHAPTER SIX

THE DAY FELT full of promise.

Out in the cold, crisp air, Brooke pushed the double stroller across the parking lot to the large event center on Winston Ranch. Already, people waited in line near the outdoor tents, where a petting zoo and Living Nativity were located. She could just make out a few reindeer in a portable corral beyond the tents. Decorated pines, garlands galore and an empty sleigh in front of Christmas trees gave the exterior of the Winston a hefty dose of yuletide cheer. This was the first holiday season since Ross died that she had even a twinge of Christmas spirit.

She hoped her leg didn't act up today. Earlier, her calf had felt twitchy, which didn't bode well. She probably should have stayed home, but this was one Christmas memory in the making she refused to miss. The girls were going to love it.

"Out, Mama!" Alice banged her little fists on the stroller bar.

"Out." Megan had clearly gotten the memo from her sister.

Brooke ignored them. The girls had been cheery all morning. She'd savored a full cup of hot coffee while they ate breakfast. Then she'd dressed them in matching outfits—something she typically didn't do—knowing the Christmas festival was sure to be packed, and it would be easier to keep track of them if they matched.

She glanced around the parking lot. Had Dean already arrived? She didn't see him or his truck. Best to wait for him in the event center. She forged ahead.

A teenager from church opened the door for her, but she still struggled to push the stroller inside.

"Let me help with that." Clem Buckley grabbed the front stroller bar and lifted it over the threshold. "Got your hands full, huh?"

"I sure do. Thanks." She usually avoided Clem. He always said exactly what was on his mind, and his words tended to cut like a saber through butter.

"How do you tell them apart?" he asked gruffly.

"Normally, I dress them in different colors. Megan is on the left, and Alice is on the right." She tried to keep her voice pleasant.

"Howdy there, ladies." His face softened as he wiggled his fingers in greeting to the girls.

Was Clem smiling? She couldn't recall a time she'd seen him smile. The girls weren't crying, so he must not be frightening them.

"You tell your mama to take you over to the kids' area. Get you some cookies and cocoa."

There was a human heart beating in Clem after all. She opened her mouth to continue the conversation, but he straightened, gave her a stern side-eye and hitched his thumb toward the table behind him.

"I've got to watch the donation jar. We're collecting for Hildy Youngkin's roof to be repaired. The insurance lapsed after Fred died, and one strong windstorm will tear those paper-thin shingles right off." He retreated a few steps. A large jar half-filled with bills sat on the center of the red tablecloth. "A tip from me to you. Skip the Living Nativity. That entire area smells. The camel stink will curl your toes, and I'm not certain your little ones won't get fleas—or something worse—in there."

"I'll keep that in mind." Brooke dug around in her purse until she found her wallet. She dropped a twenty-dollar bill into the jar, thanked Clem and pushed the stroller off to the side to wait for Dean. The girls began to fuss, and she bent to see what the problem was.

They wanted out. Which was absolutely not happening.

A tap on her shoulder made her turn. To her surprise, it was Mackenzie Howard and Cade Moulten. They'd gotten engaged in the fall and were planning their wedding for January, much to Christy's delight. Whenever Christy stopped by, Brooke heard all the latest about their plans.

She loved weddings. Her own nuptials had been small and perfect. She'd been blessed.

"Hey, guys." Brooke hugged Mackenzie, then Cade. "Did you just get here?"

"No, we decided to go through the Living Nativity first." Mackenzie smiled. "It's amazing. The girls are going to love it."

"That's funny, because Clem told me it smelled bad and the girls would get fleas."

"Leave it to Clem." Cade shook his head and rolled his eyes. "Ignore him."

"The owner assured me the camel and the alpacas have been treated for fleas and mites." Mackenzie, the local vet, took animal health seriously. "The girls will be fine."

"Good to know." Brooke hadn't considered fleas to be a problem in any way, shape or form, so she wasn't worried. Two older ladies from church stopped in front of the twins and began oohing and aahing over them, which was good since it distracted the girls from wanting to get out of the stroller.

"Mom should be here any minute. She's bringing Tulip." Cade put his arm around Mackenzie's shoulders.

"I'll watch for her." Brooke grinned. "The girls are obsessed with that little dog."

"We are, too." They caught up for a few more minutes before Cade and Mackenzie waved and walked away.

"Sorry I'm late." Dean, out of breath, came up to her. "Got here as soon as I could."

"It's no problem." Her heart practically fluttered in her chest. How ridiculous! She should not be this excited to see him. She studied him more closely. His face was flushed. "Are you okay?"

"I'm fine. I took Dusty for an early-morning ride, and I lost track of time. Sorry."

"Is that all?" She arrived late for things too often for her own personal taste. One of the girls would spill something or need a diaper change, and her careful timeline would collapse. "No big deal." She reached out and squeezed his hand, then gripped the stroller. The church ladies had moved on, and the baked goods section beckoned. "Shall we?"

"Lead the way." He stayed by her side as they strolled around to the various booths. She bought decorated sugar cookies in the shapes of dogs and cats. Dean bought blueberry muffins and peanut butter blossoms. More than one person insisted on giving the girls treats, and Brooke had to store most of them in the white paper bag with the cookies she'd purchased. The twins were hyped up enough without buckets of sugar in their systems, and both would surely want hot cocoa later.

"What do you think?" she asked. "The outdoor attractions first? Then the children's area?"

"Works for me."

"Oh, and I want to get a picture of us in the sleigh." If it turned out well, she'd frame it. A happy memory with her girls.

"I'll take it for you."

"You will?"

"Want to take it now?"

"Good idea. Let's do it while the girls are fresh. I think I'll leave the stroller in here. It's hard to push over uneven ground." After making sure Megan and Alice had their winter coats zipped and their little stocking caps on their heads, she carried Alice, and he took Megan outside.

"Good, the line isn't too long for the sleigh." Dean pointed. Megan pointed, too, and he laughed. "You're going in there, kiddo."

Brooke happily chatted with people who stopped to greet them. When it was their turn, she gave Dean her phone and climbed into the sleigh, settling Alice on her lap. Dean handed her Megan.

"Everyone say, 'Booboo.'" He held up her phone.

Megan and Alice clapped and yelled, "Booboo!"

He took several pictures, then jogged over and handed her the phone before taking Alice from her lap. "What now?"

She kept Megan on her hip as she stepped down, but her leg muscle gave out, making her trip and fall into Dean. With one arm, he steadied her. "Whoa, there. You okay?"

"I'm fine." Heat blasted her cheeks. Stupid leg. "Just tripping over my own feet."

He didn't say a word, but his eyes shimmered with concern. He kept his hand on her elbow to guide her toward the tents. She had the strongest urge to hold his hand or hook her arm in his. To lay a claim on him that wasn't hers to make. This wasn't a date. They were two friends enjoying the Christmas festival together. That was it.

"Let's check out this Living Nativity and hope we don't get fleas," she said brightly.

"Huh?"

She told him about Clem's warning as they made their way to the tent. After a brief wait in line, they were ushered inside, where John and Shirley Jones, a couple from church, wore makeshift robes. "Welcome to Bethlehem. You're about to go on a journey—a Christmas journey—similar to the one Mary and Joseph took over two thousand years ago. You'll pay your taxes and see the sights and sounds of the market. You'll stop at the inn and the stables. And you'll see shepherds worshiping a baby—our Savior, Jesus Christ."

They took it seriously, Brooke would give them that. She glanced up at Dean. With a solemn expression, he tipped the front of his Stetson and replied, "Thank you."

They carried the twins through the next section of the tent. Roger Pearl, Jewel River's dentist, was dressed like a soldier. He stepped into their path. "Halt. What is your purpose here?"

Megan took one look at Roger and started bawling. Alice joined her. Their wails were accompanied with fat teardrops on their cheeks.

"Oh, no, I'm sorry." Roger took off his helmet. "See, girls? It's me. Rog."

Brooke glanced at Dean. "I think we'll try this next year when they're a little older."

"Smart thinking."

"I'm sorry, Brooke," Roger said. "I never thought I'd scare them." He fished around where his pockets should have been, but his costume didn't have any. "Oh, fish sticks. Next time I see you, I'll have stickers for them. You two girls can have all the stickers, okay?"

"It's fine, really." The wailing continued. "We'll pet the reindeer instead."

"There's a shortcut through the back." He pointed behind him.

"Thanks."

They hurried out, and the girls quieted almost immediately. Megan's bottom lip still wobbled, but Brooke could tell the worst was over.

Brooke kissed Megan's cheek. "How about we go see the reindeer?"

Dean was rubbing Alice's back as her arms wrapped around his neck tightly. He whispered, "Shh. It's okay. I've got you."

Seeing him holding Alice, hearing him comfort her, made her stomach drop. Maybe enjoying the Christmas festival with him was a mistake.

Stop reading too much into it.

A couple of hours together wouldn't hurt a thing.

"Well, if it isn't Dean McCaffrey." A female voice carried. "I figured I'd see you around eventually."

Ten minutes after the Living Nativity fiasco, Dean turned his attention to Donna Marquez, one of his high school friends, waving to him from outside the pen.

He kept a firm grip on Alice's and Megan's hands in the reindeer pen. Brooke had been taking pictures, but had gotten waylaid by a little boy who wanted to talk to her.

"Hey, Donna," he said, slowly steering the girls her way. "It's been a while."

"Too long. How'd you get your hands on these babies?" Donna grinned and waved her hot pink gloves beyond him. "Hey, Brooke."

"Hi, Donna." Brooke grinned before turning her attention back to the little boy.

"How's your dad?" With dark curls tumbling from the hood of her coat, Donna rested her forearms on top of the fencing.

He glanced down at the twins. They were getting antsy. He swooped Alice up on his right hip and Megan on his left. "He's improving. Ornery, though."

She let out a guffaw. "Ornery is only the start of it, I'm sure. Ed lives, eats and breathes construction. It can't help his blood pressure being out of the loop for this long."

"I'm doing everything I can to keep his blood pressure as low as possible." He smiled, firming his hold on Alice as she twisted her neck to watch the reindeer behind them.

"You're doing a great job. Henry said Dan's pole barn passed inspection, and Patrick Howard's relieved his service dog training center will be able to open on time."

"Thanks, but I didn't do anything special."

"I disagree." She narrowed her eyes and made a tut-tut sound. "Since when did you become so modest?"

"What about you?" Time to change the subject. "What have you been up to?"

"Got promoted to sergeant in the spring, and I met Andy in September." She glanced back and pointed to a tall man in a winter coat standing a few feet behind her. The man didn't smile, didn't move. He did nod, though. "Hey, Andy, this is my buddy from high school, Dean. The one I told you about. His daddy had the heart attack."

"Sorry about that. Having fun, Donna?" Brooke joined them. "Hey, Andy."

The man gave her a nod.

"We're having a great time," Donna said. "Not as much fun as you two seem to be having, though."

Dean stiffened. Did Donna think he and Brooke were dating? That they were a couple?

"You're having fun today, aren't you, Meggie?" Donna asked. "You too, Alice."

The twins. Right.

"Except for the Living Nativity. Too intense for them at this age." Brooke reached for Megan, and Dean handed her over.

"Uh-oh. Did Roger scare them?"

Brooke chuckled. "Yeah. He felt terrible."

"Well, I won't keep you. Bye, girls." Donna blew them kisses, and they blew kisses right back to her. "Bye, Dean."

"See you later, Donna."

Donna and Andy continued on their way, and Brooke began walking toward the corral gate. "Are you up for the children's area? It's inside."

"I'm up for it." He unlatched it and waited for her to exit before following her out of the reindeer pen.

"Have you decorated your tree yet?" She asked about his

tree every time he saw her. And the answer was always the same. No.

But he didn't want to admit he had no plans to decorate one. "Not yet."

"Dean! You need to decorate it. Just think how nice it will be to come home to those twinkling lights."

"Mmm-hmm."

"Do I need to come over tomorrow and make sure it happens?"

"No, no." He shook his head. "I'll take care of it."

"Uh-huh." She didn't sound convinced. Inside the Winston, they unzipped their coats, found the stroller along the wall and laid the coats on top of it. Then they went to the restrooms to wash their hands.

When they returned, Brooke turned to him with wide eyes. "Oh, I almost forgot. Joey's movie. Let's go find it." Brooke looked around and pointed to the left. "It looks like the kids' area is over there. Oh, look, a hot cocoa stand."

In no time at all, Brooke situated Megan and Alice on the large rug where several kids lounged in front of a big-screen television that played a movie.

"Why don't I get us some hot chocolate?" Dean whispered, bending over so only she could hear him and not the girls.

"Would you? That sounds good." Her grateful smile sent a pool of warmth down to his stomach. What was it about her? Was it this festival? It made him feel all ooey-gooey inside, and he'd never considered himself a softie.

"Be right back." First he checked out the movie. Instrumental Christmas music played, and a cat wearing an elf's hat walked past a fireplace. The twins pointed, their mouths rounding in Os as they yelled, "Kiki!"

Then a dog with antlers walked past the fire. One of the girls pretended to bark. Probably Megan. A bunny with a red cape hopped by the fire. The twins scrambled to their feet. "Bunbun! Mama, see?"

"I see. A Christmas kitty, doggy and bunny. Don't they look cute?"

Dean tore his gaze away from Brooke and the girls. The camera panned to a window with snow falling against a night sky. Then the three animals lay side by side on a rug in front of the fireplace. The words Merry Christmas danced on the bottom of the screen for several moments, and then the movie replayed. He noted both twins staring in rapt attention at the television.

A dozen people waited in line ahead of him at the hot chocolate booth, and he took the time to study the place. It seemed the entire town had turned out for the Christmas activities and bake sale.

This morning, as he'd ridden Dusty around the trails at the stables, he'd had second thoughts about coming. But there was something special about experiencing the event with the twins and Brooke.

The line inched forward, and he bought four cocoas with whipped cream topped with lids. He brought them in a drink carrier to the children's area. Brooke had settled the girls at a child-size picnic table, where they were coloring on printed sheets of snowmen.

"Here you go." He handed Brooke one of the cocoas.

"Thank you. I saved you a chair." She gestured to the folding chair next to hers.

"Should I give them these?"

"Not yet. Let's give them time to cool down. Besides, they're busy at the moment."

He sat beside her, enjoying how the twins clutched the crayons in their chubby fingers.

"We need to set a time to work on your dad's basement."

"What do you mean? We went there a few nights ago."

She laughed as if he'd said something funny. "All we did was figure out a game plan. We actually need to go through all the stuff."

"Do we?" Although his tone was joking, inside, he was dead serious.

"How about Wednesday night? My mom should be free to watch the girls."

Wednesday? So soon? He wanted to let out a loud sigh but took a sip of cocoa instead. "Uh, sure."

Brooke winced, set her cup on the floor and massaged her left calf.

"Everything all right?"

"Yeah." She let go of her leg and straightened. Her forehead creased as she picked up her cup. "My leg acts up sometimes."

"What do you mean?"

"It gets weak. Cramps and twitches."

"Anything I can do to help?"

She shook her head, but the tightness in her face concerned him.

"How often does this happen? What do the doctors say?"

"Not that often." She shrugged. "They tell me to take it easy. I will when I get home."

"It's good that we're taking a break." He took another drink of the cocoa. Sweet. Warm. He hadn't had one in years, but could easily make it a habit.

Megan and Alice lost interest in their coloring sheets. They toddled over to Brooke and put their hands on her leg as they bounced. "Cocoa?"

"Yes, Mr. Dean got you some cocoa, too. What do we say?"

"Tank you!" Megan shuffled over to him and held up her arms.

"You're welcome." He picked her up and gave her a hug. The layer of toughness he'd forced on himself a decade ago melted away. He was beginning to understand why parents would do anything to protect their kids. These girls were precious.

"Me, me!" Alice held up her arms.

He laughed and set Megan back on her feet. Then he hugged Alice.

Brooke pointed to the table. "Once you sit down, I'll give you the cocoa."

They sat across from each other and beamed at her as she put the cups in front of them.

Alice took a sip and grinned. Megan followed. They only spilled a few dribbles. Brooke wiped them with napkins, then winced.

"Here, why don't you sit again?" He wanted to take her hand in his. Reassure her he'd take care of whatever she needed. But they didn't have that kind of relationship.

Which left him wondering, what kind of relationship did they have?

"Thanks." Her face had paled, and fear filled her gaze. "I was going to return home soon, before the girls get crabby, but I think I'd better stay here for a while."

Any other guy would leap at the chance to drive her and the twins home. He wanted to be that guy.

He couldn't offer to drive her home, though. Couldn't offer much at all.

No, that wasn't true. He could do something. It might not be much, but it was better than nothing. "I'll stay with you."

The way her eyes lit up would have made someone think he'd offered her the moon. Did she expect so little out of life that him offering to stay with her made her grateful?

"Thanks, Dean. I appreciate it."

"It's no problem." He finished his hot chocolate and pushed the empty cup to the side. "Your husband would have loved this, huh?"

"Ross?" She frowned, blinking. The twins were licking the lids of their cups. "Yeah. He'd have loved it. He would have been protective of the girls. That was his nature. And he would have spoiled them, I'm sure. It's hard sometimes, thinking of what should have been."

What should have been. She *should* have been here with her husband.

And Dean should have been alone in Texas, checking cattle. Not enjoying himself here with her.

"I wish your husband could be here. I'm sorry you're stuck with me today."

"Never be sorry. I'm not stuck with you—I'm glad we did this. It's been really nice. Thank you."

Really nice.

For him, too.

They were quite the pair. Brooke had physical issues. He had emotional ones. And she needed someone she could depend on, not a guy like him who couldn't even drive her and the twins home when her leg cramped up.

He wasn't meant for Christmas festivals and families and a beautiful woman like Brooke. He'd simply finish her projects, deal with Dad's basement and move on.

SHE'D BEEN PUSHING herself beyond her limits. And she'd let her enthusiasm about walking around the festival with Dean bulldoze the signs that she needed to slow down. It had only been an hour since she'd left the Christmas festival, but she probably should have driven home immediately after tripping as she got off the sleigh.

The signs that she needed to rest had been there, and she'd chosen to ignore them. Being off-balance, fatigued, having the muscle weakness—not good.

Brooke leaned her head against the pillow she'd brought from her bed to the couch. She stared at the ceiling with her hands on her stomach. The girls were napping in their room, and she'd put a soothing Christmas playlist on the speaker. The mug of hot tea on the end table behind her was too hot to drink.

Dr. South's advice whistled through her brain. *Be mindful of your body. Keep your stress levels low. Don't overdo it.*

She constantly referred to her list of stress relievers she kept in her phone. *Lie on the couch, listen to soft music, sip hot tea, take a long bath, read a novel, watch a movie, do gentle stretches.*

All well and good if she wasn't raising active toddlers by herself. Was she being too optimistic thinking she could raise the twins on her own?

Closing her eyes, she tried to picture Ross. His sharp jaw and amused expression still stayed in her mind. She remembered how she'd clung to him right before he left on assignment. How he'd kissed her and held her as if he'd never wanted to let her go.

But he had let her go.

Neither of them had had any idea it would be their final moment together.

The familiar sadness seeped through her body, but it didn't feel as raw anymore. She supposed she was moving on…to what, though?

Dean's brown eyes, broad shoulders and gentle way with her girls kept opening her eyes to a potential future she'd never considered.

Her ankle and calf twitched as if to remind her she'd be a fool to consider dating again. Her health problems were real, and they were too much to burden Dean with.

God, forgive me for wanting things I can't have. Remind me You're enough. You'll always be enough for me and my girls.

Her eyelids drooped. Maybe she needed a nap as much as the twins did. Monday morning, she'd call the specialist about her leg. If the weakness was signaling her body was in danger, she needed medical advice.

Once again, she wished the bathroom were finished. If she had to use a wheelchair, the bathroom and ramp would be vital for her to live here with the girls. Anxiety spun around inside her.

Dean would complete everything. She could count on him to see her projects through. They'd finish his dad's basement—providing she didn't have a medical emergency anytime soon—and then they'd go their separate ways. She'd keep her romantic feelings to herself. It wouldn't do to burden him with her house *and* her heart.

She wasn't the kind of girl who could offer marriage and more children, and he might not be the type of guy who wanted either from her.

They were best off staying just friends.

But her heart was stretching past the friendship boundary already, and she couldn't seem to stop it.

CHAPTER SEVEN

"IT'S TOO COLD to dig the holes for the new posts." On Wednesday afternoon, Terry's breath came out in visible puffs as he eyed the pile of old decking they'd finished tearing from the back porch of Brooke's house. "Ground's frozen."

Dean pushed and pulled on one of the old posts, trying to wiggle it loose. "These have to go. Did you call 811 yesterday?"

"No. I saw the forecast and figured I'd better talk to you before having the utility lines flagged."

Dean clenched his jaw. He'd specifically told him to call the number yesterday. He hadn't asked him to check the forecast. While Terry had been a big help so far, the man didn't always follow through with directions.

"We need to get these posts out and the new ones in. Soon."

"If you ask me, it should have been done in the fall." Terry pulled back his shoulders. "I've lived in Wyoming for sixty-four years…"

Here we go. If Dean had to hear one more mention of Terry's sixty-four years, he was going to march to his truck and drive to the stables to ride Dusty. He couldn't take it.

"I'm sure you're right, but this ramp needs to be installed before Christmas." He looked around the yard, trying to come up with a plan. He couldn't build the ramp until the old posts were removed. He also couldn't build the ramp until the new posts were installed. And Terry was right. The ground was frozen and probably would be through May.

Getting the old posts out wouldn't be a problem. McCaffrey Construction had machines for that. But he didn't want to tear up Brooke's yard by digging the new holes with a backhoe.

At least the bathroom was moving along. He and Terry had installed the shower tray on Monday. And yesterday, Dean had painted the walls. He'd tried to find a subcontractor to lay the tiles, but they were booked through mid-January.

He might not be an expert, but he knew the basics on how to set the shower and floor tiles. The replacement tiles had arrived yesterday. In the meantime, he wanted to get started on the ramp.

Which meant they needed to dig postholes, bringing him back to square one.

Think. This was Wyoming. Winter lasted forever. Nothing new there. Ranchers had to fix fences all the time, and that included putting new posts in the ground.

Dean pulled his phone from his coat pocket, tore off one glove and found Marc's number. He answered after one ring. "What's up?"

"Any suggestions on how to dig a posthole when the ground is frozen?"

"Are you kidding? I dig them all the time in the winter. Here's what you're going to do. Figure out where you want the holes and clear the area of anything flammable. You're going to cover those spots with metal ovens—don't worry, I've got a bunch of old metal protein supplement tubs on hand for that reason. We'll make some fires and cover them with the metal ovens. Let them burn a few hours, and you'll be able to dig those holes with no problem."

"What about embers and sparks?" Dean saw the potential in Marc's idea, but this was a residential area, and he had to keep in mind all of the nearby houses.

"I weigh down a small mesh screen over each smoke hole. Keeps the embers in."

They chatted a few more minutes and ended the call. Dean then explained the process to Terry, who brightened at the mention of fires and metal ovens.

"If we get us some marshmallows, we can make s'mores."

Dean blinked twice. Had Terry really just said that? "No marshmallows. This isn't camping."

"I didn't say it was. I just like a toasted marshmallow now and then. My mouth's watering just thinking about those burnt, crunchy edges."

Dean ignored him and dialed 811. After telling the operator Brooke's address, he pocketed the phone.

"Let's move the old deck boards to the back of my truck."

"What about these?" Terry pointed to the posts sticking out of the ground.

"We'll bring the digger over."

A grin spread across Terry's face. "Now you're talking."

Two hours later, the cement-encased posts had been removed, and all of the old materials were loaded into the back of Dean's truck. Terry waved goodbye, and Dean knocked on the front door to let Brooke know they were leaving.

"Come in." She smiled, waving him inside.

"Dee!" Megan and Alice barreled to him with their arms open wide.

He laughed and gave them both hugs. They each took him by the hand and attempted to drag him to the kitchen.

"Whoa, I can't go in there." He used his kid-friendly voice. "My boots are all muddy."

Their faces fell, and Brooke caressed the tops of their heads. "Go play for a minute while I talk to Mr. Dean."

"No, Mama." They both shook their heads. "No."

"Girls," she warned.

"Dee, Dee!" Alice clung to his hand.

"Alice!" Brooke sounded mortified. "Mr. Dean is working. He can't come in right now."

She stomped her little foot. Even when mad, the kid was cute. Dean held back a laugh. Megan whispered something in Alice's ear, and together, they ran off.

"Those two get more stubborn every day." She gave him her full attention. "What's going on?"

"The back porch is gone, so I put up a rail blocking the doorway to keep you or the girls from accidentally falling. I'm heading over to Marc's to pick up a few supplies, and I'll be right back."

"Maybe the girls and I could come with you. I wanted to pick up a novel from Reagan. She was supposed to drop it off today, but she forgot it at home."

Dean blanked. His palms grew clammy, and his chest grew tight.

Brooke could not come with him. Not if he was driving.

"Sorry," he choked out. "The truck's full." A lie, but a necessary one. "I can pick up the book for you if you'd like."

Was he imagining the question in her stare? Maybe.

"Of course." She shook her head in a self-chastising way. "You need your truck for supplies. I don't know why I thought we could all take my minivan. If you don't mind grabbing it for me, she said the book is on the kitchen counter. And when you come back, we can head over to your dad's place."

His mind raced. What was she talking about?

"It's Wednesday. Basement. Remember?"

"Oh, right." He should have made an effort to sound thankful, but he was pretty sure he sounded like a man condemned. "I'll have to meet you over there."

As the words left his mouth, he wanted to take them back. Wanted to be a normal guy who could drive her wherever she wanted to go. He couldn't, though.

"Why don't we drive over together?" she asked.

"I can't."

"Why not?"

Because I get a panic attack every time someone gets in the passenger seat. I'm thrown right back to that night when I almost killed Lia. The wreckage... How did either of us survive?

"I just can't." The words came out with the speed and precision of a nail gun.

"But it would save on gas, and we live so close to each other."

"Brooke." He inhaled through his nose, feeling the nostrils flare. Was it anger? Or fear? If it was anger, he needed to bring it down right now.

"What?"

Hedging and lying were not the way to go. He'd simply tell her the truth and trust she'd understand. Even if he didn't understand it himself.

"I don't drive with anyone else in my truck—or any vehicle, for that matter."

"Really?" She blinked in surprise. "Why not?"

"I was in a bad accident—" No, he wouldn't sugarcoat it. "I take that back. I *caused* a bad accident. And I haven't been able to drive with anyone in the passenger seat since."

"How long ago?" She didn't look horrified. Yet.

"Ten years, give or take." He kept himself still and stood tall.

"What happened?"

He gave a slight shake of his head. "I don't want to talk about it."

"Were you hurt?"

"No." Only on the inside. The emotional scars refused to heal.

"Was anyone else hurt?" The words were gentle, and her eyes warm.

"No."

"But everything changed for you, didn't it?"

"Yes." How did she know? How had she put his replies together and come up with that?

"I see." No judgment. Just acceptance.

"You do?"

She nodded, a compassionate smile on her lips. "Life changes in an instant. There's before. There's after. And no matter how hard you try or how much you want to, you can't get back to before. You're stuck with after."

"Yeah." He wanted to say so much more. Wanted to thank her for putting into words what he couldn't himself. Wanted to tell her he'd get back to before—back to when he could drive with a passenger and not have a complete emotional breakdown. Back to when he had a social life and a job with a future.

Back to when he sort of liked himself.

But she was right. He was stuck with after. And he wasn't making promises he couldn't keep.

"I'll meet you at your dad's house at six-thirty." Her chin rose slightly. "We're going to make a dent in it. You'll see."

Dean searched her eyes for any trace of disgust, but all he found was her acceptance of what he'd told her. He didn't have the heart to tell her the last thing he wanted to do was go through those boxes in the basement. Not when something was probably down there—who knew where—that he didn't want to see, didn't want to remember.

He sighed. "Yes, I'll meet you there."

SNOW BLEW DIAGONALLY across the road as Brooke neared Ed's driveway that evening. She didn't like driving in bad weather, but this was Wyoming. She'd never leave the house if she waited for clear skies. Tonight, however, it added a layer of stress she didn't need.

The leg twinges she'd experienced on Saturday had returned briefly Sunday evening. On Monday, she'd called the specialist to make an appointment. They couldn't get her in until January. When she'd called the clinic here in town, Dr. South referred her to the specialist and told her to get more rest. She'd expected it. She'd called the clinic many times about leg weakness and fatigue over the past eighteen months. They were probably sick of her.

If she was supposed to be resting, why had she insisted on working on the basement with Dean tonight?

She turned into the driveway and kept her gaze straight ahead until parking in front of the garage. Dean's truck wasn't there. Not surprising, since she was ten minutes early.

She probably should have stayed home and rested. The Christmas season had brought more activity than she was used to, and she'd been enjoying every minute of it. She'd finished wrapping all the homemade candles, and the gifts she'd ordered for the girls were beginning to arrive.

Just because she had energy, though, didn't mean she should deplete it. She'd have to take extra care not to overdo it tonight.

What Dean had told her earlier about his accident came to mind. Had he been drinking? Distracted? What had happened? And why had it affected him so deeply?

Headlights appeared in her rearview. He was here. Anticipation spread through her body.

As he parked, she got out of the minivan and retrieved her box of supplies. They braced themselves against the cold all the way to the front porch and didn't speak until they were both inside.

"What a night, huh?" Dean swiped off his coat and shook the snowflakes from his hair.

Brooke had a hard time looking away from him. She had the strongest urge to help him brush off those snowflakes. *Keep your hands to yourself.*

"What's that?" He pointed to the box she'd set on the floor.

"Tape, garbage bags, scissors, blank labels, markers." She eased out of her coat. Dean reached for it, and she smiled. He hung both their coats in the closet, and they headed to the basement.

"Oh, good. The kitchen doesn't smell anymore." She glanced over her shoulder on the way to the staircase.

"You're right." He grinned. "Scrubbing the dishes must have taken care of it."

When they reached the basement, Brooke moved to the side to catch her breath and rest a moment. Dean didn't seem to notice. He went straight to the couch where they'd found the clothes in garbage bags. Two more remained.

"I'll deal with these." He grabbed one of the bags and began untying it.

"I'll start looking through the boxes." In a minute or two. She needed to get her equilibrium first.

"Don't feel like you have to do anything," Dean said. "I'll take care of the heavy lifting."

Music to her ears. She missed having someone around to get things out of storage…and to kill spiders. She hated spiders.

Ross hadn't been around much for their marriage, though. He'd been deployed for most of it. She'd gotten boxes out of storage herself. Killed spiders herself.

Why did she long for something she'd never had?

Brooke looked at the boxes closest to her. Should she dive into them? Or work through the plastic bins?

Dean hauled two of the bulging garbage bags near the staircase, dropped them on the floor and resumed his spot at the couch.

She lifted the cover off one of the bins. A wireless phone, an answering machine, cords galore, and an empty box the phone had been packaged in greeted her. All of it looked hopelessly out of date. "I think we can safely donate this entire bin. Except for the empty boxes. I'm trashing those."

"What's in there?" He glanced up. She listed everything, and he nodded. "Donate, for sure."

"I have to ask—and I already know the answer—but have you decorated the tree at your house yet?" She didn't look up from the bin she was poking through. She wanted Dean to have the Christmas feels. Every night, she loved dimming the lights, wrapping up in a soft blanket and staring at her pretty Christmas tree after the girls went to bed.

"Not yet."

"I'll come over and help you. Just say when. I want you to walk into your house and experience that warm hug feeling you get from seeing the glow of the Christmas tree lights."

"Warm hug? From those prickly needles? If you say so."

"You know what I mean."

He smiled at her. "Yeah, I know."

They talked about their favorite Christmas memories for half an hour and moved things into piles. Trash. Donate. Sell. Keep. The things they weren't sure about, they packed together in the bins she'd emptied. Ed could decide what to do with them later.

Brooke reached for a box marked Office, but it was too heavy. "Do you mind lending some muscle over here?"

"Sure thing." His lopsided grin and shimmering eyes made her heart beat faster. It certainly wasn't the taxidermied prairie dog she'd come across in the previous box, although that had given her a scare. He carried the box over to the coffee table. "Now that the couch is cleared off, you can sit on it while you're sifting through Dad's treasures."

"I like that. Sifting through your dad's treasures." She opened one of the flaps. "If anyone went through the boxes in my attic, they wouldn't think they were treasures. They'd see a bunch of junk."

"That's mostly what I'm seeing here." He went to the other side of the couch and hauled a crate of vinyl records over. "Why do you keep yours?"

"I suppose it's not junk to me." She smiled at him. He was staring at her, and she wasn't sure why. She turned her attention to the contents of the box. "I think this one must have been marked wrong."

"Why do you say that?" He shuffled through several records.

"I spy someone's rodeo trophies," she singsonged. Then she faked an enthusiastic grin as she lifted one up.

"Nothing like gold-sprayed plastic to make you feel like you're a winner." He shoved the records back in the crate. "Vinyls are popular again. I'm putting these in the sell pile."

"Good plan." She set each trophy on the coffee table and worked through the rest of the box. An old computer mouse, too many random ink pens to count, a mug shaped like a moose head and a plastic grocery bag filled with Matchbox cars and candy wrappers. "I don't think these candy wrappers are worth anything, but the cars might be."

Dean strode over and peeked in the bag. "Seriously? Why didn't Dad throw this away?"

He took the bag from her and tied the handles into a knot.

"Little boys would love those cars." She held out her hand to take it back. "Church rummage sale?"

"Fine. I'm getting rid of the trash in here, though." He sighed and opened the bag again. Took out each car. Reached in and dug around.

Then his hand stopped. He pulled out something, stared at it with an odd expression and quickly shoved it in his pocket before wadding up the bag and taking it over to the trash pile. "We've gotten a lot done tonight. Why don't we call it quits? I'll follow you back to town. This weather could make the roads slick."

"You're probably right. I don't like driving when it's snowing and the wind picks up."

With a serious expression, he nodded. "This is going faster than I thought it would."

They both surveyed the large space. They'd cleared about a third of the floor already. Progress.

"When are you visiting your dad again?"

"Tomorrow."

"In that case, why don't we load your truck with the pile of donations? You can drop them off at the thrift shop in Casper."

She took out her cell phone, searched for ones close to the rehab center and texted him the results. "There. You have at least three to choose from."

She hefted one of the garbage bags and started up the staircase.

"Wait, you don't need to carry anything. I don't want your leg to bother you again." He reached for the bag. His calloused palm grazed the back of her hand, launching her back to her teen years and the million crushes she'd indulged in. She liked this guy. A lot.

Why wouldn't her brain get the memo that she was a widow with twin daughters, not a single woman in her prime? *If you care about him, you won't even consider a future together. You could be paralyzed or die young. And he'd be stuck dealing with the aftermath. It wouldn't be fair to him. Stop being selfish.*

"I think I can handle this. It's light." She yanked the bag her way. "You can get the other stuff."

He met her gaze for a moment too long, then nodded. She continued up the stairs. When she reached the top, she wasn't sure if her heart was racing due to overexertion or from the lingering sensation of Dean's hand grazing hers.

Either way, it was good they were calling it a night. She couldn't fall for Dean McCaffrey. Not now. Not ever. Not with her uncertain future.

CHAPTER EIGHT

"DID YOU BRING me crullers?" Dean's father finished tying his running shoes and rose to his full height on Friday afternoon. He wore dark gray sweatpants and a Wyoming Cowboys T-shirt. He looked like he'd dropped ten pounds in the short time he'd been in the rehab center. His face was still pale, though, and he took a moment to catch his breath.

"Crullers? No." Dean shook his head, pretending to be offended. "You're supposed to be eating healthy."

"Anne's crullers *are* healthy." He dropped into one of the chairs by the window. "They give me the will to live."

"I brought you the next best thing." He held up the paper bag with an Annie's Bakery sticker on the side. "Her low-sugar, high-protein applesauce muffins."

"Low sugar?" His dad pulled a face. "Are you punishing me, son?" He muttered something about tasting like cardboard, and Dean decided to ignore it.

For the first time since getting the call about the heart attack, Dean truly believed his dad would make a full recovery. Relief made him tighten his grip on the bag.

He'd spent yesterday morning at McCaffrey Construction's office in town going over unfinished business with Brenda.

Then he'd headed to the various jobsites before hurrying to Brooke's house.

Sadly, building the ramp was on hold. The utility companies were dealing with severe weather in several counties, and they wouldn't be out to her place until next week to mark the lines.

Thankfully, between yesterday afternoon and this morning, Dean had been able to install the grab bars in her bathroom, and he'd laid the shower tiles. As long as the new vanity door arrived by the end of next week, her bathroom would be finished by Christmas.

He was certain of it.

What he wasn't certain of was how to deal with the locket he'd found in that bag of toy cars Brooke had handed him in the basement Wednesday night.

He'd known what it was the instant he'd spotted it. The one thing he'd hoped would stay lost forever.

Twenty-three years ago, he'd stolen the locket from his mother the week before she'd moved out permanently. He'd been eight.

Why had he done it? Why had he taken the necklace from her? He'd regretted it almost immediately. Over the years, he'd wondered what had happened to it. And now he knew.

When he'd gotten back home after making sure Brooke arrived to her house safely, he'd tossed the locket into the dresser drawer with his socks, where it had been burning a hole ever since.

He hadn't opened it to see the photos inside.

He knew what he'd find.

And he didn't want to see them.

"I might as well try one of those tough, nasty muffins." Dad motioned for him to hand him the bag. Dean brought it over. "If Anne made them, they might not be so bad."

His cheeks still had a hollowness to them. Dean could see why he needed to be here rather than home.

"Hard day, huh?" Dean pulled a chair over to sit across from him and leaned forward to rest his forearms on his knees.

"Yep." Boy, he looked tired. "They had me on the stationary bike for thirty minutes."

"Are you sure they aren't working you too hard?" Should he find one of the nurse's aides and ask them about it?

"They're working me hard, but I need it. I feel stronger. I'm sleeping better, too. I didn't realize how out of shape I was—and how much the heart attack and surgery took out of me."

"Brooke said the same about her stroke." When Dean had finished at Brooke's place yesterday, he'd hung around talking to her for a long time. She'd explained her daily routine while in the rehab center. It made him appreciate what she'd been through even more than he had before. The woman was a fighter. A good mom. A great listener.

A friend.

His friend.

"She would know. It does make me feel better." Dad took a large bite of the muffin and didn't continue until he'd chewed it. "What's going on with the business?"

He fought a twinge of disappointment. His father always wanted updates on the construction projects, but he never seemed to want updates about him personally. Not that he expected him to care when he was dealing with so much, but Dean had a lot on his mind beyond McCaffrey Construction.

He was confused. About his future. About his feelings for Brooke. About the fact he actually enjoyed being involved with his father's business and didn't miss ranching as much as he thought he would.

"Everything's on track." Dean filled him in on Brooke's bathroom, Patrick's building and a potential new construction house Brenda had gotten a call about yesterday.

"Did you set up an initial meeting with them?" Dad finished the muffin and wiped the crumbs from his hands.

"Not yet—"

"What's the holdup? We don't turn down business if we can help it."

"I didn't turn down business." Frustration built. This was how his temper always ignited—Dad made assumptions, Dean justified himself, and before he knew it, they'd be going round and round, tempers escalating. *You're older now. More mature. You don't have to react.* "I needed to talk to you before I set up the initial appointment."

His father frowned. "Me? Why?"

"To make sure you want to take the job. Do you think you'll be able to handle adding it to your busy schedule? The couple wants to break ground this spring."

"That gives us plenty of time." He had a far-off look in his eyes. "I'll be home around Christmas. Back to work the beginning of January. I've got a few basement remodels starting in February. Yes, the spring will be fine."

Dean had his doubts. "Have the doctors told you you'll be home at Christmas and ready to work in January?"

"Doctors?" He scoffed. "I've got it covered. I'm doing my part. Sitting through the nutrition classes and listening to them jabber on about stress management. Next week, they're getting me on the elliptical machine. I'm not looking forward to it, but it's what I've got to do to get out of here and have my life back."

Dean had been avoiding thinking about it, but when Dad got his life back, where did that leave him?

"And, son, I know this isn't something we talk about, but I'd sure like for you to join me at McCaffrey Construction. You're doing a good job. Clem Buckley and Christy Moulten visited me yesterday, and they said everyone around town is impressed with how you've stepped up."

"Clem and Christy came together?" He'd chew on the compliment later. First he had to deflect the topic of him joining the family business. Didn't need a case of heartburn on an otherwise fine Friday.

"Yeah." He let out a throaty chuckle. "He's giving her driving lessons, and from what I can tell, they aren't going all that well. Those two bicker like an old married couple."

"Huh."

"You don't have to give me an answer today. Just consider it. That's all I'm asking."

Younger Dean would have brushed him off with a curt reply. Older Dean didn't have it in him. "I'll think about it."

Dad blinked several times before giving him a firm nod. "All right, then. Now, how's your horse? Christy mentioned you're stabling Dusty at Cade's stables. We did a bang-up job on that project. I worried we wouldn't finish it before his deadline, but we stayed on track and got it done. I had to bring in subcontractors from Casper."

"Dusty's thriving. Trent takes care of him whenever I can't be there."

"You and Trent used to run around together, if I recall. Have you been catching up?"

"Yeah, I see him at the stables every morning. And I went over to Ty's place when I first got to town."

"That kid's a hermit." He made a tsking sound. "He needs to get out more. Hiding away on his ranch isn't doing him any favors."

"I don't know about that." Hadn't Dean done the same for the past ten years?

"I do. Ty's broken heart is still broken. Probably always will be. But that doesn't mean he can't have a life."

"He has a life."

"The one he's living is no life."

The urge to argue tugged at him, but he kept his mouth shut. What would it accomplish?

"Dean?" Something in Dad's tone made him glance up.

"What?"

"Why are you staying in Reagan's old place?"

Oh. That.

"It's closer. Makes for a shorter drive here."

"Is that the only reason?" The vulnerability in his expression tweaked his conscience.

"No." Maybe they didn't need to tiptoe around touchy subjects anymore. Maybe they could move past them. "I wanted to be close to Dusty. Ty and I are more alike than you think."

"I know why Ty hides away. I don't know why you do."

Tiptoeing was one thing, but full transparency was another. Dad's stress levels were supposed to be kept to a minimum. Even if Dean wanted to tell him about the car crash and events leading up to it, this wasn't the time or the place.

"I'll tell you about it when you're out of here and back home."

"How bad was it?" Fear flashed in his eyes. "Whatever it was that caused you to hunker down on that ranch in Texas?"

"I'm here, aren't I?" He attempted to smile. "I'll tell you when you're home."

His father studied him for what felt like ten minutes before nodding. "I'm holding you to it. I want to know what shook you up so bad."

"Fair enough." Dean exhaled a resigned breath.

Eric, the nurse's aide, entered the room. "Are you ready for your stress management class, Ed?"

"I'm ready for a nap." His dad gave the bed a longing glance.

Eric chuckled. "Plenty of time for that later."

Dean rose and gave his dad a big hug. "I'll be back on Sunday after church."

"Okay. Oh, and Dean?"

"Yeah?"

"Bring some more of those muffins. They were pretty good."

He grinned. "Will do."

As Dean strode down the hall to the entrance, he smiled at an older woman pushing a walker. Then he nodded to a man in a wheelchair. His dad was blessed to be leaving this place in decent health. Not everyone had that luxury.

He pushed open the door and went out to the parking lot. It was windy and cold. He shoved his hands into his pockets and ducked his chin as he strode to his truck. He had the whole night ahead of him, and he knew exactly what to do with it.

He'd stop at home, change his clothes and drive out to Dad's place. It was time to get serious about finishing the basement. It was the least he could do for the man.

WHY COULDN'T SHE stay away from him? Early Friday evening, Brooke held Megan's hand and had Alice on her hip as she knocked on Dean's door. She'd been on her way to her mom's when she saw his truck in the driveway of Reagan's old house. Instead of driving past, like any normal person would, she'd pulled in and parked. To get an update on his dad. At least, that was what she was telling herself.

The truth was more complicated.

He'd been opening up to her, and she'd been sharing more with him, too. She felt safe talking to him.

That alone should have prevented her from stopping by.

Maybe she should leave. Yes, she definitely should march back down those porch steps and pile the girls into the minivan. But just as she began to turn away, the front door opened. Dean, clean-shaven and wearing jeans and a sweater with the sleeves pushed up his forearms, blinked, then grinned and held the door open for her to enter. "Come in—get out of the cold."

"Dee! Dee!" Alice twisted and held both arms out to him. Megan dropped Brooke's hand and held up her arms, too.

He laughed and took Alice from her. After settling her on his left hip, he reached down and hauled Megan onto his other one. The move was so quick and easy—the man could clearly handle two toddlers, no problem.

"What brings you here?" He turned and made his way to the couch up ahead, and she followed. The twins were trying to tell him something, but it sounded like gibberish to her ears. He gave Alice his full attention before switching to Megan. "A dog? You got to pet a dog?"

How he'd deciphered *dog* when they'd been speaking over each other, she had no clue. But it was true. She'd paid Christy Moulten a visit this afternoon, and the twins, as usual, had been enamored with little Tulip, her Pomeranian.

"Tutu go woof!" Alice opened her hands as her eyes grew round.

"Tutu soft." Megan had a shyer way about her.

"I've got to meet this Tutu, huh?" He set them on the couch and sat between them. They both nodded through sparkling eyes.

Brooke sat in an adjacent chair. "Sorry to barge in like this. We won't stay long. I wanted to see how your dad is doing."

"He's good. Today I can honestly say I think he'll make a full recovery. I can't put my finger on it, but he seems to have cleared a hurdle."

"That makes me so happy." She put her hand over her heart. She knew exactly what he meant. "I remember the moment I knew I'd be able to walk unassisted again. That day filled me with hope and purpose. It gave me the drive to keep going, even when it was hard."

"He's determined. Your mom's muffins were a hit, by the way."

"I'm not surprised. She has a special touch when it comes to baked goods. They're all amazing." The girls had climbed onto his lap and were squished together, holding hands.

Oh, my. What a picture they made. She really should have kept driving.

"He specifically ordered me to bring more of them when I visit him after church on Sunday."

"I'm on my way to Mom's now. I'll pass the message along to her." She gave the room a once-over. "Where is your Christmas tree? Don't tell me you still haven't put one up."

"I'll get around to it."

She didn't want to badger him about it anymore, but she'd say one more thing before letting it go. "I want you to have something heartwarming and joyful to see every night. You deserve to enjoy the Christmas season."

Something in his gaze brought a flush of heat to her cheeks. If she wasn't mistaken, it was attraction. She reveled in the fact he saw her—the real her, the mom, the widow, the survivor of a stroke—and he still liked what he saw.

After all her lectures to herself, triumphant was the last feeling she expected to have.

Alice held on to his sweatshirt as she pulled herself up to stand next to him. Megan, not wanting to be left out, did the same. And to Brooke's shock, the girls each planted a kiss on one of Dean's cheeks. His face grew red as he beamed at them. Then he held both of them tightly, and they leaned against his shoulders.

"Well, that was awfully nice," he said.

"Wuv, Dee." Alice nodded solemnly.

Megan nodded, too. "Dee, wuv."

Brooke's heart couldn't take it. Her girls were as into him as she was. And on that note, Brooke figured she'd better go. She stood and reached for Megan, who waved her away with a "no." Alice did, too.

Fantastic. The girls preferred him to her and were on the verge of a tantrum.

"Come on, ladies," she said. "Grandma's waiting for you to help decorate reindeer cookies."

"Gwammy!" the girls shouted.

Phew. Sticky situation averted.

Dean rose and carried the girls to the door, then set them down.

"What are you doing tonight?" she asked as she reached for the handle.

"I'm heading out to Dad's place. Figure I can work on more of those boxes."

"Want some help?"

"I couldn't ask you to do that. It's Friday night. And your mom's expecting you."

"Mom is expecting the girls. She won't mind." She watched his expression carefully. Something held him back from accepting her offer, and her earlier triumph deflated. The girls wandered back to the couch. Great. "Unless you want to be alone."

"That's not it. I guess I just feel bad." He shrugged. "Christmas is less than two weeks away? You should be watching movies and drinking eggnog, not digging through dusty old boxes in my dad's basement."

"Maybe I want to dig through dusty old boxes."

"No one wants to do that." His eyebrows drew together.

"It's not the boxes, Dean. It's the reason behind it."

"My dad."

"And you."

"Me?"

The surprise in his tone made her question how truthful she should be. Then she tossed off her reservations. She hadn't made it this far—losing her husband, raising twins on her own—to be too scared to say what was on her mind.

"Yes, you." But then reality stepped in. Her health. Her future. "We're friends. You're finishing my house. I'm helping you with Ed's basement. That was the deal we made."

The light in his eyes dimmed, and it hurt her to see it. She'd reduced their relationship to a bargain, when what she felt was far more than that.

"In that case, I guess I'll meet you over there." His tone was flat.

She'd hurt him. Why was this so hard? Why wasn't she being honest about her feelings?

Because she wasn't supposed to have these feelings.

She couldn't leave it like this, though. "Wait, that came out all wrong."

"I think it came out exactly as you intended."

"You're right. I deserve that." She stared down at her boots, then met his gaze once more. "Our friendship took me by surprise." She tried to find the right words. "And it's more than that. I feel close to you."

The shimmer in his eyes returned, and he took a step forward. "I feel the same."

"But I...well...there are things that prevent me from getting too close."

"Like twins?"

"No, not really." She wrung her hands together. "Like my risk of another stroke and what it means for my future."

"I thought that's why you've been remodeling your house."

"It is." She nodded, swallowing the fear stuck in her throat. "But it's more than that. I don't see marriage again in my future. And I definitely don't see more children."

"Why not?"

"My doctors warned me about the dangers. My stroke risk would be too high during a pregnancy and for the first three months postpartum. I'm not willing to chance it."

His mouth opened slightly then closed again. What was he thinking? Why wasn't he saying anything?

She could guess why. If he'd harbored any deeper feelings for her, she'd just squashed them.

"Come on, girls," she called. "We're leaving."

"Let me carry them to the van." He slipped his feet into slides, picked up Megan and Alice from the couch and followed her out onto the porch and down the steps. "I get it, you know."

She buckled Megan into her seat and looked over her shoulder. "You do?"

"Yeah." He handed her Alice, and she got her settled. Then she pressed the button for the sliding door to close. "I don't see marriage in my future, either."

"You? Why not?" She barely noticed the cold as she stood inches from him.

"My reason isn't noble like yours." He shrugged. "I can't marry someone if I can't even drive her to church on Sunday."

Oh. She'd forgotten about that. Tilting her head, she stared at his earnest face. "She might not mind driving *you* to church."

"I'd mind."

"Want to give it a try later?"

"What do you mean?"

"I'll drop off the girls and come back here. We'll see what happens."

"No." The color drained from his face. "No."

"One try." She held up a finger. "I'll hop in the passenger seat of your truck, and if it's too much, we'll drive our own vehicles to your dad's house."

"You don't know what you're asking."

"Okay." She held out her palms. "Forget it. I'll meet you there instead."

Reaching for the door handle, she paused as Dean gently touched her arm.

"Wait." The muscle in his cheek flexed. "I'll try. But it's not going to be pretty."

"I don't expect it to be." She opened the door, got inside and started the van. "I'll be back in ten."

He nodded. Then she backed out of his driveway with her heart racing.

She'd intended to set him straight about the limits of their friendship. Talk about backfiring. They might both be saying they didn't see marriage in their future, but did they believe it? Why did she spend time with him—even if coming back would help him get over his fear—if she wanted to keep their friendship out of the romance zone?

Too many questions she couldn't—wouldn't—answer.

For now, she had a Friday night wide-open with Dean McCaffrey, and she was going to make the most of it.

OF ALL THE stupid things to agree to, this one took first place. But he wouldn't get a plastic trophy for it.

Dean paced in his driveway as he waited for Brooke to return. He cupped his bare hands to his mouth in an attempt to warm them. His heart was beating way too fast.

He could *not* do this. He couldn't let Brooke see him shut down. Couldn't bear to witness her disgust at his incapability of doing the simplest of tasks.

Anyone with a license could drive with a passenger next to them. Anyone. Except him.

Maybe it's better this way. She'll see for herself. Then you can leave, and she'll never think of you as more than a friend again. Isn't that the goal? This will accelerate the process.

He paused. Closed his eyes for a moment.

What if he *was* willing to explore a deeper relationship with Brooke?

That would open up another bag of problems. Because she'd made it clear she wasn't doing forever with a ring on her finger again. And he wasn't a casual dating type of guy.

Her minivan pulled to a stop in front of the house. She parked and got out.

"Are you ready for this?" she asked as her dark hair blew in the breeze.

"No."

Her lips twitched into a soft smile. "I know."

Her kindness, her understanding—that was what made him straighten his shoulders and glance at the truck. He knew exactly what was going to happen when they got into it.

Maybe he was tired of hiding. Tired of pretending he was like any other guy out there.

He cracked his knuckles. "I've tried before."

She wasted no time getting into the passenger seat of his truck. He raised his face to the sky. *God, I can't do this.*

A Bible verse he'd memorized raced through his mind. *I can do all things through Christ which strengtheneth me.* He regularly read the book of Philippians from his old King James Bible, and chapter four, verse thirteen, was one of his favorites.

Okay, God, I'm counting on You.

He got in and sat in the driver's seat. Pushed the start button. Let the engine purr while he attempted to clear his mind. *Pretend she's not next to you.*

As he glanced her way, the gravity of the situation weighed on him. Brooke, with her shiny hair and trusting eyes, was sitting in his truck despite his warning.

The memory of the crash was like a jolt through him. The crunch of the metal, the hiss of the valves.

As he stared at the dashboard, his breathing grew shallow. So shallow he began to gasp. Sweat broke out across his forehead. Dizziness forced him to grip the wheel, and his hands, moist with sweat, slipped on it.

He couldn't put her in danger.

Without giving it another thought, he jabbed the start button to turn the truck off. Dropping his head into his hands, he stared at his lap, blinking, gasping, trying to find normal, but it was nowhere to be found.

Why couldn't he breathe? Was he going to die?

The foggy feeling grew worse. He dared not think about Brooke or how she was reacting to all this.

"Dean, I'm here." She slipped her arm around his shoulders and gently rubbed his biceps. "It's okay."

It's okay? Was she serious? He fought for breath as his heart pounded. Moments later, he knew he'd gotten through the worst of it. As his breathing slowly returned to normal, he became aware that tears had fallen down his cheeks, and he discreetly swiped them away before raising his head.

"It's not okay." He shot her a sideways glance. "Nothing about this is okay."

She softly rubbed his upper back. "We're still in the driveway. Nothing happened. We're safe. Come here." She shifted, holding her arms out. Feeling foolish, but needing her embrace, he let her wrap her arms around him.

Her hug was like walking into a warm room, fire roaring, during the coldest ice storm. Like being tucked into the softest bed after climbing a mountain. Like taking shelter in a bunker during a tornado.

Her embrace was the safest place on earth.

When she eased back, his hands were trembling. He stared into her big eyes, so close to his, and his gaze dropped to her lips. She didn't back away. No, her hand cupped his cheek, leaving him shaken, but not from the panic attack.

Without another thought, he slid his hand around the back of her neck and let his fingers creep into her hair. So soft. Just like her.

He needed her. Wanted to kiss her.

They'd both said their pieces earlier. This relationship couldn't go anywhere. But his heart didn't care.

"Kiss me, Dean," she whispered.

He didn't need to be told twice.

As soon as his lips touched hers, all the pain and worry and shame fled from him. She was peppermint sticks and hope and all the things he'd lacked for so many years. She pressed closer to him, and her touch made him bold. He explored her mouth and savored the feel of her silky hair between his fingers. Then he ended the kiss.

What was he doing? He could not kiss Brooke in his driveway. Couldn't kiss her anywhere.

Neither of them wanted a relationship. They both had their reasons. He'd proven to her he wasn't husband material, even if she changed her mind. Flattening both palms on his thighs, he dared not look at her.

"Wow," she said softly, sitting back into her seat with her fingers touching her lips. "Why don't you start the truck again?"

"What? No." He'd kissed her, and that was her response? Hadn't she seen him fall apart? Shouldn't she be yelling at him for kissing her? Or shaking her head in pity that having someone in the passenger seat affected him like this?

"Just start it." Her tone wasn't angry or judgmental. She sounded understanding. "We'll sit here. We'll stay parked."

He rolled the idea over in his mind. If they didn't leave his driveway, he couldn't crash the truck. They'd be safe. He couldn't see any harm in it, so he forced his finger to press the button again. The engine rumbled, and he let his head fall back against the headrest.

"How much of the basement do you think we'll be able to get through tonight?" she asked.

She wanted to discuss the basement? Now? Visions of the crash flirted around the edges of his mind, but he directed his thoughts to the boxes in the basement.

"I'm not sure. It depends on what we find."

"Are there any more trophies I should know about?" she teased.

"If there are, I don't know what they'd be for." His jaw would shatter if he didn't loosen it. "Sixth-grade archery, maybe."

"I won a trophy in fourth grade for the triple jump on track and field day. I only won it because everyone else scratched."

His mood lightened a fraction. "It's still a win."

"This was, too." Her deep blue eyes captured him. "We've been like this for almost a minute."

He dragged his gaze away and stared ahead at the garage door. "Yeah, well, a minute is nothing to be proud of."

She placed her hand on his forearm. "It *is* something to be proud of. This was excruciating for you, and I think you're brave for trying."

An incredulous laugh slipped out. "Brave? I don't think so."

"You are brave." She gave his arm a squeeze before sitting back again. "I'm going to drive over to your dad's house now." She opened the door.

"Wait." Confusion crept in. "You're leaving? Now?"

"Yeah." She stepped onto the driveway. "Why?"

"I thought you'd want me to—"

"No." Her tender smile tore at his emotions. "You don't ever have to drive me anywhere, Dean. But if you want, I have the number of a counselor you can talk to. He helped me last year after the stroke. I wouldn't have been able to move out of Mom's place if I hadn't committed to several sessions with him. He helped me see things in a different light."

"What kinds of things?"

"My fears. He gave me strategies to handle my worry about having another stroke."

Dean didn't say anything. The fact she'd spent a huge chunk of money making her home accessible made him think the counselor hadn't done a very good job. Did Brooke really believe she'd become disabled anytime soon?

"The only way I could handle moving out and raising the girls on my own was knowing I had a backup plan. My biggest fear is losing my ability to raise the twins. So I'm taking measures to retain that ability. Everyone around here thinks I'm overreacting, but they haven't been in my shoes."

Put like that, it didn't sound so extreme. Not like his overreacting to someone in his passenger seat.

He supposed they hadn't been in his shoes, either.

"I'll text you his number now. That way you'll have it." She smiled again. "See you at your dad's."

When the door shut, he allowed himself a few minutes of stillness. Brooke was right. The fact he'd been able to idle in the driveway with her in his truck had to count for something. He backed out and flicked on the radio. "I'll Be Home for Christmas" played, and he let out a soft snort.

He was home for Christmas. Brooke had seen for herself his panic attack problem. And oddly, he felt even closer to her because of it. If he could put the accident behind him, his future might look a whole lot brighter.

It was worth a try.

CHAPTER NINE

WEDNESDAY EVENING, BROOKE nibbled on a frosted sugar cookie in the shape of a bell as she sat in Christy Moulten's living room. For months, Christy had hounded her to join her book club, and in September, Brooke had succumbed to the pressure. To her surprise, she loved the books—they were Christian romance novels with happy endings. This month's selection was a Christmas romance featuring a single dad, his triplet sons and the service dog he hadn't known he'd needed.

Brooke had found the entire thing dreamy. She'd read it in two nights after putting the twins to bed. Both mornings, she'd been groggy, and her leg had been stiff.

Lately, there'd been too many signs in her body telling her she needed to take it easy. But it was Christmas. She finally felt engaged with life, and she didn't want to stay home and rest and keep her stress levels to a minimum.

She wanted to grip life by the horns and take it for a joyride.

"These candles smell sensational." Angela Zane stuck her nose in the candle Brooke had given her when she'd arrived. "I want to gobble it up. So thoughtful of you to make them for us."

"Reagan did everything. I just helped."

"I'm lighting mine as soon as I get home." Mary Corning selected a gingerbread cookie that sat beside the large frosted brownie on her dessert plate. She craned her neck to the hall. "Where did Reagan go?"

"She had to use the restroom. She'll be right back." Brooke was saving her a seat. Reagan had joined the book club in October after Brooke mentioned how much she enjoyed it.

"I remember those days," Christy said as she carried a tray of mugs into the living room. "My bladder seemed to shrink to the size of a sesame seed when I was pregnant with Cade and Ty."

"Mackenzie isn't coming?" Angela asked.

"No. I keep inviting her. I gave her a copy of the book, but I'll probably have to face the fact she's not into it." Christy handed Brooke a mug of cocoa, then gave one to her best friend, Charlene Parker, who worked at the nursing home in town. "One of these days, I'll wear her down."

Janey Denton, Charlene's daughter, who'd married one of Winston Ranch's cowboys, Lars, in the fall, took a seat on the pale gray couch next to Brooke. Her dessert plate overflowed with various cookies. A woman after her own heart. Reagan returned and promptly took a huge bite of a frosted sugar cookie with red and green sprinkles.

Christy settled into an overstuffed floral chair as Tulip jumped onto the matching ottoman near the fireplace. The little Pomeranian curled up on Christy's lap. Cream-colored quilted stockings hung from the mantel, and the Christmas tree in the corner was decorated with bulbs and ornaments in pastel pinks and greens. Brooke always loved visiting Christy's home, which overflowed with feminine touches.

"Now that everyone's here, we can get started." Christy's eyes glimmered in anticipation. "But first, let's hear the updates. Reagan, how are you feeling?"

Reagan glanced up mid-bite of a cookie. After brushing crumbs from her lips, she held up a finger and finished chewing. "Great. The first trimester was rough. Now that the nausea has passed, I'm enjoying the pregnancy."

"We can't wait to babysit." Christy pressed her palms together in the prayer position. "Can we, Char?"

"I adore babies." Charlene nodded. "I miss holding Megan and Alice. They're growing up way too quickly."

"I agree," Brooke said. "Every time they go up a size in clothes, I end up crying. I have all their old clothes packed away for the church rummage sale next summer. Unless you have a girl, Reagan, in which case you should take all of them."

"We don't know what we're having. Marc and I decided not to find out." With a loving expression, she rubbed her baby bump. "It'll be a surprise."

As the conversation veered to pros and cons of finding out the gender beforehand, Brooke's mind wandered to last Friday's surprise—sitting in Dean's truck as he dealt with his trauma. Almost immediately, she'd regretted pushing him into letting her get in the truck with him. Seeing how deeply it affected him had broken her heart.

But she'd also sensed how his panic had stolen part of his future. He'd flat-out told her he was staying single because of it. What exactly had he been through the night of the accident to affect him so terribly?

They'd been spending their evenings together, partly because he'd been working on her bathroom, and partly because she insisted he join her and the girls for supper every night. She learned more about him each day, and it was getting harder and harder to avoid her feelings. Dean shared her values. He made her feel safe, smart, important.

"How are the driving lessons with Clem going, Christy?" Mary was the only one in the room who could ask her that with a straight face. Christy was notorious for having her driver's license revoked at least three times a year. Back when she'd announced she was moving to town, Clem had offered to give her lessons. Last Brooke had heard, they weren't going well.

"Not good." Christy took a sip of hot tea. "We took a hiatus for the month of November after he yelled at me for hitting a curb while turning onto Maple Street. I told him there wasn't enough room for my Ford Escape to *not* hit the curb. He claimed that was nonsense, and I told him I wanted to Ford Escape his judgmental tone. Let's just say words were exchanged."

That was putting it mildly, if Brooke had to guess. She'd seen those two get into shouting matches that could go on for days.

"Anyway," Christy continued, "our tempers cooled, and last week he wanted me to drive to Casper to visit Ed. We didn't make it more than two blocks before he started harping on me for not braking soon enough. I didn't know what in the world he was talking about—I brake in plenty of time, and I told him so. Well, he disagreed, and I don't need that kind of negativity in my life, so I pulled into the feed store's parking lot and cut the engine. He claimed I was a menace to society every time I got behind the wheel. I told him he was a menace to society for being alive."

Everyone hung on her words. Anytime a conversation included her driving and/or Clem, it was sure to be entertaining. This one didn't disappoint.

"What happened next?" Janey asked. Her blond hair had been French-braided and tied with a red ribbon. She'd accepted the full-time position of second-grade teacher at the elementary school. To think, it would only be a few years before Megan and Alice went to school. Hopefully, Janey would still be teaching by then.

"He got that hard look in his eyes—you know, the steely one—and told me to hand over my license. I refused."

"Why would he want your license?" Brooke eyed the brownie on her plate. *Yes.* She took a bite.

"He made a scissor-cutting motion with his fingers." Christy widened her eyes and dropped her chin to emphasize her words. A collective gasp filled the room.

"He wouldn't." Charlene shook her head.

"Oh, I think he would." Christy's chin bobbed. "My license stayed tucked into my wallet, where it has remained ever since. Clem ended up driving to Casper and back. We called a truce. Anyway, enough about me. Brooke, how is your bathroom shaping up?"

All eyes turned to her. "It's great. The new vanity door came in on Monday, and Dean and Terry installed the floor tiles this week. They'll be able to finish up by Friday."

"Wonderful news. Just in time for Christmas. I can't believe it's next Wednesday already. How did that happen? Ed sure is thankful Dean stepped in and took over for him."

"I'm thankful, too." Brooke set the brownie back on her plate. "Once the bathroom is done and the back ramp is built, I'll have more peace of mind."

She didn't miss the exchange of glances among the ladies, and she didn't care. They didn't need to understand why the renovations were important to her.

"Speaking of Dean, any chance he'll stick around Jewel River after Ed comes home?" Charlene asked.

"I don't know." Brooke hoped so—more than hoped. She looked forward to each day when he finished whatever was on the agenda for her bathroom. She'd learned a lot about him, and she wanted to learn even more.

"It would be good for Ed to have him around," Angela said. "Then he'll be able to pass on the company to him."

Unless Dean didn't want to take over the company.

"I still don't understand why he quit construction altogether to work on a ranch down in Texas. We have plenty of ranches here if he wanted to work with cattle so bad." Mary shrugged.

Now that Brooke had seen firsthand what Dean had gone through by having her in the passenger seat of his truck, she knew exactly why he'd gotten that job on the ranch in Texas.

His accident had broken something inside him. Just like her stroke had broken something inside her.

"The past is in the past," Janey said. "We can be thankful he's here now."

Brooke's thoughts exactly. But when Ed returned, would Dean stay? He'd made it clear when he first arrived that this was a temporary landing for him. If he didn't settle down in Jewel River, where would he go?

Her appetite fled. She shouldn't have encouraged their friendship to blossom the way it had. Spending all this time with him was a mistake.

At least the basement was almost complete. On Friday, they'd gone through a large amount of the remaining items. Dean had dropped off several boxes to one of the church members who stored items for the church's rummage sale. He'd also taken another truckload of donations to one of the thrift shops in Casper. Without all the boxes and bags clogging up the basement, it looked bigger. The space could be used for something other than a catchall for junk.

There'd been a few times Brooke had caught Dean opening a box only to clench his jaw and pack it up quickly. His mother's things, she supposed. Wasn't any of her business. It did make her question if Dean had unresolved issues from his past, though. Brooke certainly had wounds that hadn't healed from her father's abandonment.

"Let's talk about the book." Christy's cheery tone cut through her thoughts. She turned her attention to the group. "What did you all think about the hero, Rick?"

"I loved him," Janey said. "But Dierdre got on my nerves— at least at first."

"I warmed up to her after the first couple chapters," Reagan added sweetly.

"I couldn't get enough of those triplets," Charlene said. "The only thing that would have improved the book for me, personally, is if Rick had been a cowboy."

"I hear you on that," Brooke said. She pictured Dean in his cowboy boots and Stetson. The way he hefted the boxes in

Ed's basement and carried them upstairs as if they weighed less than a bag of marshmallows made her want to fan herself. Yes, give her a cowboy any day.

And that cowboy sure could kiss.

Stop it! That was a onetime kiss.

Onetime kiss or not, Dean was one swoony cowboy, and she'd savor what they had for the moment.

It wouldn't last. But at least she'd have some good memories.

THAT SHOULD DO IT. Dean finished spray-painting the final circle on the lawn in Brooke's backyard on Friday afternoon. The company had finally made it out yesterday to flag the yard. Now that he knew exactly where the gas and electricity lines ran, he could dig the holes for the new posts. After they thawed the ground.

"Once we get the fires going good, we'll cover them with the metal ovens." Marc pointed to one of the circles. "Needs more kindling. Man, it's cold out here."

Terry wrung old newspaper tightly and stuffed it in between the split logs, where flames sputtered. "My daddy taught me all his campfire tricks. Why, I must have made half a million fires in my sixty-four years..."

Dean glanced at Marc, who pressed his lips together to hide his laughter. Dean had told Marc how well he and Terry got along—except for the age-reference thing. He didn't need any more reminders of Terry's sixty-four years.

"That newspaper trick does seem to be working." Marc pivoted and went to the driveway, where they'd set out the supplies. He came back with one of the old metal pans, some wire mesh and a few large rocks. "Here, why don't you put this over the fire, Terry?"

"Me?" The man grinned. "Sure thing."

Terry took the pan and bent over, his girth straining against his winter coveralls. Then he straightened and nudged it in place with his foot.

"Now what?" Dean asked.

"Mesh. Rocks. Repeat." Marc pointed to the other circles.

It took about an hour to get all the fires started, and once they were done, they went inside. Brooke sat at the kitchen island, sipping something hot from a mug with purple flowers as she read a book.

Dean wouldn't have minded walking into that scene every day for the rest of his life. She glanced up and smiled. "Done already?"

"Not even close." Marc approached and gave her a side hug. "I take it the girls are napping?"

"For another hour."

"You have any more coffee?"

"Fresh pot. Help yourself."

Dean hung back, and Terry asked Marc to pour him a cup, too.

"The tile looks incredible." As she held the mug between her hands, her beauty took his breath away. "Oh, Mom dropped off two dozen doughnuts. She knew you were coming over and said it would make the job go quicker if you had sustenance."

Marc had already opened the box. He chomped half a cruller in one bite and grinned. "She knows me too well." Then he turned to Terry and Dean and tossed each of them a doughnut.

Dean caught his—barely. If he kept this up, he'd have to start jogging or something. His active lifestyle as a ranch hand was a far cry from eating doughnuts and all these delicious suppers with Brooke. The fact her mom dropped off pastries here each day—and that they were the best ones he'd ever eaten in his life—didn't help.

"I'd work any job just for Anne's baked goods," Terry said. "That woman knows how to cook."

"Couldn't agree more." Marc selected a chocolate-covered doughnut. "Want another?"

Terry nodded. Dean shook his head.

"What's the verdict out there?" Brooke's tone was cheerful, but there was a strain in her eyes he wasn't used to seeing. Was she paler than normal? Dean didn't want to stare, but he couldn't help it. He worried about her.

Last Friday's kiss had affected him deeply. He hadn't stopped thinking about it—or her—since.

"Thawing the ground as we speak." Marc took a loud slurp of coffee. "In a couple hours, we can dig the holes and set the posts. We'll have to use the utility sink in the laundry room for hot water to mix the cement."

"Why?" she asked.

"To make sure it sets properly in the cold," Dean explained. "I bought special cement for it."

"Oh, I didn't realize. That makes sense." She nodded. "And then what?"

He had come to know her pretty well over these past weeks. He wanted to go over there, take her hand in his and tell her not to stress out—that he was taking care of everything. But he stayed where he was and let Marc answer.

"Then these guys can get to work building the actual ramp."

"How long will that take?"

"A couple days," Dean said. "But I won't be able to start until Monday. The cement has to cure. We're tenting the area with tarps, and we'll have insulated blankets covering the cement, too."

"Do you think it could possibly be done before Christmas?" Her voice had a wistful quality.

"I'll work on it Christmas Eve if I have to. I want everything to be completely done by Christmas. Dad promised you."

"Yeah, well, he didn't know he'd have a heart attack and be stuck in Casper. I don't want you working on my ramp Christmas Eve and missing out on the holiday."

"I won't be missing out. I'll try to get most of it done on Monday. And if I have to come out Tuesday, I'll make sure it's first thing in the morning."

"You'll join us for the Christmas Eve service that night, right?" she asked.

He hadn't thought that far ahead.

"Of course he's coming to church with us on Christmas Eve," Marc said, shaking his head as if it had been a dumb question. Part of him was relieved that they expected him to be with them, and part of him worried he shouldn't be spending all this time with them.

"He might plan on visiting Ed." She glared at her brother.

"He can do that in the afternoon."

Dean had nothing to add to the conversation. He wasn't sure how he was spending Christmas Eve yet. He probably should figure it out soon, though, since it was only a few short days away.

"I'll let you guys know after I talk to Dad." Dean stretched his back from side to side. "He was acting like he'd be home before Christmas, but I think it will be another week before they'll release him."

"And then what?" Marc asked.

"I'm not sure. Knowing him, he'll want to pick up right where he left off."

"The doctors won't like that." Brooke frowned.

"Trust me, I know they won't."

"No, I meant, what are you going to do?" Marc asked. "Are you staying in town or moving on?"

Leave it to his best friend to cut right to the heart of the matter. Dean stared at the counter. He didn't know his plans, and this wasn't the time or place to figure them out.

"You should stay," Marc said with a nod.

"I agree." Terry walked his fingers toward the doughnut box and grabbed a cinnamon-sugar twist.

Dean glanced Brooke's way. She watched him with a curious expression.

She made him want to stay. She made him want this—all

of it. The job, the friends, the town, the time with her and the twins.

But they both had too many hang-ups, too many obstacles, to pursue a relationship.

"Before I forget," Marc said to Brooke, "do you have that heating pad for Reagan? Her lower back's been aching."

"Yep, let me go get it." She stood and left the room.

Terry asked Marc when the baby was due, and Dean tuned out their conversation. He was almost finished with the basement. One more session and it would be done. As much as he wanted to ask Brooke to join him tonight, he couldn't. Didn't want her overdoing it. Especially this close to Christmas.

And every time he was in the same room as her, he had the urge to kiss her.

No, he'd tackle the rest of the basement on his own. Last Friday, he'd found several of his mother's items in the boxes. The locket was the only thing that bothered him. He still hadn't opened it. He'd dropped the rest of her stuff off at the thrift shop in Casper without a second thought.

Maybe he should open the locket and deal with whatever pain it brought up. Get it over with. Go into next year with some closure.

Next year?

Marc had brought up another thing he'd been avoiding. What was he going to do when Dad came back to town?

"Here you go." Brooke returned and handed Marc the heating pad.

Maybe he should call the counselor Brooke had recommended. Find out if the guy could help him get a new perspective.

"Let's see if the fires are still going." Marc pointed to the door. "I want you to have this ramp done. Then you won't have so far to walk from the garage. I still don't know why they built these houses without attached garages."

"The ramp will be more convenient, for sure." Brooke

wrapped her arms around her waist. "But I can't complain. The back porch has only been down for a week."

"You ready, Terry?" Marc asked. "Dean?"

He nodded, moving toward the door, but Brooke stopped him.

"Dean, could you wait a minute? I have a question about the bathroom grout." Her head tilted to the side.

"Sure." He turned to Marc. "I'll be out there in a few."

"Take your time. We've got this under control."

Dean followed her down the hall, trying to remember if any of the grout needed fixing. He'd finished the bathroom last night. Terry had helped him install the mirror and towel bars yesterday, and Dean had stuck around touching up paint and verifying everything was caulked and sealed. It looked great.

Afterward, he'd joined Brooke and the girls for a supper of homemade chicken noodle soup and warm bread. Comfort food with the most comforting woman he'd ever met. They'd talked about everything and nothing for hours.

Brooke stopped inside the bathroom and spun to face him. "I know this is weird timing—and it doesn't have to do with my bathroom or the grout, which is perfect, by the way—but Marc brought up something we haven't discussed. What *are* you going to do after Ed comes home?"

"I don't know."

"You don't know, or you don't want to tell me?" An air of dejection covered her. All because of him. "Never mind. It's none of my business."

Now he felt like a jerk. "It is your business."

"No, it's not. You're almost done with my house, and you don't owe me anything. You never did." The words came out tight, practically strangled.

"Hey, I don't mean to sound gruff." She was swiping imaginary dust from the new countertop. He gently turned her to face him. "I owe you a lot."

"No, you don't." She swallowed, still not meeting his gaze. "It's just…"

When she didn't finish the thought, he caressed her upper arms. "Just what?"

"Things in my life happen all of a sudden. It's boring, boring, same-old, same-old, and then wham! When Marc asked about your plans, it hit me that you might not be here much longer." Her big eyes, filled with vulnerability, lifted to his. He wanted to reassure her that he wasn't going anywhere. That nothing had to change. But he couldn't.

"I'm not leaving tonight," he said.

"I know. But the next couple of days will fly by, and then Christmas will be here, and your dad will return, and—" She held her breath.

"And what?"

"And what if I wake up one day and you're gone? Without a goodbye?"

He took her in his arms, wrapping his hands behind her lower back, and stared into her eyes. "I wouldn't leave without saying goodbye."

"You might."

"I won't."

"You can't promise that. You are leaving, aren't you?" Tears began to pool in her eyes, and he almost told her he'd stay forever if she wouldn't cry.

"I don't know, Brooke." Frustration began to build—not at her, but at himself. "If I do leave, I'll say goodbye."

"Ross didn't." She brought her hand to her mouth as if she hadn't expected that to come out of it.

"Is that what this is about?" His frustration vanished like mist in the morning. He brought her closer and held her, letting his cheek rest against her hair. "I'm not going to be killed in action."

"I know. I'm not being logical." She snuggled in closer. "But it's hard. Being the one left behind is hard. Picking up the pieces without any warning is something I never want to go through again."

"You think there would be pieces to pick up if I left?"

She pushed at his chest. "How can you say that? Of course there would be. I've grown close to you. And you've grown close to me. Don't try to deny it."

He wouldn't. Couldn't. He'd grown very close to her. So close, he was actually considering staying in Jewel River. Working with his dad. Pretending he didn't have an anger issue that almost killed his ex-girlfriend.

Brooke deserved someone better than him.

He sighed. "I don't have my life figured out. I don't know what next year holds. But I promise you this—I'm not taking it lightly, and you will be the first to know when I do figure it out."

She searched his eyes for a few moments and then nodded.

"I'm not being fair to you," she said.

"How so?"

"I want you to stay, but my mind hasn't changed about marriage."

"Are you sure it's your fear of having another stroke holding you back?" After her reaction to the thought of him leaving without saying goodbye, he had a feeling her stance on marriage had more to do with Ross's sudden death than anything else.

"I'm sure." She stepped back, out of his embrace, leaving his hands feeling empty. "What else would it be?"

Dean was no therapist, and it wasn't his place to share his theory.

"What about you?" she asked. "Is your fear of driving with me in the car the only thing that's holding you back?"

"Yes." The hair on the back of his neck stood at attention. What was she getting at?

His mother's locket came to mind. What did that have to do with this? Nothing.

"If you say so." Her lips set in a firm line.

"Maybe in time we'll both get more rational about our fears." Before the words left his mouth, he knew it was the wrong thing to say.

"Rational?" She blinked a few times. "What's irrational about acknowledging my risk for a stroke?"

"Nothing." He looked around the bathroom with its lowered sink, special commode and grab bars. She followed his gaze.

"Oh, I see." Her inhalation through her nose was loud. "You think all of this is me overreacting."

"I didn't say that."

"You didn't have to. Your traveling eyes said it all." She pushed past him and out of the bathroom.

"Brooke, wait." He hurried out of the room after her, but she didn't stop until she got to the living room.

She turned to him, trembling with emotion. "I know what everyone thinks. I hear what they say. It's all, 'Oh, Brooke's being super cautious,' or 'Wheelchair-accessible? She's taking it a little too far.' But you don't know. None of you were there. I collapsed in front of my three-month-old babies, Dean. If my mom hadn't been there, I probably would have died. She got me to the clinic. They rushed me in the ambulance to Casper. And my life completely changed. So if you have a problem with me preparing my house in case it happens again—which it very well could—tell me now. Get it off your chest. Because this—" she waved wildly to take in the house "—isn't going away. This is my life. And I'm not putting you or any other man through it."

Regret sank down deep inside of him. She was right. And he didn't know what to say. Didn't know how to fix it.

So he did the only thing he could think of. He took her in his arms, looked into her beautiful big eyes, and whispered that he was sorry.

The fear and anger in them disappeared. He cupped her face in his hands and gently kissed her. "I'm sorry for making you feel that way. What you and I have is all new for me, and I'm terrible at this."

"At what?" Her face twisted in question.

"At women. Relationships. I don't know what I'm doing."

"Yeah, well, I don't know what I'm doing, either." Her mouth curved into a smile. "I guess we'll have to figure it out together. Because I can't seem to stay away from you."

His thoughts exactly.

The front door opened. "Hey, Dean?" Marc hollered. "Did you get lost?"

Dean shook his head, giving her a smile. "That's my cue."

She nodded, the sparkle in her eyes returning.

As he strode to the door, hope filled him. Brooke felt something more for him, too. And they might both be messed up, but at least they weren't hiding from whatever was brewing between them.

But if it ended badly...maybe it would be better if they did.

CHAPTER TEN

"MEGGIE, HAND ME the sprinkles." Monday morning, Brooke held out her hand to Megan, who clutched a plastic tube of red nonpareils. If that child dumped out the container, Brooke was going to lose it. Her patience was already whisker-thin.

Megan's big eyes didn't waver as she slowly shook her head and stood in the space where the kitchen met the living room.

"Give them to Mommy." She thrust her hand closer to the pudgy fingers gripping the tube.

Again, the shaking of the head. These little twins were cute and all, but they were also stubborn. And both were trying her self-control something fierce today. It was terrible timing, too, since she'd felt unwell when she'd woken, which had been an hour earlier than usual.

Her stomach kept churning, and the coffee she'd brewed earlier tasted bitter. Plus, her leg muscles felt weak again.

Megan backed up a few steps. That did it.

"I said, give them here." Brooke reached out and grabbed the tube.

"No, Mama!" Megan began to cry, which only added to the incessant noise of hammering and nail guns pounding from out back. True to his word, Dean had shown up at the crack of dawn to begin installing the boards for the ramp. Each *pop* of the nail gun drilled into her head.

Maybe she should sit on the couch for a while.

The kitchen island held freshly baked cookies, bowls of colored icings, wax paper and several options for sprinkles. She'd promised the girls they'd decorate Christmas cookies, and she doubted she'd have more energy later. Best to do it now.

She spotted Alice licking a full spoon of icing. "Alice! No!"

The child dropped the spoon—icing splattering on the floor—and her lips began to wobble. Then she started wailing even louder than Megan. Soon, both of them were crying at the top of their lungs.

It was times like this she missed living with her mother. At least she'd gotten a break when Mom came home. Now? The only break she could count on was during their naps or after she put them to bed.

Brooke couldn't call any of her family to come over and help out, either. Mom, Marc and Reagan had gone into Casper for some last-minute Christmas shopping and a movie. Both her mother and Reagan had scheduled part-time employees to run their shops today. Neither was in the habit of taking vacations or even the occasional day off. They deserved a day on the town.

After inhaling a deep breath, Brooke went over to Alice, still sobbing, and gave her a hug. Then she bent to pick up the spoon. A light-headed feeling flooded her, and as she straightened, she grew dizzy and grabbed hold of the corner of the counter until it passed.

Not now. Tomorrow was Christmas Eve, and she had so much to do still.

The list of symptoms to watch out for ticked through her mind. Had she eaten? A few bites of toast counted, right? She simply couldn't stomach much at the moment. What about water? Was she hydrated?

Maybe that was her problem. She took a glass from the

cupboard and filled it with water from the dispenser in the refrigerator door. For weeks, she'd been telling herself to slow down. But she hadn't.

Megan sniffled her way over to her with Alice not far behind. Brooke took a long drink and set the glass down, then forced a smile and a chipper tone. "Let's decorate the cookies."

To her ears, her voice sounded far away. She nudged the girls toward the hall. "But first, we need to wash up."

"No!" Alice scrunched her face and stamped one foot. Megan copied her.

"We're cleaning our hands. Then we'll decorate the cookies." She didn't want to decorate the cookies. She didn't want to wrestle the girls over to the bathroom sink to wash their hands.

She wanted to go straight to her room, climb into bed and curl up in her softest blanket for a long, long nap.

By the time she'd helped them wash and dry their hands and gotten them situated at their little table, a dull ache filled her head. After spreading out a small tablecloth and putting bibs on both girls, she brought over two paper plates with cutout cookies and handed them each a small silicone spatula. She set three bowls of icing in the center.

The girls happily spread icing over the cookies. Globs of it landed next to the plates.

Oh, well. She smiled as they shook sprinkles over the cookies. Both girls licked their spatulas and dunked them into the bowls. *Mental note: throw all the icing away and only let the girls eat the cookies they were decorating.*

She was still tired, and the dizzy feeling from earlier returned. But now the dull ache in her head was intensifying, too.

The girls were a mess. They had icing and sprinkles all over their faces and hands. But they sure looked happy.

"You can each have one cookie. Then we need to get cleaned up again." Again, the words sounded strange to her ears, like they'd been spoken from far away. She sat on a stool at the island and covered her face with her hands.

She didn't feel good.

The back door opened, and she barely registered the blast of cold air that accompanied Dean. "Check it out. The ramp boards are all in, and one side of the rail is finished. I'll have this done in no time."

"I'll be there" was all she could say. Little lights flashed to her left. Did Dean have a strobe light on or something? "Clean girls."

"What?" He stripped his gloves off as Megan and Alice came at him with their arms in the air. "Oh, you two are sticky. Why don't I help?"

Brooke was vaguely aware of him taking off their bibs. They giggled as they followed him to the kitchen sink. She heard water rushing, more giggles.

A fuzzy filter seemed to cover her eyes. She couldn't see very well. Couldn't think. She was tired. So tired.

And afraid.

"Hey, are you all right?" Dean's voice was near.

Whatever she replied came out garbled. She only had one clear thought.

The doctor.

She needed a doctor.

"Doctor. Call." She pointed...somewhere.

"The doctor?" His strong arm went around her shoulders. "Here, lean against me. I'll help you to the living room."

When she barely moved, he swung her into his arms and carried her to the couch. She could sense the darkness slipping in. Could feel her body refusing to obey as she rested there. The fear grew into something worse.

"Muh phone." She lifted her arm, her finger, to the ceiling.

Seconds later, her phone was in her hands. She tried to press the buttons but couldn't.

"Doctor," she said.

"You need the doctor. Okay." He sounded worried.

Even in her groggy state, her mind warned her this was the

stroke she'd feared. The one she'd known would come. She just wished it wasn't happening so soon.

Think, Dean.

Something was wrong with Brooke. Very wrong. Her phone slipped out of her fingers and fell to the floor with a thud. The twins stood on either side of him, poking Brooke's arm and repeating, "Mama?"

"Let's give your mom a little space." He pulled out his phone and found the number for the clinic. They answered on the first ring. Relief made him raise his face to the ceiling, until he realized it was an automated system. He pressed one for the receptionist. Two for an appointment. And the dreaded instrumental music began to play.

Maybe he should call 911. He padded over to Brooke, took her hand in his and squeezed it. It was cool to the touch. She moaned and turned onto her side toward the back of the couch. He felt her forehead. Normal temperature. Tried to take her pulse, but he'd never been good at it. Was it too fast? Too slow? He didn't know. Finally, someone at the clinic picked up.

"Hi, something's wrong with my friend." *My friend?* Moron. Brooke was way more than a friend. "She's slurring her words, really tired—"

The receptionist asked him several questions. He was wasting time. "No, she's not under the influence of alcohol. She's a mom with twin girls...yes, it's Brooke." The woman advised him to call an ambulance. "Okay, I'll call them now."

He ended the call and dialed 911. The operator informed him the nearest ambulance was half an hour away. Thirty minutes? Way too long. He hung up, and worry spun inside him.

Now what?

If Anne or Marc were here, they'd drive her to the clinic. But they weren't here. And Brooke clearly needed medical attention ASAP.

What if this *was* a stroke? What if she died? What if he was waiting too long right now and she ended up paralyzed?

He had to drive her to the clinic. Him. His breathing came in shallow gasps.

The twins were watching him, wide-eyed. He would *not* be responsible for these precious babies losing their mother.

"Brooke?" He gave her shoulder a gentle shake. She groaned. "Brooke? Can you hear me?"

She gave no indication she'd heard him.

He knew what he had to do, but he didn't know if he could do it.

God, don't ask this of me. Help me!

"Come on, girls," he said, choking on the words. "We're getting our coats on. Taking a drive."

They climbed down and scampered to him. Their lips were wobbling as if ready to cry. He knew the feeling. If he wasn't so stressed, he'd want to cry, too.

"Where are your coats and boots?" he asked. They ran toward the hallway closet. He followed and helped them into their outerwear, then grabbed Brooke's winter coat and rooted around the floor for a pair of her shoes. Then he went back to the couch and eased her into a seated position.

"I need your help, Brooke. I'm taking you to the clinic. Help me get your arm into the coat, okay?" He used his gentlest voice, and it cracked with fear. At least she wasn't unconscious. She moved her arm as he asked. "Good. Now let's get your other one in there."

After placing a shoe on each foot, he left her on the couch and picked up the twins to carry them to her minivan. The cold air hadn't bothered him earlier, but it felt frigid now. He buckled Megan into her seat and Alice into hers, and promised them he'd be right back. Inside, he found Brooke's phone and cradled her in his arms, snatching up her purse on his way out. He got her settled into the passenger seat, buckled her seat belt and rushed around to the driver's side. Rooted around in the purse for her keys. Found them and started the minivan.

As soon as the engine came to life, his world seemed to retreat into slow motion. Snow had begun to fall, and he could make out each snowflake as it hit the windshield. The girls were silent in the back seat. Christmas music played on the radio. The wipers swished back and forth.

He glanced at Brooke—out of it. Lethargic. His body froze harder than the ground he'd had to thaw with Marc's and Terry's help. Except there wasn't a metal oven to thaw him. Nothing would fix this.

Drive!

His brain yelled one thing, but his body refused. His mind flashed back to the wreckage from a decade ago, this time with visions of Brooke mangled next to him. And the twins.

His throat tightened to the point he was choking. His eyes bugged out, and he tore at the zipper at his collar.

He couldn't breathe. Couldn't move. Couldn't drive.

He couldn't go through with this.

"Dee?" one of the twins asked.

He snapped out of it, blinking, gulping deep breaths, but still not getting enough air.

"Yes?" He tried to sound normal.

"Mama?"

"I'm taking care of it, darlin'."

Lord, I need Your strength. I've tried this before and failed every single time. I've failed at so many things in my life. Please, have mercy on me. I don't deserve it, but Brooke does. Get us to the clinic safely. I'm begging You!

He swallowed bile, clenched his jaw and put the minivan into Reverse.

"We're taking your mama to see the doctor." He'd never backed out of a driveway slower in his life. His hands shook. His stomach rolled. But he kept going. And when he reached the end of her drive, he waited twice as long as he normally would to make sure no cars were coming. By the time he actually pulled onto the street, his palms were slick with sweat. If he hadn't been choking on fear, he probably would have been crying.

He was a broken man.

The speedometer showed the van traveling at a solid seventeen miles per hour. He didn't even attempt to go faster. He still couldn't catch his breath. He needed to keep his eyes on the road and continue driving. All that mattered was getting Brooke to the clinic. Safely. In one piece. Without smashing the minivan into a pole or a tree and crumpling it up.

The closer they got to the clinic, the easier he found it to breathe. He checked the twins in the rearview—they weren't crying. That had to count for something. His palms weren't slick with sweat anymore, either.

The clinic's parking lot came into view, and the relief flowing through his veins overwhelmed him. Just a little farther... The van crawled into the lot, and he eased into a parking space. Cut the engine. Let his head fall back against the headrest, and closed his eyes for the briefest of moments. *Thank You, Jesus. Please, don't let me be too late.*

Now what? He couldn't carry Brooke *and* the twins. Did he leave them out here alone? He was going to have to. Brooke's health was the priority.

"I'll be right back to get you two, okay?" They both nodded. Then he got out, hurried to the passenger side, unbuckled the seat belt and swung Brooke into his arms. Using his hip, he closed the door and power walked the short distance to the entrance. Two wheelchairs were inside, and he placed her in one and wheeled her to the reception window.

"Hello?" No one was there. He pounded on the small bell on the counter. *Ding! Ding! Ding!*

A young woman in scrubs appeared. "May I help you?"

"Brooke—she needs medical help. The ambulance was thirty minutes out, so I brought her here."

"You did the right thing." The woman sprang into action, yelling for one of the nurses to get the doctor. Then she came through the door and wheeled Brooke away, calling over her shoulder, "Don't go far! We need to ask you questions."

"Give me a minute. I have to get the twins." There was so much he wanted to say to Brooke. So many things he hadn't realized until this moment. But the twins were alone in the minivan, and Brooke had already disappeared from view.

He raced outside and slid open the van door. Both girls appeared to be on the verge of tears.

"Hey, there, I'm back. We're going inside to wait for your mama, okay?"

"Mama?" Alice's watery blue eyes stared up at him.

"Yep, she's inside, sweetheart."

He unbuckled them from their car seats. Snow landed on their hoods as he made his way to the entrance. Inside, a nurse was waiting for him. She asked about Brooke's symptoms as he helped the girls get their coats off. When he'd answered all her questions, he led them over to a children's table with crayons and coloring sheets.

They showed no interest in coloring, and instead lifted their arms for him to pick them up. Glancing around, he spotted a stack of children's picture books. He snagged one and sat down, then boosted the twins onto his lap.

"I'll read you a story, but first I need to call your uncle." He gave each of them what he hoped passed for a smile. Then he slipped his phone out of his pocket and found Marc's number. It rang twice, and Marc answered.

"Hey, Marc, we have a bit of a situation here."

"What are you talking about?" His tone went from relaxed to tense instantly.

"Brooke wasn't feeling good, so I took her to the clinic."

The line was silent for two beats. "Define not feeling good."

His chest seemed to be snagged with briars as he tried

to form the words. "Tired, slurring her words, unaware of her surroundings."

Marc hissed something Dean couldn't make out.

"What are the doctors saying?" Marc asked.

"Nothing yet. We just arrived."

"We?"

"Yeah, I've got the girls."

"Oh, man, thanks. Just a sec." Dean could hear Marc telling Reagan and his mom what was going on.

"Dean? Describe what happened." Anne must have grabbed Marc's phone. In the background, Marc was protesting for her to give it back. Dean told her exactly what he told Marc. "She didn't pass out?"

"No."

"Did one side of her face seem to freeze? And did you notice if she could move her limbs?"

"Her face seemed normal. I don't know about her limbs. I think she could move them. She did move her arms. She seemed more weak and out of it than anything." The temptation to rake his fingers through his hair grew strong, but he couldn't with the twins on his lap.

"Good. That's good." Anne's voice grew muffled as she relayed what he'd said to Marc and Reagan. "Listen, we'll come home now. I'll call Christy Moulten to take care of the twins."

"I'm not going anywhere." His tone grew firm. "I'm staying right here with these two until I know what's happening with Brooke."

"Thank you, Dean," Anne's voice softened. "We'll be there in an hour and a half. Sooner if Marc has anything to do with it."

"I'll keep you posted with any updates."

They ended the call. He kept an eye on the receptionist window and the door leading to the examination rooms. What was happening? Was Brooke okay? He wished someone would come out and explain everything to him.

Alice held the book he'd selected. He might as well keep the girls entertained and calm while he waited.

"This looks good," he said. "I like Christmas and polar bears."

As he began to read, the girls snuggled into his sides. They made him want to protect them from everything life would throw their way, including what was happening to their mommy.

He'd let the doctors take care of Brooke. And in the meantime, he'd take care of her girls. It was the least he could do for the woman who'd brought him back to life.

CHAPTER ELEVEN

"How are you feeling?" A man's voice cut through the fog in her brain. Brooke forced her eyes open.

The crinkle of paper as she shifted on the examination table alerted her that she was at the doctor's office. An IV was hooked up to her arm. Dread poisoned her veins.

Was it another stroke?

Her head ached, and the grogginess from earlier lingered. She gingerly wriggled her fingers, toes, legs and arms. She could feel and move every part of her body! The realization almost brought her to tears.

"What happened?" Her throat was parched.

Dr. South handed her a small cup of water. She drank it in one gulp. Better.

"Dean McCaffrey brought you in about twenty minutes ago. He was concerned about your symptoms." Dean? That couldn't be right. He didn't drive with other people in his vehicle. "The ambulance will be here shortly to take you to Casper for further testing."

"Further testing?" She brought the hand not hooked up to the IV to her chest. "Was it...? Did I...?"

"Have a stroke?" he added.

She nodded.

"I don't think so. We took your vitals, and once we got the IV started, you rebounded pretty quickly. I'm not ruling one out, though, given your history. You need testing we don't have here. Do you remember anything from before Dean brought you in?"

Her mom. Marc and Reagan. They were shopping.

The twins. Who had the girls?

"My girls?"

"With Dean in the waiting room." His patient smile reassured her. "Nurse Jody's out there playing peekaboo and giving them animal crackers. You know she dotes on them."

Of course. No one in Jewel River would let the twins be alone. Why had she even considered it? Everyone in this community had helped with Megan and Alice at some point in their almost two years of life. It humbled her. Filled her with gratitude. She had a lot of thank-you prayers to offer God later.

"Back to earlier," Dr. South said. "What do you remember?"

"Cookies." She remembered being mad at Megan for stealing the sprinkles. And then at Alice for licking the spoonful of icing. "We were supposed to decorate cookies, and I was tired and nauseous. I felt off."

"Mmm-hmm." He typed on his laptop. "Go on."

"I let the girls frost the cookies, and I thought I'd better have some water. So I did. Then I saw little lights."

"Flashing lights?"

"Yes."

"On one side or everywhere?"

"One side."

The clickity-clack of his fingers typing filled the room. "And then?"

"Dean came inside. He's been finishing the ramp out back. I told him to call the doctor."

"I see."

"Everything's fuzzy from that point on. I felt so tired, and my head hurt. I wanted to close my eyes and rest. I... I don't remember much after that."

He stopped typing and met her gaze. "I suspect you had a migraine with aura. When you get to Casper and have the tests, they'll be able to give you an accurate diagnosis. You've had all of them before, so you know the drill. In my professional opinion, I don't think this episode is as serious as it appears."

Not serious? Was he joking?

"You told me the signs to watch for in case of a stroke. All the signs were there." She ticked through the list in her head. Well, not all of them.

"Migraines can be mistaken for strokes. Both share a lot of attributes. I don't think you need to worry."

"All I do is worry." Had she really said that out loud?

"I understand. It's reasonable, given your circumstances. I hope, in time, you won't worry so much."

"I don't see my anxiety levels changing anytime soon." She wanted to hug herself, but the IV line was in her way. "I could have a stroke at any moment."

He gave her a kind look. "You do have an increased risk, but it's not as high as you might think. You don't have the most common risk factors. Your blood pressure is normal, your cholesterol levels are great, you're at a healthy weight, and you're young."

"Yes, but I had a stroke before. And even if this was a migraine, doesn't that increase my risk, too?" She had memorized the literature. Knew all the risk factors. Understood she didn't have the typical ones that caused a stroke.

What did it matter? She'd had a stroke less than two years ago, and she'd been young. Too young. Why did what happened today not count?

"I wish someone could give me an answer. Do I have a fifty percent higher chance of having another stroke? Seventy-five? I feel like I'm walking on eggshells, waiting to be paralyzed or worse."

She hadn't realized how keyed up she was, how much worry and tension she'd been holding inside, until all of that came out.

"Fifty? Seventy-five? No." Frowning, he shook his head. "Not even close."

What had her neurologist told her? The last time she'd gotten a follow-up checkup had been in June, a year after the stroke. She'd heard *increased risk* and assumed the worst.

"Then what is it? My neurologist has told me time and again that, compared to the average person, I have an increased risk of having a stroke. All the research I've done has confirmed it, and you've said it, too."

"You're right. I can't give you an exact number, but I can tell you it's well below the percentages you mentioned. About one in four people who've had a stroke end up having another one. That includes the most at-risk group—older people. You're managing your risk factors well. I'd place you well below twenty-five percent."

"It feels like the threat is always there, waiting to take me down."

"It's normal to feel that way, but our fears don't necessarily reflect reality."

"What if I get to the hospital, and it wasn't a migraine? What if I *did* have another stroke?" Tears pooled in her eyes.

"Then it's a good thing Dean got you here when he did, because you're sitting here talking to me, and that's a good sign."

A knock on the door drew their attention. "The ambulance is here."

"Send them in." Dr. South nodded.

"Can I see the girls?"

He hesitated. "I'll have Nurse Jody bring them in—just for a moment, though."

"Can Dean come, too?" She needed to see him. Needed to verify he'd brought her here. Needed to make sure he could take care of her babies until arrangements were made.

"Briefly."

Had he really driven her here? She couldn't imagine how difficult that must have been for him.

Her head still ached, but she didn't dare close her eyes. Was it wishful thinking to believe Dr. South's conclusion that she'd had a migraine? The symptoms screamed stroke to her.

Seconds later, Dean walked in with the twins and her purse.

"Mama!" They both twisted in his arms to reach for her. She attempted a smile as she shook her head.

"I can't hold you right now, my loves. I will as soon as I can, though, I promise." She met Dean's gaze. His eyes were full of concern, hope—and something more.

That glimpse of the depth of his feelings scared her. She couldn't offer him forever. She wasn't even sure she'd have tomorrow. Look at her current situation.

"Are you okay?" he asked. Megan whined as she reached for Brooke. He kept his hold on the girls as he let the purse drop from his hand onto Brooke's lap. "I figured you'd need this."

"Thanks. I think I'm okay. They're taking me to Casper for tests."

"Was it a stroke?"

She wasn't going to lie to him. "They aren't sure. The doctor thinks it was a migraine. But... I don't know."

He nodded. Nurse Jody pulled on Dean's sleeve. "Time's up."

The medics stood in the doorway. "Excuse me, but we need to get in there."

"I'll follow you to Casper with the girls." Dean stepped closer to the bed.

"No, I want them home. The tests take forever." Brooke took Megan's hand and squeezed it, then did the same with Alice's. "Be good for Dean. Mommy loves you. I'll see you soon. Dean, did you call my mom? Oh, and call Christy. She'll take care of the girls."

He nodded. "I'll drive to the hospital later—alone."

"Please don't." She hated seeing the hurt in his eyes, but

there was no point in him driving all that way. "I'll be getting tests done, and you won't be able to see me."

With pain in his eyes, he backed up and left the room as the twins started to cry. The sound tore at her heart. Their cries faded as the medics prepared to load her into the ambulance. Minutes later, as they shut the ambulance's doors and the sirens started, she closed her eyes.

Maybe this really had been just a migraine. But what would happen next time?

She hated living in constant fear like this. She'd never put Dean through a lifetime with her health problems. She wasn't enough. Not for an amazing guy like him.

AFTER GETTING THE girls buckled into their car seats, Dean prepared himself for another panic attack. So far, no gasping of breath. He glanced at the passenger seat. Didn't see visions of wreckage. No mangled metal or crumpled bodies. All he saw was an empty seat.

He wished it wasn't empty. Wanted Brooke there with him.

He started the minivan. *Now* the panic attack would begin. He waited for the symptoms. At least this time he knew it was possible for him to drive through them. Honestly, he hadn't acknowledged what a triumph that was until this moment.

He'd done it. He'd driven Brooke and the girls—and he'd been breathless, with sweaty palms, a tight chest and the terrifying feeling that he was going to die or kill them. And they'd all survived.

Oh, God, You are good. You alone got us to the clinic. Thank You!

While the engine warmed, he called Marc to give him the update. In the background, Anne told Marc to turn around and head back to Casper. They were meeting Brooke at the hospital.

With that out of the way, he shifted the van into Reverse. His heart pumped faster, and his breathing quickened.

None of it was a surprise. These were the symptoms he knew and loathed.

What did it matter, though? He forced himself to inhale. Exhaled slowly. Repeated it. He couldn't breathe deeply, but he could breathe.

God had given him the strength to get Brooke and the girls to the clinic safely. Dean could count on Him to help him get the twins back to her house.

With moist palms and adrenaline rushing through his body, he backed out of the parking spot. Took his time turning onto Center Street. Tried not to think about his tight chest or the difficulty he was having with his breathing.

Last-minute Christmas shoppers clutched scarves as they ducked in and out of shops. If anyone noticed the minivan crawling at eighteen miles per hour, they didn't seem to care.

He was doing this. Again. Driving with passengers in the car. Sure, he hadn't cracked twenty miles per hour, but who cared? It wasn't perfect, and it didn't have to be.

He just needed to get them home safely.

Brooke's street was up ahead, and he slowed even more. Why didn't Brooke want him at the hospital with her? Didn't he mean anything to her? Didn't she want him by her side?

They'd gotten close. Only a few days ago, she'd clung to him, asking him to at least say goodbye before he left.

Maybe that was the problem. He hadn't made her any promises beyond assuring her he'd say goodbye if he left.

Did he want to leave?

No. He wanted more. Wanted long-term. Wanted Brooke.

For a decade, he'd cut himself off from relationships beyond short visits and texts with Marc and his father. But his time in Jewel River had shown him he could have more.

It's not for you to decide. Brooke isn't getting remarried. Period. And she made it clear that she doesn't need you the way you need her.

Dean pulled into her driveway, parked and carried the twins

up the front porch. Christy Moulten, shivering in a parka with a furry hood, stood on the welcome mat, waiting for him.

"Anne called." Her kind smile brimmed with compassion. "I'll take care of these little dears until we know more."

"I can take care of them if you have somewhere else you need to be." He gave a slight nod to the front door. "It's unlocked. Didn't have time to lock it earlier." He'd been too busy having a mental breakdown over the realization he had to drive Brooke to the clinic.

"It will be hours before they come back. This is where I need to be." Her understanding tone took the edge off his raw emotions. "I'm so glad you were here."

She opened the door and waited for him to carry in the twins before closing it. Together they peeled off the girls' coats and boots. He left his own on. Figured he might as well finish the ramp's railing while there was daylight. At least he'd be able to keep his promise to Brooke that her projects would be completed before Christmas.

It would also mean he wouldn't have a reason to come back.

But that was okay. He didn't belong here anyway.

"Come on, girls, you look like you need some milk and cookies." Christy took them by their little hands and walked down the hallway to the kitchen. With a glance over her shoulder, she included Dean. "You look like you need some, too."

He wanted to decline, but her tone left no room for argument, so he joined them in the kitchen.

"What happened?" She found two sippy cups and a glass from one of the cupboards, then took out a gallon of milk from the fridge and poured. Handed each of the twins a sippy cup and guided them to the living room couch.

He took his milk with him and sat in one of the chairs while Christy settled on the couch with Megan on one side of her and Alice on the other. The girls could barely keep their eyes open while they drank their milk.

As Dean filled her in on the events of the day, Christy nodded thoughtfully. "I see God's hand in this. Just think what might have happened if you weren't here. With Anne and Marc and Reagan in Casper, who else could have taken her to the clinic? I couldn't have driven them. I still have two more weeks on a suspended license. What a blessing you are to all of us, Dean."

He frowned, not expecting those words to come out of her mouth.

"You've been an answer to so many people's prayers," she said. "Ed's, for sure, since he's been recovering. But Brooke's, too. You have no idea how important it was for her to have everything in here accessible for a wheelchair. And can you blame her? Look at today. It's a good thing she's not suffering any ill effects, whether it was a migraine or not."

He finished his milk, not knowing what to say.

"Patrick and I had lunch at Dixie B's last week," she said. "He raved about the work you're doing for his service dog training center. He can't believe how quickly the work is getting done, and the quality of it, too…"

As Christy went on about the pole barn he'd finished, Dean's mind wandered. She was making him see himself in a new light. A good light. One he hadn't seen himself in for a long time. Maybe ever.

"…and it's not every day a single cowboy like yourself could handle getting toddler twins buckled into their car seats and off to the clinic while taking care of their mother…"

If only Christy had any idea how hard it had actually been—the panic, the desperation he felt having to drive those three to the clinic. Brooke, Megan and Alice—treasures, each one. His treasures.

God, I love them. He almost gasped. Kept his face schooled and nodded as Christy talked on and on.

He loved Brooke. He loved her twins.

And she didn't love him back. Didn't want him around for moral support.

"Listen, I'm going to finish up the railing on the ramp out back." He stood abruptly. "It shouldn't be more than an hour. I'll try to keep as quiet as possible. Then I'm taking off. Holler if you need me."

The girls were almost asleep. Christy beamed at him. "You are too good to be true. Thank you."

He crossed over and kissed the top of Alice's head, then Megan's, and he thanked Christy before letting himself out. For the next hour, he forced all thoughts out of his head to focus on finishing the rail. Then he loaded his materials into the truck and drove straight to Moulten Stables.

He'd never needed a long ride on Dusty more than he did this minute. After methodically saddling the horse, he led him outside. Dusty shook his mane and snorted, clearly eager to get out and stretch his legs. Soon Dean was in the saddle, and they headed through the snow toward the trails leading to the back of the property.

What was he supposed to do?

He loved Brooke, and there was no way he'd be able to convince her she wouldn't have another stroke. For all he knew, she'd had one today. When he thought about her so lethargic and incoherent and tired, it was all he could do to keep it together.

Dusty picked up the pace as they entered the woods. Though it looked like a winter wonderland, he couldn't enjoy it.

Christy's words from earlier ran through his mind. *I see God's hand in this.*

He saw God's hand in it, too. Dean had been able to drive Brooke when he hadn't been able to drive anyone for years.

God had made the impossible possible.

Lord, thank You, again, for getting us to the clinic safely.
Thank You for helping me push through the panic when Brooke

needed me the most. I don't know what would have happened if You hadn't gotten me through it.

The verse he loved came back—*I can do all things through Christ.*

Yes, he could.

He *could* drive with other people in the vehicle without crashing it and hurting them. He *had* come through for Brooke when she'd needed him most. And he'd kept his promise to finish her remodeling projects.

He'd taken a huge step forward in his personal life today.

There was one more promise he wanted to keep. With a click of his tongue, he turned Dusty back toward the stables.

Dad's basement still had a few piles to dispose of. He could get it done tonight. And later, he needed closure on something else.

The locket.

BY TEN THAT EVENING, Brooke had officially been discharged from the hospital in Casper. As her mom harassed a nurse about what she could or could not do for the next few days, she sat in the wheelchair the hospital insisted on. Reagan stood next to her and held her hand.

"Praise God, praise God…" Reagan kept saying under her breath.

Brooke wasn't as elated as Reagan. She probably should have been, but getting discharged didn't change her situation.

After performing a slew of tests, the doctors concluded what Dr. South had suspected. No stroke, but a migraine with aura. A particularly bad migraine, at that.

The doctor had written a prescription for medicine to take whenever she had migraine-like symptoms to stop the attack in its tracks. And she'd had an in-depth discussion with the neurologist about her fears. Like Dr. South, this doctor seemed to think her chances of having another stroke were much lower than she believed.

As much as she wanted to trust that the doctors were right, a little voice in her head told her she couldn't.

She never should have had the first stroke. How could anyone claim she wasn't likely to have another?

Marc pulled the truck to a stop near the sliding glass doors, and Brooke pushed herself out of the wheelchair. Reagan reached over to help her. She was tempted to fling her arm away and hiss that she could manage on her own. But shame filled her at the thought. Reagan was the most supportive person she'd ever met.

Brooke would not hurt her feelings. She'd hurt enough feelings for one day. Every time she recalled the look on Dean's face as he'd carried the twins out of the examination room, her heart twisted.

"I can manage." Brooke attempted to smile, but it felt tighter than the skinny jeans she'd worn in high school.

"Let her help, Brooke." Mom sounded exasperated. "I had the nurse call in the prescription to the pharmacy back home. We'll have to pick it up early tomorrow. I'm sure they're closing by noon, with it being Christmas Eve and all." She blocked Brooke's path. "Where are you going? You're not sitting in the back. You're up front with Marc. The back seat is notorious for car sickness, and you've been through enough for one day."

She'd gotten rid of the migraine, but her mom's fussing might just bring it back.

This was what she hated: being treated like an invalid. Being told where to sit and what to do and how much to sleep and what to eat and that she was overdoing it.

Feeling less than.

Being less than.

She silently got into the passenger seat and buckled her seat belt. Marc reached over and touched her arm. "You okay?"

She nodded and rested the side of her head against the window as her mom continued to lecture her about how she needed to stay on the couch or in bed for the next several days. Marc began to drive.

For the umpteenth time that day, Brooke wished she hadn't told Dean to stay home. Wished he were here. There was so much she wanted to tell him. There were so many questions to ask.

Had he really driven her to the clinic? He obviously had, and it cut her up inside thinking what it must have done to him. She had to apologize for causing him all that pain.

Dean was a good man. The kind of man she wished she could have. If things were different…if she could just go back to life before the stroke. Back when she'd taken her good health for granted and never could have imagined the anxiety she faced now.

Today, Dean had gotten a taste of what life with her would look like, and it wasn't pretty.

She wouldn't put him through it. She loved him too much.

Yes, she loved him.

At some point today, in between the ambulance and the tests, she'd realized her feelings had leaped to love.

But nothing had changed—she still couldn't give him forever.

Something Dr. South said earlier echoed in her mind, though, and wouldn't let go. *Our fears don't necessarily reflect reality.*

She was tired of fearing the worst. Tired of living with this constant burden.

Her family had already told her they'd watch the twins tomorrow. She planned on getting out her Bible and her journal and figuring out how to find peace or at least manage the anxiety better.

What she really needed to do was thank Dean in person. Find out how difficult driving her to the clinic had been. Apologize for putting him through it.

But under no circumstances could she tell him she loved him.

She'd keep her feelings tucked deep down inside where they were safe. For Dean's sake. And her own.

CHAPTER TWELVE

LATER THAT NIGHT, Dean sat on the couch, staring at the locket in his hand. It had been a day of revelations, and he fully intended to get closure on this, too.

Something told him he'd never be able to truly move forward until he faced his past.

Yet he couldn't bring himself to open the locket. When he did, he'd be unleashing the memories he'd shut away for years.

Finishing the basement had taken a few hours. Every box was emptied, every pile stacked along the wall, taken out to the trash or loaded into the back of his truck to donate. At this point, he was practically on a first-name basis with the staff of the thrift store in Casper, where he'd dropped off so much stuff.

He'd swept and mopped the vinyl flooring down there and arranged the furniture to function as a family room. He couldn't wait for his dad to be released. The man was going to burst with excitement when he saw the basement.

Maybe bursting with excitement wasn't a good thing—he did have a heart problem. Dean chuckled at his own joke. He was willing to take his chances.

He'd texted Marc several times, and Marc had called him before the hospital released Brooke. The tests concluded she hadn't had a stroke, and Dean had almost sunk to his knees in relief.

He'd wanted to call her. But he hadn't. Couldn't bear to hear her clipped words or dismissive tone. He'd already heard both at the clinic. And a text wouldn't work, either. What if he asked her how she was doing and she answered with a thumbs-up emoji or something? He couldn't handle being brushed off as if they hadn't grown close. As if he hadn't told her his darkest secrets. As if they hadn't kissed and opened up about how scared they were to consider a future with anyone else in it. So he hadn't reached out to her at all.

Was that worse? Did she think he didn't care? Did she think about him at all?

At this point, it would be easier to open the stupid locket than to beat himself up about Brooke.

Closing his eyes, he took a moment to clear his mind. Then he looked down at the trinket in his hand. Flipped it over once. Twice. And using both thumbs, he popped it open.

On the right-hand side, his mother smiled back at him. Brown waves of hair fell to her shoulders, and she looked so young and impossibly full of life.

A piercing pain shot through his heart. Why had she left? Why hadn't she come back?

When he was younger, he'd asked himself the same questions—and he'd always answered, *Because of this.*

And by *this*, he meant the left-hand side of the locket.

The three of them together, back when they'd been a family. Dad stood next to his mother. Neither smiled. Dean stood in front, seven years old, grinning like an idiot. It had been taken in town at the Fourth of July festival.

There was a big, black X marked through the picture.

He'd made the X.

After his parents separated, Dean had permanently stopped grinning like an idiot. His safe world had evaporated like a wisp of smoke. He remembered begging his mom to let him live with her. But she'd had other plans.

The night she'd sat him down and told him she was moving far away and that he was staying here with his father, Dean had felt a betrayal so deep, he couldn't see straight. He'd snuck into his parents' room, tiptoed past all the boxes she'd been packing, found the travel bag with her jewelry and taken exactly what he'd been looking for.

The locket.

When he was growing up, his mom had worn it all the time. But she'd stopped wearing it after they split up. Dean had been full of rage when he'd slashed that X with permanent marker.

He'd regretted it immediately. Had slipped it into his pocket and run to his room, crying until he'd fallen asleep.

Not long after, she'd said her goodbyes. He'd wanted so badly to give the locket back to her, to tell her to open it to remember him, but how could he? He'd ruined it.

His anger had ruined everything.

The first year after the divorce, she'd visited him a few times. And he'd always wondered if she'd known he'd stolen the locket. He'd worried she'd tell him he was the one who'd crossed out their family, not her.

With it nestled in his hand, he could see the situation through older, more objective eyes. He wasn't an eight-year-old kid anymore. And his mother hadn't stayed away over a ruined picture in a locket.

She'd wanted out—out of her marriage, out of being a mother—and nothing would have changed it.

Dean closed the locket and shook his head. What a day.

All the things that had been holding him back for so many years… It was as if the walls of Jericho had fallen down.

His mom hadn't cut him out of her life because he'd crossed out their picture.

And he hadn't been trying to kill Lia all those years ago

when he'd driven so fast. Yes, he'd driven recklessly, and he'd paid a steep price for it.

But he had to stop punishing himself.

God, You've forgiven me. It doesn't change my stupid choices or the mistakes I've made, but I don't have to keep punishing myself for them anymore. I'm ready to move on. Please, help me.

What if he had another panic attack the next time he tried to drive with a passenger next to him?

So be it. He'd have to trust God with it. Today, his panic symptoms hadn't stopped him in an emergency situation. He'd driven Brooke—white-knuckled—to the clinic. He'd driven the girls—slower than a snail crossing a highway, but he'd done it—back home.

He'd done a lot of things he hadn't thought possible since arriving in Jewel River. Gotten involved with McCaffrey Construction when his father needed him. Kept his word and cleaned out the basement. Finished Brooke's remodeling projects.

Maybe he wasn't such a bad guy after all.

He flipped the locket into the air and caught it. He felt lighter, more hopeful, freer than he could remember. And he recalled those words his dad had told him all those years ago about his temper. Dad had been right. At twenty-one, Dean had thought he knew everything and had chosen the easy path. He *had* let his temper get the best of him.

But the past decade had changed him. The years had taught him patience and humility. He not only could but *would* keep a lid on his anger if it neared the boiling point. He'd been through too much, punished himself too much, to ever let it get that far again.

Dean stood and took in the glow of the lamp in the darkened room as he made his way to the bedroom. He stopped in front of the dresser, preparing to put the locket back in there. Instead, he clasped it tightly.

Why keep it? He didn't need to cling to guilt or shame. Reaching into his pocket, he pulled out his pocket knife and poked the blade along the edge of the photo with the X until it popped out. He repeated it on the other side. Then he stared at both pictures for a moment and returned to the kitchen. Threw them into the trash.

Without overthinking it, he slid his feet into sliders and made his way outside in the cold air to the back of his truck. He tossed the empty locket into one of the donation boxes.

Someone else could fill it with photos that meant something to them. It no longer meant anything to him.

Back inside, he grabbed a bottle of water from the fridge and returned to the living room.

Tomorrow was Christmas Eve, and this comfortable, inviting home held no sign of it. Brooke was right about that, too. He might as well put up the Christmas tree and enjoy the season for once.

As he lugged out the decorations that Erica had left on the porch when he'd first arrived, he planned out the next day. First he'd ride Dusty and give the horse some treats. An apple and a carrot ought to do it. Then he'd drive to Casper to visit Dad. Maybe they'd get good news and find out he could come home next week. After Casper, he'd return to Jewel River and pay Brooke a visit.

She might not care about him the way he did her, but he needed to see for himself that she was okay. If he ended up wrapping her in his arms and telling her he loved her, all the better.

He loved the woman, and it might be the last time he had the chance to hold her. Not because he was leaving Jewel River. No, Christy's words from this afternoon had seeped inside him and made him realize he wanted a life right here in the community he'd once belonged to. He wasn't sure how it would all work out, but he didn't need to know at this point.

He missed his dad. Missed Marc. Wanted to hang out with

Ty and Trent and the other friends he'd grown up with. Was ready to live in a comfortable home like this one rather than a sterile, tiny cabin.

No more hiding away from life on a ranch in Texas. He'd forgotten how much he enjoyed working in construction. And how nice it was to live in a place where everyone knew him. He liked being able to grab a burger from Dixie B's and run into familiar faces.

More than anything, he finally liked himself again.

After ten long years, it was about time.

BROOKE WOKE WITH a start, jerking upright in her bed. The clock glowed 5:08 in the darkness. For some reason, Reagan's voice kept echoing in her mind. *Praise God. Praise God.*

Were the twins all right? She padded down the hall and into their room. Megan must have climbed out of her crib and into Alice's. A few stuffed animals were piled up on the floor nearby. Those girls were too smart for their own good. They were sleeping with their arms wrapped around each other—her babies, her sweethearts.

Not wanting to wake them, she quietly made her way back to her bedroom. She doubted she'd be able to get back to sleep. She felt keyed up. And no wonder. Yesterday had been all kinds of awful. By the time her family had dropped her off and made sure she had everything she needed, she'd been too tired to function. She'd hugged and thanked Christy, checked on the sleeping twins, crawled into bed and fallen asleep.

She checked her phone. There were several text messages she'd missed yesterday, but none were from Dean. She frowned. She had a lot of smoothing over to do with him. He must be upset. And she'd be mad too if she were him. To think of all he'd done for her, and she'd been so curt with him at the clinic.

She opened the text from her best friend, Gracie. It made her smile.

Reagan called and told me what happened. I'm driving to Jewel River on Christmas Day. I'll stay with your mom if you don't have room for me.

Tears pressed against the backs of her eyes. She had the most supportive group of friends and family on the planet. She texted Gracie back. There's always room for you here. Thank you!

How had she been blessed with so many people who would drop anything to help her out? Her mom, her brother, Reagan, Christy, Gracie—anyone in Jewel River.

And Dean. His selflessness, his generosity, the way he made her feel—like she wasn't a ticking time bomb ready to have a stroke at any minute—had her wanting more.

The enormity of the past three years slammed into her. All she'd been through. All she'd done to move forward. All she'd taken for granted.

God, Reagan was right. Her first instinct was to praise You. And what did I do? Sat there like a sullen child. Mad that I have health issues. Angry that my family was fussing over me. Upset that I can't have the life I want.

Feeling thirsty, she walked through the living room to get to the kitchen. The white Christmas lights still glowed from the tree, and her mother's soft snores drew her attention to the couch. The woman was covered with a thick, soft blanket, and the sight tugged at her heart. Her mom would do anything for her.

Brooke made a mental note to thank her mother and to be more patient.

As quietly as possible, she selected a journal and her favorite Bible from the shelf. Then she poured herself a glass of water and retreated to her bedroom, where she turned on a reading lamp and settled into bed.

It had been a few months since she'd logged any entries in the journal. Staring at the blank page made her pause. What should she write? A diary entry? A list of things to be thankful for? She took a drink as she tried to decide.

At this rate, it would be New Year's Eve before she wrote anything.

She had to start somewhere. And she knew exactly where to begin. The day when everything changed. The day Ross died.

She remembered details from the day like it was yesterday. How sunny and warm it had been. How she'd driven to the supermarket and debated over three flavors of ice cream before purchasing two of them. She'd been hoping Ross would be able to call her. Instead, she'd gotten the news she'd never wanted to hear.

Brooke poured it all out on the pages—the feelings of it not being real, the grief, the depression, the difficulty of those first months as a mom. She had to flex her hand again and again as it cramped while she wrote.

The sun was rising as she wrapped up the journal entry. While she flipped through the pages she'd scribbled, a newfound understanding of herself, her circumstances and God's provision for her took hold.

Lord God, You've held my hand through every step of my life. I don't know what I'd do without my family—Mom, Marc and Reagan. I love them so much.

She'd do anything for them. The same as they'd do for her.

Ross and I didn't have much time together, but I loved him, too. That will never change. Then the twins came along. They gave me so much to do, I didn't have time to think about how much I missed Ross anymore.

She hadn't really allowed herself to think back to those months leading up to the stroke. She'd been too busy moving forward, raising babies. But now she allowed the memories from that terrible time to return. And more pieces locked into place.

Not sleeping. Barely eating. Just getting through each day.

How many times had her mom and Marc begged her to eat

more during her pregnancy and in those first months of having the twins home? They'd told her she needed to keep up her strength for the babies. But she'd ignored them. They hadn't understood that everything tasted like cardboard and had the texture of chalk in her mouth. Her clothes had drooped on her bony frame.

Reality slapped her.

She kept acting like the stroke had come out of the blue. Like nothing had caused it. She'd convinced herself that she'd been perfectly healthy and—bam!—the stroke. But that wasn't what had happened. And it was time to face it.

She'd been at least twenty pounds underweight. Her blood pressure had been higher than a mountaintop. She'd been sleep-deprived for almost a year.

Was it really any wonder her body had shut down? When she'd been running on empty for so long?

Dr. South was right. She didn't have the common risk factors that would cause another stroke. However, back when she'd had one, her risk factors *had* been high.

She tapped her pen against her chin.

She'd told Dean she'd never get married again because of her health and her decision to not have more children. But these journal pages told a different story—one Dean had hinted at previously.

Face it, Brooke. You're scared. Your dad left years ago. Then you fell in love with Ross. But he died, and you were alone again. And now you have a good man who might be willing to take a chance on you, but you won't consider a future with him. Why?

Choked up, she dropped her chin to gain her composure.

I don't think I can take another loss.

Had she been using her fear of having another stroke to protect herself from loving—and losing—again?

She owed Dean an apology. And a thank-you. And so much more.

God, I'm tired of taking from my loved ones when all they do is give. And I don't give You credit for all my blessings, either. You gave me healthy twins. I don't have to worry about money. I have friends nearby who constantly look in on me, babysit for me and overall encourage me. Forgive me for taking You and them for granted. Help me show them all how much they mean to me.

Murmurs came from the twins' room. She closed her eyes and smiled. *Praise You, God!*

She stood, stretched her arms over her head and made her way to the girls' room. Only when she reached the doorway did she realize it was Christmas Eve.

The most wonderful time of the year. She smiled to herself.

Something told her better days were coming. Starting today.

CHAPTER THIRTEEN

"MERRY CHRISTMAS EVE, Dad." Dean entered his room at the rehab center. At dawn, he'd ridden Dusty and given the horse a few treats. Then he'd cleaned up and made good time driving to Casper. It wasn't even ten o'clock. "How are you feeling today?"

His father looked as healthy as he had before the heart attack. Maybe healthier. His color was good, he'd slimmed down by at least thirty pounds, and he was wearing a T-shirt and sweatpants that were clearly too big for him.

"I'm great." Dad gave him a hearty hug. "Merry Christmas Eve to you, too."

"You're in an unusually good mood." He was used to his father ranting about how the staff was trying to kill him with the nonstop exercising and small food portions. That and the never-ending complaints about when they would finally let him return to Jewel River so he could do his job.

"They're releasing me today, son. I got the all-clear to return home."

"What?" Dean couldn't imagine a better gift. Unless…this wasn't wishful thinking on his father's part, was it? "Really? Today?"

"Yes." He pointed to the corner, where two transparent plastic bags were filled with clothing. "I've already got my stuff packed. See?"

Dean couldn't believe it. His dad *was* coming home today.

With a quick knock on the open door, his father's social worker, a short woman in her late forties, entered. "Did Ed tell you the good news?"

"He did," Dean said. "Can we get out of here now?"

"Just a few more forms for Ed to sign, and then you can go." She handed his father an iPad and stylus as she instructed him on what to sign and what to initial. Several minutes later, she shook his father's hand and smiled at Dean. "Take the folder with the instructions. He's all yours."

"Merry Christmas," Dean said to her.

She smiled, nodding. "Merry Christmas."

Dad had already hefted the bags.

"Hold up, Dad. Let me get those. You shouldn't be lifting anything."

"That's what you think. I've been lifting weights—supervised strength training, they call it—for a week. I'm supposed to be active. Move it or lose it. That's what they tell me."

It made sense. Dean wasn't going to argue. He motioned for his father to hand him a bag.

His dad beamed all the way down the hall, saying goodbye to nearly every person they came across. Finally, they made it outside and crossed the parking lot to Dean's truck.

"Feels like Christmas, doesn't it?" Dad chucked the bags into the back seat and climbed into the passenger seat. Then he rubbed his hands together. "A little snow, a little sunshine. It's good to be alive."

"I couldn't agree more." Dean gave his dad a grin. "I can't believe they let you go. And today, of all days."

"You're telling me." His eyes crinkled in the corners.

Dean started the truck, and his chest tightened. He hadn't considered that he might be driving his father home. Would he have a debilitating panic attack? Or would he be able to drive through any symptoms?

After a few shaky breaths, he backed out of the spot and began the long drive home.

"I worked so hard this past week," Dad said, "that they agreed I could take care of myself at home. Between you and me, I get tired pretty easy, but that's to be expected. I promised I'd buy a treadmill. I'll order one this afternoon. Now, tell me everything I've missed since we last talked."

On the main road, Dean swallowed the fear clogging his throat and kept the speed at thirty miles per hour. Beads of sweat formed on his forehead.

At least his dad hadn't said a word about how slow he was driving. His heart thumped, but he kept his gaze ahead. "I finished Brooke's house."

"No kidding? The ramp, too?"

He nodded. "She had quite a scare yesterday. I was there. Thought she was having another stroke." He filled his dad in on the details and realized his breathing was almost normal. He lightly pressed the gas pedal.

"Good thing you were there. Anne, Marc and Reagan were here in Casper yesterday. They stopped by to visit me in the morning. Anne snuck me cinnamon rolls, and Reagan left four huge chocolate-covered strawberries."

"They're good people." Dean started to relax. Nothing but rolling hills and prairie for miles. Now was as good a time as any to keep his other promise—to tell Dad about the accident years ago. "I almost couldn't drive Brooke to the clinic."

"Why not?"

"For ten years now, I haven't been able to drive with anyone else in the vehicle. It's the reason I got that job as a ranch hand in Texas."

"What caused it?"

"My stupidity. About six months after I moved to Dallas, I caught Lia kissing Colin—you remember him?" Dean glanced at his father, who nodded. "We were at a bar. It was late. I was the designated driver, and I couldn't wait to leave. I excused myself for a minute and found them kissing. Went from bored to furious in three seconds flat. Told her to get her own ride home. We were both pretty upset. She got in my vehicle. I told her to get out. She refused, so I drove. We argued, and what can I say? You were right. My temper did hurt someone. I kept going faster and faster. Every word she said made me accelerate more until I crashed."

"What happened? Did she...?" Dad's eyebrows formed a V.

"No. She wasn't hurt. But my SUV... I've never seen anything so mangled. I don't know how she walked away without being seriously injured...or worse. I've lived with that image in my head for a decade."

He placed his hand on Dean's arm. "I'm sorry, son."

"I am, too. Her dad fired me. I got a reckless driving ticket. What a joke. I could have killed her, and all I got was a slap on the wrist? Whatever. I lost my job, my friend, my girl and my self-respect all in one night."

"That's why you got the job on the ranch."

He nodded.

"I wish you'd told me. You've been alone all these years, and you didn't need to be. We all make mistakes."

"I haven't been alone. You never gave up on me." Even when they hadn't seen eye to eye, Dad always wanted the best for him.

"Never will, either."

"God's seen me through all of it."

"You can trust Him."

"I don't want to hide my mistakes and my problems anymore. Like I said, after the accident, I couldn't drive with anyone in the vehicle with me. I tried a few times, and it was always the same. I'd gasp for breath, and in my mind, I'd see the wreckage. My heart would pound in my chest. I'd get dizzy. I was always convinced I was going to die. Had full-blown panic attacks."

"That's a lot to deal with."

"Yeah, I kept it all inside. Until recently. I told Brooke. She's— Well, she's special, and I've gotten close to her."

"Wait. Yesterday—you said you drove her to the clinic?"

"I did."

"You didn't have a panic attack?" Hope lined the words.

"No, I definitely had a panic attack."

"How'd you do it, then?"

"I thought her life depended on it. And the twins were in the back seat. I drove through all the symptoms—could barely breathe. Sweat was dripping. My heart was clenching. I kept it slow. And I got them there in one piece."

"That had to be hard. I'm proud of you. I've always been proud of you, but that's really something."

"Thanks."

"And you're driving me now. You seem fine. Are you?"

"I wasn't at first, but now? Yeah, I feel okay."

Neither spoke for several minutes.

"I like Brooke." Dad stared out the window. "I understand why she made her house accessible for a wheelchair. She needs independence, and the stroke took it from her. She needs the assurance she can raise those babies and live on her own."

Dean wished he'd been more understanding about why the remodel was important to her. He *did* understand. But he'd been dismissive, too—and he shouldn't have been.

"I'm thinking about staying in Jewel River, Dad."

His eyes grew round. "Really? You're not putting me on, are you? I can't take that kind of joke. My heart, you know."

Dean chuckled. "Seriously. I've enjoyed overseeing the projects, and in Brooke's case, I also liked doing the actual work. Laying the tile. Building the ramp. Reminded me of working with you all through high school."

"We were a good team. That's why it was hard when you

went to work for your girlfriend's dad. I'd been waiting for you to finish up college and work with me again. And I'm sorry I yelled that day. You were right. You did get your temper from me."

"I didn't leave because of you, Dad."

"I know." He frowned, shrugging. "You had a girlfriend and a good offer."

"I don't think it was that, either. I mean, it was a big part of it, but not all."

"What was it then? Why did you leave?"

"I'd buried a lot of pain from when Mom left us. I think I blamed myself. And I wasn't willing to look inward and deal with any of that. Moving to Texas allowed me to escape."

"You weren't the reason she left. I was." He jabbed his thumb into his chest. "Your mother wasn't meant for a small town. She was a social butterfly from Chicago, used to strolling out the door and sitting in a coffee shop down the street. Picking up takeout food at midnight. Catching a movie on a Friday afternoon and again on Saturday night, just because she could."

"I never knew that."

"How could you? I wouldn't talk about her." He shook his head. "I did you wrong, Dean. I didn't know how to talk about your mother. Pretending it didn't happen didn't make it go away."

"It's in the past. I've made my peace with it."

"You forgive me?" Dad asked.

"There's nothing to forgive." He glanced at him. "Do you forgive me?"

"There's nothing to forgive." He grinned. "Now, let's talk about your role in McCaffrey Construction. I say we make it an equal partnership…"

Once they worked out the particulars, Dean turned on the Christmas station, and they caught up on everything that had happened over the past couple of days. Before long, they arrived at his dad's house and were opening the front door.

"Before you go to your room, there's something I want to show you." Dean set his dad's bags on the floor.

"What are you talking about?"

"Come on." Dean led the way to the basement, and when his dad reached the bottom of the staircase, his jaw dropped. He walked forward, turning this way and that to take it all in.

"I can't believe it." He blinked, staring in wonder. "It's clean. All the boxes and bags and piles are gone."

"What do you think? Are you okay with it?"

"Okay? I'm more than okay. I'd let it become a dumping ground for years. You cleared it all out." His face brightened like the sun shining through a break in the clouds. "Knowing all that stuff was down here bothered me. I kept telling myself I'd tackle it a little here, a little there. But it was daunting, so I avoided it. The only time I ventured to the basement was to add more junk I wasn't sure what do with."

"I know exactly what you mean. That's how I felt, too. But I also felt really guilty. You've been asking me to help for years, and I've never taken the time."

"It wasn't your problem."

"But it was yours, and you mean so much to me, Dad. I love you, and I should have helped you with it sooner."

They hugged. "I love you, too, Dean. I'm speechless. I can't get over how clean it is down here. You know what this place needs?"

"What?"

"New furniture." He snapped his fingers. "A big-screen TV. I'm picturing it now. A man cave."

Dean laughed. "I'm always up for buying a new television. *Man cave* has a nice ring to it."

They went back upstairs, and his dad pointed to the hall. "I'm going to rest for a while."

"Good. I'm heading to Brooke's."

"Are you two a thing?"

"I want to be."

"I wish you well."

"Hey, Dad."

"Yeah?"

"Merry Christmas Eve. It's good to have you back."

"Merry Christmas Eve to you, too. It's good to be back."

"WHAT ARE YOU DOING?" Brooke's mom yawned as she entered the kitchen later that morning. Earlier, Brooke had changed the girls and gotten them each a sippy cup with milk. Thankfully, her mom had been able to get some much-needed sleep after yesterday's drama. "You're supposed to be resting."

Brooke adjusted the heat on the electric griddle and flipped a pancake. She gave her mom a smile so big, her mouth cracked at the corners. "Merry Christmas Eve, Mom. Thanks for staying over."

"Of course I stayed." Her mother bustled across the room, reaching for the spatula. But Brooke held it up and away from her. Mom stepped back and gave her the don't-test-me stare, but Brooke simply shook her head. Mom glared. "Brooke, go rest on the couch. I'll take over from here."

"I'm making pancakes. Why don't you pour yourself a cup of coffee and have a seat?" She pointed the spatula to the stools opposite where she stood at the island. Her mother didn't take orders well, and that was probably the reason Brooke didn't give them very often.

"I don't like this. Yesterday was a big wake-up call. You've been overdoing it, and—"

"Mom," she interrupted in as gentle a tone as she could manage, "I'm okay. It was a migraine. That's all."

"But next time—"

"There might not be a next time."

"But what if there is?" Her eyebrows twisted in worry.

"Then I'm prepared. The house is ready for the worst-case

scenario." A sense of peace filled her with strength. "I can't spend every minute of my life worrying about having another stroke."

Her mom let out a humph, poured herself a mug of coffee and took a seat on the stool. Megan and Alice ran into the room.

"Gwammy!" They wrapped their arms around her mom's legs.

"Oh, my little darlings." She kissed the tops of their heads.

"Are you getting hungry?" Brooke leaned over to see their reactions. Wide-eyed, they nodded. "Good. We're having yummy pancakes. And we're going to sing Christmas songs and color pictures and watch cartoons."

"Yay!" They clapped and hopped up and down.

"But first, I have to finish making these." She straightened, and her heart burst with love for her babies. "Go have a seat at your table."

They scampered off and took a seat. Her mom got up and gave them each a wooden puzzle to play with while they waited. Then she returned to her spot at the island.

"Mom?"

"What, hon?" She sipped the coffee.

"I'm making some changes."

"Don't ask me to get behind anything that's going to hurt your health." She shook her head, her mouth drawn into a tight line.

"Why are you assuming I would want to hurt my health?"

"I'm not." She sighed. "I just… I worry about you."

"I know." The pancakes were golden. She slid them onto a plate, dolloped butter on the griddle and poured batter for new ones. Maybe she needed to approach this conversation from a different angle. "Why didn't you ever remarry?"

Her mom sputtered into her coffee, set the mug down with a thunk and pounded her fist into her chest as she coughed. "What?"

Talk about being dramatic.

"After Dad left, you never got close to anyone. Why?"

"I was busy. The bakery took up all my time."

"Even after we grew up? Marc was busy running the ranch. I fell in love with Ross. Moved out of state. You had time then."

"Dating wasn't on my radar. After your dad left us, Marc and I went into survival mode. It took years to get to a place of stability. And I really never gave dating much thought. I focused my energy on you kids and the bakery."

Brooke flipped the pancakes. Was that what she wanted her life to become, too? Focusing on the twins to the exclusion of everything else?

"What do you think of Dean?" She wasn't sure why she was asking her mother about him.

"I give him credit for stepping in to help when his dad needed him. Do I wish he was settled, with a career? Yes. But he's your brother's best friend, and it's none of my business what he does with his life."

"He's not a shiftless drifter."

"I didn't say he was." Her eyebrows rose as she lifted the mug to her lips again. "He's not exactly established, either. We don't know what he'll do once Ed comes home. He might not even know yet."

All good points. If Brooke had her way, Dean would stay right here in Jewel River.

"I hope he stays," Brooke said.

"I wouldn't count on it."

In the past, she would have gotten disheartened at her mother's skepticism. However, today it only reminded her she didn't have all the answers. She could trust God with her future, whether it included Dean or not, whether she had another stroke or not. God would be holding her hand. He'd get her through everything.

"I'm in love with him, Mom, and I think I'm going to tell him."

"In love with him?" She set the mug down. "So soon? What

are you talking about? Does he know? Does he feel the same? Is he going to stay here? How does he feel about the twins? He's not ready to be a father. He might not want to be one at all. I don't think you've thought this through. This is all too sudden."

The rapid-fire questions and statements took a minute for Brooke to process, and when she did, they hurt.

"Why do you assume the worst? About him and about me?"

"I'm not. I'm just being realistic."

The clacks of wooden puzzle pieces and the sizzles from the griddle filled her ears. She wasn't sure she even wanted to respond to her mom if this was how the conversation was going to continue.

"I don't want to see you hurt," Mom said softly.

"I know. And don't think I haven't noticed your sacrifices. The past two years especially have upended your life, and I appreciate all you've done to take care of me and the girls. I don't know how I would have managed without you."

"Those weren't sacrifices. I love you. I'm your mother. I'm always here for you."

"I know. But they *were* sacrifices. I think it's time I accept the fact I'm healthy. As healthy as I'll probably ever be. I don't need to be in survival mode anymore. I don't need to spend every day fearing another stroke. I'm taking care of myself, and I think it's time to move forward."

"Wishful thinking won't prevent another stroke from happening."

"No, but let's face it. My body was shutting down when I had the stroke. I'm healthy now."

She transferred the new pancakes to the plate. Then she turned off the griddle and found the syrup. Cut up pancakes and put them on snowmen plates for the girls. After she got them settled in their high chairs, they dipped the bites into syrup and began eating.

Brooke stacked three pancakes on a plate and slid it to her

mother, then added three to her own plate and drizzled syrup over them. She rounded the island and sat on the stool next to her mom.

"I don't know if Dean and I have a future," she said, "but he's patient and understanding. He took charge yesterday when I needed him the most. I've gotten to know him, and I..." She couldn't think of what else to add. Shaking her head, she scooped a bite of pancakes on her fork.

"I think it's moving awfully fast." Mom's eyes glistened with worry.

"I agree." She nodded. "But we've both had life experience. I don't want to spend the rest of my life alone, not when I could be really happy with him."

Her mom shifted her gaze to her plate. "That's a good point."

They ate in silence until the girls banged on their trays. "More?"

"Hungry today, huh?" They nodded. "I'll get you some more."

By the time she'd loaded their plates with more cut-up pancakes, her mom had finished breakfast and was watching her.

"What's your plan? With Dean?"

"I don't know yet. I didn't think it would be fair to put a man through a lifetime of worrying I could have a stroke at any minute, but now?" She shrugged.

"What changed?"

"Nothing. Everything. I guess Dean opened my eyes."

"Are Marc and Reagan still picking up the girls at noon?" Mom stood and took her plate to the sink.

"Yeah."

"Invite him over. Talk it out. You'll know what to do."

"Thanks, Mom."

"I'll always be here for you." Her mother came over and hugged her. "No matter what."

"Thank you. I'll always be here for you, too." With tears

in her eyes, she exchanged an understanding smile with her mother. "I don't know what I'd do without you."

"I think you should wear your burgundy sweater to talk to Dean. It's your color."

"Oh, yeah?" If her mother was suggesting outfits, Brooke knew she'd be on board with them dating before long. She just hoped Dean would be on board, too.

CHAPTER FOURTEEN

DEAN'S PHONE DINGED as he cut the engine to his truck in Brooke's driveway. She'd sent him a text. Can we talk sometime today?

He grinned. Yeah, they could talk. Right now.

He snatched up the flowers he'd bought from the grocery store. A Christmas bouquet with red and white roses, greenery and silver glittery spiral things. He would have liked to buy her two dozen roses, but this was all they had. It would have to do.

Sometime between dealing with his mother's locket and opening up to his dad about the accident, Dean had changed. He no longer felt unworthy of having a full life—with a career, a home, a community, a wife and two little girls.

Now all he had to do was convince Brooke that she deserved it, too.

After two quick knocks on her front door, Brooke opened it, and her big blue eyes widened at the sight of him. She backed up for him to enter, then closed the door behind him.

"You're here." There was a glow about her that had been missing yesterday. Her dark hair fell in big curls over her shoulders, and she wore a burgundy sweater and dark pants.

"These are for you." He thrust the bouquet into her hands. "Is this a good time to talk?"

He craned his neck to see if the girls and her mom were around. No signs of anyone.

"These are beautiful, and yes, it's a great time to talk." With a gentle smile, she pivoted toward the kitchen. "Marc and Reagan took the girls to the ranch. Mom went home for a nap."

"You're alone?" He followed her until she stopped in front of the sink. She reached up and took a vase from a cupboard and filled it with water. "You're feeling okay?"

"Yes to both." As she trimmed the stems, she sighed. "Dean, I'm so sorry about yesterday. I feel terrible."

For what part? His panic attack while driving? Not wanting him with her at the hospital?

She adjusted the flowers and set the arrangement on the island. "I put you in an awful situation. I can only imagine how terrible it was for you to have had to make the decision to drive me to the clinic."

"It forced me to get real about my problem."

"Why did you do it?" Her soft voice and shimmery eyes lured him closer.

"Because you needed me, and I wasn't going to let you down."

"At what cost, though?" Worry lines creased her forehead as she stepped toward him. She reached up and brushed her fingers along the hairline at his temple.

Her touch, her words, her demeanor made his heart pound. This was why he loved her. She was more concerned with him having to drive her than she was with her own health.

"I won't deny I had a panic attack. I could barely see straight in the driveway. Then I glimpsed Meggie and Alice in the back. They looked scared. I couldn't let them—or you—down, so I forced myself to drive. It was slow going, but I got you there. God got us there."

"I will never put you through that again."

"I know you won't." He grinned, reaching for her hand.

"Because when I drove them home, it was easier. I still drove slowly, but I didn't have a complete breakdown."

"You mean it?" She searched his eyes. "You could drive me somewhere right now and not be affected?"

"I can't say I wouldn't be affected, but yeah, I could drive you." He brought the back of her hand to his lips. "I have so much to tell you, but first, what did the tests show? What did the doctors say?" He led her to the living room, where they sat side by side on the couch with her hands in his.

"The tests confirmed Dr. South's suspicions. It was a migraine with aura. A bad one. I now have migraine medicine on hand in case it happens again."

"So there won't be any long-term issues? Do you have to do anything different?"

"No and no. Rest for the next couple days. That's it."

He pulled her into a hug, sinking his fingers into her hair, and whispered against her ear, "Praise God."

She twisted out of his arms. "What did you say?"

"I said, 'Praise God.'"

She covered her mouth with her hands. Then her shoulders shook, and she cried.

What had he said? He wrapped her in his arms, caressing her back and murmuring shushing noises.

He wasn't sure why she was upset, but he'd caused it—he knew that much.

When she regrouped, she wiped the tears away and sniffed. "You probably think I'm a mess."

"No."

"Reagan said the same thing last night when we learned it wasn't a stroke. She kept saying, 'Praise God.'"

It didn't seem out there to him that they would all want to praise God for her health, but what did he know?

"I realized how tight-fisted I am with my praise to God. My first thought was that this time it was a migraine, but what about next time? I was angry for having to live in constant fear. But Reagan—and Marc and Mom and all of my friends, and now you—are thankful it wasn't worse news."

"We're thankful you're alive, Brooke. You're a special person. Of course we're going to praise God that He watched over you and kept you safe from harm."

"I know, and I feel so ashamed. Because I should be the one praising Him. I woke up early this morning—before dawn—and I took out a journal and really thought over the past couple of years. They've been so hard. And blaming everything on the stroke was easier than accepting the other fears I have."

"Like what?"

"You already know. You called me out on it last week. I'm afraid of being left behind. Of loving someone and losing them. My dad saw no reason to be a part of my life. And Ross died when we'd barely gotten started."

"I'm sorry, Brooke. You've been through so much."

"You have, too."

"Not like you have." He wanted to kiss her, but he had things to say. "I understand why you needed to remodel the house. The ramp is done, by the way."

"It is? Completely?" She brightened. "I forgot to even check."

"Yes. And I also understand why you've decided marriage is off-limits."

"Yeah, about that—"

"But yesterday and today have given me a whole new perspective. And I'm not leaving until I convince you that you can trust me with your forever. I love you, Brooke. And nothing's going to change it."

HER SHARP INTAKE of breath kicked up her adrenaline. Dean loved her?

"But you saw what happened to me." She lowered her chin, needing to be transparent with him. "Everything I experienced yesterday was similar to a stroke."

"I know, and I want to be the one here in case it happens again. I don't want you to be alone. I don't want to be alone. I've been alone for ten long years, Brooke, and I'm tired of living like that. You changed me."

"Why?" She didn't know what she was asking. All she knew was up until yesterday, he'd refused to consider forever. And she'd refused, too.

His lips curved slightly, and his eyes crinkled in the corners. "Turns out coming back to Jewel River was exactly what I needed. I've had to make peace with things I'd been running from."

"The accident?" She moved closer to him, wanting his arms around her again, but content to watch him as he talked.

"Yes, but other things, too. The basement was part of it. I found something of my mother's down there that I'd been avoiding. It forced me to admit I'd believed I was the reason she left. But I was just an eight-year-old kid. I've let that go."

She nodded in understanding.

"But Dad—did I even tell you he's home?"

"No, really? What terrific news!"

"Yeah, they released him this morning. He was blown away when I showed him the basement. He's online shopping right now for a treadmill and a big-screen TV. Said it's going to be the man cave."

She chuckled, even though she wanted to get back to the subject at hand. The two of them. Love.

"Anyway," Dean continued, "I told him about what happened in Texas. And I told him I'm staying here in Jewel River. I'm ready to have a life again."

Hope almost choked her. He was staying!

"Listen, Brooke." He caressed the back of her hand with his thumb. "I get your fear about having another stroke, and I'm sorry I was dismissive the other day. I didn't fully understand what you're up against and how difficult it is to live with that kind of fear."

He was saying everything she'd needed to hear, and she loved him all the more for it.

"I'm not living like that anymore," she said.

"What do you mean?"

"You faced your fears and your past, and I did the same. I've been lying to myself. I wasn't healthy when I had the stroke. You can ask Marc or my mom. I'd lost a ton of weight, wasn't eating, wasn't sleeping. My body couldn't take it anymore. And all this time, I've convinced myself I could have another stroke any day—and truthfully, I could—but the doctors have assured me I've kept my risk factors to a minimum. I need to trust God with this, Dean. I need to let go of this constant worry."

"What are you going to do?"

"I'm going to praise God." She closed her eyes briefly as the sweet rush of peace stole over her. "Every morning, I'm going to praise Him for another day. And I'm going to trust Him. If I have another stroke, I know He'll take care of me. I'm done limiting my life."

She searched his eyes and saw nothing but admiration. Squeezing both his hands in hers, she held his gaze. "I love you, Dean. Your courage and generosity humble me. I know how tough it was for you to come back. All the worrying about your father. Then you took on his construction projects. None of that was easy. And I'll always be in your debt for driving me and the girls to the clinic. You're the best guy I've ever met, and I don't deserve you, but I love you. I promise you if you'll give me a chance, I'll do everything I can to make you happy."

He crushed her to him, and she sank into his embrace, grateful beyond measure he'd come into her life.

Then his hands lightly framed her cheeks, and he was kissing her. She kissed him back, pouring all her emotions into it. Sensing his conviction. This was a man who would never let her down, never walk way, never give up on her.

When they ended the kiss, she took a minute to regroup. "I never asked how you felt about the twins."

"You don't have to." He shook his head. "I love them. They wriggled into my heart from day one."

Just as she'd hoped. But there was one more issue to address, and it was important. "The doctors advised me not to have more children. It would be too dangerous."

"You already have two beautiful girls." His face broke into a smile. "I'd say that's a good-sized family."

"I would have liked more," she admitted, enjoying the way he was stroking her back.

"I never thought I'd get married, let alone have kids, so as far as I'm concerned, the twins are the icing on the cake."

"Are we talking about marriage?" she asked, surprised she'd already accepted the thought.

"If not now, we will be soon, I hope."

She didn't have a chance to respond. He'd claimed her lips with his again. And nothing else mattered.

CHAPTER FIFTEEN

"HEY, MARC, CAN we talk for a minute?" Dean pulled Marc from the crowd after the Christmas Eve service that night. Brooke held Megan on her hip, and Anne held Alice. The girls were wearing frilly dresses, white tights, shiny black shoes and ribbons in their hair. To say they were cute would be an understatement. A group of people stood in a circle talking to Dean's dad, and every now and then, Ed's hearty laugh filled the air.

"Sure, what's up?"

They retreated to the coat rack, where a few stragglers were zipping up before heading to the door.

"I hate to have this conversation here, but I wanted a word before we head over to Brooke's," Dean said.

"What's going on?" His expression shifted from merry, like the holiday signaled, to worried in a split second.

"I'm in love with your sister." He probably shouldn't have blurted it out like that, but he'd been holding it in for hours. This was a conversation he needed to have in person with his best friend, the man who'd been there for him since he was a child.

Marc blinked a few times, and Dean held his breath, unsure if he would be upset or okay with the situation. Then a grin slowly stretched across his face, and Dean relaxed.

"That's great!" Marc pulled him in for a bear hug. Then he stepped back, nodding with twinkling eyes. "Does she know?"

"Yeah, we had a long talk this afternoon."

"And she's on board with...what exactly is happening between you two?"

"She's on board. We're dating. More than that, really. I love her, and she loves me, and I plan on proposing in the near future."

He let out a low whistle. "You aren't messing around, are you? Do you think you might be rushing it? Brooke has been pretty clear that she doesn't want to get remarried. I'd hate for you to get your hopes up."

"The past few days have changed her mind. And if she needs to go slow, I'll wait as long as it takes. I love her, and I'm not letting her go."

"Good. She's worth the wait." He adjusted his necktie, looking like he wanted to yank it off and toss it in the trash. "Does this mean you're staying in Jewel River?"

"Yeah. Dad and I worked out a plan. I'm officially becoming a partner after the new year."

"Yes!" Marc pumped his fist in the air. "Where are you going to live?"

"I'd like to keep renting Reagan's house if she's okay with it."

"She'll be thrilled. She doesn't like seeing it empty." He shook his head in wonder. "I feel like I just won a million bucks. You're moving back. Dating my sister. Merry Christmas to me."

Dean chuckled. "I'm the one who's the winner. Thank you, man. Thanks for all the ways you were there for me through the years."

The Christmas Eve service had touched him—the fact God would send His Son to save a sinner like him made his heart burst with gratitude. His empty, closed-off life had become full. Full of light, energy, opportunities and love. He didn't deserve it, but he sure was grateful for it.

"Are you ready?" Brooke came over. "The twins are getting restless."

"Let's go." Dean took Megan from her, and she snuggled her cheek onto his shoulder.

Fifteen minutes later, Dean and his father, Anne, Marc, Reagan and the twins sat in Brooke's living room. Anne carried a tray with cookies and bars around to everyone, and Dean helped himself to several.

"I made these special for you, Ed." Anne pointed to some square treats in the corner of the tray. "Pumpkin bars. They're low in sugar."

"Thank you. Those muffins you sent with Dean were some of the best I've ever had. I didn't know healthy could taste so good."

They laughed. Then the twins started yawning. Brook stood. "I'd better get these two in their pajamas. I'll be right back. Come on, girls, let's get your comfy pj's on."

They raced ahead of her to the hallway.

"I'll help." Dean placed his hand against the small of her back as they continued to the girls' bedroom.

She looked at him and smiled. "I can do it by myself, you know."

"I know." He slid his hand around her waist. "But then I'd miss you."

"Miss me?" She laughed. "With everyone back in the living room?"

"I only want to be with you."

She paused in the girls' doorway and turned to him. "I feel the same way."

He tugged her closer and gave her a kiss. Little giggles made them separate. Brooke glanced at Megan and Alice, who were on the floor yanking off their tights.

"Welcome to my world." She shook her head with a smile.

"Your world is the only place I want to be."

"Then come on in." She waved him into the room.

"You don't have to ask me twice."

"Praise God."

Praise Him, indeed.

EPILOGUE

"HE'S GOING TO make a good daddy."

Brooke followed Christy Moulten's gaze to where Dean stood talking to Marc, Cade and Dalton in the community center. The blustery February evening hadn't deterred the Jewel River Legacy Club members from gathering. Her mom was watching the twins so Brooke and Dean could make their announcement.

"He certainly is." Brooke gave Christy a smile.

"I wish Ty would find someone. Every month I remind him of the meeting time. And every month he avoids it. Not that he's going to find a girlfriend at the Legacy Club, but he should be getting out more." Christy made a clucking sound with her tongue. "At least Cade found his forever love. With Cade and Mackenzie married, maybe they'll think about having babies."

"I hope so." Brooke had enjoyed their wedding last month, probably because Dean had been her date.

Erica Cambridge stood at the podium and waited until she had everyone's attention. Dean slid into the seat next to Brooke's, and he slung his arm around her shoulders. He was always nearby, which was just one of the many things she loved about him. She could count on him.

His father sat on his other side. Ed was thriving now that he was back home. He'd bought a treadmill, converted the basement into a man cave and thrown himself back into McCaffrey Construction with gusto.

"Sorry to bring you out on a cold night like this, but it's Wyoming, right?" Erica opened her hands as if to say, *What can you do?* "Clem, would you mind getting the meeting started?"

He stood and led them in the Pledge of Allegiance and the Lord's Prayer. After everyone had settled in their seats, Erica went over meeting minutes and old business.

"Erica?" Angela Zane raised her hand.

"Yes, Angela?"

"What are we going to do about the meat market closing?"

"I talked to Bob at the supermarket, and he assured me they'll continue to stock local beef and pork."

"What about the building, though? I had this idea—"

Clem raised his palm. "Don't say it."

Angela shot him a glare. "As I was saying, I had an idea. For a meat locker."

"A meat locker?" Erica looked confused.

"Yes. It's like a storage unit for your meat. For anyone who doesn't have enough freezer space."

"Everyone has enough freezer space." Clem narrowed his eyes.

"Actually, that isn't true." Ed joined the conversation. "You'd be surprised at how many people don't have enough room to store their frozen meat. A quarter cow takes up a lot of space."

Angela's chin rose, and she sent Clem a smug look. "Joey and I discussed it at length during last month's storm, and he took the liberty of making a promo video."

"Not another video." Clem shook his head. "Does your grandson ever study?"

"He's on the honor roll." She took out her phone. "Let me send you the video, Erica."

While Erica and Dalton got the screen and equipment ready, Dean leaned over to Brooke. "What's going on?"

"I'm not sure. But if Joey's involved, it means there will be some explosive special effects."

Christy turned her head and gave them a thumbs-up. "I was hoping Joey would have something for us tonight. Livens things up."

The lights went out, and the screen glowed with an outside view of the meat market. A man's low voice narrated. "No meat market? No problem. Jewel River has a whole new way to store your meat." Lightning bolts crisscrossed the screen while the sound of thunder boomed. "Ice lockers. Big. Small. For a bag of wings or a full deer. You decide."

Dynamite blasts erupted, and an animated Coming Soon banner unfurled across the screen.

Erica turned on the lights. "Marc, you're on the town planning committee. What do you think?"

Marc launched in on the permits involved. Brooke yawned. It had been a long day, and she really wanted to make their announcement and head back to her place to snuggle up on the couch with Dean and watch a TV show.

When the meeting was about to wrap up, Erica asked if there were any announcements. Dean rose and helped Brooke stand.

"We have an announcement." Dean looked around the room. "Brooke and I are engaged. I asked her to marry me over the weekend, and she accepted."

Congratulations filled the air. When the chatter died down, Ed stood, too.

"I'm thankful to finally have a daughter." Ed's eyes were moist as he beamed at Brooke. "And granddaughters. I'm a blessed man. Also, the paperwork has been finalized. Dean and I are officially partners at McCaffrey Construction."

Everyone stood to congratulate them, and when the meeting ended, Brooke took Dean's hand as they made their way out the door.

Her leg had been weak all day, but she wasn't letting it

worry her. She'd taken it easy and was more than happy to lean on Dean's strong arm at times like this.

"Are you okay?" He looked into her eyes, tightening his grip on her hand.

"Yes. Thank you."

Out in the cold wind, he put his hands around her waist and swept her off her feet in a twirl. "I love you, Brooke."

She laughed, her hands resting on his shoulders, and kissed him. "I love you, too."

"I can't wait for you to be mine."

"News flash, Dean. I'm already yours."

His grin said it all. He kissed her again.

"And I'm yours. Praise God, I'm all yours."

* * * * *

Christmas On The Ranch

Jennifer Slattery

MILLS & BOON

Jennifer Slattery is a writer and speaker who has addressed women's and church groups across the nation. As the founder of Wholly Loved Ministries, she and her team help women rest in their true worth and live with maximum impact. When not writing, Jennifer loves spending time with her adult daughter and hilarious husband. Visit her online at jenniferslatterylivesoutloud.com to learn more or to book her for your next women's event.

Books by Jennifer Slattery

Restoring Her Faith
Hometown Healing
Building a Family
Chasing Her Dream
Her Small-Town Refuge

Sage Creek

Falling for the Family Next Door
Recapturing Her Heart
Christmas on the Ranch

Visit the Author Profile page at
millsandboon.com.au.

For we that are in this tabernacle do groan, being burdened: not for that we would be unclothed, but clothed upon, that mortality might be swallowed up of life.

—*2 Corinthians* 5:4

Dedicated to my sister and friend, Jesseca Randall,
who showed up for me during some of
my hardest moments.

CHAPTER ONE

FOLLOWING HER PHONE'S GPS down a long, two-lane highway, Evie Bell slowed as she neared the wooden archway of Bowman's Rough Stock Ranch.

New Day Caregivers hadn't been joking when they'd referred to her assignment location as "off-the-beaten path." She'd expected country lodging but assumed she'd at least be near a shopping mall or steakhouse. Her brief drive down Main Street had dashed all hopes of weekend entertainment. Sage Creek, Texas, boasted little more than an old-fashioned diner, a coffeehouse/bookstore, a library and a handful of boutiques.

Decorated for Christmas, the town itself was beautiful. But she still had to wonder, what did the locals do for fun? Horse riding and hunting?

She'd hired on as a traveling in-home caregiver, hoping to blend her love for people with her passion for adventure.

She'd anticipated diverse backgrounds and cultures and exploration of new locations during her off hours. She had *not* expected to land in horse country, as Sage Creek's welcome sign had so proudly proclaimed. Until now, she'd turned down rural assignments. But this one came with a significant financial bonus.

She feared this assignment would be her loneliest yet.

At least she'd only be here three weeks, during which time she hoped to earn enough favor with her boss to secure the next big-city assignment. Then she'd enroll in nursing school, which would widen her options and increase her salary.

Maybe she could even work at a local hospital. *"And meet a handsome and available doctor?"* She laughed as her mom's teasing words replayed through her mind. But the statement did carry some truth. The closer she came to thirty, the louder her biological clock ticked. She was ready to find a life partner, to build a family.

Dust kicked up behind her as she drove toward the sound of bellowing cattle. As she passed pastures bisected by a fence and stables, two large barking dogs raced after her. She sucked in a breath, her gaze shooting from them to the handful of cowboys talking outside an arena. She assumed one of them was Monte Bowman, the ranch owner and the man responsible for her being here.

She sensed this was going to be far from a spa experience. What had she gotten herself into?

She mentally reviewed the details from her client's file. Monte was a single father in his late twenties, raising twin five-year-old girls. His great-aunt, age seventy-five, had stage 3C ovarian cancer.

The aunt and kids, Evie could handle. But if the guy was expecting her to do any type of ranching, he was in for a disappointment. New Day Caregivers wasn't paying her enough for that.

She followed the curve of the road past more grassland bordered by mature trees to a blue single-story with a timber-frame portico. The covered porch bore simple fir garlands woven through the railings and accented every couple feet with red bows. Two vibrant poinsettias burst from pots wrapped in gold paper and were positioned on either side of the front door.

She wasn't surprised by their lack of lights. Monte had probably struggled to manage his family, let alone worry about decorations. Although she did find it odd that Tracy, their former caregiver, hadn't made the place more festive.

Maybe that would be a way she could connect with the Bowman children. She could make hot cocoa, turn on holiday music and invite them to adorn their Christmas tree with ornaments and tinsel.

She parked behind a maroon four-door with a large smiley-face sticker in its back window. A red pickup sat in the shade of a large gray shed a few feet away. The dogs, one with long black fur and pointed ears, the other splotched with three shades of brown, yapped near her door, as if daring her to step outside. Hopefully, someone would hear them and come out of the house to escort her in.

Until then, she'd stay put.

She shot Mr. Bowman and his great-aunt a text to let them know she'd arrived—in case they hadn't gathered as much from all the ruckus—and pulled her makeup bag from her purse.

When she was young, her dad used to make a game of counting the freckles on her face. "Sun kisses", he called them. Said she got her auburn hair and porcelain skin from her mom, her silver-blue eyes from him, and her quiet nature from the good Lord above.

A tap on her side window startled her, and she turned to see a broad-chested man with light brown eyes rimmed in green peering at her from beneath a gray cowboy hat, espresso-colored hair curling up under the brim.

With his strong jaw, thick brows and slight smile, he looked like he belonged on the cover of a clothing catalog.

Donning a professional smile despite an unexpected flutter through her midsection, she lowered her window. "Hello. I'm Evie Bell." She handed him her business card.

"Figured as much." He tipped his hat at her. "I'm Monte Bowman. Martha, your patient, is my great-aunt."

"Nice to meet you." They'd spoken briefly by phone a few days ago.

He opened her door for her. "Welcome to what most folks around here refer to as horse country."

Her gaze shot past him to the dogs, seated on either side of him, ears alert, eyes trained on her.

"Don't let these loudmouths fool you none." He flicked a hand toward the larger of the two. "They're a pair of biteless beasts." He chuckled. "The black one's named Max. He's as big of a baby as they come. This other guy's Finn, and he likes to think he runs the place and single-handedly keeps our fif-teen-hundred-pound bulls in check."

She glanced at the animals grazing in the nearest field. "Wow. They're massive."

"About half a truck."

She eyed the fence. It didn't look as robust as she'd like, con-sidering all the muscle contained inside. "They ever get out?"

He gave a slight shrug. "Once in a while, if a corner post gets knocked down."

Not the most encouraging response he could've given. She was quickly regretting accepting this assignment.

"Come on in." He motioned her forward. "Let me introduce you to my aunt and girls."

She grabbed her purse from the floorboard. "That sounds great."

He climbed the steps and paused on the stoop. "Excuse the mess. If my aunt was feeling better, there wouldn't be a dish out of place. But you know how it is."

"I understand completely, and I hope I can alleviate some of your stress." People tended to crave order more when their lives felt chaotic. Experience had taught her that. Tidying up their living spaces was one of the easiest ways she could in-crease their peace.

Opening the front door, he indicated for her to precede

him. He smelled like an enticing mixture of leather, cedar and citrus.

Once inside, he took her coat and hung it up for her. "Weatherman's predicting high sixties next week. I'd say that's one of the blessings of hill country winters. My girls would disagree. They're always hankering for a white Christmas."

"I'm with them. Snow always makes things seem more festive. But then again, I don't spend nearly as much time in the elements as you do." She hoped he wouldn't expect her to take on outside chores.

He moved a pile of children's clothes and a well-loved blanket to clear space on the brown leather couch. "Have a seat."

Coloring pages, pencils, crayons and partially eaten bags of crackers cluttered the coffee table. A mound of shoes gathered near the door, and dust danced in the sunbeams slanting through the window. A fake-looking tree stood in the corner. The sporadic and low placement of ornaments indicated the children had helped.

Although the home was slightly disheveled, it was cleaner than she'd expected, all things considered.

Monte looked from the empty kitchen that extended from the den to a back hall. "I'll go see where the ladyfolk are."

Nodding, she set her purse at her feet and sat with her back straight, ankles crossed, fingers intertwined over her knees. These initial encounters always felt like job interviews, this one even more so, considering the termination of their previous caretaker.

He returned. "My aunt's catching a nap. Lucy Carr, a family friend from church, must've taken the girls to their tree house. Can I get you something to drink? Cup of coffee, sweet tea or iced lemonade?"

"Whatever's easiest, thank you."

He nodded and retreated into the kitchen. The sound of a cupboard door then fridge opening and closing followed. "Supper's in a couple hours."

"Can I help with that?"

"I'll just pull out some leftovers. The local quilting club brought us enough food to about feed half of Sage Creek."

"That's thoughtful."

He returned with two tall, steaming mugs and handed her one. "You okay with hot chocolate?"

She inhaled the rich, soothing scent. "That sounds lovely."

He sat kitty-corner to her. "Figured you might want something to help fight off the chill. As to our church family, not sure what we would've done without them." His expression tightened. "You heard what happened with Ms. Tracy Gray, the gal you're replacing?"

"I know she was let go."

"I came home from a rodeo to find her gone, my aunt sleeping, and the girls running amuck."

"That must've felt like a betrayal."

"She said that was just the once." He scoffed. "I'm just glad my Callie—she's the risk-taker of the two—didn't get caught between a fence railing and a fifteen-hundred-pound bull."

Evie could tell he didn't trust her. Why should he, considering what had happened with the last caregiver? He'd had plenty cause to sever his contract. The fact that he hadn't showed how much he needed help.

He studied her for a moment. "I 'spect your outfit gave you the rundown on my great-aunt. She'll turn seventy-six this February, and this is her second bout with cancer. They say that makes it harder to fight, but if anyone can beat this monster, she can. She's one tough lady. Proud, too, which means she might not ask for help when she needs it or speak up when she's in pain."

"I'll keep that in mind."

"Bonus points if you can make her laugh. She especially loves it when the girls put on shows for her."

That had to be hilarious and adorable. "Does she have children?"

He shook his head. "Never married. Always said she got her

kid-fix working for the school system. Taught sixth grade for nearly four decades. When my ex-wife, now deceased, left us three and a half years ago, she moved in to help me raise them."

Left as in died? Except the way he frowned when he spoke suggested she'd taken off before her death.

"I can't imagine how challenging that must have been, running this ranch as a single dad." Then to have his great-aunt get sick? Poor guy probably felt like life had kneed him in the chest then hurled him in white water rapids without a vest.

Considering his good looks, she was surprised some pretty woman hadn't pranced into his world already. Did the fact that he was single mean he had commitment issues?

That wasn't any of her business.

"Aunt Martha was a godsend." He rubbed the back of his neck. "As you can imagine, she means the world to my girls. And they do a great job of keeping her entertained." He chuckled.

"I look forward to meeting them." She took a sip of her drink, her gaze drifting to a series of photos displayed on the far wall. In one of them, he stood beside two brunette toddlers sitting on a spotted horse. "They're twins, right?"

"Yep. Turned five this past September. Two days shy of the kindergarten cutoff."

"Are they in preschool?"

"Start next week. I was late getting the girls signed up. When I finally did, they put us on a waiting list. They're good kids, but they're a handful. 'Specially Callie. That girl's always climbing up something, and she's got two gears—full speed ahead, or stop. Whether she's running her legs or her mouth." Fatherly humor lit his eyes.

She laughed. "Sounds like she'll keep me on my toes."

"That's a fact." He lined three crayons lying on the table side by side. "You have much experience with children?"

His pointed expression revealed his concern. "Some." Only not as a caregiver. She'd primarily worked with dementia clients, although telling him that wouldn't increase his confidence in her.

Good thing all parties had signed the personal care agreement, because if this had been a job interview, she felt certain the man would escort her out.

While she didn't fault him his apprehension, she needed to demonstrate her competency before his last threads of trust in the company shred completely.

She'd already spent her recent bonus—the incentive for taking this job—on car repairs.

"FIGURE WE'VE SPENT enough time chitchatting." Taking their mugs, Monte stood. "Up for a brief tour of the property? Thought you may want to stretch your legs some. Course, if you'd rather take a moment to unwind…"

"A walk sounds lovely, thank you." She grabbed her purse, a shiny purple bag decorated with iridescent beads that matched her shoes, and stood.

He retrieved her jacket, which carried a slight floral scent, from the closet and handed it over.

Her wavy hair, streaked with hints of blonde, reached just below her chin and flecks of silver shimmered in her blue eyes like an early morning frost. Standing, the top of her head reaching his shoulders, she looked fit but not all that strong. Her clothing was better suited for the city than a ranch. At least she wasn't wearing heels.

He hadn't expected her to be so beautiful. Not that it mattered. He was much too busy raising world champion bulls, God willing, to fall for a gal that'd be gone quicker than a drought could turn pasture to dust.

Besides, he'd fallen for a city girl once, and was left with a heartache that took two years to bounce back from. And his girls were left with a gaping mama-hole.

Was Evie's attire evidence of her trying to leave a good first impression, or was she that ignorant about ranch life?

He'd find out soon enough.

She waited in the entryway while he wrote a note telling Lucy and Aunt Martha whom the car out front belonged to and where he was taking Evie. He figured they'd assume the part about the vehicle but might wonder where they'd taken off to. After depositing their mugs in the dishwasher, he poked his head in the fridge to note supper options.

Lucy probably would pop the casserole she'd brought over into the oven before she left, and they still had plenty of pickled beets and fresh tomatoes from lunch.

He loved knowing his girls would grow up in such a loving community, with fresh air, land to explore, and the satisfaction that came from working with their hands. That made all the struggles and setbacks he'd experienced raising bucking bulls worth it.

So long as he earned enough to pay the bills—a constant concern for any cattleman, those raising animal athletes especially.

That reality had caused his ex-wife deep frustration.

This ranch hadn't been enough for her. *He* hadn't been enough for her. So, when a wealthy horse breeder from Dallas started paying her attention, she'd bailed on Monte and her daughters. She was killed in a car accident a year later. He probably shouldn't have grieved her like he had, considering how she'd betrayed him.

Unfortunately, his heart had taken a while to catch up with his head.

Shaking off the thought, he turned and strode back through the living room to where Evie waited.

He opened then held the door. "After you."

She smiled then stepped onto the porch and down the stairs. Max, his ten-year-old Lab-mix, trotted ahead of them, tail wagging, while Finn, his younger buddy, chased after a squirrel scampering up a nearby fence post.

Evie fell into step beside him on the gravel road that led to the barn and stables, alerting him to her soft lavender scent.

She gazed toward the east pasture where about half his herd grazed. "How much land do you own?"

"Two hundred fifty acres."

She raised her eyebrows. "That's a lot."

He shrugged. "Might sound like it, but the average cattle ranch in Texas is near double that."

"Wow."

"Big animals need a lot of forage." He picked up a stick, waved it at Max, then tossed it a good twenty yards ahead. "I have seventy-five head of cattle. Thirty bucking-bred, twenty-five yearlings, three champion sires, twelve PBR" –she probably didn't know what that meant. "Professional Bull Riders, Inc. competitors, and the rest heading that way. Then there's half a dozen chickens, five horses, a donkey and two pigs."

"Your ranch's name, Rough Stock, is there a story behind it?"

He cast her a sideways glance. "You asking how I got started in this business?"

"That, and why you call it that."

He frowned. "Rough Stock?"

She nodded.

She was even greener than her city-gal getup implied. "That's what they call bucking broncs and bulls—like those cowboys ride in rodeos."

"Is that where you sell them, then?"

"Some. For others, I form partnerships with investors. They buy in for a thousand, I raise and train the bulls until they're old enough to compete. Then, based on how they do, we decide whether to keep them or auction them off."

"They get paid on their performance?"

He nodded. "My investors and I split the winnings. Not every bull's a champion, obviously. But if you get yourself a superstar, they can bring in hundreds of thousands of dollars."

"I had no idea. Or that they could be trained for that matter. Ever have a dud?"

"For sure. Sometimes, you'll get one that refuses to buck or won't calm down in the bucking chute. Got to auction them off, at a loss. It takes a lot of money to raise competition bulls. Ever spent time on a ranch, Evie?"

She shook her head.

Max trotted back and dropped his stick at Monte's feet.

He threw it again, farther this time. "This can be a dangerous place for greenhorns."

Running a hand up and down the back of her arm, she looked away.

A few months ago, he was convinced New Day Caregivers was the best outfit to care for his aunt. They'd asked him pages of questions, related to everything from medical needs to family preferences. They promised to pair the Bowmans with the best possible match, and in many ways they had—with Ms. Gray.

Until she turned irresponsible.

Seemed, when it came to Evie, the decision-makers had sent the next available body. Then again, he doubted they'd had much choice. Ms. Gray's negligence had left everyone scrambling. Regardless, he didn't have many options. As much as he loved Sage Creek, he doubted the town was high on caregivers' must-visit list.

And that was why Evie was here, filling in until her company sent a longer-term replacement.

Lord, we need You. Give Aunt Martha strength to fight this, keep the girls safe, and help me be the father they need without neglecting the ranch.

Because if his bulls didn't perform well, he stood to lose a lot more than his dream of raising PBR champions. Keeping this place in the black and paying for the level of care Aunt Martha and the girls deserved didn't come cheap.

He should be grateful Evie had come on such short notice,

so close to Christmas, and to an environment that clearly made her uncomfortable. Poor woman's face had paled a full degree when he answered her question about the bulls ever getting past the fence.

Under other circumstances, her vulnerability probably would've triggered his protective side. To an extent, it did. And her delicate beauty stirred a reaction he might otherwise welcome. If she wouldn't be gone before his neighbor started planting his spinach seeds.

Regardless, he'd hired her for one purpose—to care for his family. He didn't have the luxury of thinking about anything else.

He showed her his pastures first. "Most of the year, we rotate our cattle, so they don't overgraze." Although you wouldn't know that from looking at them. The dry fall had hit everyone hard, hay and grain producers included. That led to higher-than-normal prices, which made him think seriously about which bulls he could keep and which ones he'd need to cull.

Droughts always forced ranchers to make hard decisions. At least he was able to supplement their diet with burnt cacti. He'd learned about the plant's high protein content years ago while ranch handing.

Max started to trot back toward him then got distracted by a flock of wild turkeys and took off after them.

"We wean our calves at eight to ten months of age," Monte said. "Then we put them on our pro-performance feed." With how dry it'd been, that cost a pretty penny as well. When he needed to turn a profit more than ever. "About three months later, we start training them—getting them used to being handled, the bucking chute and whatnot."

"Do you keep all your bulls together?"

"Yep."

"They don't fight?"

"Sometimes, least till they establish their pecking order.

After that, so long as they've grown up together, they get along well enough."

They passed the tree house he'd built for his girls the summer before. Behind this snaked a creek that swelled in the spring and shrank come August. It cut through the back corner of his land, through the trees, and wound behind the windmill that pumped water from the ground to irrigate his pastures and keep his cattle hydrated. When the well didn't run dry.

"Stables are over there." He pointed to a large red building lined with glassless windows adjacent to the arena. Three of his horses, along with their Shetland and donkey, grazed nearby.

"They're beautiful."

He suppressed a chuckle, amused by the obvious delight in her eyes. "Want to feed them a treat?"

"Absolutely." She must've intended to hide her enthusiasm, because she straightened, and her almost childlike smile turned formal. "Thank you."

With a slight nod, he led the way to the tack room where he kept grooming tools, feed, saddles and other gear. He pulled some keys from his pocket and unbolted the door guarding a large tub of grain, a container filled with peppermints, and an old and partially dehydrated bag of carrots. "Got to keep this area locked up so my girls can't get to it and give the horses a belly ache."

Whinnies and nickers drifted toward them as he deposited a scoopful of grain into a bucket. "My Callie's quicker than lightning. One minute, she's helping me muck the stalls. The next, she's double-fisting candy."

"For herself or the horses?"

"Both."

She followed him to the railing where two of his mares stood, ready and waiting, ears forward, big brown eyes trained on them. "They know what's coming, huh?"

"They hope, isn't that right, Applesauce." He scratched the

paint's neck then turned to Evie. "Want to become her new best friend?"

"Sure."

He poured grain into her outstretched hands.

Lady Mule gave a loud hee-haw, startling Evie. "Oh, my. Someone's hungry."

"Always got to get her nose in the action. She's our self-appointed pasture protector. Isn't that right, girl?" He tickled her upper lip.

"Really?"

He nodded. "Donkeys are fighters. Highly territorial, too. They can take on a coyote any day. They also help drive away disease-carrying possums."

"Now that fable about the mule, the monkey and the mountain lion makes much more sense."

"Haven't heard that one."

She relayed the story, initially told to her during the "worst camping experience ever."

"It wouldn't have been so bad if I hadn't attracted every mosquito in Washington State," she said. "Or our parents hadn't made us clean our own fish." She wrinkled her nose. "Suffice to say, sleeping on the ground is not my idea of a relaxing vacation." Her gaze swept across the horizon before landing on his recreational trailer parked near the tree line. "I take it you're a big outdoorsman?"

"The girls' mom and I used to call that old, rusted hunk of metal home. We bought it from an older couple who must not have used it or aired it out in decades. We burned at least a hundred scented candles that first year."

She used to joke that his bulls had better accommodations than they did. He'd told her they were their route to a real home and promised to build her one as soon as their animal athletes began earning more than they ate.

He'd made good on that promise a year later and thought for sure they were steadily heading toward the life they wanted.

Clearly, she'd never shared that dream. Not that he could blame her. Ranch life required a special kind of woman, one with grit, who wasn't worried about breaking a nail or getting mud on her blue jeans.

He cast Evie a sideways glance. Did the woman even own a pair of jeans? Or boots, for that matter?

CHAPTER TWO

WHEN THEY RETURNED to the house, they were met by Monte's girls, who simultaneously looked identical and vastly different. The one lingering in the open doorway wore a yellow-and-white striped dress with blue flowers, glittery shoes that appeared as sturdy as they were delicate. Her brown hair was secured into two long braids.

The other, and likely the child who double-fisted peppermints, barreled down the stairs like an excited puppy. "I'm Callie." Her wide grin extended to her chestnut eyes, her hair looking like it could use a good brushing and her jeans and T-shirt, gray with a tractor printed in red, in need of a wash. "You our nanny?"

Evie's widened eyes pinged to Monte.

He picked the girl up, swung her in the air, then deposited her, giggling, on her feet. "This is Ms. Bell, and she's here to care for Aunt Martha."

"But not when she's in bed?" The child turned to Evie. By now, her sister had joined her. "Then you'll play with us? And take us to the creek to look for frogs and lizards and go exploring in the forest."

"The forest?"

Monte laughed. "That's what they call that thin stretch of trees bordering our land. Near the camper and gazebo."

"Right." She lowered to the twin's eye level. "I'm sure we'll have plenty of time for adventures." So long as they didn't involve bulls.

As a nontraditional caretaker working for a private company, she found that her job often included tasks related to "daily living." Usually that meant cooking and light housework. While she had nothing against children, she'd heard enough stories from some of her coworkers to leave her apprehensive. Overly concerned family members had nothing on helicopter parents. Thank goodness Monte didn't seem to hold unrealistic expectations—as of yet.

"Luna and I made a fort." Callie flung a hand toward her sister, then leaned closer with a hand cupped around her mouth. "It's private. Girls only. Want me to show you?" She spoke so fast her words blended together.

"Later." Monte's voice was kind but firm. "Let's give Ms. Bell a chance to get settled." He strolled to the rear of Evie's car, as if expecting her to pop her trunk. "I'll grab your things while the girls show you to your room."

"I can get that, but thank you."

Before she could say more, or move his direction, the wild-haired child was tugging her up the porch stairs talking about the "care basket" she and her sister had made. Seemed rude leaving Monte with her luggage—of which, admittedly, she'd brought more than necessary. Yet, dampening the girl's enthusiasm for whatever "surprise" she and her sister had waiting inside didn't feel much better.

Monte's further insistence persuaded her to honor the child's obvious joy. The slight nod of approval he offered as she allowed Callie to pull her up the stairs assured her she'd made the right choice.

Inside was quiet, and the living room cluttered with more

toys than when she'd initially met with Monte. A handful of blankets lined the carpet in the hallway.

"This is me and Luna's room." Callie stopped in an opened doorway to their left and motioned to a space with equal parts dolls, pink frills and plastic animals, tools and trucks. Upon one bed lay a rainbow comforter, the other decorated with horseshoes, stars and spurred boots.

Evie glanced behind her to offer a smile to the other child, clearly much shyer, who lingered nearby. But her breath caught when her gaze landed on Monte, who was standing behind her. He was lugging an overstuffed suitcase in each hand, his biceps straining against his shirt's short sleeves.

"Should've figured my Callie-girl would make a pit stop or two." He rustled Luna's hair, then poked his head into the room. "Ms. Bell and I are scooting on. May want to skedaddle ahead of us, if you're wanting to be there when she sees her welcome gift."

"Oh, yeah!" Chattering with even more animation than before, Callie dashed past them.

Monte grabbed her by the shoulder before she ran off. Holding a finger to his mouth, he glanced toward a slightly cracked door down a ways on the left. "Sh. Aunt Martha may be sleeping."

Callie slumped with a groan as if he'd just told her she couldn't have chocolate for the rest of the month. "But she's always doing that. And she said it's no big deal and that kids will be kids and not to make such a fuss."

Monte frowned.

The child sighed nearly as loudly as she'd groaned. "Yes, sir."

Evie would've laughed—if the entire interchange, and every other moment prior, since she'd arrived on this ranch, wasn't promising a rather exhausting next three weeks. The child had already proven that her legs moved about as quickly as her mouth. On land spanning 250 acres, that could lead to a lot of steps.

If Callie could sneak handfuls of peppermints while working alongside her dad in the stables, how long would it take her to wander out among the bulls while Evie tended to her great-aunt?

If this assignment proved more challenging than Evie could manage, would she lose her job?

They rounded the corner to find Callie hopping onto and off the bottom step of wooden, retractable railless stairs that led, she presumed, to the attic. She glanced around, then to Monte, who'd stopped beside his daughter, then to the rectangular opening above her.

"Out of the way, munchkin." Monte set one of the suitcases down and moved the child aside.

Evie shivered as thoughts of cobwebs and spiders lurking in corners and creeping across the floor came to mind. *Please tell me that's not where I'll be staying.*

Her concern must've shown on her face, because Monte said, "Don't worry. You won't be holed up in some dark corner. I turned the attic into a comfortable guest room, with carpet, brightly painted walls, a nice reading nook and plenty of window space. Even installed a half bath."

She raised her eyebrows. "Really?"

He nodded. "Hope you won't mind using the one down here for showers."

"Not at all." She watched as he began lugging her belongings up the stairs, understanding why he'd insisted on carrying everything for her. And she was quite grateful.

She wasn't sure how many more "surprises" she could handle. Sent to a town that was probably occupied by fewer people than her old high school and hours from the nearest shopping mall, or movie theater for that matter. To stay on a ranch. That raised bulls that bucked. To help care for two adorable little girls, one of whom would exhaust a day care's entire, highly caffeinated staff.

And sleep in what Mr. Cowboy assured her was an upscaled attic, but an attic just the same.

She followed after him and the girls.

Pausing to preemptively hide whatever grimace might try to force through a professionally appropriate smile, she sucked in a breath and poked her head through the opening.

Her tense shoulders relaxed with her exhale. A genuine smile took form as she surveyed the cozy and aesthetically pleasing space. "Lovely."

Lace-trimmed curtains matched the painted walls, three of which were pink, the fourth, a rich burgundy. A bench seat topped with a long, floral cushion stretched beneath the far window, and various books filled corner shelves. A pink and lavender quilt with blue trim was spread across a queen-size bed. Decorative pillows added to its charm, and rather than the musty smell she'd feared, the room carried a slight scent of lemon and cedar.

Monte grinned and offered a hand. She took it, his skin, warm and rough against hers, sending a jolt of electricity through her. Heat rushed to her face as she tried to break contact as soon as possible.

"Are you hot?"

Evie turned to find Callie standing beside her, studying her. "What?"

"Your face is red, like mine gets when I run real fast for a long time."

That caused her cheeks to flush even more. Thankfully, Monte either thought nothing of the question or had missed it entirely, because he began talking about how he turned the space into a livable loft.

"I added those dormer windows to bump up the ceiling height and brighten the room." He pointed. "A contractor buddy helped me get the flooring up to code."

"Impressive."

She feigned interest as he continued talking about bridging joists, rerouting ventilation, and other renovation details she didn't understand. Then he shifted to why she came.

"I made a binder of about everything you need to know in regard to my aunt, the girls and the ranch." He grabbed it off her bedside table and handed it over. "We'd be much obliged if you'd help us with cooking and basic household chores. It's more than Aunt Martha can manage of late."

"Understandable."

"I could really use a hand getting the girls ready and off to preschool in the mornings. Aunt Martha will need you to drive her to her treatments in Houston once a week. Those are near all-day deals. Her platelet count was pretty low last time. Not sure she'll be up for her next dose of chemo."

"Okay."

"Doc'll be out Wednesday or Thursday to draw blood."

"Wow. That's quite a drive. I'm impressed."

"He's local—her regular physician. The treatment center's pretty good about letting her do whatever she can, here in Sage Creek."

"That's great." Evie flipped through the binder as he thoroughly explained his aunt's care plan and the family's typical routine.

"May want to snag some time before supper to rest from your drive."

"I appreciate that."

He turned to his daughters. "While you two clean the tornado you made below."

"What about the surprise?" Callie asked, Luna all bright-eyed by her side.

"Totally forgot." One hand resting on his belt buckle, he glanced about. "Where'd you two put it?"

Callie cupped a hand around her mouth and whispered, "Somewhere secret." She looked at Evie. "Close your eyes."

She complied, her smile expanding at the sound of little feet scurrying across the carpet. After this, she heard whispered bickering, a firm, "Girls," from Monte, and Callie's instructions to open her eyes on the count of three.

She did, laughing at their, "Surprise." The most delightful giggles followed as the twins gave over a basket filled with snowflakes cut from paper, hand-drawn pictures, slices of gum, a partially burned candle and a few other random items. They must have scoured the house in search of "treasures" to give her.

How precious.

"Do you like it?" Callie bounced on the balls of her feet.

"I absolutely love it." Her gaze shot to Monte, and her breath caught to find him watching her with an intensity that turned her insides to jelly.

That was yet another reason she was grateful she'd soon be away from this ranch—and this much too handsome cowboy.

The longer she stayed, the less likely she'd leave with her heart intact.

THE OVEN TIMER DINGED. Monte exchanged the steaming casserole with a sheet of prebaked biscuits. His mouth watered as he inhaled the cheesy-garlicky steam rising from the dish.

He glanced into the living room to find Luna picking up scattered pieces to a board game while her sister stacked a series of rectangular blocks end on end.

Standing in the archway, he crossed his arms. "Callie, that doesn't look like cleaning up to me."

She glanced up. "Oh. I forgot." Her wide-eyed look of surprise indicated she was telling the truth.

That girl could get distracted walking from the couch to the television.

He surveyed the remaining mess. Experience told him Luna had already tackled more than her fair share. With that assumption, he excused her to let Evie and Aunt Martha know supper was almost ready.

He turned to Callie. "Do what you can now. You can finish the rest after we eat."

"By myself?"

"Yep. That way you can catch up with what your sister already did."

Slumping with a sigh and frown, she began tossing her blocks into their tub, making her frustration known with every overdramatic clunk.

Suppressing a chuckle that otherwise would only irritate his daughter further, he shook his head and went to the pantry for a couple cans of green beans and emptied them into a bowl. He was removing them from the microwave when the twins entered with their aunt.

He greeted Aunt Martha with a kiss on the cheek. "How was your nap?"

"Much longer than I expected." Yet, she still looked tired, or discouraged.

Probably both. Considering the dark place he'd started to slip into upon hearing her cancer had returned, he could understand. But the more positive they stayed, the greater their strength and perseverance for the long battle ahead.

"The more rest the better, right?" He beat her to the table and pulled out her chair.

She quirked an eyebrow, humor dancing in her eyes. "What's good for the goose? Because it seems to me you've been burning the candle at both ends and in the middle besides."

He laughed. "Nah. A man can hardly call it work when he's doing what he loves." The last thing he wanted was for her to start worrying about him.

He noted her frown as she watched him place food on the table. Fearing she might feel guilty that she hadn't been the one to prepare it, he told her about Evie's arrival. This initiated an animated retelling of the twins' surprise from Callie.

"Sorry to keep you waiting."

He turned as Evie entered, captivated by her almost shy smile. She'd pulled her hair up in a messy bun, a few streaked, strawberry blond strands framing her face. Although she wore the same blouse and slacks she'd arrived in, without the blazer, her trim yet curvy form was more noticeable. And her apparent embarrassment at thinking she'd arrived late added a beautiful flush to her cheeks.

The same delicate blush he'd caught in the loft. One he wasn't any more comfortable with, nor how it affected him, now than he had been then.

He cleared his throat and raked a hand through his hatless hair. "Perfect timing." He introduced her to his aunt.

"Pleasure to meet you." Evie's smile widened as she approached his aunt initiating a handshake.

"Thank you for coming all this way," his aunt said. "How was your drive?"

"Easy-peasy. No road work or traffic between here and Dallas."

Monte raised his eyebrows. "Now, that's a surprise. Seems every time I'm on I-35, the DOT's doing something."

Callie frowned. "A dot?"

He laughed. "Department of Transportation."

"Oh." This led to a plethora of questions that shifted to one of Callie's obsessions—tractors and other heavy machinery. Somehow this morphed into a rather extensive listing of various nicknames she'd heard.

"Daddy calls me his little Cowpoke." She grinned. "Cuz I'm so tough, right, Daddy?"

"Stiffer than leather." He ruffled her hair.

"And Luna likes to smell books."

"Do not." Her sister crossed her arms with a pout.

"Do so." Callie swiped her hair away from her face with her forearm. "Just ask Ms. Lucy."

He narrowed his gaze on the child. "What Ms. Lucy says is that your sister is a bookworm. And you know good and well she speaks the words in love."

Callie huffed. "Reading is stupid and boring. That's why I don't want to go to school. Cuz they have to do boring stuff and sit behind a desk all day. You don't even get snacks when you want. Plus, Max will miss me."

Aunt Martha chuckled. "I'm sure he'll survive."

The child frowned. "Who will he play with?"

"He'll have Finn, dear." The woman's hand trembled slightly as she lifted her glass.

Callie shook her head. "He'll be too busy minding the bulls with Daddy. And you'll just stay in bed."

Aunt Martha flinched, and her gaze dropped to her largely untouched plate.

"Callie Rose Bowman." Monte's tone was firm.

"But it's true." Tears filled the girl's eyes, suggesting she'd merely intended to state facts as she saw them, not to be rude.

She still needed to learn to use a filter. His aunt felt bad enough about her inability to do more for the girls.

"I said enough." He looked around. "Shall we bless the food?" When everyone had bowed their heads, he led them in prayer, which, based on the thump-thump-thumping coming from Callie's direction, must've exceeded her patience level.

As usual.

"This kitchen is lovely." Evie's gaze swept the room, lingering on the hand-embroidered towel hanging from the stove handle. It was green with lace trim, and a reindeer stitched in silver thread.

"Mostly thanks to Aunt Martha's loving touch." Although, Erin, his ex-wife, had chosen the paint colors—white cabinets and cupboards set against celery green walls, his aunt had sewn the checkered and lace curtains.

On the wooden countertop left of the sink, a wicker basket she'd found at a garage sale held fruit. Next to this, a ceramic crock she'd painted during a ladies' church event held various cooking utensils. She'd purchased the tall glass canisters that were now filled with various foodstuff at the local pawn shop.

Aunt Martha took a sip of her drink. "Where are you from, Evie?"

"Holland, Michigan."

"Your folks still there?" He spooned green beans on his girls' plates with a look that communicated that he expected them to eat them.

She nodded. "Although at this precise moment, they're with my siblings—I've got three—hiking the Myakka Trail in Florida."

Aunt Martha looked up, lowering the fork that never quite made it to her mouth. "I imagine winters are quite lovely there. I'm sorry you couldn't join them."

Did she worry she'd cost the woman her vacation? Thankfully, Evie refuted that idea quickly enough.

"I could have." She spread butter onto her biscuit. "If I'd wanted to trade nice crisp sheets for a musty old sleeping bag."

Callie studied her with a tilt of her head. "What does that mean?"

Evie shifted in her seat and gave a nervous laugh. "Guess I'm just not the roughing-it type."

"I believe what she's saying is that she'd prefer to spend her nights in some posh hotel somewhere with Wi-Fi and air-conditioning," Monte said. Rather than on the land the good Lord gave them. "That the gist of it?"

She grinned. "Exactly."

"Yet here you are. On a ranch." He'd intended his tone to hold more of a teasing lilt. Her look of surprise indicated he'd failed. Yet, neither of them could deny this wasn't their first choice. He'd asked New Day Caregivers to send someone more accustomed to country living. And he suspected, Evie preferred much more concrete and the lifestyle that tended to accompany it.

They'd both have to make the best of a less than ideal situation for the next few weeks. He'd be happy so long as she cared for Aunt Martha and the girls. It didn't take an animal science degree to do that. Just a compassionate heart, an attentive eye and basic medical knowledge, all of which her field already required.

"Maybe God wants us to teach her how to have fun." Callie gave one quick nod. "Cuz hotels are even boringer than school."

He fought to contain his grin. "Is that a fact?"

"Uh-huh. Cuz you have to be quiet and not jump or run in the halls or up and down the stairs, unless all the old people are still awake."

Evie laughed. "You have a point." Her gaze shot to Monte, catching him watching her.

He quickly focused on his plate. "How long you been working as a traveling caregiver?"

"Almost three years now."

Aunt Martha moved her green beans around her plate. "I bet you've visited some interesting places."

"It's been a fun way to explore the United States."

"I can do twenty pushups," Callie said. "Want to see?" She sprang to her feet and threw herself on the floor before Evie could respond.

"That's enough." Monte softened his firm voice with kindness.

"Yes, sir." Her words came out on a loud exhale as she marched back to the table.

When she launched into a story about how she was the fastest kid in her Sunday school class, Monte nudged her plate toward her. "Eat your supper, now. And hold your words." While he didn't mind her enthusiasm one bit—rather enjoyed it, actually—he knew the child could wear other people's ears out.

"Our little Callie likes to talk." Aunt Martha unfolded her napkin and spread it across her lap. "Isn't that right, sweet pea."

She nodded, seeming not the least bothered by the reprimand. "Cuz I've got so much stuff bouncing around in my head." She patted her skull. "That can be hard to keep in sometimes. But Ms. Lucy said that's when I can use my strength. Said if I can barrel race and mutton bust with the best of them—I'm not the best yet, but Daddy says I will be, soon 'nuff. And Ms. Lucy says if I can rodeo as good as I do, then I can keep my thoughts in my head no matter how hard they're fighting to come out."

Evie laughed. "I see." She swallowed a mouthful of food. "What's a mutton bust?"

Luna's head snapped up.

Callie's brow furrowed. "You don't know for real, Ms. Evie? Or are you joshing us?"

"Can't say that I do."

A few hours ago, that might've surprised Monte. But after her questions regarding bulls and rough stock, he probably would've been stunned if she had known.

The child opened her mouth to say more, but Monte raised a hand, palm out. "How about you give your sister a chance to speak, darling."

Callie slumped with a huff, and soon her feet took to swinging again.

That child was sure to keep Evie on her toes—an unsettling thought considering her lack of experience with children and ranches. Hopefully, common sense would override any ignorance that could otherwise prove dangerous.

Monte offered his other daughter a warm smile. "Luna, want to answer Ms. Evie's question?"

"Yes, sir." She spoke a decibel above a whisper. "Mutton busting is where you try to stay on a sheep—"

"Bareback." Callie grinned.

Evie's eyebrows shot up. "That must be quite challenging."

Luna shrugged. "You only have to stay on for six seconds."

"'Cept Luna and I haven't done that. But I'm close, right, Daddy?"

"You both are." He wiped his mouth with his napkin. "Keep strengthening your grip swinging from tree branches, caterpillar." He scooped up a forkful of casserole, a string of cheese trailing from his plate.

"You should come watch us," Callie said.

Monte swallowed a bite of food. "Doubt she'll be here long enough for that."

"Does that make you sad?"

"What?" She looked from the child to Monte, to his aunt, then back to Monte. "Oh, yes, of course. That was so kind of you to invite me." She tore off a chunk of biscuit. "I've never been to a rodeo."

Monte's jaw went slack.

Then Callie gave a soft giggle that warmed his heart. "You're being silly. Ain't you?"

"Aren't," Monte corrected, although he was equally interested in the answer.

Callie sighed. "Are-en-t you?"

Evie shifted and occupied herself with her food. "Nope. I'm serious."

"Not even to see the bull riding or barrel racing or steer roping or nothing?"

She shook her head.

The girl stared at her as if she'd said she'd spent the prior years of her life locked up within her house or something. Monte would've laughed if not so flabbergasted himself. But he wasn't entirely surprised, considering all her questions while touring the property.

"Well, now." Aunt Martha quirked an eye at him. "Seems we've got to do something about that. Don't you agree?"

"Yes! Yes! Yes!" Callie bounced in her seat, and Luna brightened.

Monte's pulse kicked up a notch. He had a strong feeling he wouldn't like where his aunt was steering the conversation.

He knew she worried about his rather pathetic social life and longed to see him married—for his sake and the girls'. Was that why she wanted him to take Evie to the rodeo—to force them to spend more time together? Then again, she had to realize her caregiver wouldn't stick around long.

He was probably overthinking Aunt Martha's suggestion.

"Could be a good opportunity to take some of your new classics to the Christmas rodeo." Aunt Martha looked at Evie. "That's what they call four-year-old bulls." She resumed eye contact with Monte. "Get them used to a new arena and a crowd."

"Not sure a charity event's the best place to debut them."

His aunt gave a one-shoulder shrug. "May not meet any potential sponsors, but the girls would sure have a great time."

"I'm not comfortable leaving you home alone that long."

"I'll be fine." She flicked a hand. "Like Callie said, I'll probably do a lot of sleeping anyway. And there's always a ranch hand close by, if I need anything."

"Even so."

"I'll reach out to Lucy. She's been bugging me about watching old musicals with her, anyway. This would be a great way for you to build memories with the girls while giving Evie a taste of cowboy culture, holiday-style."

He scratched his jaw, looking from his girls, to Evie, to his aunt, to his girls, then back to his aunt. Aunt Martha was right about the twins. He'd been much too busy and distracted, of late. Regardless of the reason, his girls needed their dad.

He was all for a fun weekend with them both. He wasn't so sure how he felt about Evie tagging along. But his aunt would never let her stay, not when Evie was the reason for the idea.

Luna clasped folded hands beneath her chin. "Can we, Daddy? Please?"

Why was it so hard to tell that child no when she turned those big chestnut eyes his direction? Maybe because she rarely

asked for much. Unlike her sister, who had about ten requests
for every situation.

He sighed. "I'll see what I can do."

"And Ms. Evie, too?" Callie asked.

He looked at her, trying unsuccessfully to gauge her feelings on the matter. "If she'd like."

Callie sprang from her chair and hurried to Evie's side. "Do
you? It's real fun. They've got clowns and horses and cookie
decorating with lots of different colored frosting and sprinkles
and stuff. And Daddy always buys us corn dogs for supper."

Aunt Martha caught her eye. "Seems a good opportunity
for you and the girls to bond."

Way to guilt the woman into accepting. He'd been too frustrated with himself to realize he'd wanted to know her interest level.

"Sure." She forked a cheese-covered noodle. "That sounds
like fun."

"Yay!" Callie jumped up and down, fist pumping the air.

Monte urged the child back to her seat. "I'll make lodging
arrangements."

Why did the thought of spending a full weekend with Evie
leave him feeling so off-kilter? So what that she was the most
beautiful woman he'd encountered in some time, even more
so than his ex, if he were being honest. And just as averse to
his way of life.

CHAPTER THREE

THE NEXT MORNING, Evie descended the stairs to find cartoons playing on the television in the living room and Monte and the girls in the kitchen. The smell of fresh brewed coffee and hot chocolate made Evie crave a mocha. Maybe she could take the twins to that cute café/bookstore she'd seen on Main Street.

Would Monte want to join them? The thought sent an unwelcome flutter through her midsection, which she quickly shut down. She didn't need to start feeding her attraction to the man by entertaining absurd questions. Besides, she was here to help with the aunt and children so he could focus on his ranch.

She paused in the archway separating the living room and kitchen to watch him and the girls. The children's behavior and bedclothes differentiated them. Callie, dressed in a navy and superhero-print nightgown, spoke fast and hopped from one foot to the next. Luna sat quietly at the table coloring a snowman picture. She wore gradient pink and purple pj's decorated with sparkly stars.

Monte looked all cowboy in his jeans, boots and flannel shirt. He was humming "Jingle Bell Rock." His playfulness only added to his appeal.

He opened the fridge and moved some items around, Callie lingering at his side.

"Sorry, nugget." Facing her, he tapped her on the nose. "Guess y'all ate the last of the French toast sticks. I can nuke some of the breakfast burritos the church gals brought over."

Callie groaned. "Those are yucky."

"You liked them well enough Sunday."

"I changed my mind."

"Cereal it is."

"But we don't have any good kinds." Her tone carried a whine.

"Then you must not be that hungry."

"Yogurt?"

He opened the fridge again, grabbed a tub, popped the lid and sniffed. "Whew. That's rancid." He tossed it in the nearby trash can. "Guess we're out of that, too."

"Aw!" She fisted her hands at her sides. "We never have anything to eat."

Evie bit the inside of her lip to keep from laughing. Apparently, the child hadn't seen all the filled food containers in the fridge.

Monte's phone rang. He pulled it from his back pocket and glanced at the screen.

She stepped into the room. "I can make French toast sticks."

He turned toward her with what looked like a smile tinged with gratitude. "Thank you. And good morning." His cell chirped again. "I need to take this." He tapped his screen on his way to the pantry. "Hey, Jesse. Thanks for returning my call."

He retrieved a loaf of bread and set it on the counter. "Nope. No fires to put out. Just wanted to let you know I won't be around this weekend. I'll keep my cell handy, should you need anything."

He placed a large bowl from the cupboard onto the counter, stuck a wooden spoon inside it, and motioned Evie over.

With a nod, she set out the remaining ingredients.

"Oh, I'm sure they will." Phone to his ear, he pulled a pocket notebook from the junk drawer and started flipping through the pages. "They've never been to one of these holiday shindigs. Guess that tells you how long it's been for me, huh? Figured, as long as we're going, may as well bring some of my bulls."

He started talking about bucking chute etiquette, bull intensity and other things Evie assumed were related to the rodeo.

Like the one he'd asked her to attend.

Only he hadn't. His aunt had forced the invite, and of course Monte had given in. He probably didn't want to be rude.

She doubted he was thrilled to have her tagging along. Why did that fact leave her with a hint of disappointment? It wasn't like she wanted to go, either.

Except she did. But only for the new experience, not because her pulse spiked whenever the cowboy's brown eyes held hers. Or she watched them soften when he spoke to his daughters, or twinkle with mirth when they said something funny.

What had gotten into her? She was here to fulfill a role, for a short period at that, not to fall for a man she'd never see again once she left Sage Creek.

"Want me to get you a frying pan?"

She startled at Monte's voice, then blushed when she realized she'd been standing there lost in preposterous thoughts.

Releasing the spoon, she cleared her throat and placed slices of bread onto a cutting board beside the sink. "I got a little distracted." *Thinking about you, as absurd as that is.*

Although he *was* handsome. There was nothing wrong with acknowledging that.

So long as she remained wise and professional—more nonchalant than elevated heart rate.

He refilled his coffee cup and leaned back against the counter, legs crossed at the ankles. "The girls have a Christmas party this afternoon. At their new preschool. The director invited them. Said it could help them feel more comfortable for their first day."

"How thoughtful."

He nodded. "Aunt Martha and the ladies from church will want pictures. Think you can get them dolled up a bit?"

"Sure."

"Luna will comply with no problem. She loves anything frilly. Callie might take some cajoling. Feel free to bribe her with a visit to the 'forest' after. Once she's changed, of course, which she'll probably do the minute we get back."

"Behind the gazebo?"

"Yep. Just keep them away from the water."

"Okay. Anywhere else off-limits?"

"Nope. Other than the creek, so long as you're with them, they can pretty much go wherever you're comfortable. Don't figure you'll be venturing near the bulls?" His tone held a teasing lilt.

She laughed. "Absolutely not."

"Expect Callie to tiptoe right up to whatever boundary line you set. But she'll mind you so long as you're firm and consistent. You'll never have to worry about Luna. She came into the world looking for rules to follow."

He watched as Callie lined stones across the wood floor. "I doubt their party will last more than a couple hours. Supper's at six. Know how to fry chicken?"

"Probably not as well as Aunt Martha, but yeah."

"If you can cook even half as well as her, we'll eat good tonight." Taking a sip of his coffee, he regarded her with mirth-filled eyes.

This lighthearted side of him, wrapped up in his rugged cowboy exterior, left her even more unsettled than his steady gaze.

He glanced at Luna, his expression tender as he watched her color. "The girls may want to hang with me while I do chores this afternoon."

"You're okay with that?"

"May help if you stayed with them, but yeah. They can help me muck a stall and feed the animals. They'll probably want a turn on the ATV when I drag the arena. I've got some cowboys coming to ride some of my mature bulls. Practice for everyone involved. If that interests you, you're welcome to watch."

Her eyes widened as thoughts of men getting stomped on flashed through her mind. "That sounds dangerous."

"So's driving through rush hour traffic in Dallas, yet you survived." Laughter lines crinkled around his eyes. "But don't worry. I won't force you to ride. Least, not this early in your stay."

Her heart gave an unexpected lurch at his playful banter, which seemed to have replaced the edge he'd displayed when she first arrived. Hopefully that meant that he was beginning to feel more comfortable with her as a caregiver. Walking beside a family member fighting cancer was hard enough. She fully intended to lessen that load however she could.

Her demonstrating her competency would reduce his concerns.

Regardless, the handsome cowboy had alerted her to something. If she continued working with New Day, she'd need to stick with elderly patients in the future. And work extra hard at maintaining her professional demeanor in the present.

Because seeing the blend of warmth and strength with which Monte interacted with his girls was threatening to turn her insides into mush.

Good-looking, she could handle. Attractive merged with playful affection was another matter.

She finished making breakfast, the scent of cinnamon and butter filling the air, while the girls played a modified game of checkers.

After a few more phone calls, Monte snagged a couple French toast sticks, and drizzled them with enough syrup to create soup. Taking a bite, he raised his eyebrows. "Not bad."

"Yeah?"

He nodded. "Might even be a match for Aunt Martha's." He glanced through the archway, his lips twitching toward a smile. "Don't tell her I said that."

Her grin emerged before she could cover her enthusiasm with a nonchalant smile. "Your secret is safe with me."

He popped the last of his rushed breakfast into his mouth and washed it down with a swig of coffee. Depositing his dishes in the sink, he glanced at the time on the microwave. "Guess I best get going."

Callie slid from her chair and rushed over. "Me, too, Daddy?"

He scooped her up. "Not this time, Cowpoke." With her feet dangling, he kissed her neck, causing the child to giggle and squirm. "I'm running behind this morning." He deposited her back on her feet.

"But I can help."

"Oh, I'm sure you'd be a help, all right." He shot Evie a wink, sending a jolt through her. "But I think it's best if you, Luna and Ms. Bell get more acquainted."

She frowned. "We already did. Last night at supper."

Evie didn't take the child's statement personally. Of course, she'd want to spend time with her father. She adored him and he her. But the better she and the girls got along, the easier her job would be—and the more confidence Monte would hold in her abilities.

"We'll be together plenty today." He wrapped an arm around her waist, gave a squeeze, then kissed her and Luna goodbye.

Once the twins finished eating, Evie sent them to the bathroom to wash the syrup from their hands and faces, and for Callie, out of her hair. Then she walked down the hall to check on Martha.

The door stood ajar, and the woman sat propped up in bed reading.

Evie knocked softly. "Good morning, ma'am. Can I get

you anything? Juice or a banana?" Both should be easy on her stomach, if she felt queasy.

"Not at the moment, but thank you." She looked tired. Frail.

Respecting her space, Evie nodded and slipped away. She caught a glimpse of Callie as she walked past the bathroom. The child stood gripping the sink, face under the faucet, water dripping off her loose strands of hair.

Evie frowned. "No more, please."

Callie looked at her as droplets continued plunk-plunk-plunking on the floor. "But I'm thirsty."

"Then come finish your juice. After you clean up the puddle growing beneath you."

This wasn't a great sign regarding how the rest of her day might proceed.

Callie sighed and turned off the water. "Okay. But then will you play with me?"

Evie smiled. "Sure. What would you like to play?"

"Pick-up sticks. No, stack the boxes. Wait! Go Fish!"

"My brothers and sisters and I used to play that a lot when we were growing up."

"Really?"

She nodded, and once Callie had cleaned her mess, followed the child to the cupboards beneath the television. Inside, puzzles and board games were stacked on top of tubs of toys. An endearing image came to mind of Monte and his girls gathered around a board game.

She could tell those girls, and his aunt, were his entire world. He'd probably been an attentive and loyal husband as well. What had happened with his ex-wife? And why had he remained single?

More importantly, why did her brain wonder about things that weren't any of her business?

"Here it is!" Holding the cards high, Callie skipped into the kitchen and climbed onto a chair. Luna followed and sat beside Evie, periodically casting her the most adorable, shy smile.

The twins were as different as sisters could be. That was
a good thing. Two Callies could about wear a person into the
ground. Although Evie had to admit, she found the child delightful. So full of life and joy. Traits Luna balanced with her
quiet, observant nature.

Curiosity sparked in Luna's eyes. "You have brothers and
sisters?"

Warmth spread through Evie's chest. That was the first time
the sweet child had initiated conversation with her since she
arrived. Was she feeling more comfortable?

Evie shuffled the cards with a nod. "Two older brothers
and a younger sister."

"Do you still play with them?" Seemed fitting Callie would
ask that.

"In a way, I suppose."

"And your daddy?"

"Over the holidays. Trivia, mostly. Only I'm not very good."

Callie studied her. "Does that mean you lose?"

She laughed. "Pretty much. My brother, on the other hand,
is like a walking library."

Luna's eyes lit up. "I love the library. Some days, Aunt Martha takes us to story time."

"Only not anymore." Callie frowned and crossed her arms.
"Cuz she's always so tired and stuff."

Evie placed a hand on her shoulder. "That's hard."

She nodded. "But she's going to get better now that you're
here. Daddy says that's why you came."

Wow. No pressure there.

She always felt uncomfortable with these types of conversations, especially with children. They were almost as difficult
as those that occurred when patients were placed on hospice.
She hoped that wouldn't occur here. In the meantime, Evie
needed God's guidance on how to support this family amid
all the uncertainty they faced.

That always felt like a heavy assignment.

Her training had taught her that the best way she could comfort a person was to remain present. That she could do.

And she could pray.

She had just finished asking God to encase each of the Bowmans in His love when Callie shifted to talking about the upcoming rodeo.

She jutted her chin. "I'm going to hold on to my sheep for all six seconds. I've been making my grip strong. That's what they call it when you can hold on to stuff for a long time." She opened and closed her hand. "Want me to show you?" She grasped onto Evie's arm and squeezed so tightly her face scrunched up.

Evie fought to hide her amusement. "Impressive."

Callie grinned and refocused on their game.

After a few rounds of Go Fish, the girls decided to play school with their stuffed animals. This lasted about fifteen minutes before they asked to watch their "absolutest-favorite cartoon ever!" Assured their father wouldn't mind and anxious to tackle some housework, since that was part of her job, Evie agreed.

She cleaned the kitchen and dusted the living room before the girls decided to make a fort from furniture, couch cushions and sheets.

Callie peered up at her with eyes filled with such innocence, the look had to be well-rehearsed. Especially considering the context. "Daddy lets us so long as we put everything back when we're done."

That was probably the best activity to keep the little ball of energy occupied for any length of time—both in the construction and cleanup.

This also could provide the bribe Monte suggested Callie might need to don the outfit he wanted her to wear for the Christmas party. "After you put on the clothes your dad laid out on your beds and brush your teeth and hair."

Luna scampered off, with a disgruntled Callie lagging behind.

Those girls were as energetic as they were adorable. How had Monte managed them by himself after Tracy left?

No wonder he'd expressed such urgency that New Day Caregivers find a temporary fill-in.

With the children well entertained in their fort, filled with books, iPad, plastic and stuffed animals, and numerous pillows, Evie entered the kitchen to check the fridge and pantry for supper ingredients.

She'd clean up their disaster and tackle the mound of laundry overflowing the hamper while they were at the party. Finding the meat drawer bare, she pulled chicken legs from the freezer and set them in a sink of water to thaw.

After surveying his supply of veggies and salad fixings, she shot Monte a text offering a few options for sides.

Her phone dinged a response: Any of those sound great. The girls will probably ask for pickles. You'll find some of Aunt Martha's home-canned in the pantry.

Sounds delicious.

A loud crash came from somewhere outside the kitchen. Dropping her cell on the counter, she hurried into the living room. "Luna? Callie?" She lifted a corner of their fort and peered inside to find them lying on their bellies, Luna focused on a book while her sister watched something on her iPad.

Evie's chest tightened. Martha.

She raced down the hall and knocked on the woman's partially opened door. "Ma'am?" She stepped inside and surveyed the empty and disheveled bed. Where had she—the bathroom.

"Ma'am, are you all right?"

She was sitting on the floor, face in her hands. Beside her was an overturned countertop organizer, its contents spilled out. Intermixed with this lay shattered pieces of a small, ceramic cactus.

Evie rushed to her side and placed an arm around her shoulders. "What happened?"

Martha straightened with a visible breath. Surveying the mess all around her, she shook her head. "I got dizzy and reached out to steady myself and…and… I'm so sorry." She struggled to stand. "I'll clean this up."

Supporting her beneath her elbows, Evie helped her to her feet. "No big deal. I'll take care of it." She kept her voice soft, soothing. "Let's get you back to bed."

Martha hesitated, like she wanted to protest. Poor woman had probably spent so much time tending for others, she didn't quite know how to respond on the receiving end. But with her feeling even slightly lightheaded, Evie wasn't comfortable with her up and moving around.

She guided her back to her room.

"I think I'd rather sit in my chair, if you don't mind."

"Of course." Evie walked with her to the dusty rose recliner tucked in the corner beside the window and helped her get settled. "You cold?"

"A bit."

Evie grabbed a knitted throw blanket from a wicker basket nearby and laid it across Martha's lap. "How about I make you some chicken broth?"

"Maybe you should."

The woman wasn't up to eating but likely understood, especially after her fall, her need for calories. Not that there were many in broth, but that was better than nothing.

Evie dashed back into the kitchen. Glancing at the girls' fort en route, she paused to listen to Callie's cartoon, emanating from beneath it. And most likely, Luna still lay stretched out beside her, flipping the pages of one of the many books she'd brought in.

Five minutes later, Evie carried a steaming bowl and half a sleeve of saltines to Martha. Sensing her sorrow, she sat on the edge of her bed and waited, should Martha want to speak.

She'd found, if one waited long enough, without pushing or prodding, others often opened up. This proved true in this instance as well, because just when she was about to excuse herself, Martha began to speak.

"I'm not normally this weepy." She offered a hint of a smile.

"Considering the circumstances, I'd say it's normal—and healthy—to shed a few tears now and again."

Martha studied her for a moment then gave a slight nod. "I suppose you're right. And here, in my room, Lord knows I've done that."

Evie caught the words left unspoken: But not in front of Monte and the children. That was relatively common, as well. Those with cancer often hid their own pain so as to not cause their family further distress, while their loved ones did the same. Unfortunately, that tended to leave everyone alone in their struggle.

But that was why Evie was here. While it wasn't her place to advise them on how to handle the situation or their relationships, she could listen, without judgement or offering unsolicited advice. And so, asking God to pour His love through her, she listened as Martha shared some of her fears and anxieties.

Evie glanced at the clock on the bedside table. She was as reluctant to end what felt like a sacred conversation as she was to leave the twins unattended for long.

Thankfully, the woman made the decision for her. She held up a nearby book on deepening one's intimacy with Christ. "If you don't mind, I think I'll catch up on some reading."

"Not at all." Evie smiled, gave the woman's shoulder a gentle squeeze, and strolled out of the room.

She stopped at the end of the hallway and cocked an ear. Silence.

With what she knew of Callie, that couldn't be a good sign.

"Girls?" She entered the living room and peered beneath their fort. Lots of toys and books. No children.

She hurried down the hall. They weren't in their bedroom, either.

"Is everything all right?" Martha asked from her opened doorway.

Evie forced a confident smile. "Yes, ma'am. I need to take care of something real quick." *Like making sure the girls hadn't wandered into one of the pastures with the bulls or somewhere else equally dangerous.*

Evie dashed out of the house and down the porch steps, grateful Monte wasn't in sight. She'd hate for him to see her without the kids and ask about them. Telling him she had no idea certainly wouldn't earn her points in the trust department.

And if the twins had wandered into one of the pastures with the bulls...

She didn't want to think about that.

Unfortunately, with the way her experience here had been going, Martha would probably once again get dizzy and fall—while Evie was searching for Monte's missing children.

Scanning the visible property, Evie cupped her hands around her mouth and called out to the twins.

First real day on the job, and she'd already lost them. Surely Monte knew how challenging Callie was! He'd been parenting her for five years, after all. Unless he always had others, like the ladies from church, a nanny, or someone from a caregiving service to rely on. Even so, the child had to have slipped away from the most attentive adults a time or two—or twenty.

Evie paused and held her breath. She heard their voices. Following the high-pitched sound—laughter merged with hollering—she raced around the house then froze.

Callie stood over a mud-filled plastic pool, looking as if she'd been swimming in the stuff. And Luna, who was running toward Evie, crying, had smears on her face, droplets on her dress, and globs in her hair. The shivering child looked like she'd lost a mud fight.

Based on Callie's hands, coated to past her wrists, that was precisely what had occurred.

And with less than twenty minutes before their father would arrive to take them to their party. To make matters worse—as if that were possible—Max was covered in mud as well and chose that very moment to try to shake it off.

Catching Evie in the spray.

She should've known better than to wear her white pants.

Taking in a deep, slow breath, she counted to four, then exhaled. She dropped to one knee in front of Luna, who now stood before her, and placed a hand on her shoulder. "What happened, sweetie?" Not that figuring that out took any kind of sleuthing.

Thank goodness today was relatively warm, one of the blessings of the south.

The little one leaned into her, causing moisture, likely a lovely shade of brown, to seep into her pink shirt as drips from the child's hair snaked their way to Evie's elbow. "Callie got me dirty."

Evie straightened, at a complete loss for words.

Callie seemed momentarily tongue-tied as well, although she came up with a story soon enough. "We were pretending to be pigs, and—"

"No, I wasn't." Luna stomped a foot.

"Yuh-huh!"

"Enough." Evie spoke with more force than she'd intended, and both girls stared at her with wide eyes. "Let's get you both washed up." Maybe if she worked quickly, and Monte was delayed, she could get the girls scrubbed clean and changed before their father arrived.

Without tracking mud through the house. Had this been summer, she would've simply hosed the girls off.

The sound of someone behind her clearing their throat a moment later indicated it was too late for that.

Evie turned around to find Monte glaring at her. "I can explain."

He looked from her to Luna, whose teeth were chattering, to Callie, both girls covered in mud, then back to Evie. "I'd love to hear you try."

He crossed his arms, and a muscle in his jaw twitched.

Evie's mind went blank.

"Daddy." With an all-out sob that was likely part princess, Luna raced into his arms.

He swept her up and held her close as she quickly relayed her version of the situation, barely pausing to suck in a stuttered breath. Callie raced over and adamantly asserted that her sister was wrong and had been an equal participant in their "game."

Grateful they'd temporarily diverted Monte's attention, Evie tried to think of a scenario that wouldn't make her appear irresponsible. Sadly, however she tried to spin it, she'd lost sight of the girls.

On her first day.

She'd be surprised if he didn't send her away before the night's end, and she wouldn't blame him one bit.

CHAPTER FOUR

"Sir, I'm really sorry—"

"No time for that now." This was not a great start to what he'd hoped would be a special, memory-making event. "Help me get the twins inside and cleaned up."

"Yes, sir." Taking Callie by the hand, Evie pivoted toward the front of the house.

"Not that way." He pointed to the back door.

The last thing he needed was for them to dirty the carpet.

He couldn't believe Evie had allowed this, especially so close to when he and the twins needed to leave. But he'd rather assume that than the alternative—that she'd left them unattended.

This felt like Tracy Gray all over again.

Clearly New Day Caregivers wasn't as wonderful as they claimed. One irresponsible employee, he could understand. He knew from working with numerous ranch hands over the years that people who seemed great during an interview could be the biggest dud of the bunch.

But two loafers in a row suggested a pattern.

At the entrance to the mudroom, he surveyed his property. Erin, his ex, now deceased, had taught him that not everyone considered this country setting a slice of heaven on earth.

What if the organization couldn't find competent staff willing to come out here? Sure, he could try another company, but then he'd have to begin the process all over. Making phone calls, asking questions, filling out forms and getting all the necessary medical documents transferred.

They'd probably stick him on a waiting list.

And who was to say another outfit would send him anyone better?

Evie and the girls followed him inside and stood in the center of the tan-and-cream tile while Monte warmed the water in the industrial-sized sink next to a row of boots. Above this hung a series of basket-filled cubbies.

Dropping to one knee, he shucked off Luna's outfit—the one she'd picked out specifically for today—and tossed it into a plastic hamper next to a large bag of dog food. The tears in her eyes tore at his heart.

Some might call him overly sensitive, reacting to her sorrow as he was. But he knew how excited she was for today's Christmas party, and to see her new school. He'd been hoping the event, and the opportunity to check out the facility for themselves, would ease his girls' first-day jitters. Late start or not, beginning preschool was a big deal.

Without a mama to see them off, that transition would be hard enough.

Jaw tight, he shot a glance at Evie as she tended to a chattering Callie. The child seemed intent on giving her version of events. As far as he could tell, Evie didn't know much more about the girls' mischief than he did.

Yet another indication that she'd left the twins unattended for a stretch of time.

Long enough for them to fill their plastic wading pool with enough dirt to plant a garden, add water and march around.

He wrapped his girls in stained towels to stop them from dripping water.

Throwing those into the hamper as well, he made eye contact with Evie. "You run a bath while I pick out their clothes."

She hurried to comply.

Grabbing a child under each arm, he followed. "All right, my little piggies. Time to leave the sty and return to the land of humans."

The girls giggled. Callie, the one who likely initiated their make-believe game, did so most enthusiastically.

He deposited the twins onto the pale blue linoleum where they waited for Evie to test the water and plug the tub.

"Can we have bubbles?" Callie's voice was sweet, as if she'd just come from cleaning up her toys without being asked, rather than swimming through mud.

Made sense considering she probably hadn't thought anything wrong with her fiasco, until she saw the adults' faces. Nor would she understand why Monte was so concerned.

Thank the good Lord for that. The last thing they needed was to feel untended to.

Regardless of how true that was.

"Everything all right?" Aunt Martha's voice, soft and kind, drifted from behind.

Evie looked up, tears pooling behind her long dark lashes. Torn between compassion for her obvious regret and frustration over all that had occurred, Monte took in a slow deep breath.

He explained what he'd found, upon returning to the house. With a full day booked, besides. While he'd happily made time for the party, his schedule didn't allow for an extensive cleanup. Or the fit Callie might throw when he tried to get her in yet another presentable outfit.

"Oh, my." His aunt laughed—her momentary amusement a gift in an otherwise unpleasant situation. "Can't take your eyes off them for a moment."

"That's a fact." He looked at Evie. "Which begs the question, how long were they out there, playing in the mud. And where, exactly, were you?"

She blinked rapidly, her gaze shooting from him to Aunt Martha, then back to him.

At least she wasn't firing off excuses. "This isn't a playground where you can let them do whatever they please."

"I know—"

"Do you? And if they'd been hurt while you were on social media or texting some guy, or doing whatever it was you were doing—other than what I'm paying you for. What then?"

The tears she'd fought back spilled over her lashes.

"Monte, that's enough." Aunt Martha spoke with more force than he'd heard from her in some time. She released a sigh, her shoulders and expression sagging. "She was helping me." Her entire body conveyed defeat.

He turned to Evie. "What happened?"

She looked at his aunt, as if seeking permission. When his aunt gave a slight nod, she told him about an incident he hadn't anticipated.

"Is this normal, getting dizzy like that?"

Evie shrugged. "It's not terribly uncommon. Could be a sign of dehydration or low blood sugar." She made eye contact with his aunt. "That's why it's so important that you do your best to eat."

Aunt Martha nodded again.

"It could also be from anemia, which can be a side effect of chemotherapy, or from anxiety and stress." Tub filled, Evie turned off the faucet.

Monte scrubbed a hand over his face, his irritation at finding his girls covered in mud replaced with deep gratitude for Evie's attentiveness with his aunt.

"I shouldn't have gotten so upset with you." He sighed. "The good Lord knows, those girls have landed in mudholes under my watch a time or two."

"Or ten?" Aunt Martha quirked an eyebrow at him.

He chuckled. "Or fifty-five. Thankfully, kids and clothes wash up well enough."

"But that was my favorite dress." Moisture pooled in Luna's eyes.

"And it was so beautiful." Evie smoothed the child's hair from her face. "In fact, I think it would be perfect for your first day of preschool. This will allow you to keep it a surprise while showing off one of the other dresses I saw in your closet. My favorite is the red one with the wide white bow. It's so Christmassy! Which do you like best, other than your first day of school surprise?"

Luna's face brightened. "I like the red one, too."

Evie clapped her hands together. "Wonderful! I can't wait to see it on you!"

Monte's heart warmed as he watched Evie interact with his daughter, and how the child's shyness began to melt away with her smile.

Maybe New Day had sent a more competent—and compassionate—caregiver than he'd thought.

"I want to wear my favorite clothes, too." Callie crossed her arms with a frown that warned him of an upcoming battle.

"So long as that means something without grass, food or dirt stains, sure." That about knocked out everything she considered comfortable. "Bonus points if it's red or green."

Spending the next thirty minutes sifting through her drawers would only leave them both frustrated. It'd probably trigger Callie's stubbornness as well, a trait he celebrated when it came to rodeoing, not so much when it complicated daily parenting.

"Anything I can do?" Aunt Martha asked.

He shook his head. "You go rest. With four hands for two girls, we've got them covered." He watched her leave, ready to accompany her if she seemed unsteady on her feet but unwilling to unnecessarily encroach on her independence.

Assured she was okay, he leaned toward Evie, inhaling her

soft lavender scent. "You mention anything about taking them to the forest?"

She shook her head. The slight flush to her cheeks suggested she was as aware of his nearness as he was.

Clearing his throat, he widened the distance between them. "Tell you girls what." He lifted his daughters, one by one, into the tub. "How about I take you little explorers to your fort when we get back from meeting your teacher? May even catch us a glimpse of some deer or wild turkeys."

"Max and Ms. Evie, too?" Callie's eyes shimmered with hope.

"Doubt I could keep that dog from tromping around with you girls, even if I tried. As for Ms. Evie, if she wants. And isn't too upset about that fit I threw a moment ago."

She dropped her gaze and rubbed the back of her arm. Obviously, his invite had made her uncomfortable. She was probably searching for a polite way to decline.

He opened his mouth to save her the trouble when she offered the twins a wide smile. "That sounds fun."

He blinked. Not the answer he'd expected, and one that triggered much too intense a response within him.

Seemed he couldn't be near that woman without his palms turning sweaty. Last time he'd reacted that way around someone had been fifteen years ago, when he first met his ex. Although they attended the same high school, their paths hadn't crossed until his mom hired her to tutor him in biology.

He'd fallen for her hard and fast, and by the time they turned seniors, they were both dreaming about their future together. If only he'd known how quickly she'd bail, after they said their vows, he could've saved himself a whole lot of heartache.

But then they never would've had the twins. Those girls were well worth the grief their mama had caused.

His phone rang, and he glanced at the screen, then to Evie. "I need to grab this call." His friend wasn't one for chitchat, which meant, if he reached out, he had good reason.

"No problem."

With a nod, he slipped out, grateful for the excuse to distance himself from the woman whose pull on him only seemed to be getting stronger.

Considering his reaction after having spent less than forty-eight hours around her, he was increasingly uneasy regarding the next few weeks. And frustrated with himself for not doing better at keeping his emotions in check.

Midway through another ring, he answered. "Hey, Sean. What's up?"

His friend's sigh reverberated across the line. "It's Ian. He's acting up again, worse than ever. My sister and brother-in-law are at their wits' end. They don't want to give up on the kid, but nothing they've tried seems to work. My nephew's bent on destroying his life."

"Man, I'm sorry to hear that."

He ambled into the living room and paused to take in the scene. His kids had stretched a sheet from the coffee table over the back of the couch, and another from the table to the armchair, the edges anchored with their marble box, his Bible and a jar of coins. While not a fan of the mess, he did like to see that Evie allowed the children's creativity.

He picked up a sheet of paper. On it, one of the girls had drawn three stick figures, two smiling children standing on either side and holding the hands of an adult. Above this, they'd colored a heart.

While his girls would call about anyone a friend, it was nice to see the three of them getting along just the same.

"I'm hoping to find a positive outlet for my nephew to channel his energy into. Give him something to shoot for, know what I mean?"

"Makes sense. How can I help?"

"Actually…" Sean paused. "I was thinking it might be good to get him into bull riding. Think you can show him the ropes, maybe even let him help out on the ranch to compensate your time training him?"

"As to putting him to work, I'll have to think on that." Normally, Monte would welcome the opportunity to mentor a troubled teen, but that would require a good deal of supervision. With all he had going on, he wasn't sure he had the time or energy necessary for such an arrangement. "But I can coach him up, no problem. How about you bring him by Friday afternoon?"

"That'd be great. You have no idea how much I appreciate it."

"My pleasure." Ending the call, he scooped up an armful of stuffed animals and returned them to the girls' room.

Bath done, they met him there. Luna was already putting on her lace-trimmed red dress while Evie helped Callie sort through her clothes in search of something event-appropriate that didn't cause the child to scrunch up her face in overdramatized disgust.

"Isn't this adorable?" Evie pulled a short-sleeve dress from the closet with a denim top and green-and-white checked cotton from the waist down.

He leaned a shoulder against the doorframe. "That's cowpoke attire for sure."

Callie studied it with a furrowed brow that indicated her refusal would soon follow.

"Remember what I told you about taking you and your sister to the forest after." He glanced at the time on his phone. "If you cooperate. Which includes not spending the next thirty minutes fussing over what to wear."

Callie slumped. "Okay." She shrugged on the dress, making the process appear much more difficult than it could possibly be.

He grabbed a brush from on top of her dresser and secured her hair in a ponytail while Evie braided Luna's, upon her request. Ten minutes later, he was grabbing snacks for them to eat on the way and ushering them to the door.

Evie followed. "Sorry about the mess." She glanced back at the living room. "I'll clean up while you're gone."

Luna frowned. "You're not coming?"

His daughter only issued such requests to those she felt comfortable with. Had Evie managed to capture the child's heart already?

Biting her bottom lip, Evie looked at him, probably trying to gauge his preference.

The thought of her coming triggered a sense of anticipation that was almost a gut reaction—which in turn made him want her to stay home. Otherwise, he feared it wouldn't just be his children's hearts she'd capture.

"You know," Aunt Martha said from behind him, "might not be a bad idea for her to join y'all. I imagine she'll be helping the girls with their schoolwork and all and the one to pick them up, should they get sent home sick."

Monte rubbed the back of his neck. He fully intended to remain engaged in his daughters' education. He also disagreed that Evie needed to know their teacher to see they practiced their penmanship or studied their spelling words. But whenever his sweet Luna turned her big, brown eyes, brimming with hope, his way, he felt ready to give her the world.

"Okay." He gave her braid a gentle tug, then turned to Evie. "That is, if you're up for it."

She glanced again at the mess.

"Don't fret about that none." Aunt Martha flicked a hand. "This house has seen worse, believe me." She eyed Evie's muddied clothes. "Although you might want to change first."

Evie looked at Monte, as if seeking an invite.

"Go get yourself fixed up. We don't mind waiting." He grabbed his car keys from a bowl on the entryway accent table. "As to all this—" he indicated the disheveled living room "—it'll still be here when you get back."

Evie laughed, a melodious sound that reminded him to keep a stronger rein on his emotions before they got away from him.

CHAPTER FIVE

EVIE SUSPECTED LUNA wasn't often quick to invite acquaintances into her world. Nor did Evie underestimate the importance of this event. She'd seen enough Instagram reels to realize that entering preschool was a huge transition. The girls probably were equally nervous and excited.

Most importantly, they wanted Evie to come. How could she possibly say no? Attending the party this afternoon would go a long way toward building trust, which was an important part of her job. Perhaps the most crucial, in fact. While it might appear the children had little say over her employment, she'd learned, a parent's heart was often deeply connected to their kids. As one of her friends often said, "You love my babies, I'll love you."

Plus, the Bowman girls were adorable. There were worse ways Evie could spend the afternoon.

She tossed Luna a smile. "I would love to come."

The child's bright-eyed grin squeezed her heart.

"Yay!" Callie jumped up and down, clapping. "You can see the playground. It's got two slides, swings, a jungle gym, and a rock wall. I climb up real fast." Her words trailed behind her as she skipped out of the house and down the stairs. "Daddy showed it to us after church last week. Said, with all

the climbing we're bound to do, I'll get stronger and stronger."
She flexed her nonexistent biceps.

Evie laughed. "I see." She looked up to find Monte watching her. When their eyes met, his gaze intensified, lingering on hers long enough to send a rush of heat to her face.

A man who, only moments ago, had seemed ready to give her the boot, and who still could, should another mud incident arise. Which wasn't unlikely, considering the setting.

With a deep breath, she tucked a lock of hair behind her ear and followed him out and onto the porch. Callie waited at the bottom step and slipped her hand into Evie's, flooding her chest with warmth. That child was as precious as she was rambunctious.

Monte's pickup, a metallic green with an extended cab, was parked in the shade of his shed. He opened the rear, driver's-side door, and the girls clambered in and fastened themselves into their car seats.

He rounded the front as if intending to open Evie's door for her, but she beat him to it. She was having difficulty enough maintaining her professional focus without him doing anything to increase his charm.

His cedary-citrus scent that accompanied him when he slid behind the wheel wasn't helping.

Fastening her seat belt, she focused on a series of questions Callie was firing off rather than the handsome cowboy sitting less than two feet away. The child's inquiries barely lasted five minutes before the girls started singing embellished lyrics to "Rudolph the Red-Nosed Reindeer."

Normally, she probably would've sung along, but she felt self-conscious doing so in front of Monte.

An awkward silence followed.

"So…" He drummed his fingers on the steering wheel, his pause suggesting he was trying equally hard to think of a conversation starter. "What were some of your favorite Christmas traditions?"

"Hmm... That's a tough one. I have so many special memories." She gazed out her window, mentally sifting through over two decades of family celebrations. "Probably eating my great-grandmother's home-baked cookies. She always brought a massive tubful. Oatmeal Raisin. Chocolate Chip. Soft and lemony sugar cookies. I also looked forward to finding and decorating our Christmas tree."

"Y'all had live ones?"

She nodded. "The morning after Thanksgiving, we got all bundled up. Winters can be quite cold in Michigan."

"I imagine."

"Mom would fill a bunch of thermoses with hot cocoa. Then half of us would pile into my dad's truck, the other half followed in our station wagon. We'd head to a family-owned farm outside of town to find the best Christmas tree possible, not that any of us agreed upon which one that was."

He laughed. "Y'all did a bit of bickering, I take it?"

She nodded. "Which usually ended in a brutal—and fun—snowball fight. Initiated by my dad."

"That's one way to redirect squabbling siblings."

She angled her head. "Huh. I never thought of it that way, before. My dad was such a sneak!" She grinned, more impressed with her father's gentle parenting than ever. "What about you?"

On their right, two women in jeans and sweatshirts power-walked side by side. Beyond them, a man hung lights from his gutters while a woman and two teenagers decorated the porch and bordering bushes. A golden retriever supervised from where he lay in the yard.

"I've got to copy your cookies answer." Monte shot her a grin that halted her breath. "The ladies usually baked them together while we guys watched football and pestered them for spoonfuls of dough. I loved the smell of melted chocolate and vanilla that swirled throughout my grandparents' house."

His memories were allowing her to see a different, more

nostalgic side of him that she found endearing. For that reason alone, she'd be wise to shift to another topic. But her curiosity, tinged with a growing fondness, won out. "What was the best gift you ever received?"

"A twenty-piece electric train set."

"You answered that quickly. Must've been quite the toy."

He nodded. "It was actually for both my brother and me. Because of how expensive it was. Not that my parents were poor or anything. But they were always careful to keep the main thing the main thing."

"Jesus?"

He nodded. "Like they reminded us a thousand times, it was His birthday, after all. In Christ, God the Father had already given us the best gift possible. They never wanted us to forget that."

"I respect that."

"I didn't always like their logic back then, but I appreciate it now. I want to raise my girls the same way—to value faith and family more than some fancy gadget that they'll lose, break or grow bored of."

"They're blessed to have you."

He chuckled. "Doubt they'll feel that way once they hit the teen years. You know what they say about parenting?"

"It's a long game?"

He gave a slight shrug. "Isn't that the truth. But what I was going to say was if your kids aren't upset with you about something, you're doing it wrong."

"Ah. So, if you come home to find the kids pitching a fit, you'll recognize that as a sign of my competency?" Their easy banter had eradicated the insecurity with which she'd climbed into his vehicle. That felt like a dangerous shift, considering how appealing she found the man, and more so with every encounter.

He turned onto a residential street lined with numerous houses that clearly went all out for the holidays. One had a large wooden display of Santa in a sleigh overflowing with brightly painted boxes. Another had decorated the massive tree anchoring their lawn with fake candy canes.

But had the town held a competition, the prize would've gone to the homeowners two blocks down. Their yard looked like a winter wonderland, with a snowflake-adorned multi-sectioned archway stretching the length of their walk, and giant lollipops staked in the grass.

They passed the local high school, another short stretch of houses, then turned into a small circular lot filled with about a dozen other vehicles. The brightly painted sign on the single-story building said Bright Start Preschool. Someone had painted large ornaments with silver tops and holly with bright red berries on the windows. But she most loved their nativity scene, with Mary and Joseph kneeling on either side of baby Jesus's manger.

"Here we are." He parked next to a station wagon with plastic taped over a partially busted rear window and cut the engine. "Your new school." He flashed his daughters a smile. "Big girls only."

Evie slipped out, opened Luna's door and helped her climb from the truck. Apparently, she'd increased her connection with the child, because, although not as exuberantly affectionate as her sister, she remained at Evie's side as they strode toward the entrance. Callie, on the other hand, raced ahead, then back, then up ahead again before hanging by her knees from a bike rack.

Reaching her, Monte tickled her ribs, scooped her up and dangled her, laughing, over his shoulder. "Come on, little monkey."

Once inside, he placed her on her feet, catching her by the arm before she darted ahead once again.

"Hold on, Cowpoke. Let's find out where we need to go before you go blazing off and wind up in the custodial closet."

Callie angled her head, brow furrowed. "What's that?"

"Lots of scrubbing, sweeping and mopping, that's what."

Evie laughed. "You're great at positive redirection." Had he answered the child any other way, she probably would've been more determined than ever to go exploring.

He grinned. "Kinda have to be, raising that fireball on a bucking bull ranch and all."

His statement reminded her of the challenge that lay ahead. Keeping that girl out of mud-filled pools was the least of her concerns.

"Well, look who we have here." A tall, lanky woman with curly gray hair approached with a wide smile. She wore a sweatshirt with a decorated tree on it and a lanyard bearing her name and the phrase I Can Help.

"Mrs. Gutierre!" Callie ran toward her with her arms outstretched.

Laughing, the woman dropped to one knee and pulled the child into a firm embrace.

"Ma'am." Monte tipped his hat. "I didn't realize you worked here." As she stood, he introduced her and Evie to one another.

"I don't. Just volunteering." Stepping forward, Mrs. Gutierre drew Luna into a hug then took Evie's hands in hers and gave a gentle squeeze. "It's so nice to meet you."

"Mrs. Gutierre volunteers in children's ministry one Sunday a month," Monte said. "As you can tell, the kids love her, mine included."

"And I them." The woman turned her warm, kind eyes to Evie. "Thank you for taking care of our sweet Martha. As you probably know, this town would be devastated without her."

These types of conversations were as touching as they were stressful. Evie loved seeing the legacy of a life lived well, evident in the depth of relationships formed. And yet, hearing such adoration also served as a reminder of how many people were placing their hopes not just in Aunt Martha's treatment, but in Evie's caregiving abilities as well. Logically, most understood there was only so much she could do. The real battle lay with the doctors, the chemotherapy and Martha's strength to fight.

But in these situations, the heart often disregarded the head and people grasped on to every bit of hope possible.

The adults engaged in conversation a moment longer, but then Callie became restless and began pulling on her father's arm, urging him forward.

"Patience, Cowpoke." The amused glint in his eyes contradicted his stern tone. "You'll have plenty of time in this building, believe me." With a chuckle, he took a flyer Mrs. Gutierre offered, glanced at it, then used it to bop Luna on the head. "Ready, kiddo?"

Face bright with wonder and a hint of anxiety, she nodded.

Together, they followed brightly colored, hand-drawn signs past a gym/cafeteria, around the corner, and to the last classroom on the left. The melody to "Frosty the Snowman" and the sound of voices floated toward them.

Inside, Ms. Vargas, the pre-K teacher, greeted them. About thirty years younger than Mrs. Gutierre, she had blond hair, green eyes and a petite frame well suited for her forest green cotton dress. She wore ornament earrings and a light-up Christmas necklace.

Monte introduced her to Evie. "Kate here attends Trinity Faith. We've known each other for at least fifteen years, wouldn't you say?"

The teacher nodded. "Ever since Drake's younger sister Elizabeth started inviting me to youth group. Back when I had a crush on his best friend." Her laughter indicated she was referring to Monte.

His slight blush confirmed that. "A long time, that's for sure."

Why did their warm familiarity prick Evie with a twinge of jealousy? So what that he had a pretty friend—and the two didn't seem any more than that. It wasn't like Evie had any claim on the man, or that she'd stick around long enough to change that.

However, her reaction did increase her desire to get into nursing school and get hired on at a local hospital. One in a city with a thriving art and music culture, great restaurants and opportunities to meet someone and fall in love.

God willing, someone with the strength, kindness and integrity she detected in Monte.

Hand resting on his belt buckle, he surveyed the classroom. "Quite the setup you've got here."

Empty cubbies stood along the wall between them and a corner reading nook designated by a tiered book display. Beanbags and a mural of a tree house occupied the corner. Square tables, each with four chairs arranged around them, and colorful plastic caddies filled with various craft supplies were arranged in the center. On the far wall hung a decorated bulletin board, a window to its right, bins of blocks and other manipulatives to its left.

"I like to provide the children with ample opportunities to engage their curiosity." Ms. Vargas began explaining some of the sensory stations placed about the room. "They learn best through play and a sense of wonder."

"Impressive," Monte said. "The girls will think every day's a party here. After seeing all this, they'll be biting at the bit for their first day."

Ms. Vargas grinned. "Then I've accomplished my goal."

To Evie's left stood a do-it-yourself photo booth type of display designated with a fake fir adorned in ornaments and tinsel, a yellow bench and a framed chalkboard with the words *Merry Christmas* in bold lettering.

"Girls, look." She pointed. "Let me take some photos for your aunt Martha."

Luna's eyes brightened. Callie slumped but complied with minimal coaxing.

Evie snapped a picture of each child by herself, with one another, and then their dad.

"Can I take one with you, too?" Luna asked.

Evie's heart melted. "Absolutely." But the warmth the child's request brought turned to nervousness once she was standing behind the twins, shoulder to shoulder with Monte.

As if she were part of their family.

Thank goodness, Callie's impatience broke the moment before it became too awkward.

"Daddy?" She tugged on her father's arm. "Can I go paint?" She pointed to a series of standing easels where two other children had gathered.

Monte looked at Ms. Vargas, who turned to his daughter with a warm smile. "Absolutely."

"Yay!" Callie skipped off and introduced herself to a round-bellied, chubby-cheeked boy with spiked black hair and a red-headed girl in a turquoise T-shirt and rainbow-print skorts.

While Ms. Vargas described various activities she'd planned for her students during the months ahead, Luna lingered between Evie and her dad. Her gaze locked on a lady and her child working a puzzle set up in one of the corners.

"Is this open play time?" Evie asked.

Ms. Vargas glanced at the clock on the wall above her. "For about fifteen more minutes, yes."

Evie made eye contact with Luna. "Shall we go join them at the puzzle table?"

The child's eyes widened for a flash of a second, then she gave a weak shrug.

Poor girl wanted to make friends. She just needed someone to help her gain the courage.

"Come on." Evie took the child's hand in hers and guided her across the room to where the mother and her daughter sat around a circular table covered with colorful puzzle pieces. "Mind if we join you?"

The mom looked up, her eyes warm and friendly. "Not at

all." She stood and initiated a handshake. "I'm Brooke, and this is my youngest, Destiny." She motioned to her daughter. "I also have a third and fifth grader. They're at home playing video games with their dad."

Based on the way Destiny leaned into her mom, as if wanting to hide behind her, she was about shy as Luna. That could make them a great match.

Or lead to awkward silence.

Choosing a navy chair short enough to bring her knees to her ears, Evie introduced herself and Luna. "I bet you both have a lot in common." She tried to think of something that would help the girls connect. "Do you like animals?"

Sitting a tad straighter, Destiny nodded. "I've got a dog named Big Bear."

"What about you, Luna?" Brooke found a corner puzzle piece and snapped it into place. "Do you have any pets?"

She nodded. "Two dogs. Max and Finn." Her voice was soft.

After a few more gentle proddings, the girls relaxed and soon meandered over to a dress-up area on the other side of a colorful rug, leaving Evie and Brooke to complete the puzzle.

"Do you have other children?" the woman asked.

"Oh, no. The twins aren't mine." She explained her relationship to them.

"The Bowman ranch?"

She nodded.

"That must be hard."

"It can be. But my job can also be deeply fulfilling. It feels good to know I'm making a positive impact on someone."

"No, I mean living out there and seeing what those poor animals are forced to endure." She shook her head.

Evie frowned. "I don't know what you mean, or what it's like on other ranches. But from what I can see, Mr. Bowman treats his animals well."

"You've never watched them buck, I take it?" The woman went on to tell her about a flank strap she felt certain caused the bulls pain. "No offense, but it makes me ill to think about it. Can't understand the type of man that would subject a creature to such torment."

Jaw slack, Evie looked at Monte, who'd moved to the easel area and was squatting down, eye level with Callie.

Was what Brooke said true? From what she'd observed, that seemed hard to believe, although she had seen a hint of a temper during the mud incident. At the time, she hadn't thought his reaction extreme. Not to mention, he really seemed to love his bulls, and his girls.

Then again, she didn't know Monte well, nor would she stick around long enough to change that. In the meantime, common sense told her to disregard any and all small-town gossip, which was what this felt like.

Still, her inner caretaker couldn't help but bristle at the idea that Monte's personality carried even a hint of cruelty.

MONTE GLANCED UP to see Evie talking with Brooke Sanders and frowned. Terrific. He could only imagine the type of garbage that busybody was spewing. So convinced he was a heartless rancher, she'd made it her mission to harass and badmouth him every chance she got.

Regardless that her perspective was skewed, her falsehoods were perpetuated by animal rights groups and those who were clueless when it came to raising rough stock. Had Mrs. Meddle taken the time to check her assumptions, he would've kindly set her straight. Even given her a tour of his ranch. But then she'd have to find some other way to satisfy her self-righteous hunger for superiority.

Evie, he hoped, had enough wisdom to disregard, or at least question, the woman's prattle.

Refocusing on Kate, who was in the middle of explaining her online communication system, he waited for her to pause. "Would you excuse me for a moment?"

"Yes, of course."

Why was he concerned with what Evie thought, anyway? It wasn't like they had, or ever would have, anything other than a working relationship.

Although their interactions would be much more pleasant if she didn't think of him as a callous jerk.

Both women glanced up as he approached. "Ma'am." He greeted Brooke with a tip of his hat. "Is Destiny excited about starting school?" Some guys might try to avoid their enemies. He figured his display of human dignity was one of the best ways to expose her immaturity.

Expression hard, Brooke gave a shrug that almost resembled a twitch. "She's always been an enthusiastic reader."

He expected her to use the opportunity to brag about her daughter. Instead, she turned to Evie with a stiff smile. "It was nice meeting you. And if you'd like more information on my book club, don't hesitate to give me a call."

Great. The two had exchanged numbers.

Suppressing a huff, he eyed the partially completed puzzle spread across the table, then glanced at Callie. She and two other children were playing with an educational display made from cords, clothespins and various circle cutouts.

"Can't imagine my little cowpoke will find anything boring about this place."

Evie nodded. "Your friend has created an inviting environment, that's for sure. And apparently, she can turn almost any lesson into a game."

"I'm not surprised. Kate's always been creative. Here I've been fretting about getting Callie to school without a fuss each morning. Now I'm thinking I'll have a tough time enticing her to come home."

"Well, there's always Max."

"True that. And Aunt Martha. Doubt either of them could stay away from her long."

Evie dropped her gaze with a hint of a frown.

"All right, everyone." Now standing in the center of the

room, Ms. Vargas clapped her hands. "How about a fun game of pin the carrot on the snowman?"

The children cheered and hurried over, Callie among the first in line. Luna, not surprisingly, hung back. For a moment, he feared she wouldn't participate. But then Brooke's daughter took her hand and said, "Come on."

While not exactly thrilled by her choice of a playmate, he was thankful that she had found a friend. Besides, it wouldn't be right to judge a child based on her mother's behavior.

After three more games and cookie decorating, Ms. Vargas released the children to once again engage in whatever activities they pleased. Callie joined a group of boys playing with tractors and dump trucks while Luna and her new friend gravitated toward the dress-up area again.

Feeling a bit out of place as the only father in the room, Monte lingered near the door, reading through his emails.

"Daddy!" Callie hurried over with bright eyes, a newfound friend at her side, followed by a woman he vaguely remembered from one of the story time gatherings at the library. "Can I go to Bobby's house to play? His mama said it's okay."

He assumed she was referring to the boy with short brown hair standing beside her. "Hello." He shook hands with the child's mother. "I'm Monte."

"Abigail." She pulled her son's index and middle fingers from his mouth and turned to Evie. "Seems our kiddos hit it off. I'm part of our local moms' club. We get together for park days and playdates. This afternoon, I'm hosting a get-together at my house. You and your daughters are welcome to join us." She glanced Luna's way. "Callie mentioned her twin."

Evie blinked, apparently taken aback. "Oh, I'm not her mother. I'm their aunt's caregiver."

"Cancer," Monte said.

Sympathy lines stretched across Abigail's forehead. "I'm so sorry. I know that can be quite the battle."

"I appreciate that."

"Can I go?" Callie clenched folded hands beneath her chin. "I'll be real good and will mind my manners and not talk too much or interrupt. Or jump on their couch, either."

Her enthusiasm made him smile. "Really, now? Those are some mighty big promises." He bopped her on the nose.

"But I mean it."

He rubbed the back of his neck, thinking through the rest of his day. He wasn't keen on sending his girls off with a woman he didn't know, nor of Evie accompanying them. They'd left Aunt Martha untended long enough. Plus, he still had a lot to take care of, back at the ranch.

"Another day, Cowpoke."

She groaned with an overdramatic slump. "How come?"

He explained and looked at the time on his phone. "Speaking of, we best round up your sister if y'all want to hit the playground before we leave."

Her frown indicated she didn't consider this a fair trade, although her mood lightened considerably when he reminded her about playing in the creek later.

On the drive home, however, she was uncharacteristically quiet.

He glanced at her through the rearview mirror to find her staring out her window. "You all right back there?"

She didn't respond right away, then she released a heavy sigh. "I want a mama like everyone else."

His chest squeezed, and his throat turned tight and scratchy.

Lucy had warned him events like this could remind the girls of what they didn't have. Told him to think about how he might answer their hard questions. But no words, no matter how logical, could ease his little girl's ache.

"I know." His near whisper came out hoarse.

He wanted that for them, too.

CHAPTER SIX

THE DOCTOR WAS at the house when they returned. Seeing his gray station wagon sitting near the shed tightened Monte's muscles with a burst of adrenaline. Had Aunt Martha fallen again? He never should've taken Evie with him and the girls to that Christmas party, especially after her dizzy spell this morning.

What had he been thinking?

Clearly, he hadn't been.

Parking a foot from the porch steps, he looked at Evie. "See to the girls?"

She nodded, her wrinkled brow indicating she sensed his concern. "Everything all right?"

He glanced at his daughters to find their big eyes trained on him. "Yep."

The twins tended to take their emotional cues from him. If he acted all worked up, they'd become frightened. One of the best ways to teach his girls how to have faith was to keep it himself.

Seemed that was all he'd been clinging to, of late.

Stepping out of the truck, he pocketed his keys and ascended the steps two at a time. The front door and screen stood propped open, the interior dim compared to the afternoon sun.

"Aunt Martha?" As he hurried toward her bedroom, a splash of color filled his peripheral vision, along with quiet voices. With a deep inhale, he stopped and turned back around.

Doc Tackett met Monte in the archway separating the living room and kitchen. "Howdy." He wore jeans and a blue, collared shirt.

Aunt Martha sat at the table behind him, looking tired but less so than before her fall. Less discouraged, too.

"Doc. Thanks for coming." He shook the man's hand, then went to his aunt. "You feeling better?"

"Much." She smiled. "The party go well?"

By now Evie and the girls had joined them, and Callie began telling her about pert near every detail of her classroom.

"I made a friend." The child grinned. "We both like climbing trees, catching lizards and making mud pies."

Remembering their morning fiasco, he stole a glance at Evie and was captivated by the soft blush on her cheeks.

Clearing his throat and his head, he turned back to the doctor. "We weren't expecting you until tomorrow."

Doc gave a one-shoulder shrug. "My schedule freed up unexpectedly today. Made plans to go skeet shooting with a buddy of mine that lives one county over. Figured I'd stop in here on the way."

Apparently, this reminded Callie of Monte's promise to take her and her sister to the woods, because she abandoned the story she'd been telling Aunt Martha and dragged her sister off with her to change into playclothes.

Monte slipped a hand into his pocket. "Everything check out?"

Doc looked at Aunt Martha, and his eyes softened. "Don't know yet what her blood work shows, obviously. But considering her numbers last week and her fall this morning..." Straightening, he shifted to face Monte. "She's asked to cancel this week's treatment, and I'm inclined to agree. Give her time to grow stronger."

Monte scrubbed a hand over his face. "Okay." Every delay felt like a setback. While he knew logically her cancer wasn't likely to spread due to a one-week layoff, it didn't alleviate his anxiety any.

Then again, he doubted anything would until he heard the words they were fighting toward—remission.

The doctor gathered his things. "In the meantime, I encourage you to eat foods that naturally help increase blood platelets. Spinach. Broccoli. The Literary Sweet Spot's got a tasty papaya smoothie. With just enough fresh fruit to make the ice cream base healthy."

Aunt Martha sighed. "For a small fortune, I'm sure."

"May do you good to get out of the house now and again." The doctor leveled his gaze on her, then turned to Evie. "On another note, welcome to Sage Creek. I hear you won't be staying long." He made eye contact with Monte. "Make sure she tries a piece of the Herrings' fresh peach cobbler before she leaves."

"Will do." He walked him to the door, his aunt and Evie following. "We really appreciate you stopping by. We know how busy you are. Nurse Geneva out on maternity yet?"

"As of last week, yep. And it sounds like she's not planning on coming back, least not for a few years."

Aunt Martha gave a compassionate shake of her head. "Sorry to hear it. I know how challenging it can be to find compassionate and competent help."

"'Spect you do."

Wasn't that the truth. As far as Monte knew, New Day still hadn't found Evie's replacement. They never came right out and said that, but they hadn't sent him any information on anyone, either. Although, considering what had happened with Ms. Gray, they probably were being extra cautious.

He appreciated that—so long as they sent him someone by the time Evie was fixing to leave.

Monte waited until the doctor got into his car. With a last

wave, he stepped back inside and closed the door. He studied his aunt, struck by how much she'd aged over the past few months. Course, it didn't help how little she was eating.

"You up for a smoothie?" He eyed the browning bananas in the fruit bowl, then faced Evie. "We've got strawberries and blackberries in the freezer. Enough for her and the girls. They'll want a frozen treat, too. But we'll probably need more for the days ahead. If I write you a list, can you hit the grocery store when you get a chance?"

"Absolutely."

By now, the girls had returned dressed in playclothes. As usual, Callie had her butterfly net that she used to catch lizards, frogs and whatever other creepy-crawlies she could find. She'd probably snag the small red cooler still sitting by the porch stairs where she'd last left it. Noting Luna's tote, likely filled with at least one book, he was struck once again by how different those two were.

He expected they'd both start out in their fort, which he'd helped them build in an alcove of trees. That was the only time they'd allowed him near their "secret, girls-only" hideaway. Inevitably, Callie would grow bored of their imaginary play and become engrossed in building a "critter habitat" of sorts from sticks, stones, mud and straw. Meanwhile, her sister would find a smooth rock to sit upon and flip through one of the illustrated nature books borrowed from the library.

"Are you coming, too?" Callie looked up at Aunt Martha with hope-filled eyes.

He could tell she was struggling to respond, probably feeling the same ache he did at how much had changed. But only for a season.

He placed a hand on his daughter's shoulder. "Not today, Cowpoke. Your aunt needs to rest."

"She can rest there, and read books with Luna, like she used to."

"Another time."

Callie's frown deepened. "All she does is sleep. She never does anything fun anymore." She dropped her net on the floor and stormed down the hallway.

Monte wasn't sure what tore at his heart more, seeing his daughter's pain and obvious longing for how things used to be, or the defeated look on his aunt's face.

He reached for her hand and gave it a gentle squeeze. "She'll be all right."

Aunt Martha offered a slight nod.

In situations like this, he wished his kids had a mama to help them process, because he hadn't a clue how to respond. He couldn't make sense of his own emotions half the time.

"Do you mind if I talk with her?" Evie asked.

He released a breath. She must've sensed his inner angst, evident by the fact that his feet remained planted.

He shrugged. "You probably have more experience with these types of things than I do." True, she hadn't worked with kids much, but she'd probably been trained in what to say, or not to say to family members with loved ones fighting cancer.

"I don't know about that, but I have been told I give a mean hug." As if to prove this, she wrapped an arm around Luna, who stood in the center of the kitchen, taking it all in, and pulled her close. Worried expression smoothing into a hint of a smile, the child leaned into her.

He quirked an eyebrow, grateful for the lightened mood. "Mean hug. Isn't that an oxymoron?"

She laughed, a gentle, melodious sound. "Touché."

He watched her leave, his other daughter trailing after her, then turned to his aunt. "Mind if I add one of those protein shakes I bought into your smoothie?"

"That's fine." Her tone indicated she didn't have much of an appetite.

Knowing Evie might be occupied with Callie for a while, he pulled his aunt's food processor from the cupboard and added enough ingredients to fill three glasses.

The whir of the machine mirrored the anxious thoughts swirling through his brain. He'd known going into it that his aunt's battle against cancer would be tough, but he'd not expected the emotional weight of all the unknowns.

His aunt had to feel discouraged. Hearing the doc recommend delaying treatment would've been difficult enough. Then to think her very fight for life was inflicting pain upon the girls she adored more than anything.

They could all use a pick-me-up. Matter of fact, a bit of fresh air would do his aunt good. She had always loved spending time with the twins at the creek. It was a lovely December day. The sky was clear, the sun was out. If only the walk there wasn't so long.

He brightened. She could drive the Side-by-Side. Why hadn't he thought of that sooner?

Feeling like he was about to give Callie a new set of boots, he placed his aunt's drink on the table in front of her, kissed her temple, then hurried to his daughter's room.

The image that greeted him squeezed his chest. Evie sat on the floor, legs stretched in front of her, a twin under each arm. She rested her chin on Callie's head while, on her other side, Luna nestled in close.

"What do you love most about going to the forest with your aunt?"

Callie grinned. "Showing her all my tricks. I can climb trees and hang upside down by my knees, with no hands. She says I'm like a little monkey." She turned serious. "That means strong and fast."

"It feels good to know she's proud of you, doesn't it?"

Callie nodded.

Evie glanced down at Luna and smoothed the hair from her face. "And what do you love most?"

"When she reads to me."

It was probably because of his aunt that his daughter loved books so much. For the same reason Callie enjoyed "showing off." Aunt Martha had a way of making them all feel like they were the most important people in the world.

They felt the same about her.

"Is there another way you can make her proud of you?" Evie asked.

Monte stepped into the room. "Y'all could put on one of your shows for her."

"Yeah!" Callie sprang to her feet. "Like the *Three Little Bears*. Or *Santa Lost His Reindeer*." She continued listing other titles. "Can we have real curtains, like Ms. Vargas's?"

He liked hearing her speak so positively about their classroom. That and their pleasant experience that afternoon should help eliminate any first-day anxiety tears.

He and Evie exchanged an amused smile that felt far too intimate. He was touched to see how much she seemed to genuinely enjoy his girls. Then again, that was her job. She wouldn't be that great a caregiver if she didn't actually care.

Then again, Ms. Gray had played the part and had fooled them all.

But she'd never looked at the twins—or himself—the way Evie did.

What was he doing? He had no business thinking this way, and especially not about someone he'd soon never see again.

Cheeks flushed, he cleared his throat and began tossing stray toys into their bin.

Once certain his blush no longer showed, he told the girls about his forest solution.

"Yay!" Callie once again began skipping around the room, her mouth moving faster than her feet. Calling out to his aunt, the child rushed out with her sister following close behind.

Evie stood. "I'd say that just won you Father of the Year award."

"Maybe if I'd thought of that before the drama..." He laughed to hide the smile her kind words and the note of admiration in her voice triggered.

Considering how he reacted when the woman offered even a hint of a compliment, he'd be wise to limit their time together. Yet, here he was, about to spend the afternoon with her at the creek.

He hoped the girls would provide enough of a distraction to keep him from thinking about things he had no business entertaining.

Like the way Evie's face brightened whenever one of the girls engaged her in conversation. Or how her head tilted ever so slightly when Callie did something silly. Or the way her eyes softened when she looked at his aunt, or seemed to intensify when they shifted in his direction.

As if he intrigued her.

A ridiculous thought. If anything, she was trying to figure him out and what he wanted. He was sort of her boss, after all.

And she was here to save his aunt's life, which was what he needed to focus on.

OUTSIDE, EVIE AND the others waited on the porch while Monte trotted off to get his ATV. Apparently, he'd left it out by the arena. Callie used the slight delay to alternate between jumping off the bottom step and playing fetch with Max. Luna lingered between her and her aunt, glancing from one to the other, before climbing into her aunt's lap.

Had she been contemplating sitting with Evie? The thought caused her heart to swell. Prior to coming here, she'd felt certain kids weren't her thing.

Granted, she was far from an expert—and still had to make it through her end date without the girls experiencing anything catastrophic. She was finding her time here on the ranch much more pleasant than expected.

Unfortunately, she was finding her interactions with Monte more enjoyable than anticipated, or helpful, as well.

Now she had a new concern. Were the twins becoming

too attached to her? She didn't want to set them up for a hard goodbye.

The low rumble of an engine caught her attention. She turned to see Xavier approach in a swirl of dust. Grinning, he stopped in front of the porch, a disarming combination of boyish playfulness and rugged cowboy.

Her breath stalled as an image flashed through her mind of the two of them horse riding across his property, him in front, her arms wrapped around his middle, her cheek pressed to his back.

He had much too strong an effect on her.

This forest adventure was a bad idea.

"I can manage the girls while you take care of whatever you need to on the ranch." The breeze stirred a lock of hair in front of her eye. She swept it away. "I'll text you with any concerns."

He gazed down the dirt road leading to the far side of his property and scratched his jaw. Seemed he didn't want to come any more than she wanted him to, although likely for a vastly different reason. He had a ranch to run, after all, not act as caregiver.

That was why he'd hired her.

On a temporary basis, after which she'd never see him, his aunt or the adorable twins ever again.

The fact that this disappointed her only amplified her concerns regarding this little outing.

He pulled his phone and looked at the screen. "I do need to fix a leak in the hay barn and should probably ride the fence." Her confusion must have shown on her face because he added, "Check for places in need of repair."

She nodded, relieved and disappointed by his response.

And much too pleased when the girls' pleading changed his mind.

Mercy, she was a mess.

He swung a leg over to dismount his vehicle and climbed the porch steps in long, easy strides. "You ready, Aunt Martha?" He reached out a hand to help her rise then walked beside her, to the ATV-like vehicle he referred to as a Side-by-Side.

Evie and the girls followed and lingered, the dogs nearby, as Aunt Martha got settled on the vehicle.

"The dust won't bother you?" Monte asked.

Evie was once again struck by the tenderness he showed his loved ones. But what about his animals? Was what that woman from the party said true?

Granted, she'd seen how kind he'd been to his horses and dogs. Did he treat his bulls differently? How'd he get them to buck, anyway?

How he ran his ranch shouldn't matter, nor would it affect how she did her job. It could, however, temper her attraction to the man.

Compassion for his animals aside, that would be a good thing.

CHAPTER SEVEN

THE NEXT MORNING, Monte followed the scent of cooked bacon and buttery flour into the kitchen. Seemed Evie was already making use of the groceries she'd picked up the evening before.

He paused before entering to smooth his hair, then chastised himself for it—along with the slight spike in his pulse at the thought of encountering Evie.

The woman was his aunt's caregiver, nothing more. Maybe if he told himself that enough, logic would overpower his growing affection toward her.

With a sigh, he turned and stepped into the room, mentally processing the image of his aunt standing at the stove. With her normally slumped shoulders squared, she almost appeared like her formerly strong self.

She glanced at him with a genuine smile. "Morning."

He greeted her with a kiss on the cheek. "You're looking bright-eyed and bushy-tailed. Does this mean you're feeling better?"

"I'm looking forward to a week free of nausea."

He admired her positive outlook, but also worried she might be acting braver than she felt. She had to be frustrated by her delayed treatment, but probably didn't want to increase his anxiety. She always put others first.

Regardless, the delay was temporary—so she could grow stronger.

Doc's advice carried weight. He was as knowledgeable as he was trustworthy, and he loved Aunt Martha near as much as Monte and the girls.

He poured himself a mug of fresh-brewed coffee. The rich aroma soothed him. "The girls still asleep?"

Aunt Martha chuckled. "Oh, my, no. Callie and Luna were up by five thirty and whisked Evie off to help them gather chicken eggs."

"Impressive." And yet one more indication of how much they'd taken to Evie.

As if on cue, the front door clanked open, and enthusiastic voices drifted toward him. The twins and Evie appeared a moment later, the latter carrying a basket half-filled with eggs.

Evie's eyes danced with laughter, as if spending time with the girls brought her joy. She wore her hair down, and he felt an unexpected urge to run his hands through her soft, silky waves.

With a mental shake, he greeted her with a nod he hoped didn't appear rude or awkward and focused on his daughters. "What kind of mischief have y'all been up to this morning?"

Not surprisingly, Luna was already dressed in the newly cleaned—and stain-free—outfit her sister had splattered with mud the day before. Callie, on the other hand, remained in pajamas, which now had bits of straw attached to them.

Frowning, his daughter stomped to the stove. "You didn't wait for the eggs."

Aunt Martha placed steaming bacon onto a paper-towel-covered plate. "Y'all told me you didn't want any this morning, remember? So that you could save tummy space for pancakes."

"I changed my mind."

His aunt placed a hand on Callie's head. "Then this'll be a great lesson on following through on what you say."

Seeing how his daughter was already disappointed, Monte figured it'd be a good time to tell her to change into her school clothes. As expected, she slumped with one of her melodramatic moans but complied.

Shaking her head, his aunt set food on the table. "Someone should sign that child up for acting club. If you can keep her off a bull long enough to get her on the stage."

He laughed. "Now, that would be the challenge of the century." The way Evie was watching him indicated she wanted to say something, so he invited her to do so.

She still seemed hesitant.

"Come on now," he said. "Spit it out."

She placed a pitcher of orange juice on the table. "Are you worried she'll take your statements seriously and wind up bull riding when she gets older?"

He pulled a stack of plates from the cupboard and distributed them at each place setting. "You saying her rodeoing would be a bad thing?"

She lowered her gaze. "I misunderstood. I apologize."

"If you think bull riding is too dangerous for my girls, I'd say so's felling trees, fighting fires and chasing criminals. I wouldn't deter the twins from working in any of those fields. I'd rather teach them to follow their heart, and the good Lord, wherever He leads, than to live enslaved to fear. Or to think that some things are off-limits to females."

"I meant no offense."

"None taken." Her question had been harmless enough. But he'd known what she'd been thinking. Why had her statement gotten him so riled up? It wasn't like he hadn't heard others convey similar thoughts.

However, her comment *did* remind him of why, if he fell in love again, it would be with a woman who loved the country. That was one lesson Erin had taught him well.

Yet, no one had ever directed their statements at his girls, which by association meant at him as a dad. That was an area in which he often felt he failed, especially since his aunt had become sick.

Regardless, he wouldn't raise his girls to believe they weren't fit for certain careers, or to feel compelled to prove their value as females. He'd seen enough cowgirls to know that could lead to reckless behavior more dangerous than getting into the bucking chute.

Besides, he wouldn't act a hypocrite by directing them from an industry in which he invested most of his waking hours.

He sipped his coffee. "I trust so long as I teach them to seek God, when they need to make those types of decisions, He'll show them where and when to step."

"Yes, of course." Poor woman looked like she'd been sent to the feed lot.

He was about to ease the tension invading the room when the twins burst back in, Callie asking about bringing her "laundry rocks" to school.

Evie looked from one person to the next with raised eyebrows. "Laundry rocks?"

Monte chuckled. "Crumpled pieces of paper she sticks in her pocket that get run through the wash. Come out hard and small like pebbles from the driveway."

"I see."

Aunt Martha placed a stack of pancakes in the center of the table and sat. "The first time was an accident. But she liked the results so much, she's been doing it ever since."

"Good info." Evie looked at the child with as much seriousness as if they'd been discussing precious stones. "When I do laundry, I'll make sure to leave your treasures be."

Grinning, Callie climbed into the chair beside her and revealed small, compacted wads in her palm. This led to a discussion on show and tell, an activity that excited both girls. He hoped that would counter any first-day anxiety that could otherwise make it challenging to get them off to school.

"You know, you and the girls should add something fun and

relaxing to your to-do list," Aunt Martha said. "I'm sure Evie would love to experience some of the perks to ranching life." She looked at Evie. "It isn't all mucking stalls and corralling bulls, you know. Y'all should have plenty of extra time, seeing how I won't need a ride to Houston this week."

Once again, Monte wondered if his aunt was trying to find reasons for him and Evie to spend more time together. He suppressed a sigh. Despite the nonexistent state of his love life, he didn't need a matchmaker. Nor did he have any intention of building anything more than a professional relationship with their temporary caregiver.

"Speaking of treatments." He forked a chunk of syrupy pancakes. "Last night, a friend forwarded me information on clinical trials for ovarian cancer. I haven't read through the material yet but will prioritize doing so today."

His aunt frowned and looked at her plate.

Did she think he'd lost faith in her current treatment plan? He shouldn't have said anything until he'd learned more.

Although he shifted the conversation to something more pleasant, the spark he'd seen in her eyes first thing this morning seemed faded.

He sensed she could use a dash of humor this afternoon.

Accompanying Evie as she walked the girls out of the house, he encouraged the twins to give one of their impromptu plays once they returned from school.

"Can you and Ms. Evie be in the show, too?" Luna asked.

Callie jumped up and down. "Yeah! With the stage and curtains, remember?"

He did recall her request that he build her something like that, but not how he had responded. "That'll take time, Cowpoke. I was hoping y'all could pull something together today."

"But that won't be real."

Apparently, her visit to Ms. Vargas's classroom had elevated her expectations.

"You promised," she whined.

While he doubted that, considering he'd forgotten his reply, he felt it best to concede in case she was right. He couldn't teach them to stand by their word if he wasn't willing to do the same.

"Okay. I'll start working on that this afternoon."

Callie skipped ahead, then turned back around to make eye contact with Evie. "Will you make the curtains?"

"I don't have anything to make them with."

"Aunt Martha has a sewing machine and bunches and bunches of fabric in the attic."

"I don't know how to sew."

The girls stared at her with wide eyes, as if this was the strangest thing they'd heard since she told them she'd never attended a rodeo.

Luna slipped her hand into Evie's. "That's okay. They have YouTube videos."

Evie burst out laughing, and the sound was so contagious, soon they all joined her.

"Okay." She gave a quick nod. "I'll see what I can do."

"Yay!" Both girls cheered and started jumping up and down.

Her expression sobered. "Don't get too excited yet. When it comes to anything creative, I'm all thumbs. But I'll do my best."

His heart swelled at the lighthearted interaction the four of them shared. This was precisely the type of moments he'd dreamed of enjoying with his wife. He'd been devastated when she left, and he had decided he was done with women for good. Too bad Evie didn't plan to stick around. She was the type of gal that could make a man rethink how he planned to spend the rest of his life.

ONCE BACK AT the house, Monte excused himself to exercise his bulls and Evie spent the morning cleaning and tending to his aunt. After the doctor's recommendation from the day before, Evie would've expected her to feel discouraged. Yet, she seemed chipper, even energized.

Had the smoothies Evie made for her helped that much? If so, she needed to make sure the Bowmans kept plenty of fruit and protein shakes on hand.

Laundry taken care of, she followed the sound of humming into the living room to find Martha sitting in an armchair, knitting.

This reminded her of the girls' request from that morning.

Martha glanced up as she approached. Smiling, she looked around. "Everything appears all clean and tidy. Might be an opportunity to take some time to yourself. Have you been to the lake, yet? There's a lovely walking path."

"Actually, I was wondering if I could borrow your sewing machine."

"Of course, dear. It's in the attic. The door on the wall across from your bed leads to our storage area. Don't worry, it's not as small and dark as one might expect. But if you're more comfortable, I can ask Monte to retrieve it for you."

"That's not necessary, but thank you."

"We have a lovely fabric store in town. Although I have a lot of unused supplies tucked away in tubs that you're welcome to."

"I appreciate that."

Once in the attic, she was grateful to find it more spacious, and with a flick of a switch, brighter, than she'd anticipated.

An antique chest like the ones people once used as suitcases when they traveled and various other items from a similar time period occupied the corner nearest a small window. Along two walls, numerous tubs stood one on top of the other, and sagging boxes lined the third.

She picked up a Raggedy Ann doll with yellowing fabric, a threadbare foot and a fraying apron. Had this once belonged to Martha? Books, some with thick, maroon or green hard covers, others leatherback, were stacked in front of a pedestal table with a scallop-edged surface and intricately carved legs.

She crossed the room to where a handful of quilts, some pastel, others in vibrant designs, hung from a rack. Behind this stood a series of tubs, some labeled Fabric, others Buttons and Threads, and still others, Patterns. Intrigued, she knelt and opened the latter. Amused by the styles, she imagined for whom Martha might have created the clothing.

Where might they have placed her sewing machine? As she glanced about, she noticed a picture frame lying on the ground beneath an old chair. She picked it up. Although faded by time, the photograph was of a slightly younger Monte, on his wedding day. He was leaning in to kiss a woman with long blond hair, wearing an elegant white gown with intricate beading and lace flowers.

That had to be his ex.

The two looked so happy. What had happened between them?

Did he still love her?

It wasn't her business.

She returned the frame and continued her search for Martha's sewing machine. Ten minutes later, she'd found it and also some forest green velvety fabric that would make great stage curtains. With the cloth draped over her shoulder, she started to carry the machine down the retractable stairs but then thought better of it.

She wouldn't be able to run after Callie, were she to stumble and twist her ankle, nor did she want to accidentally drop and break Martha's machine. She'd ask Monte to bring it down for her when he came home.

In the hall, she paused, a jolt shooting through her at the sound of his voice. Resisting the smile tugging on her mouth, she forced confidence into her steps and strode down the hall toward the kitchen.

"I know it's been a difficult journey."

The concern in his tone halted her before she rounded the corner.

"I'm missing so many precious moments with the girls." Martha sounded deflated.

"They understand. And once you beat this thing, you and the twins will have plenty of time together. Just keep fighting for a little longer."

"I don't have any fight left."

"You're just tired."

"It's more than that. I don't want to spend however few days—"

"Years. Decades, probably."

"You remember what the oncologist said. Even if—"

"He was just being cautious. You know how doctors are. They've got to tell you about the worst-case scenario. But he doesn't know you like I do. You can do this."

"I don't want to waste the rest of my life lying around in bed. I want to enjoy the girls while I still can."

Evie turned the corner to see Monte kiss his aunt's cheek. "You're probably hungry."

He glanced up as Evie entered, and setting the fabric on a nearby counter, she asked for help lugging the machine down, after she'd just assured Martha she could manage that herself.

"No problem." He dashed out and returned with the machine as if it were as light as a box of cereal. He placed it in the center of the table. "Think you could make my aunt a shake—with protein added?"

She donned her widest, most encouraging smile. "I would love to. Would you like one as well?"

He looked at the time on the microwave. "You know what? Why not? I could use a break."

They occupied the next hour or so sharing stories—mostly about when Monte was a little boy. He'd spent a good deal of his summers at his aunt's and, apparently, had been as energetic as Callie. He'd also fantasized about becoming an entomologist when he grew up. Then, of becoming a pilot, then an astronaut, and finally, a country-Western singer.

Laughing, he shook his head. "That last one is hilarious, considering how much I hate standing in front of crowds. Meaning, groups with more than five people." He looked at his aunt. "You should have given me a reality check."

"I had no intention of teaching you not to pursue your dreams. I knew the good Lord, your passions and life experiences would lead you where you needed to go. Not that I ever thought that would be to a ranch in Texas."

He turned to Evie. "I grew up in the Golden State."

Her eyebrows shot up. "Really?" He didn't seem the Californian type.

"Son of a teacher and an accountant."

"How'd you get into the rodeo world?"

"Had a friend who lived out of town. His parents raised horses and were deep into local cowboy culture. Didn't take me long to catch the bug." He snatched a cookie from a plateful Martha had placed in the center of the table. "But I didn't ride bulls until I came to Texas for college. Started on a dare."

His aunt rolled her eyes. "It's only by God's grace y'all are still breathing, with how you boys used to challenge one another." She looked at Evie. "Thankfully, he always told me after the fact." She leveled a gaze on her nephew. "I suspect you only shared a fraction of your escapades."

He chuckled. "Didn't want to give you too much cause to worry."

This led to all the ways Callie was similar, which his aunt joked was God's way of getting him back for all the lack of sleep he'd caused her.

Monte gulped down the last of his smoothie and stood. "Guess I best get back to it." He faced Evie. "Walk me out?"

Her pulse increased a notch, and she fought a silly smile threatening to break through. She nodded and followed him to the porch.

He released a sigh. "Seems my aunt could use more encouragement than I realized." Rubbing the back of his neck, he gazed into the distance, then brightened. "I've got an idea. I'll build us a bonfire tonight. Got me a sizeable burn pile I need to take care of anyway. I'll bring my guitar and we can sing silly songs, roast marshmallows and make s'mores."

"You play?"

"Just for fun."

Could this man be any more charming?

He must've taken her delay as disinterest, because he added, "If you don't want to come—"

"No, that sounds fun." She'd spoken with too much enthusiasm. Heat seeped into her face. "I love spending time with your girls."

And you.

She shouldn't be thinking that way. Why was it so difficult to remember that she was here for a brief period of time—perhaps even shorter, if his aunt decided to stop treatment.

If that occurred, Evie could be gone by week's end.

CHAPTER EIGHT

MONTE WAS CHECKING his cattle for illness and injury when he saw Evie drive by, heading to pick up the girls.

Was it that time already? The day sure seemed to be galloping by, and he hadn't even made it through half his herd. His periodic trips to the house, including nearly an hour for lunch, hadn't helped his chore list any.

But he'd been concerned for his aunt.

While that was true, it didn't explain why he found himself looking for Evie the moment he stepped inside. Nor why he had to fight an almost goofy grin whenever she engaged him in conversation, regardless of the subject.

Had he ever reacted this way with the twins' mom? In the beginning, maybe. Toward the end, their interactions had more frequently brought sorrow than joy as he slowly came to realize his love wasn't enough to hold her.

Would she have stayed, had he been willing to give up his PBR dreams?

Would he have?

She'd never given him the chance, which proved she'd set her heart on leaving. She'd never been the country-loving type.

That was a trait Evie shared, it seemed, which was the very

reason he remained focused on his bulls despite a ridiculous urge to chase after her now.

He'd just finished inspecting the leg of a limping derby, unfortunately one of his more athletic, when his daughter called out to him.

Wiping dust from his hands, he jogged across the pasture and through the gate to wait for them. Luna raced toward him and reached him out of breath, face red. Callie followed at a pace much slower than usual.

"Well, now, look who blew in with the tumbleweeds." Grabbing them beneath their arms, he lifted the girls one after the other, swung them in the air, then dropped them, laughing, to their feet. "You have fun at school?"

Luna nodded and told him about all the art supplies she'd used and books she'd read.

By now Evie, who'd followed at a more casual pace, had joined them, her eyes gleaming with amusement. Honey-toned streaks in her strawberry blond hair shimmered in the sun.

"That sounds like quite a day." He turned to Callie. "What about you? Was it as boring as you'd thought?"

She shrugged and squatted down, picked up a stick and began to draw in the dirt.

Not the enthusiasm he'd hoped for, but at least she didn't say she hated it. "Make any friends?"

"Sort of."

Either the child was plumb tuckered out or she was in a funk about something. Had someone teased or excluded her? "Did you play with anyone at recess?"

Her eyes brightened as she launched into a story about challenging her classmates to races and rolling down the sloping hill behind the school.

He quirked an eyebrow at her. "That explains the grass streaks on your outfit."

She glanced at her jeans. "Sorry."

He couldn't say her appearance surprised him. That child

could soil an outfit faster than she could walk out the door. Almost made him wonder why he didn't just let her wear her playclothes.

But Aunt Martha would never let Callie leave the house looking like a prairie dog digging through the turnip patch, as she liked to say.

"Dirt, fabric and little girls wash up well enough." He bopped her on the nose.

She scrunched her face, probably thinking of her upcoming bath.

That was his Callie.

After some prodding, whatever mood she'd arrived home with lifted, and she began jabbering on about what the other students brought for lunch.

"*Everyone* gets juice boxes?" he asked.

"Unless they buy chocolate milk. Only Pete said it smelled bad, so nobody wanted any." She was halfway through a story about a boy who stole someone else's dessert when Max caught her attention.

She darted off toward him.

Reaching the porch, Monte shook his head. "To think, in ten years or so, I'll hardly get a word out of her, if what folks with teenagers say is true."

Evie laughed. "I can't imagine that child holding her tongue at any age."

"Good point." Taking Luna by the hand, he led the way up the steps and into the house, pleased to see his aunt in the living room working on one of her scrapbooks. Lucy had encouraged her to do things that brought her joy as a way of increasing her resiliency.

That reminded him… "Y'all up for a good ol' weenie roast for supper?" He relayed his bonfire idea.

"It won't be too cold?" Aunt Martha asked.

"Not with jackets. Weather app said high fifties."

His aunt's face lit up. "That sounds lovely. Let me check on our chocolate bar stash."

Hand cupped over his mouth, he leaned toward Evie, and her soft floral scent momentarily halted his thoughts. "She's got a secret hiding place, so the girls can't get to it."

"Smart. If you're out, I can run to the store."

"Sounds good."

He really had no logical reason to stick around, not with the amount of ranch work he still needed to tackle. His reluctance to leave didn't make much more sense, either.

Nor would he waste time considering the emotions emerging behind it.

"Guess I best get." He gave Luna a sideways hug, hollered an *I love you* to his aunt, and spent the next couple hours trying to focus on his herd. But his thoughts kept pinging between Evie, who always made him smile, and his aunt, which knotted his stomach.

He understood how tough everything had been for her, physically. He knew well how devastating it must've felt when she first learned her cancer had returned. That news had nearly wrecked them all. He also realized how, considering the what-ifs conveyed with her diagnosis, she might feel as if too much was stacked against her.

But she couldn't quit treatment.

Father, give her strength. Please.

The girls had already lost their mother. They couldn't lose their beloved aunt as well.

He wouldn't let that happen.

Eyeing a truck that belonged to one of his ranch hands, parked a few feet from his, he scanned his property for sight of the guy. Hopefully he was repairing that rotten pole barn post. Travis was handy that way. Tended to be intuitive with the bulls, too. Had a gut instinct as to which were the winners and which they needed to send to auction.

With the man's help, with Monte's growing experience and

what was looking to be a genetically solid herd, his animal athletes stood a shot at bringing in sizable earnings. Then, maybe he could hire a full-time nanny.

Evie's smiling face popped into his mind. With a mental shake, he returned to the pasture and the bull he'd been inspecting prior. Noting swelling, he abandoned his hopes that the issue would resolve itself and called the vet.

He explained what he'd found and when he first noticed it. "Thought maybe he needed a shot of Lutalyse."

"He competing this weekend?"

"No, thank goodness." Although he had hoped to enter the bull into the Christmas charity event he planned to take Evie and the girls to.

"Okay. Because I might not be able to come out until early next week. Unless I can squeeze in a stop by your place on my way to the Johnson ranch."

"That sounds great."

"Need me to call before I come?"

"Nah. If I'm not around, one of my ranch hands will be." The less fuss he caused, the more likely the doc would find room in his already busy schedule.

He'd barely hung up when his phone chimed a text. Seeing it was Evie, he grinned, then chuckled when he read her question. Seemed the girls were trying to hornswoggle her into believing they always had ice cream with their s'mores, and Evie wanted to know if he thought it too cold for that.

He replied with a series of laughing emojis that soon led to a hilarious GIF exchange.

One that had him looking forward to the evening much more than he should've been—and every night after.

Until it came time for her to leave.

EVIE PLACED GRAHAM CRACKERS, chocolate bars, marshmallows and thermoses of hot cocoa into one of Martha's totes.

She'd moved to the fridge to gather condiments for hot dogs when her phone rang.

She glanced at the number on her screen, smiled and answered. "Savannah! How are you? Still causing mischief in Memphis?"

"You know me. Always got to play big." Savannah laughed and shared a few of her most recent escapades, most of which involved food. "How's life in the country? Met any handsome cowboys yet?"

An image of Monte's easy grin and hazel eyes came to mind, sending a rush of heat to her face. She shook it off with a nervous chuckle and shifted the conversation to a much safer topic—the children. "Callie is as wild-spirited as she is adorable. One of these days, she's liable to find her way into one of the pastures and try to climb onto a bull's back."

"Sounds like you've got quite an assignment. Guess you're glad it'll be over soon."

Her heart sank at the thought, but then she reminded herself of her long-term goals. "I'm just hoping next time, they'll place me somewhere close to a reputable nursing college."

"Actually, that's why I'm calling. Mr. McGee asked me if I'm interested in going to Philadelphia for an extended gig. While he wouldn't promise anything, he said to plan on at least nine months, and likely longer. Isn't that one of the cities you put on your preference list?"

She felt a burst of excitement tempered by a twinge of sadness knowing her time in Sage Creek would soon come to an end. Yet, why hadn't their boss called her? "Yeah. When is the start date?"

"Ten days from now."

"That's quick. And so close to Christmas."

"I don't know the full story, but the grandson caring for the woman suddenly decided it's more than he can manage on his own."

"Alzheimer's?"

"Dementia. It's a part-time deal but with full room and board, obviously. Figured it'd be perfect for you, with you wanting to go to school and all."

"Only problem is my replacement isn't due for another couple of weeks." That was probably why their boss hadn't reached out to her.

"Think you can finagle an earlier end date? Maybe talk the family you're with into cutting you loose early? That wouldn't leave them on their own for long. Didn't they manage well enough between when they sent Tracy packing and you arrived?"

Monte probably would let her leave early if she told him why. "I doubt Mr. McGee would be open to that."

"Oh, I don't know. You *have* bailed him out a few times when others dropped the ball. Your current placement is proof of that. Seems to me, he may be willing to accommodate you just to keep you happy. So you'll stick around. You *are* one of his better, and longest-lasting, caregivers."

There tended to be a high turnover rate in this field, mainly because people eventually tired of all the travel. She also knew Mr. McGee wanted her to earn her nursing degree almost as much as she did. That was, if she remained with New Day. Contractually, she'd have to, if she accepted the company's tuition reimbursement.

This conversation was causing a hollowed feeling in her gut. From guilt, or was she disappointed at the prospect of leaving the ranch earlier than anticipated?

If so, that was one reason she felt tempted to follow Savannah's suggestion. The longer she stayed, the harder it would be to leave when the time came. But she wasn't willing to do anything that might add to Monte and his family's stress. Integrity demanded she honor her commitment.

She'd simply have to trust that God would present her with something even better than the Philadelphia placement—in His perfect timing. She'd log into the company database this week to review other upcoming opportunities. Hopefully, another city with a great nursing college would be listed soon.

But it still stung to think her being here had prevented her from what sounded like a perfect assignment.

Callie burst in and began rummaging through the cupboard where the Bowmans kept their food storage containers. Leaving a handful of bowls and tubs scattered on the floor, she darted into the pantry. All her clattering suggested she was making another mess.

Evie didn't know whether to feel frustrated or amused. "I've got to go before one of the munchkins breaks something. Or hurts herself."

She ended the call and went to Callie, who stood on the chair, on tiptoes, reaching for a galvanized bucket. "Need help?"

The child nodded. "Can you get that down for me?" She pointed. "I want to make an ocean habitat."

Evie immediately thought of the mud experience. At least Callie was wearing her playclothes. "I love your creativity." She surveyed the items already pulled from the shelves, imagining the living room in a similar state. "How about you choose one container and put the rest away. Then, if you give me a minute to check on your aunt—"

"She's talking to Ms. Lucy on the phone."

Evie nodded. "Then, we can design something together."

Callie frowned and angled her head as if not entirely pleased with the suggestion—most likely because of the tidying up it involved. But the activity won out. With Luna joining, the three of them traipsed outside to gather twigs, brush and whatever other nature items the girls found useful.

This soon led to the twins searching under rocks for bugs.

By the time Monte returned home and everyone headed out for the bonfire, the sun was sinking beneath the distant tree line and painting the sky in vibrant pinks and purples.

Wearing jackets, the girls rode ahead on Side-by-Side with

Aunt Martha, who sported a scarf around her neck. This led Evie and Monte to stroll through the grasslands alone, an action their beautiful surroundings made much too intimate. Carrying a tote filled with s'mores supplies, she eyed the guitar hanging from a strap over his shoulder.

She was anxious to hear him sing. Not that she needed reasons to find him more endearing.

Averting her thoughts, she plucked up a long blade of straw and began snapping it into smaller pieces. "It sure is peaceful out here." She inhaled the clean-smelling air. "It's almost like God feels closer, know what I mean?"

He smiled. "I do. That's one of the things I love most about ranching. It's a lot easier to hear from God when there isn't a lot of noise competing for my attention. Makes life a lot... clearer, and whatever steps He leads me to take, firmer."

"I admire your desire to follow Christ."

"Figure that's a necessity in my business. It comes with a lot of uncertainty and unknowns. A man can do everything right, working hard from sunup to sundown, and still land himself in debt. But with one talented bull, he can become wildly successful as well."

"Sort of like coaching humans, huh?"

He laughed. "That's exactly what it's like. Always hoping for the Olympic champion, running the drills, building the endurance. Praying for the day when talent, drive and preparation merge into the next superstar. The hard truth is, I can't afford to invest in every calf. Each year, I have to cull my herd, trusting God will help me know which ones to auction and which to train."

She raised her eyebrows. "Train?"

He nodded. "They need to learn when to turn it on, when to chill. How to behave themselves in the bucking chutes."

"Interesting. What makes for a great bull?"

"They're scored on spin, how high they kick, that sort of

thing. But the champions are intuitive. They sense when the cowboy's weight shifts, and react accordingly."

They reached the top of his property, where Monte had built a sizable mound of branches and twigs. Aunt Martha and Luna were sitting side by side, each on one of the stumps positioned as chairs while her sister climbed a nearby tree.

Upon seeing her dad, Callie raced over. "Can I help light the fire?"

"Yep." He led the way to the wood debris, and soon, orange and red flames danced against the darkening horizon.

Sitting with Callie to her left, Monte to her right, Evie took a slow, deep breath. "The smell of smoke reminds me of my church camp days, back when I was a little girl."

He pierced a marshmallow with his roasting stick. "Happy memories?"

She chuckled. "Mostly, minus a belly ache or two."

Initially, he led them in silly songs about bellowing bullfrogs and slippery soap, adapting the lyrics to whatever phrase one of the girls tossed out.

Laughing, Evie joined in. "Then along came a salamander, slithering up the tree then down, before falling to the ground." She could get used to evenings like this.

"Bam!" Callie sprang to her feet and clapped her hands.

Everyone laughed.

Evie had done a lot of that lately. It felt good to be silly. She couldn't remember the last time she'd allowed her playful side to emerge.

Maybe she needed to view the Philadelphia gig and her time in Sage Creek differently. Less like a letdown and more like something of a God-given vacation.

Minus chasing after a wiggly, squiggly, easily bored little girl, not that she minded. In fact, she'd enjoyed every moment much more than she'd expected. Plus, she wasn't having any trouble getting her steps in. That was an unexpected bonus she couldn't say when caring strictly for the elderly.

"Daddy?" Luna's face glowed in the light of the campfire. "Can you sing the song you wrote for my birthday?"

Monte smiled and slowed the tempo. A tranquil hush fell over the space as he began to sing about his love for his daughter. He spoke of the moment he first held her, of the overwhelming emotions that had invaded his heart. He relayed the day she released her grip on his finger to stumble forward into her first steps. Of hearing her first words and watching her appreciation for beauty draw her to the wildflowers sprouting along the fence line.

Looking from one twin to the next, he broadened the verse to include them both:

"I'll always fight for you. See the best in you.
And when your legs feel ready to give way,
By your side I'll always stay,
I'll take you by the hand,
Lend my strength till you can stand,
Until the bright rays of dawn break through."

Tears stung Evie's eyes, feeling, through his words, the depth of love he felt for the twins.

What would it feel like to have someone sing like that to her?

Maybe someday, she'd find out. Although her gut told her there weren't many men like Monte in the world.

CHAPTER NINE

SATURDAY MORNING, AFTER tending to the animals, Monte invited the girls to help build their stage. They urged Evie to join them, evidence of how quickly they'd become attached to her.

He could understand why. She was kind, gentle, attentive and witty. And unlike his ex-wife, she wasn't afraid to act silly. He recalled the night before, her melodious laughter, and the soft glow of the campfire's light on her face.

For a moment, he'd fantasized about sending the girls and Aunt Martha back to the house, so that he could have Evie to himself. Then, of holding her hand as they walked back together under the starry night sky.

He needed to stop thinking that way.

"You girls want to help me drive in some nails?" He handed them each a hammer, set a large sheet of plywood on top of two pallets he'd placed side by side, then motioned them over. He gave them a nail then marked Xs where they'd drive them, with enough room apart so that they wouldn't accidentally whack one another. "Watch your fingers, now."

Taking her father's advice to heart, Luna gently tapped while Callie, ever the risk-taker, used enough force to make him wince. "Careful, Cowpoke. You'll need all ten digits for mutton busting."

"This weekend?"

He shook his head. "Next."

She groaned. "That's a long way away."

He chuckled. "Forever. I know."

"Can we practice?"

He and Evie exchanged an amused look, her smile making him feel like they'd just shared a moment. "How do you figure, seeing how we don't have any sheep?"

"Sebastian does. He's in my class, and we're best friends."

"Are you now?"

She nodded. "We both like playing with our dogs and catching crawfish and eating strawberry ice cream. And running fast at recess."

He smiled, picturing the two of them racing up and down the hill behind the school building.

"Well, now." Evie raised a brow. "That sounds like a match made in heaven."

Callie nodded. "He wants me to come to his house to play, only he's not sure his mom will let me. She gets grumpy when he acts too rowdy or doesn't listen like he should."

"I hear that," Monte teased.

His daughter used her forearm to swipe her hair out of her face. "He's probably afraid we'll have too much fun and he'll forget the rules."

Evie laughed. "An understandable concern."

His daughter set down her hammer and looked at Monte. "Can you come? Then you could watch us and his mom wouldn't have to worry."

Invite himself to someone else's home? That sounded all kinds of awkward. "I'll think about it."

"Can we go after supper?"

"Nope. Got someone coming to learn bull riding."

"Ms. Evie can take me."

He shook his head. "It's her off night, remember?"

"No fair. I wish I had a mama. Then I could go see friends whenever I wanted."

A lump lodged in his throat at the thread of truth to her words. While having a mother wouldn't give her the limitless social life she claimed, he figured her lack had probably cost her more than a few playdates. He'd heard the ladies at church making plans with one another often enough to know that. He doubted any of them excluded his girls intentionally. They were simply friends who met on occasion and brought their kids along.

Was Callie merely frustrated that he hadn't responded to her request as she'd hoped? Or did she know about those get-togethers and feel left out?

If so, what could he say to help her understand without hurting her further?

His aunt would probably tell him it was time he started dating. When was he supposed to do that? He was having a tough enough time managing everything as it was. Besides, he didn't want to subject the girls to more loss. What if he became involved with someone, his daughters grew attached, and then the lady bailed?

They'd already had one woman walk out on them.

No one spoke for a while after that, the steady clanging of metal against metal almost loud in the absence of conversation.

"Mind if I play some music?" Evie raised her phone.

"Not at all."

He was intrigued when she played something from the seventies.

He paused to listen. "Reminds me of the summer I worked at an ice cream store. The owner had a track of maybe ten songs he cycled through. That era was one of them. Played so often, lyrics rolled through my head at the oddest times."

She laughed. "Hope I'm not bringing back traumatic memories."

"Nah. Those were fun times."

"This music reminds me of summer road trips with my grandmother."

"Y'all go anywhere exciting?"

"She thought so, although my ten-, eleven-and twelve-year-old self didn't appreciate quilt museums, historical homes and factory tours as much as she did. Yet, just being with her made everything fun. Special. The long car rides included. Probably because I had a captive audience." She threw him a playful grin.

"You were a big talker, I take it?"

"Oh, my, yes. She called me her little storyteller. Said I could spin a tale better than Shakespeare himself. Except mine were true. Mostly."

"No wonder you and my Callie get along so well." He winked at his daughter, who'd looked up upon the mention of her name. "You and your grandmother close?"

"We were. She passed a few summers ago. Heart attack."

"Sorry to hear that." She probably understood, in a way Tracy Gray had never seemed to, all the emotions he and his girls felt related to his aunt's diagnosis. He hated knowing Evie could relate to their pain but was grateful to think this would intensify her desire to fight for his aunt's life.

Her being here now, helping build this stage—and agreeing to the children's performance plans—was evidence of that.

To think he'd been so frustrated when she first arrived. Now he was beginning to wonder if God had sent her here as a gift.

Too bad she wasn't staying.

But would she—could she—if asked? Seemed that might be the most efficient option for everyone. Why go through the trouble of sending someone to replace her, unless she was already scheduled somewhere else.

She most likely was. He sighed and checked the time on his phone. Brushing dust from his hands, he straightened. "Best corral my bulls into the sorting alleys so I'm ready for the kid coming to ride."

Callie sprang to her feet. "Can we come?"

"Don't see why not."

"Yay!"

Luna appeared equally excited, although, unlike her sister, her feet remained planted on the ground. She turned to Evie. "Are you coming, too?"

Assuming she'd rather spend the rest of the day relaxing, he started to give her an out.

She responded before he could.

"That sounds interesting." Her bright-eyed grin indicated she wasn't just trying to be polite.

Maybe country life was growing on her.

He rested a hand on his belt buckle. "You sure?"

She nodded. "I'd love to see more of what you do."

She may as well have said she was interested in *him*, with how her statement accelerated his pulse—a reaction he immediately chastised himself for. Why did his heart and head keep toying with thoughts of something that would never be?

Smiling, Luna slipped her hand into Evie's while Callie darted ahead. After a few paces, she turned back around. "Are you going to run them, too?"

He gazed at the nearby pasture. "May not be a bad idea to tucker them out some."

Evie's eyes widened, probably envisioning him chasing after the massive creatures on foot.

He stifled a laugh. "On ATVs."

Her taut expression indicated she didn't find that prospect any less concerning. But she didn't say anything or make a dash for the house.

After he'd circled the pasture a few times, the girls giggling and whooping him on, the bulls darting this way and that, Evie's posture had relaxed considerably.

He'd even caught an amused glint in her eye a time or two.

He had just parked near the arena when his phone chimed a text from Ian.

Monte looked at Evie. "Y'all want to go for a spin? The guy I'll be working with tonight's going to be late." And hadn't bothered to let him know until five minutes before he was due to arrive. Then again, his uncle had indicated the young man wasn't the most responsible in town.

Her eyes widened, and her hand flew to her neck. "Oh, no. I couldn't possibly."

"I do! I do!" The twins jumped up and down, chanting in unison.

"Come on, then." He motioned for them to follow him.

"Wait." Evie darted after them. "How about we go inside for some cookies. And I'll help you build a fort, or we could play that bouncing hippo game you both like so much." Her words tumbled out so fast, she seemed to run out of breath.

Actually, she looked near terrified.

Did she think he meant on a bull?

He stifled a chuckle. "I meant on ATVs."

Her cheeks turned the most endearing shade of pink. "Oh. Right." She offered a shy smile. "That sounds fun. If you've got time."

"Yep. Got our two-seaters in the equipment shed."

As expected, Callie had made it halfway there before the rest of them reached the chicken coop.

Luna slipped her hand into Evie's once again, an action Monte was apt to feel jealous of, if he didn't keep his head on straight.

"Ms. Evie," his daughter said, "can I ride with you?"

A lump lodged in his throat at the tender, almost maternal way Evie looked down at his child. "I would love that."

If only he could meet someone like her in Sage Creek, he'd be more inclined to follow his aunt's dating advice.

But something told him finding a woman like Evie was about as rare as raising a PBR superstar.

WITH EVIE ON the ATV, the engine rumbling beneath her and vibrating her handlebars, Luna climbed on behind her and grabbed on to either side of her seat.

Beside them, Monte and Callie idled on a similar vehicle, a 2UP, he called it. "Ready to kick up dirt?"

A burst of excitement erupted into a wide grin. She glanced back to find her little friend smiling just as wide, eyes bright. "What do you say? Think we can take them?"

Her thin brow furrowed. "Where?"

Monte laughed. "She means race us, peanut. And to that, we'd say…" With a mischievous twist of his mouth, he revved his engine and the two of them took off.

"Hey, no fair!" Turning the throttle, she followed as fast as her newbie nerves allowed.

Initially, she tensed with every jostling pothole, slowing when rounding the corner. By the time they reached the far pasture, blessedly free of bulls, she gained confidence to accelerate to twenty-five miles per hour.

She loved the feel of the crisp wind on her face and blowing through her hair and the scent of the earth swirling up around her.

Dropping back to meet her, Monte gave her a thumbs-up sign. "There you go!"

Behind him, Callie extended her legs and chanted, "Faster! Faster!"

Monte continued to match Evie's speed. It felt like they were experiencing this moment together, as if he was enjoying spending time with her.

She'd once read that shared adventures formed and strengthened bonds. Was that why she felt increasingly drawn to him now?

Did he feel the same connection to her that she was feeling, at this moment, to him and the girls?

That was ridiculous, of course. If anything, he was delighting in his children and some good, clean fun, and nothing more.

She needed to view this little jaunt in the same way.

Yet, her experience with Monte *was* revealing something she'd sensed increasingly during the past year—she was tired of living single. She longed for someone with whom she could share laughter, frustrations, tears and dreams. And God willing, children to fill their home with giggles, silly songs and ATV rides in the country.

But there was a problem. Rural settings didn't tend to have nursing colleges, and she couldn't give up her goal to earn a degree, even if he were to ask—and she highly doubted he ever would.

If she detoured from her plans and things didn't work out between her and Monte, or any man, for that matter, she could easily land in a hot mess, financially speaking.

Nearing the tree line, Monte slowed. "Probably should head back now. See if my bull-riding student actually showed."

She nodded. "I better check on Aunt Martha. And get supper started." She was thinking of trying a new recipe she'd found online.

Monte chuckled when Luna's groan matched her sister's. "Another time."

The thought sent a jolt through Evie, and she fought against an overly enthusiastic smile.

Focusing on the pasture ahead instead of her growing feelings for Monte, which she had no intention of exploring or feeding further, she accompanied him back to the arena. As he'd predicted, a tall, broad-shouldered guy who didn't look much older than eighteen, was waiting for him.

He wore dingy blue jeans that seemed to hang from his frame, boots and a sweatshirt that sagged sideways. Chin-length black hair extended at least three inches beneath his sweat-stained ballcap.

Monte introduced him as Ian, a friend's nephew. "This here's Evie Bell. Drove down from Dallas."

She gave a nod. "But I'm originally from Grand Rapids, Michigan."

The guy widened his stance. "River City, huh? What brought you to Sage Creek?"

Monte answered for her. "She's taking care of my aunt for a spell."

"Speaking of, I should probably check on her now."

Feet on the bottom rail of the arena gate and hands gripping the top, Callie hung backwards. "Can we stay with you, Daddy?"

"So long as you're not underfoot and don't go running off without asking."

Luna looked from her dad to Evie, as if torn between the two. But then, probably looking forward to some extra time with her father, chose to remain. The fact that Evie factored into her decision at all touched her.

She returned to the house to find Aunt Martha in the kitchen, singing along to Southern gospel playing from an old-fashioned, portable radio. She wore a red-and-green checked apron and her hair was pulled back beneath a silky green bandanna. Flour, sugar, a mixing bowl and other items cluttered the counter to the right of the sink. To her left, she'd set out vegetables, a cutting board and a chunk of some type of meat wrapped in butcher paper.

She glanced over as Evie entered. "Hello, dear. Y'all sure seemed to be having fun out there this afternoon." She motioned with her spatula to the window. "The girls will build up an appetite tonight. I'm making their favorite. Beef potpie. And pound cake drizzled with cherry pie filling for dessert."

"Sounds delicious." Evie went to wash her hands. "I've not made any of those before, but I'm a quick learner. Just tell me what to do."

When the oven beeped, Martha placed a cake pan filled with creamy yellow batter inside and set the timer.

"I've got this." She waved a hand. "You go enjoy more of that lovely evening air. I'm rather enjoying myself. It does a heart good to make food for one's family, don't you think?"

Evie couldn't say, as she hadn't had that experience yet, unless one counted the times her parents had forced her to cook during her teenage years. Back then, she would've much preferred to spend time with her friends.

But she could see how much pleasure Martha was experiencing doing something that she might not have felt well enough to do previously.

While Evie knew that if pushed, the woman would allow her to participate, she also sensed Martha preferred to be left alone to create. And, based on the way she'd been singing a moment ago, to connect with God.

"Okay," Evie said. "If you're sure."

"I am."

She watched her for a moment longer, happy to see Martha's increased energy and enthusiasm. This was quite a change from the day she'd fallen. Was this due to the smoothies she'd been drinking or the break in her treatment?

Maybe both.

Hopefully, it would last. The woman deserved every drop of joy and vigor possible.

Of course, it hadn't slipped Evie's notice that Martha also seemed particularly pleased whenever she and Monte spent time together.

Apparently, both her and Martha's hearts were struggling to remember how fast Evie's departure date was approaching.

Discarding the thought, she stepped onto the porch and gazed toward the arena. A few bulls waited, seemingly calm, in the alley, as Monte called it, while he stood in a nearby grassy patch next to Ian. It looked like Monte was showing his student, who sat on a big stability ball, body positioning and drills.

Appreciating the pleasant temperatures, which were considerably warmer than Michigan's winters, she decided to use her unexpected free time to catch up on some reading. Her mom had recommended a book from a new author and would probably want to talk about it when they next spoke. Evie loved those discussions as much as her mom.

Sitting in the rocking chair near the end of the porch, she rested her feet on the edge of a flowerpot and opened her phone's e-reader. A few chapters in, something the heroine said reminded her of her conversation with her coworker.

She decided to check the company database.

Only about half a dozen open assignments were listed. Unfortunately, two started before her current placement ended. One was for a small town in Arkansas she'd never heard of, and another wouldn't begin for six weeks. The final listing wasn't in a bad location, but it would only last for one month. Still, it might be a good backup, because while she'd love to hold out for a Philadelphia-type assignment, she did have bills to pay.

Calling her boss, she stood and rested her elbows on the porch railing, her eyes on the horse stables and surrounding pastures.

Expecting his voice mail, she was surprised when he picked up. "Evie, hello. How are things in the Lone Star State?"

"Fine, thank you." She broached the subject of future assignments.

"Things are a tad slower than we'd expected. Has rural living grown on you any?"

Monte has.

The thought jolted her and was entirely unwelcome. "It has its pluses."

"Enough that you might give the opening in Arkansas a harder look? I know you're aiming for the city, and we'll get you there. May not be this year, but I promise you this—we won't forget your preferred list, or how you filled in for the Bowmans."

"That's what frustrates me. Knowing my coming here cost me such a great location, in terms of my long-term career goals. And as far as Arkansas goes, you know I prefer to avoid small towns." Although she had to admit, this ranch had grown on her. "Current placement aside," she amended.

"I get it, and I'll do everything in my power to see you in an area with a fabulous nursing school."

"I appreciate that." Rubbing her temple, she ended the call.

Determining not to let what felt like an unfair setback dampen an otherwise lovely day, she released a breath and turned around to find Monte standing near the steps.

Based on his tense expression, he'd caught at least part of her conversation and wasn't pleased. Why would he be? She might as well have said that she regretted coming here.

Her stomach felt queasy, almost like she'd betrayed a friend.

He looked at her a moment longer, then turned and left without a word.

Oh, well. Maybe his overhearing her wasn't entirely a bad thing—if it provided the emotional distance she was struggling to maintain.

CHAPTER TEN

SUNDAY MORNING, MONTE returned from feeding the animals to find Evie and the twins in the kitchen. The girls stood on chairs pulled up to the counter, Evie positioned between them. Luna was already in her church dress, her hair brushed. Not surprisingly, Callie remained in her pajamas and displayed a comical flurry of bedhead.

Evie had her wavy locks up in one of those clippy deals, loose spirals escaping. She wore a pink skirt that hit just below her knees, a white blouse and one of Aunt Martha's floral aprons. Both girls were chattering up a storm. He couldn't remember the last time he'd seen Luna this animated with anyone other than him, Aunt Martha or Lucy.

Watching the three of them interact stirred a longing within him reminiscent of dreams he'd once expected to fulfill with his ex.

Tempting him to think that maybe, just maybe, he could someday experience lasting love. The good Lord knew, the girls needed and deserved a mom. Someone who would listen to their random stories, answer their endless questions and readily invite them close.

Like Evie did.

Why was it, when he'd finally met someone he could see

himself falling for, that person was beyond his reach? Too bad there wasn't some way that she could stay.

Unless… He thought back to her phone call from the other day. While he'd come in on the tail end, he'd caught enough to know New Day had given someone else an assignment she'd wanted. Did that mean she'd have a lapse in employment, once she left here? While he knew little about the in-home care industry, the fact that she was here now seemed to indicate that, along with how much she disliked rural living.

Although he got the impression the hill country was growing on her.

Maybe she wasn't as opposed to ranch life as when she'd first arrived. Would she stay, if asked? If she didn't have anything else lined up after, probably. That would save New Day, and him, the expense of sending someone else down.

Yet, that would merely delay her departure—making it harder for him and the girls to say goodbye once that time came.

Evie turned and caught him watching her. His emotions must've shown in his expression because her cheeks flushed, and her gaze faltered.

"Good morning." She pulled a mug from the cupboard. "Would you like some coffee?"

Face heated, he cleared his throat and went to the sink. "That sounds great. Thank you." He washed his hands, lathering long enough to hog-tie his wayward emotions. He peered at the bowl positioned between her and the girls. "What're y'all making?"

"Crepes." Luna beamed. "With blueberries and whip cream."

"Really?"

She nodded. "Do you know what those are?"

"I've had them once or twice." He glanced around. "Where's Aunt Martha?"

"Lucy picked her up about ten minutes ago." Evie placed a

pan on the stovetop. "When she heard your aunt wasn't feeling nauseous, she insisted on treating her to breakfast."

"It's good she's taking time to connect with friends. I know she was bummed about last week's canceled appointment, but I'm glad to see her strength returning. That'll make her treatment this week all the more effective."

Evie looked like she wanted to say something, but Callie hijacked her attention to ask if she could pour the crepe batter into the pan.

He glanced at the clock on the stove. "I best jump in the shower."

By the time he returned, a plate full of crepes that looked like they'd lost a battle against the whip cream centered the table. At least, he assumed crepes sat under the massive white mound.

Twenty minutes later, the girls had washed their hands and faces and Callie had changed. When they arrived at church, they found the lot and sanctuary three-quarters full. Elementary-age kids ran around in the grass, teens gathered in groups of threes and fours, and adults and families filed into pews or conversed in the aisle.

Evie accompanied Monte when he deposited the girls in their classroom. He introduced her to people they encountered there, most of whom gushed with gratitude for her coming to Sage Creek and all she was doing to help his aunt.

He agreed with the sentiment.

Reaching an empty pew, he motioned for Evie to proceed before him.

She slid in, set her purse at her feet and rested her Bible beside her. "It's obvious how much everyone adores your aunt. From what I know about her, with good reason."

His heart swelled as he thought of the legacy his aunt had formed, not just with the girls, which itself was priceless, but also in this community.

"She loves people well." He smiled. "Always has. When I

visited her back as a kid, I used to get annoyed by all the folks she'd talk to. Always felt like they carried on for hours—as if hearing to a person talk about their grandkids, or their job, or whatever, was such a terrible thing. Now that's one of the things I admire about her most."

"Listening to someone is one of the best ways to speak value and care."

"They teach you that in your caregiving training?"

She nodded. "Often, when we see people in distress, our first urge is to try to alleviate their pain. By all means, that's a big part of my job—at least for physical discomfort. When it comes to things like sorrow or grief, however, I've found what people need most isn't our answers or so-called solutions but for someone to sit with them in their pain."

"I 'spect you're right."

"I've taken the classes and would've said I'd had plenty of practice walking beside those who hurt. But compared to the people in Sage Creek—" she waved a hand to indicate the other church members "—I'm a novice."

"Can't find this depth of community in a big city, that's for sure."

Her eyes widened for a flash of a second before she frowned and dropped her gaze—almost as if he'd chided her.

Had he offended her in some way? Made her feel like he didn't think she excelled at her job? Or maybe she thought he felt his way of life was superior to what she'd experienced in the city?

Then again, he did. He wouldn't give up this place, the people or his land for any high-rise, no matter how fancy. But that didn't mean he thought anything less of Evie.

He'd simply been encouraged to know she was beginning to see the benefits to country living.

He'd been letting his rebellious heart take the lead, and in the process, had offended the one person he'd been most wanting to impress.

With a sigh, he focused on the front as the choir rose, indicating for everyone else to do the same.

After service, Declan, a guy Monte had talked with a time or two but didn't know well, approached as he was exiting the sanctuary. "Hey." The man had a large Adam's apple, a hooked nose and bony frame that reminded him of the cartoon character Ichabod Crane. "How're you holding up?"

Monte shook the man's hand. "Same ol'." He introduced Declan to Evie, which led to a brief discussion of various jobs through which people traveled the country.

"So," Declan widened his stance and popped his neck. "I heard you're introducing my buddy Ian to bull riding."

"Trying to." Ian had little patience for drills and learning things like body mechanics or ways to avoid getting stomped on—like bolting out of the arena once bucked. Or rather, to reduce the likelihood, because as Monte's mom used to say, it wasn't a matter of *if* a competitor got hurt, but *when*.

He'd known the risks and had taken care to mitigate them. But Ian was showing no such concern.

Declan laughed. "I hear that. Dude's got an invincibility complex if I've ever seen one."

Monte shrugged. While not wanting to talk badly about the kid, there was a lot of truth to that statement. Ian was either rodeo-ignorant or assumed he'd be the only man in bull-riding history not to get injured.

Declan went on to give examples to prove just how out of touch the kid was. "Dude's convinced he's going to become the next Roy Arlington. Just wait until he breaks his jaw or busts his ribs. That'll wisen him up right quick." He shook his head. "Least he's got a great coach. I'm sure you'll steer him straight. Got time for any more students?"

"I don't actually do this on a professional basis. I'm just doing a favor for a family friend." Monte sensed Evie watching him and cast her a sideways glance. Her expression hinted at concern or confusion. Likely the latter, considering her nearly nonexistent exposure to cowboy culture.

The question was, did this conversation, and his way of life, intrigue her? Enough for her to want to stay?

He thought back to his first year of marriage and how hard he'd tried to help Erin love the country as much as he did. He'd ended up with a heap of disappointment, heartache and an ultimatum—grant her a divorce or she'd take the kids with her.

Had he fought her, he would've landed in the same place—without her or custody of the twins, and carrying enough debt from legal fees to about swallow him whole.

He'd gotten so caught up in his thoughts, he'd missed Declan's question. "What's that?"

"Bull riding lessons. You ever think about starting something like that? Could be a real moneymaker."

"I wouldn't even know how to begin."

"Word of mouth goes a long way."

An interesting idea. "I'll think about it." He had a handful of guys he invited out to ride. They helped him get his bulls practice time, and they did the same for the men. But Monte had never charged anyone, or instructed them, for that matter—other than Ian.

And he was a long way from calling the experience a success.

Declan gave a greeting nod to someone who walked past. "My buddies and I would love to come learn a thing or two, if you're open to teaching us. We'd pay, of course. We're going to dig in our spurs in San Antonio this February. Ride or die, as they say." He chuckled. "Consider this an opportunity to help a group of knuckleheads live long enough to swap stories about the bull that nearly did us in."

In other words, they were going to enter the bucking chutes coached or not. And Declan thought Ian was foolish. Monte's parents had said the same about him, when he first started riding. But at least he'd had others to learn from.

A couple with a toddler and a child near the twins' age walked by.

Monte rubbed the back of his neck. "When were you thinking?"

"This weekend be too soon?"

To get anything worth investing that much time into organized, yes. "Taking the girls and a few of my derbies to Dripping Springs."

"The Saturday after?"

"That sounds like a lot of work."

"I'll do the heavy lifting. Gather up the fellas, put flyers around town and such. Probably could even get my buddy at the county paper to write up a community interest piece. All you'd have to do is provide the space and do the coaching."

The idea did sound fun, and like a relatively easy way to boost his shrinking bank account. Plus, an article could help him establish his brand while attracting potential investors.

He shifted his weight from one foot to the other. "You don't think everyone will be too busy to come, with the holidays and all?"

"We could sell it to folks as an early Christmas present."

"You'd do all the leg work?"

"I'd loop my buddies and our girlfriends in to help, but yep."

"All right, then."

"Yeah?" Declan grinned.

"Yep. We can give it a shot." He watched a preschooler dart out of his mom's grasp. That was something his Callie would do. "I best get my girls before their teacher thinks I forgot about them."

"And I better get moving on Sage Creek's first annual winter bull riding clinic."

Monte chuckled. "Let's not get ahead of ourselves here."

He excused himself with a handshake, then, with Evie accompanying him, headed down the hall leading to one of the back classrooms.

"Drake Owens, a local contractor who handles a lot of the church's repairs, built this add-on to make space for the growth of families." The extension had increased the church by nearly one thousand feet. "His wife, Faith, painted the murals." He indicated the cartoonish Bible story scenes decorating the halls. They stopped in the doorway of his daughters' classroom. "The Jenkinses, who owned the local hardware store, donated the carpet."

"That's amazing." Her voice carried a note of admiration. "It sounds like you have a wonderful church family. That's something I really miss."

Sounded like that was another reason she might be willing to stick around. "'Spect it's hard to put down roots when you're always on the move."

Based on the phone conversation he'd overheard, she didn't have anywhere to leave to, at least not for a while. But even if she did stay for the full time he and his family needed, what would happen once Aunt Martha got better?

Seemed the question wasn't *would* Evie be leaving, but *when*. Knowing that should counter any fantasies he had regarding her becoming part of his world. So why did his mind keep envisioning the two of them building a life together?

Because he was hankering for heartache, apparently.

Suppressing a sigh, he turned his attention to the handful of children still waiting to get picked up. Callie and her friend Ramona were sitting in the far corner, creating a structure with magnetic tiles. Luna and a couple other girls were coloring at the table.

"Monte."

He turned at the sound of a familiar voice and smiled at the twins' preschool teacher. "Kate, good to see you."

She greeted Evie.

"Your nephew visiting again?" Monte asked.

She nodded, her gaze shifting to a blond-haired boy who

was stacking overturned plastic cups into a tower. "He's staying with me this weekend."

"Ah. Fun."

"And tiring." She laughed. "That kid has more energy than a Boston terrier!"

"Sounds like Callie." He chuckled, then sobered, thinking of her uncharacteristic behavior Friday afternoon. "The girls doing okay at school?"

The way Kate averted her gaze and fiddled with her bracelet concerned him.

His shoulders tensed. "Did something happen? One of the kids giving Callie gruff?"

"Oh, nothing like that."

"Then what is it?"

"Have you ever considered getting her evaluated for ADHD?"

He frowned. "No. Why?"

"I've noticed she likes to fidget. She seems to have difficulty sitting still. And paying attention to details."

"She's an active five-year-old used to having the run of the ranch."

"I understand. I just think it may be a good idea to get her tested. So that, if necessary, we can adapt accordingly."

He relaxed his tight muscles in an attempt to keep his irritation out of his voice. "I appreciate your concern."

Kate was wrong. He loved his daughter's lively personality and inquisitive spirit. Did she get bored easily? Sure. But that was just because her brain was always running. That was a good thing. A gift that would take her far, once maturity balanced her out.

"Auntie Kate." Her nephew broke the awkward silence stretching between them.

Monte used the opportunity to excuse himself. He thanked the Sunday school teacher and crossed the room, with Evie, to where Luna sat drawing.

"Hey, kiddo." He squatted down to her eye level. "What've you got there?"

She'd drawn a colorful picture of a woman standing in front of what resembled a stove or counter, a child on each side.

Luna beamed up at him. "This is my thank You art. God takes care of me just like He took care of the hungry widow the prophet Elijah lived with." Turning her smile to Evie, she relayed the basic details, with slight error.

He smiled "I see. Like Aunt Martha and Ms. Evie cook food for us."

Luna nodded. "In the story, the widow's son died. That was really sad and scary. But God brought him back to life."

A lump lodged in his throat as he considered how hard and confusing Aunt Martha's cancer must feel to the twins. But he was also grateful to know they were clinging to hope in their all-powerful Savior.

Luna handed her paper to Evie. "It's for you. I'm glad God sent you to take care of us. Before, Daddy was tired and cranky, but he's happy now. Aunt Martha, too."

Moisture filled Evie's eyes as she accepted the heartfelt gift. "Thank you. I love it."

Luna stood and wrapped her arms around Evie, cheek to her belly.

Seeing them embrace flooded Monte with emotion.

His daughter was right. He'd been stressed and over-whelmed the past few months, worrying about his aunt, his girls, the ranch. Before Tracy came and in the space between her dismissal and Evie's arrival, he'd barely had time to cram a sandwich in his face, let alone be an attentive father to his girls. When they most needed nurturing, he'd been distracted or easily irritated.

But he also had to admit to the truth of Luna's assessment regarding how things had changed. After what felt like a long stretch of inner angst and gloom, he *was* happy. These days he regularly sprang out of bed well before the sun rose. And then rushed about to finish his morning chores so that he could get back for breakfast with Aunt Martha and the girls.

And Evie.

How often had he found excuses to pop into the house numerous times each day, to see her smile, catch a whiff of her soft floral scent, and in some way to bring out her sweet, almost musical laugh?

Despite his good sense, he found himself once again thinking about what life might look like, were Evie to stay. Along with how he might convince her to do that.

Yes, she was a city girl, and about as unaccustomed to ranching life as a newborn calf was to the bucking chutes. But he'd also watched those same bulls come alive in the very places they'd once avoided.

He tensed as his thoughts shifted to his ex-wife, but he gave himself a mental shake. It was true Erin had captured his heart then trampled it in the ground, abandoning him and the girls. But he'd never sought God's will like he learned to do once she left. Nor had she. If they had prayed more—for each other and their marriage—things might've turned out differently.

Regardless, the Good Lord had brought Evie to Sage Creek. She was the clearest answer to prayer he'd experienced in some time. He'd always assumed God brought her here for a season. But what if He was doing an even greater work?

What if He was teaching Monte to trust once again?

And maybe even to allow himself to believe he could find someone to spend the rest of his days with.

CHAPTER ELEVEN

THE NEXT MORNING, Callie fussed about not wanting to go to school, then did so again the day after, and the next. Come Thursday, she refused to get out of bed, declaring that she was already smart enough. When this didn't work, she said she didn't feel well. When pressed, however, she named enough "ailments" to confirm Evie's suspicions—the child was fibbing.

Martha entered and sat on the edge of Callie's bed. "What's wrong, dear?" Dressed and hair done, she looked livelier than Evie had yet seen her.

Martha's time with her friend had done her good. Evie needed to encourage her to go out more often.

Callie clutched her blanket beneath her chin as if ready to fight for it. "I don't want to go to school."

Martha smoothed the child's hair out of her face. "But your friends and Ms. Vargas will miss you."

She shook her head. "My teacher doesn't like me."

"Don't be silly. Of course, she does," Evie said.

Callie's frown deepened. "She likes Luna better."

"That's only because you get in trouble so much," Luna said from across the room where she sat putting on pink, lace-topped socks.

Martha's expression turned stern. "Seems the solution, then, is to stop misbehaving."

"That's what I try to do," Callie whined.

"I suggest you try harder." Martha stood and planted a fist on her hip. "And get yourself up and moving. Otherwise, you won't have time for breakfast, and I'm pretty sure we can talk the chef into making chocolate chip pancakes." She shot Evie a playful smile.

Bribing them with food. Smart.

She nodded. "With whip cream."

Both girls perked up at this and darted for the door.

Martha stopped them. "Not until you make your bed, you don't."

As expected, Luna readily obeyed, and Callie whined. But she must've complied, because by the time Evie poured batter into a heated frying pan, both girls were playing happily in the living room.

Monte walked in a few minutes later, stopping first to see the twins. "Y'all about ready for school?"

Luna informed him they hadn't eaten yet, along with what was on the menu.

"So that's what smells so good. How'd you finagle that?" His teasing tone carried a hint of tenderness.

"Callie threw a fit," Luna said.

"Did not."

"Did so."

"You're a tattletale."

"Am not."

"Yes, huh. And a stupid head."

"No. You are. I'm smarter than you."

"I'm stronger and faster."

"Enough." Monte's firm voice silenced them. "Why don't you girls watch some cartoons while you're waiting?"

A moment later, the television came on.

Monte ambled into the kitchen shaking his head. "Those

two. Best friends one minute, bitter enemies the next." He grabbed a mug from the cupboard and poured himself some coffee. "What set them off this morning?"

Evie relayed Callie's attempts to stay in bed along with what Luna had said about their teacher.

He released a breath. "That child. She can be a stubborn one. She's also prone to forget her manners, especially when she's got words firing through her brain but it's not her turn to speak. I sure hope she's not being disrespectful to Ms. Vargas."

Evie bit her lip, remembering his conversation with the teacher the day before. One to which he hadn't seemed that receptive. Most likely, he'd been caught off guard. That probably hadn't been the best time to talk with a father about his daughter's misbehavior.

While Evie didn't have experience with learning disabilities or anything, what the teacher had said made sense.

"Have you given Ms. Vargas's question any more thought?" She flipped a pancake over.

"Which was?"

"About getting Callie tested for ADHD."

He snorted. "The child's fine. Maybe more active than most, sure. But what would you expect? She's had five years of chasing after the dogs, climbing trees and splashing about in the creek. She'll acclimate to her new environment soon enough."

She should probably let this go. These weren't her kids, nor did she have any business giving parenting advice. But she'd seen the pain one of her closest friends, growing up, had experienced, fighting her way through school. For years, she assumed she was stupid while her parents called her lazy. Come to find out, her difficulties came from dyslexia.

Grabbing a platter from the cupboard, Evie took in a slow, deep breath. Exhaling, she faced him. "But if she does have a learning disability, wouldn't you want to know? So that you can help her get the resources she needs?"

"You implying I don't know my own daughter?" She hadn't

heard such hostility in his voice since the day of the mud incident. "Or do you just think you know better how to raise them?"

Her stomach felt queasy. "I'm sorry. I shouldn't have said anything."

"You're right about that." He deposited his mug on the counter with a clank and stomped off.

Although his mood appeared to have improved by the time he returned to breakfast, he seemed more interested in eating than conversation. Seemed maybe her statement had hit a nerve.

He was probably just stressed about his aunt's appointment today. Considering his family's circumstances, his reaction hadn't been abnormal. Most people struggled to manage their emotions in these situations.

Was his aunt's condition and all the uncertainty related to it triggering because he'd lost his wife? Regardless of why their marriage had ended, he had grieved her twice, first when she broke things off, then again when, upon her death, her absence became irrevocably permanent.

He grabbed his plate and stood. "I'll walk the girls to the bus stop. Y'all can leave for Houston now, if you'd like. Give yourself some leeway, in case you hit traffic."

Evie made eye contact with Martha. "On the way, do you want to swing by that bakery you told me about? The one with the ginormous slices of caramel-apple-spice-cheesecake?"

"I want some!" Callie pushed her half-finished breakfast aside as if wanting to save room for the heavenly treat. "Can I, please? I'll mind my manners and won't give Ms. Vargas any trouble." When her aunt didn't respond, she added, "I'll clean my room, too, without giving you lip. And the chicken coop."

Mouth twitching toward a smile, Monte raised an eyebrow. "All that for a bit of dessert? Seems like a fair trade to me." He tossed his aunt a wink.

Frowning, she dropped her gaze and began gathering the dirty dishes. "We'll see."

This led to more begging, pleading and whining from Callie, which Monte silenced with a warning that she'd get nothing but broccoli if she kept it up.

"I'll take the girls to school," he said. "So y'all can get a head start on traffic." He opened the door for the girls. "No dawdling, now."

They shrugged on their backpacks and shuffled out, Callie slumping like she'd lost an entire year of recess privileges.

Evie laughed. "That child sure is food motivated, huh?"

Martha sighed. "That complicates things."

Helping clean up, Evie furrowed her brow. "What do you mean?"

"Never mind." She placed the last of the used silverware into the dishwasher, slipped her purse strap over her shoulder and smoothed a hand over her up-done hair. "Shall we?"

"Yep. Just give me a sec to grab your medical binder."

Ten minutes later, they were passing by Monte and the girls who were waiting for the bus, and then they were en route to Houston.

The fields stretching on either side of them blurred into endless streams of green periodically accented with dilapidated barns, two-story farmhouses and towering grain silos. They came alongside a train rumbling down the tracks to their left bearing the marks of red, orange and green graffiti.

Aunt Martha pulled papers from her purse. The first one contained printed directions.

Evie tossed her a smile. "I plugged the address to the treatment facility into my phone's GPS."

"That's not where this'll take us." She showed her the second page, a map. "You ever been to San Marcos?"

Evie shook her head.

"You're going to turn left on Texas 71. Heading west. Should be coming up in a mile or so."

Evie looked at her phone held in the dashboard mount. "You mean east?"

"Nope."

"But…" Glancing at she papers again, she caught the to and from locations printed at the top. "Your appointment's at ten, right?" Had she entered it wrong into her calendar? Even so, this was supposed to be an all-day thing, which meant they didn't have time for an out-of-the way pit stop.

"I canceled."

"What? When?" Was her primary care physician still concerned with her blood count? It would've been nice if someone had let Evie know.

"A few days ago."

But why hadn't she told her? Or Monte, for that matter, because he thought they were heading to Houston.

Evie pulled onto the shoulder and parked. "What's going on?"

Martha sighed. "I can't do this anymore. I won't waste what little time I have left with Monte and the girls holed up in bed."

She could understand Martha's discouragement, especially considering her fatigue and extreme dizziness the week before. Followed by a brief reprieve when, as far as Evie could tell, she'd regained some of her energy and maybe even a bit of joy. And she still had a long, challenging journey ahead.

"I know this is hard," Evie said. "But you can do this. You're strong and brave, and you've got a lot of people standing with you."

Martha frowned. "Look, I know you mean well, but I've made up my mind. I'm done fighting. I want to start living, while I still have life left in my bones."

Evie didn't know what to say. Besides, Martha probably had considered every aspect of her options, ten times over. She knew what stopping treatment meant.

Monte would be devastated. Martha knew that more so than anyone. This couldn't have been an easy decision.

But it was hers, and hers alone, to make.

They sat in silence for a moment with cool air blowing through the dashboard vents and the hum of an occasional vehicle passing by.

"You ever driven along a hill country highway in spring?" Martha asked.

She shook her head.

"It's a sight, let me tell you. All those wildflowers dancing in the sun. Splashing the surrounding countryside with vibrant color."

"I've seen pictures of long, wide rows of bluebonnets stretching as far as the eye can see. They're gorgeous. They're the state flower, right?"

Martha nodded. "They're often the first to bloom each spring. Folks say that's when the sky falls on Texas. Seems fitting to me, only I'd swap the word *heaven* for sky." She smiled. "Those delicate yet hardy flowers remind us of the God who brings beauty and life following the longest, most barren winters."

"I love that."

After a while, Martha produced a handwritten list from her purse and gave it to Evie.

"What's this?"

"My bucket list."

She read the items. Cruise Canyon Lake's River Road. Visit the Sugar Shack in Bastrop. Take a glass boat tour. She glanced up. "This is a lot more than a one-day excursion."

"As the saying goes, Rome wasn't built—or a bucket list accomplished—in one day."

Only problem—Evie wouldn't be around to drive her much longer. That meant, once she left, Martha would need to have this same conversation with the caregiver that came after her.

"Enough about that." Martha took her list back and returned it, folded, to her purse. "I'm ready for that glass boat tour. Followed by the biggest ice cream cone I can stomach."

"Think we should swing by a local bakery? To get something for the girls?"

"May be wise. Our little Callie probably will be dreaming of cakes and pies all day. May even have half the house tidied up by the time we get back."

"And her entire apple eaten."

"Oh, lands." Martha feigned an eye roll. "We certainly can't let that go unrewarded. The girl may decide to boycott all fruits and vegetables for the remainder of her childhood."

"What about Monte? You going to tell him?"

Martha's gaze dropped to her hands. "When the time is right. And I get my courage."

Evie couldn't imagine how hard this was for her. But she also hoped Martha would make good on that promise, because the thought of keeping this from him made her feel ill.

Yet, she had no choice in the matter. Martha was her patient, and as such, she had the right to privacy, a right Evie was legally bound to uphold.

Either way, Monte would be heartbroken. Maybe even blame her, if not hate her. Knowing there wasn't anything she could do about that didn't make her feel any better.

ON FRIDAY, MONTE loaded three of his bulls into a trailer and gave his ranch hands, Travis and Jesse, last-minute reminders. He also verified, again, that Lucy still planned to stay with his aunt while he was away at the Christmas rodeo. He would've felt much better had he been able to wait until she arrived, but he needed to pick the girls up from school and get on the road.

Sliding into his truck beside Evie, he couldn't contain his grin.

"That mischievous look on your face tells me you've pulled a prank on your guys."

He chuckled and shifted into gear. "Just thinking about how excited the girls must've been today. It's been a while since I've taken them to the rodeo."

Aunt Martha had been right. This would be a memorable weekend for them all.

In his case, potentially too memorable. The more time he spent with Evie, the more he wanted to be around her.

Suppressing a sigh, he turned onto the two-lane highway leading into town. "Listen, I'm sorry I was such a bear yesterday, when you suggested Callie might have ADHD." After a bit of a restless night trying to decipher why he'd acted like he had, he realized his frustration had nothing to do with Evie, or anything Kate Vargas had said, for that matter.

"No big deal." She offered him the sweetest, most genuine smile, as if she'd already forgotten what a jerk he'd been.

That almost made him feel worse.

He'd filtered her and Kate's words through his parental insecurities, taking a simple suggestion as a statement against him as a father. Part of him felt like he should've been the first to detect any learning disability the child might have. Another side determined that Callie wouldn't have one at all, had he been less wrapped up in the ranch.

Eventually, common sense won out, overpowering his defensiveness with gratitude that God had placed caring and attentive adults in the twins' lives.

For now.

The fact that he'd known, from the moment Evie arrived, that she wouldn't stay long, didn't make remembering that now any easier.

The parking lot at the preschool was nearly full.

"Want me to hop out and get them?" Evie reached for her door.

He glanced at the trailer hitched to his truck. "Sure would be a lot easier than trying to finagle this beast."

With a quick nod, she jumped out and strolled down the sidewalk and toward the building. Ten minutes later, she returned, holding the girls' hands, unfiltered, unconstrained joy radiating from each of their faces.

He wasn't the only one who'd come to adore the woman. That meant he wouldn't be the only one who'd feel gut-punched when she left.

Convince her to stay.

The thought landed so strong and clear, he wanted to believe it came from God—because then he could hold it like a promise. But it was far more likely the notion came from within his renegade heart.

And yet, could he entice Evie to change her plans and remain in Sage Creek—forever?

Was that what he wanted? Bigger question—could he, the girls and the ranch be what *she* wanted?

He got out as they drew near and greeted each of his daughters with an off-the-ground hug. "Y'all ready for some mutton busting?"

"Yeah!" Their enthusiasm sent a rush of warmth through him.

"You best get in then, because this wrangler's ready to go." Helping the girls climb in, he winked at Evie, delighted by the sparkle in her eyes and the slight flush in her cheeks.

Once everyone was strapped in, he veered around the vehicles idling in front of him and through the adjacent neighborhood. As they continued toward Dripping Springs, homes gave way to pastureland dotted with longhorns and clusters of leafless trees.

Initially, the girls chatted about everything from kettle corn and walking tacos to barrel racing and how long they planned to stay on top of their sheep. Unfortunately, Callie soon grew bored and began asking, repeatedly, how much longer before they arrived.

"Ten minutes less than when you asked last time, Cowpoke."

Evie made eye contact with him. "You're patient."

The admiration in her tone made him sit a mite taller. "I figure her questions stem from her excitement. And frustration with sitting still for any length of time. That girl came into the world looking for a challenge to conquer and a race to win."

"I love that about her."

He did, too, and it touched him to know that Evie saw the strength, the spark, in what others might deem a weakness.

"I have an idea." She twisted in her seat to look at the twins. "Have you ever played the alphabet game?" When they said they hadn't, she explained it to them.

They immediately began calling out the letters, starting with *A*, in various license plates and road signs.

He joined in.

By the time they reached the rodeo, they'd played four rounds, along with "I spy." Evie had also led them in a game she called "Add and pass", where she started a story, and they each took turns adding to it.

He pulled into a large gravel lot filled with horse and cattle trailers, pickups and RVs, then waited his turn to back into the appropriate loading chute. "Once I get these fellas taken care of, I'll drive you and the girls to the regular entrance. Figured you might like to catch a behind-the-scenes glimpse."

He checked the time on the dash. They'd arrived plenty early for this size of a shindig. "Some guys bring their bulls out the night before, to get them acclimated and whatnot." He would've, too, had this been a larger rodeo or PBR event.

Evie took everything in with wide eyes. "This is so cool. I'm really looking forward to this. Thank you for taking me."

His breath hitched. He cleared his throat and gave one firm nod. "Couldn't let you leave Texas without experiencing a bit of cowboy culture."

He'd rather she not leave at all.

Seeing the almost childlike wonder in her expression made him think, if this weekend went well, he stood a chance at stopping that from happening.

CHAPTER TWELVE

EVIE TOOK THE girls to the Coyote Arena to check them in for their event while Monte did whatever it was he needed to do with his bulls. The air smelled like dust, kettle corn and animals. People, most of them dressed in country attire, filled the bleachers and streamed up and down the stairs.

With an hour to spare, she and the girls left to explore the fairgrounds.

They returned with lemonade and funnel cakes to find Monte waiting near the arena entrance. "Do I get some of that?" he teased Luna.

The child's face fell as she looked from him to her treat, which was large enough to give her a bellyache twice over.

Shoulders slumped, she nodded and reluctantly raised her snack.

"You can eat your own, thank you very much." With feigned annoyance, Evie held out her plate, topped with two funnel cakes dusted with a healthy dose of powdered sugar.

Monte grinned. "Thanks for thinking of me. And my stomach."

Heat rushed to her face at the truth of his statement. She *had* been thinking of him, and not only when standing at the food stand. Her thoughts turned to him much too often.

Worse, there'd been numerous times when, instead of fighting them, she'd let various fantasies play out of the two of them together, sitting in the gazebo, her nestled against his strong chest, watching the sun set. Or riding horses across the pasture, or sipping coffee on the porch while Luna colored and Callie played tug-of-war with Max.

Callie grimaced as Monte secured her helmet onto her head. "It's hot and heavy and itchy."

Monte shot her a stern look. "No helmet, no riding."

Her torso deflated as she released an exasperated breath. But then she turned to Evie with a wide grin. "Will you watch me?"

"I wouldn't miss that for the world." She turned to Luna. "You, either."

The child's face lit with such joy, Evie couldn't help but give her a quick squeeze. Funny, prior to coming to Sage Creek, she'd felt certain she wasn't ready for kids. Hadn't been entirely sure she ever would be.

Now she found herself looking forward to the day when she had a family of her own.

When the time came, Monte accompanied the girls into the bucking chute while Evie watched from the bleachers.

The announcer proclaimed Callie's name, age and from where she came, as she burst out of the gate, arms and legs wrapped around the sheep, her head turned and cheek pressed into the thick gray wool. She stayed on for six and a half seconds. Based on the enthusiasm of the announcer and the crowd, that must've been good. Although Luna lasted just shy of five, her bright smile indicated she was pleased with herself.

Both girls received ribbons they proudly displayed to Evie.

"Way to go!" She gave them each a high five. "I knew you'd rock it. Both of you."

With a hand on each of the girls' shoulders, Monte seemed to stand a bit taller. "That's my little wranglers, all right."

"What's next?" Evie asked.

"Bull riding's always the last event. That's the rodeo director's way of making sure people stick around." He laughed. "You ever seen horse cutting?"

She shook her head. "But it sounds interesting."

"This way." He led them out of the Coyote Arena and into the open air, then stopped. "Mind if I call one of my ranch hands right quick? Make sure they haven't encountered—or created—any fires I need to walk them through?"

"Not at all."

They migrated past a handful of food booths decked out in Christmas lights to an empty picnic table.

With a foot on the bench, Monte pulled his phone from his back pocket and tapped the screen. "Hey, Travis. How're things going?" He paused. "Sounds great. Did Lucy make it over okay?" His eyebrows shot up. "Really. That's good to hear." He smiled. "I agree with you there." He straightened to standing. "Holler at me if you need anything."

He ended the call and looked at Evie with an adoration that about stole her breath. And her heart. "Good news, I take it?"

"Seems Aunt Martha's been busy. Brought the fellas fried chicken and homemade coleslaw for supper then headed out with Lucy for ladies' bunco night at the church. According to my ranch hand, looking more alive than he'd seen her in some time."

"Yeah?" Her stomach soured as she thought about the reason for his aunt's increased energy. "That's awesome."

"It is, thanks to you. To say you've been an answer to prayers would be an understatement. With you by her side, she'll beat this cancer, for sure." His eyes deepened in intensity. "Say you'll stay?"

Her heart squeezed with equal parts hope and concern. "What?"

"I didn't mean to eavesdrop, but I assume from the conversation I overheard the other day, you don't have another assignment lined up for when you leave here."

"Not yet." That did concern her.

"Doesn't make sense to me for your company to send some-one else out, when you're already here, and doing such a great job. I'd like to think that maybe country living has grown on you, least enough to entice you to stick around through the end of my aunt's treatment."

And when he learned, according to his aunt, that day had already arrived?

It made her nauseous, keeping something so big from him, especially considering his high hopes. But she didn't have a choice.

Would he understand that, once his aunt told him about her decision?

Regardless, he was right about one thing. It didn't make sense to ask another caregiver to come all this way, poten-tially costing her an assignment elsewhere, only to learn the Bowmans didn't need her after all.

"I think it's wise to keep things as they are for now."

"Meaning, tell New Day not to send your replacement?"

She nodded. Once his aunt told him about her decision, there'd be no need for the company to send anyone else. This way, if Martha delayed her revelation, whoever was supposed to come out next could find another assignment.

His grin widened. "Awesome." He pulled her into his strong arms, his heartbeat thudding against her ear, and she melted against him.

Apparently, the embrace surprised him as much as it had her, because they simultaneously stiffened and pulled apart, his cheeks as red as hers felt.

Taking half a step back, he cleared his throat and gazed toward a red building with white trim. "Let's go see us some horses."

With a deep breath to center her tumbling thoughts and slow her accelerated pulse, she followed, wishing things could be different.

That she truly could stay as more than a temporary caregiver, not that Monte had asked for that. But the way he'd looked at her a moment ago, as if she was the most beautiful woman he'd encountered, made her think maybe, just maybe that was what he wanted.

Would that change once he learned of his aunt's decision—and that she hadn't talked her out of it?

MONTE HAD JUST finished loading up his bulls and was about to text Evie when a tall, pot-bellied man with gray hair and mustache approached. He wore a black cowboy hat, a collared, blue shirt, dark jeans and boots that looked fresh out of the box. The man's swagger suggested he was someone with money and influence.

When the guy reached the truck, Monte lowered his window and greeted him with a nod.

"You Mr. Bowman, from Bowman's Rough Stock Ranch?"

Monte sat up taller. "I am."

"You got some mighty fine bulls."

"Thank you."

"Your wife said this was Jackhammer's first competition?"

His what? His shoulders tensed as an image of Erin, his former wife, came to mind. But then he smiled. The guy must be talking about Evie.

His wife. Monte liked the sound of that. As if that were even an option.

Could it be? Maybe, if she stayed through Aunt Martha's treatment, and he managed to capture her heart during that time. Those were some serious ifs—a definite challenge, but not impossible.

He corralled his thoughts back to the present. "With a rider, yes, sir." Monte had entered him in a handful of futurities, during which his performance had been hit-or-miss. The animal hadn't been much more consistent with riders brought onto the ranch for practice.

Monte hadn't been expecting much different tonight. He'd been pleasantly surprised.

The man eyed his trailer, then refocused on Monte. "I'm Cord Mariluch."

Monte introduced himself as the two shook hands, although clearly the guy already knew who he was. The name of his ranch, at least.

Cord rested a hand on his large, silver-and-turquoise belt buckle. "I hear you're looking for investors."

A jolt shot through him. "Yes, sir."

Had Evie been acting as salesperson while watching from the stands? The thought warmed him and made him feel like they were a team—something he'd never felt with his ex. Oh, Erin had said she supported him, in the beginning, anyway.

But she'd bailed before his first homebred bulls started practicing with dummies.

Prior to the girls learning to potty train, count to ten, or form their letters.

And he'd thought her the loyal type. Boy, had she fooled him.

Cord widened his stance. "You got any information on you?"

"I do." He grabbed a file folder with pictures and details on some of his best bulls.

The man studied each page, then flipped back to the first, where Monte had printed his phone number, email and website. He asked a few more questions, including how long Monte had been in the bucking bulls business and how many bulls he had available for partnership.

"I'll give all this some thinking on. Can I keep this?" He raised the folder.

"Please do."

Cord nodded and started to walk away.

"Mind if I reach out to you in a week or so?" Experience

told him, an interest was more apt to turn into a sale when he followed up later.

Cord turned back around. "Sure." He handed Monte a business card, tipped his hat and strolled away.

Thank You, Lord. While this wasn't a check in hand, it was a great lead. A wealthy investor paired with a bull as intelligent and athletic as Jackhammer was looking to be would go a long way toward establishing the Bowman name in the bucking bull business.

He reached for his phone to call Evie, then paused. When a potential blessing fell his way, she'd been the first person he wanted to tell.

That was how much she'd come to mean to him. And if he couldn't talk her into staying?

That wasn't an option.

He shot her a text to let her know he was heading her way, even more anxious to hear what she thought of his bulls than he was to tell her about the potential investor.

She climbed into his truck carrying the floral scent that always set him off-kilter, her eyes bright in the dim overhead light of his cab.

She handed him a hot dog doused with ketchup, mustard and jalapeños, just the way he liked it.

He grinned. "How'd you know?"

"The girls told me."

He glanced back at them through his rearview mirror. Smears of ketchup and mustard on their faces, they looked droopy-eyed but content. "Y'all did good."

Evie snapped on her seat belt. "You're not going to believe this, but I met a guy who invests in bucking bulls. Callie overheard him talking on the phone to someone about Jackhammer, told him he belonged to her daddy, the 'best and strongest and smartest cowboy in all of Texas.'"

He laughed. "Did she, now?"

Evie nodded. "He seemed interested and started asking me questions, none of which I had answers to, unfortunately."

"Well, you came off knowledgeable enough for him to think we were married."

"What?" Her eyes widened, and he wondered if he'd see a blush on her cheeks, if his cab wasn't so dark. "I guess that makes sense, me sitting with your girls and all."

"So, what'd you think? Was this what you expected?" He motioned toward the fairgrounds.

"Better." She smiled. "And I was much relieved to overhear a couple of guys talking about how the bulls are treated. That lady I met at the twins' party made it seem like they were tortured into bucking."

He snorted. "Hardly. An animal in pain doesn't perform any better than an injured human would."

"I suppose not."

He turned onto a winding country road. Luna fell asleep less than ten miles out. That was about the time Callie's energetic chattering began to slow before dying entirely.

He glanced at her in the rearview mirror. "Out cold."

Evie craned her neck to glance behind her. "I'm not surprised, with all the jumping up and down those two did. They were your personal cheerleaders and made sure everyone in the vicinity knew it."

"Luna included?"

She nodded.

"Wow. She must've been pretty excited, for it to overpower her shyness like that."

"They're both quite proud of their father."

A lump lodged in his throat. "Hope they always feel that way."

"I'm sure they will. You're a great dad."

The lump grew. He cleared his throat to hide the rush of emotion her honest admiration caused. "Thanks. And for coming. It meant the world to the girls."

"I had a wonderful time." He could hear the smile in her voice. Could picture it on her delicate, pink lips.

"Does that mean country life has grown on you?"

"Maybe." She was silent for a moment, but it didn't feel awkward or like either of them needed to fill it. "Callie told me you used to be quite the bull rider. Better than any of the cowboys competing tonight."

He chuckled. "That child can spin a tale."

"Were you any good?"

"I made some money. And broke some bones."

"Is that why you stopped?"

He frowned. "Nope." He didn't want to ruin a nice night talking about his ex. "Like my pops used to tell me, whenever he heard I was heading out to another rodeo, I'm either too stubborn or too stupid for my own good. Figure I'm a bit of both."

"You a born risk-taker, too?"

"Not really. If you're asking what got me started, I'll come clean now and say it was for the ladies. Thought sliding into the bucking chute made me more of a man. I also hoped to win some easy money."

"From what I saw tonight, seems to me there are a lot easier ways to make a living."

"I quickly found out just how right you are. If you're not any good or draw some exceptionally rank bulls, the sport can cost a pretty penny—by way of hospital bills."

That was one of his ex's most frequent arguments. She was convinced it was only a matter of time before he got seriously stomped on, potentially, to his death. Her concerns weren't entirely unfounded.

He turned onto the highway and set his cruise control. "What attracted you to the traveling health care industry?"

"The sense of adventure. Initially, it was only supposed to be for a year—to visit a few places, meet interesting people, try fun foods. Not that I don't enjoy caregiving. I do. I just didn't think I'd be up for living out of a suitcase as long as I did."

She'd changed her plans once. Would she consider Monte and the girls reason enough to do so again?

She'd also spoken in the past tense. Did that mean she no longer enjoyed hoofing it from one place to the next? "And now?"

"What's next, you mean?"

He nodded.

"I'm still trying to figure that out."

He liked hearing that. "You thinking you may change careers?"

"I don't know." She sighed. "I love working with people. Years ago, my grandmother had a heart attack that resulted in a double bypass. We were all scared at how close we'd come to losing her. Some of the hospital staff treated her like she was nothing but a task on their to-do list."

"I hate to say this, but I know exactly what you mean."

"But there was this one guy. The night nurse. He was amazing. It was like he carried supernatural tranquility with him. Changed the atmosphere in the room simply by entering it. When I learned later that he was a Christ-follower, it made sense. He brought the Prince of peace with him, simply by showing up. I wanted to be like him. To bring hope and encouragement to people in the most difficult and frightening seasons of their life, especially."

He placed his hand on hers. "You've done that for us. And I cannot express how grateful I am."

She seemed to be shutting down. She pulled her hand away.

"I didn't say that to pressure you into staying. I'd never do that." While he'd do anything to keep her in Sage Creek, with him, he wanted her to want that, too. If he pestered her into making a decision her heart wasn't set on, she'd come to resent him.

Erin had taught him that, and he wasn't looking for a re-peat lesson.

Silence stretched between them.

Sensing her watching him, he cast her a sideways glance. "Why do I get the feeling you're fretting about something?" Was his question too direct? In light of their conversation, and the fact that she'd already withdrawn from him, probably.

"I know it's not any of my business, but what happened with you and the twins' mom?"

He tensed, and the desire to deflect traveled all the way down into his gut. But the fact that she asked indicated she was contemplating building a relationship with him. Made sense she'd want to know why his marriage had failed.

He rubbed the back of his neck. "Erin and I hung with the same friend group in high school. I was a football player. She was a cheerleader, and once I finally convinced her to give me a chance, we spent a lot of time together riding the bus to and from games. I fooled myself into thinking she liked me for myself. But she was only interested in my persona."

"A status thing?"

"Maybe so. Back then, I wasn't very future-minded and hadn't a clue what direction to head. So, when she got ac-cepted to a Texas university, I followed. I took agricultural classes and made friends with some local cowboys. I'd done some riding prior, but that's when I really fell in love with the sport. At first, Erin was thrilled. With the line-dancing, coun-try-music side of things."

"She lost interest in what became for you a driving pas-sion?"

"Exactly. For her, the lifestyle was nothing but a passing phase. As was I. So, when life got tough, she left. I tried to fight for her. Was even willing to go to counseling, but she wasn't interested. I later learned she'd fallen for someone else. Less than a year after, she and her boyfriend died in a car accident."

"I'm sorry."

He shrugged. "It's in the past."

For a time, Erin had left him jaded to love.

Then Evie had arrived with her sweet smile, soft laugh and engaging personality and had started chiseling away at the protective walls barricading his heart.

He fully intended to do whatever possible to make her fall for him as hard as he'd fallen for her.

While he hadn't yet figured out how to do that, one thing he knew for sure—were she to leave, he'd never recover.

CHAPTER THIRTEEN

MONDAY MORNING, CALLIE was as reluctant to get ready for preschool as she had been the week prior. Evie sat beside her on the bed and rubbed the child's back in slow, circular motions. "I understand how you feel, sweetie."

"You didn't like school when you were my age, either?"

"I was a bit older, but yeah. I went through a period where I was nervous about going."

"Cuz you were stupid?"

Her heart clenched. "Oh, sweetie, you are *not* stupid. You're bright, creative and full of life. You're just learning when to let your energy loose and when to rein it in."

"Like Dad had to teach Kit Kat?"

She frowned. "Who's that?"

"His friend's horse. His old owners didn't take good care of him or ride him or nothing. So he thought he could do whatever he wanted, even if it wasn't good for him and made people not want him anymore." Sorrow filled her eyes. "That's how Ms. Vargas feels about me."

"That's not true."

"Yuh-huh. She says she likes me, but I can tell she doesn't."

"Because she corrects you?"

She nodded.

Evie offered a gentle smile. "She's a teacher. That's her job. And you're a kid, which means you're going to make mistakes."

Callie sighed. "I make a lot of them."

"I wouldn't expect any different."

"More than Luna."

"She's got her struggles, too."

"Like what?"

Evie wasn't looking to bash one child to make the other feel better. "What's important is that Ms. Vargas loves you. So do I."

The child sat straighter. "You do?"

Evie's heart squeezed at the realization of just how true her statement was. She nodded.

"So do I, Cowpoke." Monte entered smelling like leather, citrus and the faint aroma of hay.

His gaze shifted to Evie, and the intensity in his eyes suggested he felt the same about her.

Dare she believe it?

If so, then what? She thought back to his request that she stay—through his aunt's treatment, which technically had already ended. Not only was that far from a declaration of love, but whatever fondness he did feel for her could easily sour once he learned the truth.

Callie crossed her arms, her bottom lip poked out. "I still don't want to go."

"Unfortunately, you don't—"

Evie interrupted him with a forceful cough and shake of her head.

He furrowed his brow but remained quiet.

She smoothed the hair out of Callie's face. "How about if I talk to Ms. Vargas? I have some ideas I think may help you feel less…confined."

"Like what?"

"Let me chat with her first." She didn't want to plant hope

she had no power to fulfill or to inadvertently pit the child against her teacher.

"What if she says no?"

"Then we'll figure something else out. But I can promise you this, Ms. Vargas wants you to enjoy school as much as possible."

"How do you know?"

"From seeing all the decorations, toys and sensory stations she's got in her classroom."

"I like the manipulatives area. That's what she calls the building blocks and marble pipes and stuff."

"See?"

Callie nodded.

"Do we have a deal?"

She gave a slight shrug.

"I'll take that as a yes." Evie shot Monte a grin. Her breath caught to see him watching her with the same intensity as before.

Maybe even a look of adoration.

She stood, suddenly shy. And saddened at the thought of losing the man she'd fallen so hard for, despite all her efforts to remain emotionally detached.

Hand on her hip, she faced Callie. "How about you get dressed while I make you and your sister chocolate chip pancakes?"

"With bunny ears?"

She laughed. "Sure."

She exited the room. Monte followed close behind.

Aunt Martha was already in the kitchen stirring something in a large ceramic bowl. Beside this lay a package of grated cheese. Diced mushrooms, onions and tomatoes waited on a nearby cutting board.

"What's all this?" Monte greeted her with a kiss to the cheek.

"Figured, with all of the high-sugared breakfasts you've stomached of late, it was time I made one of your favorites."

"Omelets?"

She beamed at him. "Yep. With bacon and hot buttery toast."

He looked between her and Evie with a sheepish expression.

Aunt Martha's brow furrowed. "What's wrong?"

Evie told her about the deal she'd struck with Callie.

"Well." Aunt Martha eyed her fresh chopped vegetables. "I guess that simply means we'll serve both. You can bring your ranch hands whatever we don't finish."

"Great plan." He poured himself a cup of coffee then leaned back against the counter, one foot crossed over the other. He made eye contact with Evie. "Mind if I join you when you take the girls to school?"

To the contrary, as the sudden flutter that swept through her midsection verified. "Of course not. They are your children, after all."

Would he take her gentle teasing as flirting?

Did she want him to?

She suppressed a sigh. This was exactly why she'd never been a fan of dating. She stank at it. Whereas some women came off sweet and demure, she excelled at being painfully awkward.

He alleviated her insecurity with some playful teasing of his own, and by the time they were ready to leave, she no longer felt tempted to hide behind a mound of dirty dishes.

His cell rang as he stepped onto the porch, and he glanced at the screen. His eyebrows shot up, his lips twitching toward a hint of a smile. Holding up a finger to Evie, he answered. "Mr. Mariluch. Thank you for getting back to me." He listened for a moment, asked the man to hold, then cupped his hand around the phone. "You mind?"

She waved his question aside. "Not at all. I'll drive the twins. That way you won't feel rushed."

He grinned, mouthed *Thank you*, and returned to his call.

Luna skipped on ahead, her braids bouncing against her shoulders, while Callie hung back, shoulders slumped.

Evie took her hand and gave it a squeeze. "Let's go see about making this an amazing day. What do you say?"

"I guess."

"What's one thing you're looking forward to?"

She frowned, as if deep in thought, then smiled. "I know. When I get home, you, me, Daddy and Luna can give Aunt Martha our show. With the stage and curtains and everything."

"Sure. Although I meant during school."

"Oh. Recess, I guess."

Evie laughed. "That sounds fun."

As to their afternoon production, she wasn't sure how she felt about that. She had a feeling Monte would be more endearing than ever. Seeing his playful side made her wish she could stop time and delay her assignment indefinitely. But that was also why these interactions created substantial inner angst.

She knew the more attached she became to him and his girls, the deeper the ache would be once she left.

MONTE WAS REPAIRING a section of fence when Evie drove by in a swirl of dust. He felt an urge to drop what he was doing and jog after her. Instead, he reminded himself that he was a grown man and calmly, albeit quickly, finished.

Then hurried home.

As he passed the east pasture, his two ranch hands ribbed him, making it clear they knew precisely the reason for his rushed pace.

Inhaling, he raised his chin, squared his shoulders and slowed his feet.

This provided the added benefit of allowing his breathing to return to normal before reaching the house.

He followed the sound of Evie and his aunt's voice down the hall.

"I understand completely." Evie sounded concerned. "I just think the sooner you do so, the better."

He poked his head into his aunt's room. "The sooner you do what?"

Evie startled and both women looked at him with wide eyes. He chuckled. "Didn't mean to scare you."

"We're fine." His aunt tidied up her bedside table. "Did you need something, dear?"

"Well, as long as you're asking... Any chance I can talk you into making some of your awesome strawberry-rhubarb pie?"

"Was already planning on it, along with a couple pans of brownies and two big ol' pots of chili."

"That sounds like too much work."

"It'll bring me joy, and you know it. And when the gals from church heard about your bull riding clinic, they insisted on bringing desserts. The Herrons plan on supplying some of their famous peach cobbler, and the girls from youth group are supposed to be bringing the fixings for a hot cocoa bar, too. Although the weatherman's predicting a beautiful day."

"I'd hate for them—"

Smiling, she held up a hand. "Before you say some rubbish about not wanting to put folks out—they insisted. It is the Sage Creek way, after all."

"True, and for that, I'm grateful." He told them about the call he'd received. "The guy sounds really interested, and he's looking to invest in more than one bull. But he wants to see some of the other boys perform. I invited him to come out this weekend."

Evie frowned. "But won't you be busy?"

"I told him that. He didn't seem to mind, so long as I planned on letting the guys ride, which I assured him I was. Besides, my 'wife' will be here." He grinned. As always, her blush only increased her beauty. "Figured Mr. Mariluch would be in good hands, considering what a great sales lady she was last time."

Aunt Martha frowned. "What're you talking about?"

Monte laughed and relayed how the man had referred to Evie the night of the rodeo.

"Hmm…" His aunt tapped her chin. "An interesting thought, for sure."

The pink in Evie's cheeks deepened, and she fiddled with an afghan on the chair that didn't need folding. She immediately excused herself to tackle household chores.

He tapped down a sudden urge to help.

He was in deep.

In no hurry to leave the house, he told his aunt more about his time at the rodeo. "We might have ourselves a superstar. The other bulls did well, too, but Jackhammer came out of the chutes ready for business."

"I'm glad. And based on that blush I saw on Evie's face a moment ago, and the way you both kept stealing glances at one another, I'm guessing the competition wasn't the only highlight."

"You're reading into things."

"I'm not and you know it. But I'll drop the subject so your face doesn't grow more flushed than it already is."

He turned toward the door before proving her statement true. "As entertaining as this conversation is, I've got work to do."

Her soft chuckle trailed him as he strode out of the room and down the hall. He stepped outside as Evie was climbing the porch steps.

"Hey." She paused with her hand on the railing. "I forgot to tell you, Callie asked if we could put on a show this afternoon."

"Bribery to get her to school?"

"Something like that."

"So long as you take the solo."

Her eyes widened. "What? As in singing?"

He laughed. "Just kidding."

She released a breath. "Thank goodness."

"Callie said she'd join you."

"Uh-huh. Right after your ballet intro, right?"

He tossed out a few other quips, reluctant to end their play-

ful banter. But then his ranch hand pulled up in his pickup
and shot him a knowing look that heated his face double what
Aunt Martha's teasing had.

Travis parked and stepped out of his vehicle. He greeted
Evie with a tip of his hat that revealed eyes hinting at laughter. "Ma'am."

She waved, said she had a date with a carrot, and saun-
tered off.

Travis watched her leave, then turned back to Monte.
"Dude. Seems someone had a great weekend."

Monte rolled his eyes. "What are you, ten?"

"I saw the sparks flying between you two. It's about time,
too. Because, let's face it, you're not getting any younger."

"You, my friend, are regressing by the minute." The best
way to get the guy to leave him alone? Throw him a task. "How
about you quit flapping your jaw and make yourself useful?
I need you to help me feed these boys." He supplemented the
bulls' diets with a high-protein grain. "Then we need to move
them to the east pasture before they eat the grass to the ground
and we end up with a mud pit come the next hard rain."

"What? This subject hitting too close to home?"

Shaking his head, Monte headed toward the barn where he
stored the feed.

He spent the next few hours battling to keep his mind focused on the upcoming clinic, rather than the afternoon he'd
spend with Evie and his girls. Their time together always felt
so natural.

Would she say the same? Had she thought more about his
request that she stay?

Could tonight help tip her decision in his favor?

Every day she remained meant more opportunities to capture her heart. He couldn't remember the last time he'd thought
this way regarding a woman.

Actually, he could—his ex. He'd chased after her plenty, before she finally gave him a chance. Look how that had ended.

Except Evie was as different to her as ranching was to high-rise living.

She was also accustomed to a world he knew little about.

With a sigh, he reviewed his pre-event checklist on his notes app. Although he was making good progress, he still had to take care of numerous details. Next up? Ensuring he had enough training equipment to accommodate the fifteen or so guys Declan had rallied together.

He phoned a buddy that worked at the local gym. He made small talk, asking about the guy's business and family, before explaining the reason for his call. "Any chance I can rent your medicine balls? Got some balance drills I want to run the riders through."

"Sure. How many?"

"How many can you spare?"

"Got two twelve-pounders, one fifteen, and one twenty."

Four total. Adding his and the three he was borrowing from friends meant he could accommodate nearly half his students. "That'll work." He'd put the men through a rotation.

He'd just finished locating a handful of fifty-five-gallon drums to convert into practice bucking barrels when the hum of Evie's car drew his attention.

Deciding to take a brief break, he strolled back to the house. From the looks of things, everyone—Callie included—was in a great mood.

Not surprising, considering she'd probably spent much of her day imagining how they'd perform the best show possible for Aunt Martha. That child was as creative as she was mischievous.

"Daddy!" Callie jumped into his arms.

Noting Evie's immediate grin, and feeling one come on himself, he gave his daughter a squeeze, deposited her back on her feet, and did the same with Luna. "You two have a good day?"

Callie nodded, eyes bright. "Ms. Vargas gave me fidget toys

to play with and lets me stand up during reading if I want, so long as I go to the back and don't distract the other kids. Plus, she let me clean the white board and help hand out papers and stuff."

In other words, she found ways to allow for movement. Smart. And kind.

He looked at Evie, even more struck by her beauty now than when she'd first arrived, because now he knew the heart beneath her appearance. That made her radiant—and well worth holding on to.

After Luna shared the highlights of her day, they transitioned to discussing the show they planned to perform for his aunt. The girls had brainstormed quite an act.

Callie skipped ahead to the porch steps then stopped and turned around. "Can we practice now?"

He glanced at Evie.

She smiled, although she appeared a tad shy. Then again, the situation would probably feel awkward for them both, especially with Callie directing.

But they'd promised.

He rustled Callie's hair. "Fine with me."

When Evie gave a similar answer, both girls cheered and barreled inside, likely to rummage through their dress-up clothes for all manner of silly attire.

"This'll be interesting." He held the door open for Evie. "I appreciate your willingness to participate."

"I wouldn't miss it for the world."

The warmth in her expression suggested she was growing as fond of him and the twins as they were of her.

Maybe even fond enough to see herself becoming part of their lives for good.

CHAPTER FOURTEEN

THREE ENCORES AND escalating shenanigans from the girls later, Evie found herself laughing so hard she developed a side ache. Thanks to her role as the "galloping reindeer," she was also feeling every bite of the supper they'd eaten prior.

Monte appeared equally amused. But he also seemed a bit protective of his aunt and, after a quick glance in her direction, suggested the theater call it a night.

The girls groaned, and Callie flopped onto the floor with enough melodrama to make Bette Davis proud.

"That's boring," she said.

"Come sit by me." Martha patted the couch cushions next to her. "How about we watch a movie?"

"Pretty Polly Prankster?"

"Yes!" Luna plopped down on the other side of her aunt.

"I'll make popcorn." Monte darted into the kitchen and soon returned with a large bowl wafting buttery steam. Standing in the center of the living room, he eyed the open spot on the love seat next to Evie. He looked at Callie, now spread on her belly, occupying the second half of the couch. Was he debating asking the child to move over?

Seemed an easy enough request, unless he actually *wanted* to sit by Evie.

Her face heated, and her flutters extended beyond her stomach to her spine. She felt similar to how she had the day Mark Pitts had asked her to prom.

But despite her jitters, she also felt a sense of rightness when the cowboy sat beside her.

Wisdom, anchored in the reality that she wouldn't remain in Sage Creek long, encouraged her to keep her emotions in check. Yet, here she was, contemplating the question Monte had asked on their drive home from the rodeo. Common sense told her he wanted a stable caregiver for his aunt and the girls. But the way he'd been looking at her lately suggested his invitation went deeper.

If so, would she consider putting down roots in Sage Creek? And not just for him, as tempting as that was.

Could she actually be happy here? She knew from watching her parents and friends that marriage wasn't always silly fun and romantic evenings. Sometimes things got tough, especially on a ranch.

Then again, she'd encounter plenty of storms, regardless. Her mom and dad had also shown her that while loving someone didn't mean a problem-free life, it did mean not having to weather the rain alone.

There was no one she'd rather get drenched with than Monte.

As if he could read her thoughts, he slipped his hand under hers and interlocked their fingers.

She startled, her gaze shooting to his, any jitters she felt soothed by the warmth pouring from his eyes.

He leaned toward her, close enough that she could feel the heat radiating from him. "Something on your mind, Evie?" He kept his voice low.

Why did the way he spoke her name make her want to melt against him? "Just caught up in the storyline, I guess." The one she'd been fantasizing about between the two of them.

"Taking notes from these animated jokesters regarding what kind of mischief y'all may get into later?"

"Ha. Seems to me you fit that role better than I do."

"Hey, now, I resemble that remark." He laughed, then sobered. "Want to step outside for some fresh air?"

Yes! But she quickly tamped down her enthusiasm with a slow breath.

"Um…" She glanced at Aunt Martha, who, thankfully, either hadn't heard his question or didn't think anything of it. Then again, it was a bit warm in here, although she doubted that had anything to do with room temperature. "Sure." She stood and, with her hand still securely held in his, accompanied him onto the porch.

A cool breeze swept over her, and she shivered.

"Hold up." He dashed inside and returned with a throw blanket, which he wrapped around her shoulders.

He motioned to the bench swing, then sat beside her. "I appreciate what you did for Callie today. With her teacher. And that you helped me see that she needed help."

"Of course."

"When you first came, you mentioned you didn't have much experience with kids. You could've fooled me. I don't think I've ever seen Luna warm up to someone so quickly."

"She's precious. They both are."

"Pretty sure they think you're awesome as well. And I agree. The way you got Aunt Martha laughing…"

"As if your silly voices and accents didn't play a part in that?" She playfully bumped her shoulder against his.

"I knew my middle school days would prepare me for something. Seriously, though. I can't believe how well she's feeling. Whatever you're doing, keep it up."

She frowned and looked at her hands. Martha still hadn't told him. The longer she waited, the higher his hopes would rise. That would also give them much farther to crash.

"Hey." He gave her hand a squeeze. "Did I say something wrong?"

If only she could tell him. It wasn't like he or his aunt would file charges or even report to her boss that she'd broken confidentiality. But that wouldn't make sharing Martha's decision with Monte right. No matter how much she wished otherwise.

Yet, her silence was the only thing keeping her here. Was that influencing her behavior?

No. She'd signed an oath, and while the Bowmans might not disclose her actions, God would know. She chose to trust that if she followed His ways, He'd take care of everything else—even if that meant losing the best man she'd ever met.

Sensing Monte waiting for an answer, she shook her head. "Just thinking."

"About?"

"Lazy evenings and how beautiful it is here." That was true enough, as the thought entered her mind the moment she gazed at the star-dotted sky.

"I'm glad to hear that. Your company called today to verify that our needs hadn't changed before sending out your replacement. I asked them if it was possible for you to stay."

She sucked in a breath.

"Not that you have to, or even that I expect you to. I just wanted to know where things stood, contractually."

"And?"

"The gal said she didn't have authority to speak to that but that she'd relay my question to those who did. You may receive a phone call in the next day or two."

"Okay." Most likely, her company would love his idea. They wouldn't want to replace a caregiver a client trusted with someone with whom he might not click.

What if his aunt never gained the courage to explain her choice? Granted, she wouldn't be able to keep that hidden forever. Eventually, her condition would reveal itself. Although she could leave him to assume the chemo hadn't worked. Most people wouldn't even question that, based on the prognosis of recurrent ovarian cancer.

But Evie would know. Could she live with that, were they

to develop a relationship? Or would she feel haunted that she'd willingly, maybe even for decades, kept such a devastating secret from the man she loved?

She was overthinking things. The guy had asked her to extend her assignment, not pledge her life to him. Yet, she couldn't stop entertaining the possibility—along with all the what-ifs accompanying the scenario.

"Something wrong?" He regarded her with a furrowed brow.

She swallowed and shook her head. "Just processing."

"Anything related to what I asked on our drive back from Dripping Springs?"

"About a lot of things." She felt like a tangled mess of hope, sorrow, guilt and anxiety.

He smoothed a breeze-stirred lock of hair from her face, his thumb tracing the contour of her cheek. "Think you can handle hanging around a bit longer?"

She opened her mouth to respond, but he pressed his index finger to her lips. "Just give it some prayer."

"I can do that." His statement reminded her of all the times she'd told God of her longing to find someone with whom she could envision spending the rest of her life. She couldn't imagine a better, more loyal man than Monte to unite her life with, and she adored those girls. Martha, too.

As astounding as it was, considering her impression when she first arrived—she felt like she belonged here. With him.

Lord, please give Martha the strength to be honest with her nephew, preferably before he starts planning her remission celebration. And don't let him hate me when she does tell him.

MONTE BREATHED IN the clear night air, Evie's soft floral scent drawing him to her. He could tell his request left her conflicted. He liked to think that meant she too was considering where God might take them.

He'd be wise not to push her, regardless how "urgent" the issue felt.

His gut told him God had brought her here for more than Aunt Martha's care. He needed to trust his Father would work everything out, if not before her replacement came, then after somehow. As numerous Bible stories so clearly demonstrated, again and again, seemingly impossible situations merely served as backdrops to display God's power.

He sure could use divine help, because he had no intention of losing the most beautiful woman, inside and out, he'd ever met.

The fact that they could sit, content to gaze up at the stars without feeling the need to fill the moment with mindless chatter counted for something.

The creaking of the swing merged with the occasional call of a great horned owl. The nearly full moon cast the land in a silvery glow, reminding him of why he'd never want to live anywhere else.

He hoped Evie was beginning to feel the same.

Watching for her reaction, he held his breath, placed his arm around her and gently nudged her closer. She tensed, then exhaled and leaned back against his chest. Arms around her waist, hands interlocked at her belly and her strawberry-scented hair tickling his face, he closed his eyes and prayed for many evenings just like this.

Evie's breathing slowed and deepened. She remained so still, he wondered if she'd fallen asleep. The thought increased his reluctance for their time together to end.

But then she sat up straight.

"We should probably get inside." She stood.

"Right." He'd been selfish to leave Aunt Martha to watch over the girls for this long, especially since she tended to get so fatigued by day's end. This was probably doubly true now, after all this evening's activity, her belly laughs included.

He dashed to the door to open it for Evie, then followed her inside. They entered as the credits started to play on the twins' movie.

Callie sprang to her feet. "Beauty parlor time!"

Monte crossed his arms. The child was well practiced in coming up with reasons to delay her bedtime. "It's a little late for that."

His aunt smiled. "Tomorrow. That'll give me time to run in town for those fancy nail stickers you girls love so much. An early Christmas gift."

Callie groaned but complied, and soon was chattering on about what colors and designs she'd choose and how she wanted her hair done. By the time they left for school the next morning, Luna had caught her enthusiasm, and they were both planning yet another show—this one fashion.

Midmorning, Evie called him to tell him she was running into town to purchase dress-up clothes from the local thrift store.

He met her at her car when she returned, his heart swelling at the obvious joy radiating from her face, and not just because she was gorgeous. It was the cause of her joy that most deeply touched him. She was excited to surprise the girls.

Because she loved them.

Grinning, she stepped out of her vehicle. "Wait until you see what I found." She retrieved two full bags from the back seat and began pulling dresses out one by one and draping them over her shoulder.

The first was a red gown that would be the perfect length for the twins. The second was satiny blue with an intricate lace design over the skirt, and another was decorated with beading and gold embossed flowers.

He chuckled. "They'll love them. How much do I owe you?"

"Nothing. When the store owner learned who I was and why I was buying all this, she refused to charge me. Said your aunt has done more for her and her family over the years than she could ever repay."

A lump lodged in his throat at the reminder of yet another

life his aunt had touched, and how this community always cared for their own. "Wow."

"That's what I said. Sage Creek has some of the kindest, most thoughtful people I've ever encountered."

"Best place to live, hands down."

If she sensed his hidden message, she didn't let on.

She glanced at her phone screen. "That time already?" She returned her purchases to the bag. "I best go pick up the girls."

She dashed into the house and returned empty-handed.

"Mind if I join you?"

"Not at all."

The way she smiled back at him made him think she welcomed the idea.

He took her hand, her skin soft and warm against his. "How about we take my truck?"

She turned to him with a furrowed brow, her eyes searching his.

He held his breath, mentally preparing himself for the sting of rejection.

But then her posture relaxed and, with her fingers intertwined with his, she resumed walking.

This time he couldn't hold back his grin—at least, not until he glanced toward the arena and he caught Travis watching him with a teasing smirk.

He frowned, but refused to release Evie's hand. He was starting to believe she might stay, which meant he might as well get used to Travis's ribbing.

They talked comfortably on the drive to the school, mainly about the upcoming clinic. Evie seemed to be looking forward to the event, as if she felt personally invested.

He'd never felt that with Erin. Although she'd acted supportive, her enthusiasm had always felt off. Evie was different. She seemed to care, not just about what mattered to him, but about him as a person.

As if she were happy and content to be in his presence,

whether that meant sitting around the breakfast table or driving into town to pick up the twins.

At the school, he and Evie went in to get the girls together. While he hadn't had the best relationship experience prior, his heart told him this was what true love felt like.

As expected, the girls hadn't forgotten about the "beauty parlor" activity. Although they wanted to hurry home and start first thing, he told them they'd need to finish homework first.

"You mind helping the girls on your own this afternoon?" he asked Evie. "I need to catch up on some things." One thing he knew for sure, he wanted to be around when she showed the girls their dresses.

"Got it covered."

"Maybe hold off on the rest until I get back?"

"Absolutely."

He didn't know what he was looking forward to most—watching them light up when they saw all the bling, or catching Evie's reaction once they did. The fact that he'd get to do both made him work extra hard and triple fast.

An hour and a half later, he arrived home out of breath and feeling more sentimental than he'd expected at the thought of Evie dolling up his girls. Like he'd seen countless moms do with their daughters in various social media reels.

He'd not realized how much he longed for the twins to experience the same thing until this very moment.

"Hey, there." Evie emerged from the kitchen holding a toy rolling pin. "The girls and I just finished making playdough cookies."

Luna approached him holding out a plate of purple-and-green-splotched circles. "You hungry, Daddy?"

"Starved." He shot Evie a wink, delighted by the blush this triggered. "Where's Aunt Martha?"

"Visiting the horses."

He blinked. "Really?"

Her gaze faltered. "She hasn't been out long."

Was she worried he'd be upset she'd allowed his aunt to venture off without her? "That's great." With how cheerful his aunt had been lately, he wasn't about to tell Evie how to do her job.

"I'll go get her now." She handed Callie the rolling pin. "Seeing how the beauty parlor's about to open."

"Yay!" Both girls began jumping in place.

He was surprised to see Callie so enthused for such a "girly-girl" endeavor. Then again, she *did* love anything with a dramatic element, and, it seemed, that involved Evie.

He could relate.

Their excitement multiplied once Evie returned and showed them her thrift store finds. She'd also purchased scented lotions. Declaring the salon open, she treated them all, Aunt Martha included, to a manicure.

"Can we play rockstar now?" Callie asked.

Evie frowned. "Rain check? I need to catch up on the laundry. I promised your sister I'd wash her favorite dress for tomorrow."

The twins looked so dejected, he couldn't help but laugh. "You relax." He waved a hand. "I know how to run clothes through the machine."

"You sure?"

"It'll give me something productive to do while I make some phone calls."

She thanked him, and he strolled down the hall to the sound of the girls' cheers erupting once again.

He carted all three hampers, one at a time, into the mudroom, and dumped their contents into the large industrial sink for sorting. Not surprisingly, almost all of Callie's new clothes were smudged with dirt and grass stains. Equally predictable, none of Luna's were. He could easily envision her and her friends daintily swinging while her sister found a hill to tumble down or sandbox to dig through.

With room for a few more colored items, he grabbed a pair

of his aunt's pants. A crinkling sound reminded him to empty her pockets. In one, he found a wrapped piece of ginger candy, tissue and a few coins. In the other, he found two receipts. He was about to throw them into the trash when two words—San Marcos—caught his eye. He read the receipt more carefully, noting the date and time.

Odd, and certainly not anywhere his aunt would've been recently, especially not midmorning last Thursday. She'd probably picked up someone's litter.

After tossing a few more items into the machine, he added detergent and adjusted the settings. With one load washing, he grabbed the empty hampers and strolled back down the hall, whistling a tune to a commercial that had popped into his mind.

As he neared the living room, the sound of his aunt's laughter stopped him midstep.

She'd been in high spirits lately—ever since the doctor came out to check her blood and ended up canceling that week's appointment. He'd expected her to feel as bummed with the delay as he'd been. When she hadn't appeared so, he thought she'd been trying to remain positive for his sake.

But she'd also told him she was done fighting. Never knowing her to give up easily, he'd assumed her comments had stemmed from momentary fatigue she'd soon overcome.

What if she'd been serious?

No. Evie would've told him.

His gut felt hollow as he stood, watching her paint Callie's toenails.

His aunt glanced up, worry lines immediately stretching across her forehead. "Monte, what's wrong? Has something happened?"

He stepped deeper into the room. "I never asked. How'd your treatment go this past Thursday?"

She and Evie exchanged a look of guilt if ever he saw one before his aunt covered with a tight smile. "We've all heard the saying, 'Hurry up and wait.'" Her chuckle sounded forced. "You know how it is."

"Actually, I don't. How about you tell me?"

She picked up a sheet of stickers from the coffee table and studied it as if it contained the most fascinating designs she'd ever seen. "It's a busy clinic, is all. With so many people coming and going, I bet the doctors barely get a moment to catch their breath."

"You saying they rushed you?"

"Oh, I've never felt that."

She was trying hard not to outright lie, but that didn't make her evasive responses any less deceptive.

Heat surged through him. "You never went, did you?" And the fact that she tried so hard to keep that from him proved she'd made a deliberate choice.

She startled at his raised tone. "Monte, please." Her voice quivered. "I told you I couldn't do it anymore. You have to understand."

"Understand what? That you're giving up because this is hard?" Her tears pierced his heart, but he wouldn't allow emotions—not hers, his, or anyone else's for that matter—dictate such an important decision. "The girls and I need you." He shook his head. "I'm not letting you give up on yourself. Or on them."

Her shoulders trembled as she covered her face with her hands, her crying turning to deep-chested sobs.

He hurried to her and rubbed her back. "I shouldn't have gotten so upset. I recognize how difficult this has been, and I promise you that I'll walk beside you every step of the way. I won't leave you to face this battle alone. Now is not the time to declare defeat."

He turned to Evie. "How could you keep something like this from me?"

She was now standing, facing him. "She's my patient. I'm bound by confidentiality."

"Yeah, well, I'm technically your boss. As such, I'm telling you to call the clinic first thing tomorrow to get her treatments rescheduled. And see to it you get her there next time."

She took in a deep breath as if steeling herself. "I know this is painful to hear and even more so to accept, but this is her decision."

He scoffed. "Yeah, well. Then it's your job, as her paid caregiver, to change her mind."

"Actually, it's not." Her voice carried barely above a whisper.

He felt like he'd been whacked in the chest with an iron bar. "Then I guess your services are no longer needed."

CHAPTER FIFTEEN

THAT NIGHT, EVIE tossed and turned, rehashing her conversation with Martha the day she'd revealed her bucket list. Should she have tried to talk her out of her decision? Her training said, ethically, that was the last thing she was supposed to do. Give detailed information and answer questions honestly, yes. Pressure someone with a potentially terminal illness into spending the last few years, if not fewer, of their lives sick from chemo?

No. She couldn't do that to Martha, regardless of how much she loved Monte.

And she did love him, which was why it hurt so badly knowing how much he hated her now. Eyeing her opened suitcase lying on the floor, she told herself she'd eventually heal and forget all about him and her time in Sage Creek. But she feared that would never happen. Nor would she ever encounter another man like Monte Bowman—of that she was certain.

Feeling as if her heart were tearing in two, she cried herself asleep and awoke with bloodshot and puffy eyes. She emerged downstairs to find Martha's door closed, the girls watching cartoons in the living room, and Monte making coffee in the kitchen.

He turned toward her as she entered. His expression

would've implied lack of emotion, if not for the pain in his eyes. "Morning."

"Morning." She should've known he had too much integrity to give her the silent treatment. "Monte?"

He almost seemed to wince at her mention of his name.

"I wanted to tell you."

"I don't want to talk about this now."

"I know you'd like me to leave, but I also know you were expecting me here, able to help, when you scheduled your clinic. I'd like to stay through that, if you'll let me."

He released a breath and rubbed a hand over his face. Then nodded. "I appreciate that."

For the next few days, their conversations remained equally short. When the girls asked why their father wasn't around for meals, Evie said he was busy preparing for his upcoming event. While true, she also feared he was avoiding her.

She woke early the morning of his clinic to find him in the kitchen and the rest of the house asleep.

She poured herself a cup of coffee and lingered near the table before sitting across from him. "I've been praying for this weekend."

He glanced up from the notebook pages from which he'd been working, and for a moment, she saw a hint of his affection toward her. But then his expression deadpanned. "Thanks."

Lord, give me the words that will help him understand.

Yet, she knew he did, and that he wasn't truly angry at her. He was grieving the woman who had been there for him and the twins when they needed her most. The one who, up until recently, had in many ways held the family together.

Unrealistic or not, Monte had hung all his hopes on Evie.

She wrapped her hands around her mug. "What time will people start arriving?"

"Eight. I'll set up a folding table in front of the porch. I printed off a bunch of liability forms for people to sign. Minors need a signature from a parent or guardian."

"Okay. I heard a storm may come through."

He gave one firm nod. "Hoping it'll hold off until tomorrow night. If not, we'll have to cut things short. And reimburse folks."

"I'm sorry."

He shrugged. "Can't have them, or my bulls, slopping around in the mud. Nor am I willing to tear up the arena. Until then, we'll pretend like the forecast predicted nothing but rainbows and sunshine."

Had they had this conversation a few days ago, she might've made a teasing comment regarding how rainbows formed.

He pushed back from the table and stood. "I'm about to run into town to pick up ice and whatnot. Mind cleaning out the girls' wading pool? I'd like to use it to keep drinks cold."

"Of course."

He held her gaze. "I appreciate your help."

Tears pricked her eyes at the grief in his—and on a day he should feel excitement. Then again, that was what made cancer so difficult. It tended to taint everything gray. "It's the least I can do."

By the time Martha meandered into the kitchen, he'd already left. "I'm sorry about what happened the other night. I meant to tell him. I just didn't know how to get the words out."

"I understand."

"He'll come to as well. Just give him time."

She nodded, but they both knew she didn't have that. She'd finally met a man that she could envision spending the rest of her life with, and it had to be here, and now? When she knew the only possible outcome would be her leaving with a shattered heart?

The twins didn't emerge until nearly nine. They stepped outside fed, dressed, and with their hair brushed—verifying what Monte had said the night he learned about Martha's decision.

They didn't need her anymore.

Evie was already sitting behind a card table, handling check-ins. She flashed the twins a smile. "Morning." A handful of eager cowboys were lined up in front of her and more still gathered outside the arena.

"Can we help?" Callie hovered at her side, Luna half a step behind her. Still in their pajamas, they had to be cold.

"Once you get some warm clothes on, absolutely." Turning back to the man filling out a form before her, she excused herself and returned with two of the rockers from the porch.

The girls returned wearing boots and jackets and looking as proud as the evening they'd gone mutton busting.

And Evie had admitted to herself how she felt about Monte.

Averting her thoughts before the pain swelling within left her undone, she spent the rest of the morning alternating between keeping the girls entertained and acting as event director so Monte could focus on attendees.

About an hour before lunch, half a dozen ladies from the church arrived, all bearing a dish. They set these out, along with the massive pots of chili Martha had made. Not long after, a couple who owned a local peach orchard came bearing large pans of still-steaming cobbler.

Setting out napkins and paper plates, Evie surveyed it all. "Wow. You all are amazing."

One of Martha's friends smiled. "We're happy to do it. The Bowmans have always been the first to help a person in need. And after all Monte has done for sweet Martha…" She gazed toward the arena. "It's nice to see the good Lord bless him in this way. Matter of fact, we can cover things from here."

"I appreciate the offer, but I'm okay."

"I'm sure you are. But the girls are liable to get bored hanging around here soon enough, and everyone knows how Callie behaves when that happens."

She laughed. "I'll take her and Luna to their tree house shortly."

"May want to hurry. Despite how the sky looks now, if things don't shift, we're in for rain."

"Hopefully it'll hold off until after Monte's event." He didn't need disappointment added to his grief.

"Ms. Evie, watch what I can do."

She turned around to see Callie, arms outstretched, using the porch railing like it was a balance beam.

"Down please." While a fall from that height wouldn't be life-threatening, it could result in an injury.

Callie groaned and made no move to comply.

Evie narrowed her eyes. "I mean it."

"Fine." She jumped off, landing frog-like in the gravel. "But there's nothing to do."

Evie relayed where she planned to take her and her sister.

"Yeah! Come on!" Callie grabbed Luna by the hand and they raced off, with both dogs following close behind.

The guy who'd brought the cobbler chuckled. "That's one way to keep that child out of trouble."

"That's the plan."

Although she needed to hurry and catch up with her. Experience verified it wouldn't take long for the girl to create mischief.

Out of breath, she reached them at their tree house. Luna was in the tire swing while Callie was pushing with all the strength her forty-some-pound frame could muster.

"Hop on and I'll push you both."

This occupied them long enough for Evie's arms to grow tired. She was about to tell the twins she'd ran out of oomph, when they decided to "go to their fort"—an alcove in the trees they'd turned into a secret hideout.

"Girls only," Callie said. "Except for Daddy. But he needs a ticket."

Evie tried to mirror the child's serious expression. "I see. And how much does that cost?"

The girls looked at one another with furrowed brows.

"A dollar?" Callie asked her sister.

"Or ice cream." Luna grinned.

"With marshmallows and chocolate syrup. The kind that gets hard once you pour it on."

Evie laughed. "What'll you charge me?"

The girls once again exchanged a quizzical expression, but then, Luna said, "Nothing. Cuz you're our friend."

Callie nodded. "And a girl."

Tears pricked her eyes to think of the relationship God had helped them build in such a short time. When she'd arrived on the ranch, she'd prayed for the ability to earn their trust. She'd never anticipated how attached the twins would become to her, or her to them.

To Monte, as well. In fact, she'd spent a great deal of will-power trying not to fall for the man. Until the day she'd stopped fighting her emotions and let herself dream of what they might become.

This would be her hardest goodbye yet.

Taking a deep breath, she swallowed down the wave of sorrow threatening to overtake her and sat upon a sun-warmed rock while the girls pranced to and from their fort playing pioneer. The dogs followed, sniffing about as if engaged in a highly serious mission.

Inhaling the soothing scent of decomposing wood and damp earth, Evie removed her shoes and socks and immersed her feet in the cool creek water. She reflected upon her mental quip, upon first arriving, that this assignment would be far from a spa experience.

Her prediction had been right. This—breathing the fresh air, listening to the birds chirping and the girls laughing, golden rays filtering through the trees—was far better. A soul-deep sanctuary she'd never experienced in the city.

A shadow fell upon her as windswept clouds engulfed the sun. A droplet landed on her head, then on her shoulder, then another.

She surveyed the sky, noting the thick blanket of gray advancing toward them. "Girls, it's time to head back."

They groaned.

"Five more minutes?" Callie was squatting beneath an umbrella of trees, picking at a fallen and decaying branch patched with sage-toned lichen.

Shaking her head, Evie put her socks and shoes back on. "It's about to rain."

"We don't care."

She studied the sky again. Those clouds looked ominous.

She stood. "How about if we get some of that peach cobbler Aunt Martha's friends brought over?"

Although clearly disappointed, Luna complied. Callie, however, darted back into the woods. "Come find me!"

Evie made eye contact with Luna. "Wait here, please." She hurried after her sister. "Now is not the time for hide-and-seek." As she stepped beneath a canopy of enmeshed branches, bushes and vines sprouting between them, the wind picked up and the sky unleashed an icy onslaught.

Thunder boomed.

Evie shivered as rain slicked her clothes to her skin. "Callie, I mean it. One. Two."

Branches rustled, and a moment later, the child reemerged, drenched, muddy, shivering, and with twigs tangled in her hair.

"Come on." She reached for the child's hand and tugged her back toward the creek.

She turned at a yelp and a yank on her arm to find Callie sitting on the ground, holding her ankle, clearly fighting tears.

Evie rushed toward her and squatted to eye level. "Sweetie, are you okay?" It appeared she'd stumbled into a cavity formed between a jumble of thick, exposed roots.

"It hurts."

Max sniffed at the child's face, then licked her cheek. She pushed him away.

"Can you walk on it?"

She tried to stand, then winced.

Lightning lit the sky, and the wind moaned through the

leaves. Behind them, Luna called out for her, frightened, and likely near frozen.

A surge of adrenaline shot through Evie. "We're coming."

Callie wasn't heavy by any means, but neither was Evie all that strong. Yet, she needed to figure out something, or it'd take forever for them to find shelter.

She turned so that her back faced the child and patted her shoulders. "Hop on."

With icy arms wrapped around her neck and legs around her waist, she rose with a grunt, her thighs burning beneath the strain. Rain pelting her face, she hustled back to the creek to find Luna sitting on the rock, lips slightly blue.

By now, the sky held a dark, greenish tint, and the gravel road leading to the house felt impossibly long. Passing the stables, she briefly contemplated seeking cover among the horses.

Did tornadoes ever hit the hill country in mid-December? They needed to find shelter, quickly, just in case. But she assumed the thin wooden walls could be more dangerous than protective.

Plus, what if Monte freaked out and came looking for them? That would put him at risk as well.

As if on cue, a muscular form resembling their dad raced toward them. He met them drenched and with piercing, determined eyes.

He looked at Callie and the crevice between his brows deepened. "She hurt?"

Fighting to keep her voice steady despite her mounting fear, Evie told him what had happened.

"Give her to me." He lifted his daughter off Evie's back with the ease of someone carrying a down-filled pillow. "Y'all run on ahead."

She frowned, fear for him and the other child making her reluctant to leave.

But his directive made sense. The best way she could help was to get Luna inside and hunkered down in a back closet.

That was why, when he repeated the command, with more force this time, she nodded, took Luna's cold hand in hers and jogged off as fast as the girl could keep up.

Martha was waiting for them on the porch, soaked, and looking even more terrified than Evie felt, if that were possible. "Monte and Callie?"

Evie explained, ushering the woman back inside. "They'll be here shortly." She scanned their surroundings for a secure area far from windows. The pantry was too small for all of them. The twin's closet would be better. She urged Martha and Luna deeper into the house. Remembering her emergency preparedness training, she dashed into the kitchen for a pitcher of sweet tea—the quickest and easiest liquid to grab.

With every second feeling like a hundred, she prayed that, if a tornado was indeed coming, God would hold back the storm until Monte and Callie arrived.

MONTE BURST INTO the house as a living room window shattered, and the howling wind and battering hail grew louder. Callie shrieked, tightened her grip and buried her face into his chest, as if his body could shield her from the storm.

If necessary, it would. He'd cover her faster than it took lightning to flash. But he'd much rather get her someplace more secure—and check on the others.

Thank goodness he'd had enough common sense to send everyone from the workshop home once the sky started darkening.

Running down the hall, he called out to them. If they replied, he couldn't hear them above the storm. At least they'd all made it inside. He hated to think what might've happened if Evie hadn't responded as quickly as she had. Or if he hadn't found them in time to carry Callie back.

All three of them could've been whacked and buried by falling branches.

The thought nauseated him.

Had he been thinking straight, he would've taken the ATV. He tore into the twins' bedroom, pulse pounding in his ears, lunged for the closet and threw open the door. Relief nearly buckled his knees. Aunt Martha, Evie and Luna were all huddled together under the child's favorite velvety blanket. Head resting against Evie, his daughter clutched her stuffed elephant under her chin.

They all scooched over, and he deposited a shivering Callie next to Evie on her other side. She wrapped an arm around the child's shoulder, held her close and began to sing. A trained ear might call her off-key and unmelodious. Yet, he wasn't sure he'd ever heard—or seen—anything more beautiful.

CHAPTER SIXTEEN

THE WIND DIED down as quickly as it arrived. Monte released a breath, not knowing what state he'd find the house in but more grateful than he could express that God had kept the four people he most cared about safe.

He tried anyway—thanking His Father while asking for help in making sense of the confusing thoughts the storm had evoked. He'd known, when he told Evie she needed to leave, that he'd be devastated once she did. When the storm hit, he'd realized he might actually lose her, and not just to a relocation. He'd felt like he was about to lose everything that made life worth living.

That included Evie.

But she'd come to do a job and had failed—for lack of trying. Then kept that from him. Maybe she thought he would grieve and move on, but what about the girls? Seemed to him, if she really loved them as much as she seemed to, she would've found a way to talk his aunt out of giving up.

While he wasn't thrilled with his aunt's decision, he could at least understand it. She was tired and discouraged. Evie should've expected that. When she'd arrived, he'd stressed the importance of acting as his aunt's cheerleader.

Instead, she'd defended his aunt's choice.

How could he let that go?

He stood on legs cramped from a burst of adrenaline followed by confinement in a small space. "Y'all stay here while I check things out."

They nodded, and he left to survey the damage. Everything remained untouched except the living room, where a thick branch protruded through the window, and glass shards and a splattering of hail spread across the carpet. The Christmas tree had fallen against the wall, but it was intact and the handful of presents beneath it seemed okay.

Outside, the hail had dented the vehicles and left ice balls nearly the size of a quarter. A section of the shed had ripped off, and a couple trees were down, one of them uprooted.

Looked like they'd be having another bonfire soon.

Heaviness weighted his chest as he thought back to their last one—the four of them, Evie included, gathered under the stars. Her being there had felt so right. Like she'd belonged.

He'd trusted her. Believed in her. One of the gals in his Bible study class had even declared her an answer to prayer.

Seemed to him, if that were true, his aunt wouldn't be surrendering to a terminal disease.

She's not. She's coming home.

The thought, soft but clear, hit him with such force, his gut said it came from God.

Jaw clenched, he shook his head. *I can't believe that. I won't.*

He'd never been one to argue with the Father. But neither was he ready to attribute divine origin to a whisper that drifted through his mind.

Because he wasn't certain or didn't want to hear it?

With a sigh, he resumed his brief inspection of his property. He suspected the dogs had hunkered down in the stable, and the cattle within eyesight seemed okay. He'd check them more carefully for injuries later.

Thankfully, it would take a mighty strong wind to toss about fifteen hundred pounds of muscle.

The dogs trotted out of the barn, looking a little disoriented but unharmed.

Relieved, he turned back to the house to clean up the glass in the living room.

He found Evie already doing that as the twins' boisterous voices drifted toward them.

She stood as he entered. "How extensive is the damage?"

"Not bad." He joined her near the busted window and squatted down to help.

"I've got this. I'm sure you have plenty to deal with outside."

True. He also needed to call his insurance agent. "I appreciate it."

He rose and was heading back out when his aunt's voice stopped him, asking him to wait for her.

When she met him at the door, he regarded her with a frown. "You're not planning to help me haul debris, are you?"

With a quick glance behind her, she shook her head and nudged him onto the porch. "Wanted to talk with you a minute."

He nodded. He wanted to think the storm had the girls asking questions she wanted him to prepare for—like were the dogs and horses okay or what happened to squirrels and such. But after all that had occurred, he feared the conversation would land much heavier than that.

Aunt Martha motioned toward the rocking chairs. He complied.

She sat as well and folded her hands in her lap. Her delay intensified his concern.

"I know how painful things have been—and still are." Her eyes searched his with a tenderness and compassion that clamped his heart in a vise. "I never meant to hurt you. I was trying so hard not to, wanting to find the right words and time to tell you what I knew you'd been praying against."

Guilt churned his gut. She was the one dying, yet she was comforting him. That had always been her way. As much as he longed to change her mind, he wouldn't make this conversation harder for her.

She'd suffered enough.

She took his hand in hers. "Sweetie, I didn't make this decision lightly."

"I know." She'd probably spent many sleepless nights and anxious days fretting and praying over it—and all on her own. "I wish we could've talked through this together."

"I'm sorry."

He shook his head. "No, I mean, I wish I hadn't been so bullheaded, so that you wouldn't have had to stress about how I would respond."

She offered a gentle smile. "You've always loved fiercely."

"Must be hereditary." He released a heavy breath, fighting to suppress the grief that otherwise could overwhelm him. Wanting to show his aunt the same strength she was displaying now.

After all she'd given to this family, and all she'd endured, it was the least he could do.

He rubbed at his thumb knuckle. "What now?"

"Not sure. I'll call the doctor tomorrow. But I suspect you and the girls will have to put up with me for a little while longer." She gave his arm a playful slap. "Then, we'll have hospice come in."

The word squeezed the air from his lungs. Fortifying himself against the threat of tears, he nodded. "I'll make sure you have the best care possible."

She paused. "Speaking of..."

He shook his head. "I know what you're about to say, but I can't."

"She didn't betray you, nor did she do anything wrong. To the contrary. She acted with the utmost integrity, even though doing so tore her up inside. You staying mad at her won't keep me around any longer than the good Lord allows. But it will drive away the gift He deposited on your doorstop."

"I'm not upset with her. Not anymore." Truly, he never had

been. He'd merely blamed her for a situation he didn't want to accept. "I just don't think my heart can handle more loss."

"You mean when she leaves?"

He nodded.

"Then convince her to stay."

"You make it sound so easy."

"Oh, I think it will be. Matter of fact, I'm certain that sweet woman in there is waiting for you to give her reason to unpack that suitcase of hers for good."

A flicker of hope sparked within him. "Guess now I'm the one who'll be praying for the right words and timing."

"That's my boy." She stood. "How about you do that on your way into town for some window plastic before another storm blows through or a hefty rain turns our carpet and furniture soggy."

"I'll do that."

This was one discussion he didn't want to flub, especially after how he'd spoken to Evie a few nights prior, and how he'd treated her since.

What if she didn't want to hear anything he had to say?

Or if she listened, understood and rejected him anyway?

But what if Aunt Martha was right and God had brought Evie here, to this ranch, to give him a second chance at love?

EVIE HAD JUST finished depositing a cardboard box of glass shards into the outside trash when Monte returned from his trip to the hardware store. A twinge of anxiety tempted her to hustle back inside, but she'd determined long ago not to allow fear of potential conflict dictate her actions.

Besides, there was no point in delaying the conversation. Now that his event was over, cut short by the hail, he'd probably want her to leave immediately.

Then again, he might give her until first thing in the morning. That would lead to a strained and painful supper—if he joined them.

Swallowing a sigh, she waited for Monte at the bottom of the porch stairs. "Hey."

"Hey. Care to take a walk with me?"

"Sure." Her stomach felt queasy as she fell into step beside him. She glanced at the empty arena as they passed. "Sorry you weren't able to hold your full clinic."

He shrugged. "Managed to finish half of it. And I'll offer a makeup day to those who want it and reimburse the others. Several had already said they were hoping I'd host another event soon, and some talked about bringing their buddies along. Since I didn't spend much to put it on, it was almost all profit."

"That's great."

"Next time, I'll have to figure out how to feed everyone on the cheap. Otherwise, the stomachs in those guys could easily land me in debt."

"I wouldn't be surprised if your church family took care of the food again."

"Those gals do like to cook and bake, that's for sure. You try any of the Herrings' peach cobbler?"

"Not yet, but I plan to. They slipped a pan into the fridge for us. Said otherwise, they feared we might be too busy to snatch ourselves any before the cowboys demolished it." She asked if the man from the rodeo ever showed.

"Yep. Must've liked what he saw, because he walked away the proud sponsor of five of my derbies. Plus, I got four other investors and three strong maybes."

"Awesome!"

He nodded. "Seems the good Lord heard my prayers after all and plans to keep the ranch running a spell longer."

She frowned, knowing he wouldn't say the same in regard to his aunt.

If his words from the night he found out still conveyed his feelings, he blamed Evie.

Tears pricked her eyes. She blinked them away. "I'm really glad everything went so well."

"I had a lot of help."

"Your community is truly amazing."

"You think so?"

"Absolutely."

"Enough to consider sticking around?"

Her heart stuttered. Had he really asked what she thought he had?

She stopped and faced him, unsuccessfully trying to contain her hope. "What are you saying?"

"I'd like you to stay."

She wanted to as well, more than anything. Only not as a caregiver, although she realized Martha would need one. She also understood why Monte might feel reluctant to bring in someone new and unknown. And she felt a level of responsibility to accept his invitation.

But if she stayed, it had to be forever. Otherwise, she feared she'd never recover once she drove away.

Besides, with his aunt no longer receiving chemo, she wouldn't need help for a while. She told him this, as gently as possible, as they both recognized she meant once Martha went on hospice.

"Evie." Eyes locked onto hers, he took her hands in his. "I never should've lashed out at you like I did. You were doing your job, and you've been great. More than great." His Adam's apple bobbed down then up. "It's no surprise that you captured my aunt's and girls' hearts. What did surprise me, however, was how you seized mine."

The tears she'd been holding back slid down her cheek. "Oh, Monte."

He thumbed them away. "You are the most beautiful, caring, insightful, kind and compassionate woman I've ever met. I can't count how many times I've caught you looking at the girls with adoration in your eyes. Or making my aunt laugh, even if that meant acting like a galloping horseman." He quirked a teasing smile.

She crossed her arms in mock annoyance. "And whose idea was that?"

He chuckled. "Guilty. But you went along with it easily enough."

"It was fun."

"See what I mean? Entertaining, hilarious, creative."

"Did someone give you a thesaurus?" she teased.

"I'm just getting started. I have a list of accurate adjectives at the ready."

"Do you, now?"

"Yes, ma'am. And there's only one way to get this rambling cowboy to shut up."

"What's that?"

"Tell me you'll stay. Permanently." He pulled a small box wrapped in shiny red paper from his pocket.

"What's that?"

"An early Christmas gift."

"But I didn't get you anything." She'd meant to take the girls into town so they could pick out something together. But then the beauty parlor night had happened.

"There's only one gift I want this year." He motioned for her to open her present.

She complied, to reveal a velvet jewelry box. "When did you—?"

"Stopped in one of the boutiques—they've got a jewelry section in the back—before the hardware store." He dropped to one knee. "Evie Bell, will you marry me?"

She held out her hand, warmth spreading through her as he slipped a simple but gorgeous diamond ring on her finger. "Oh, Monte."

"Is that a yes?"

"I'm not going anywhere. Ever."

A grin erupted on his face, and his eyes widened. He stood, and his expression sobered as he cupped her face in his hands and kissed her.

EPILOGUE

A year later

EVIE'S HEART SWELLED as she helped her sister set Callie's hair with gold-wire pins accented with silk bluebonnets hand-stitched by Aunt Martha. When Evie had suggested silver barrettes found online, Monte had strongly opposed the idea. As he hadn't voiced much of an opinion during their wedding planning, she'd happily conceded. She hadn't discovered until that morning that his aunt had lovingly made the pieces—for her and the girls.

She still teared up, thinking about all the hours Martha had spent, crafting each piece. Knowing her, she'd probably prayed for her, Monte and the twins, as she did.

If only she were here to see how beautiful Callie and Luna looked, and how proudly they wore their cherished pins.

When they weren't giggling about some surprise they and their father had concocted.

They also insisted Evie allow them to lead her, blindfolded, to the trailer, where she and her bridesmaids were now getting ready. One of Monte's ranch hands and groomsmen drove her there on the ATV while her mom and sisters brought her gown, veil, makeup, snacks and anything else she might want.

This would be her most memorable Christmas ever, by far.

Ms. Lucy, a woman Evie had come to love as much as Monte and the girls did, entered the trailer, looked at her and pressed a hand to her chest. "Oh, my. Aren't you a vision?"

Wearing a silver-beaded lavender dress and blazer, she approached with outstretched arms and enveloped Evie in a hug. "That man of yours is liable to about lose his mind and his words, once he catches a glimpse of you." She glanced at Luna and Callie, for once looking identical from the top of their heads to their shoes. "And those precious munchkins of his. Still can't believe y'all got Callie to get dolled up without any fuss. Or that you let them plan the decorations."

Evie smiled. "I think it's wonderful he involved them."

"Some gals may worry about childish results."

"Is that a clue?" Lucy had to have seen the area on her way to the trailer and had probably paused to view it more thoroughly. "Because I'm pretty sure that's breaking the rules."

Monte had made it clear that anyone who stepped foot on the property was not to ruin his surprise.

"You aren't concerned at all?" Her sister's eyes held a teasing glint.

Evie shook her head. "I'm thrilled to see their creativity emerge. And am deeply touched by the gesture." This was also a great way for Monte to ensure the girls felt included and valued.

Ms. Lucy took Evie's hands in hers. "That, my dear, is one of the many reasons Monte adores you. And why Martha did as well."

Her heart squeezed as she thought about the woman responsible for her coming to the ranch.

"You have no idea how much joy it gave her to know this day was coming," she said.

Evie's laugh deepened with emotion. "Actually, I do. She told us often."

Ms. Lucy gave one quick nod. "That sounds like her. Watching out for her loved ones, right to the end."

She had, in so many ways. "I'm so glad I got to know her. To love her."

Ms. Lucy softly patted Evie's cheek. "Let this be her legacy."

She liked thinking of it that way, and of course, Ms. Lucy was right. While Martha hadn't raised Monte, she'd certainly influenced the man he'd become. She'd positively affected Evie as well, in so many ways.

For that, Evie would be eternally grateful.

It felt good to know Monte's community had welcomed her as their own. To think, when she first arrived at Sage Creek, she'd felt as if her boss had sent her to one of the worst locations ever. She now knew that assignment had been a gift sent from God—one that led to the best treasure of all.

Someone knocked on the door. Her mom answered to find Evie's father on the other side. Upon seeing Evie, his face sobered, and his eyes moistened. "Wow, darling. Just wow." He maneuvered around the others crammed in the tiny space and pulled her into a long, firm hug. Then he pulled away. "You too old for me to count those sun kisses?" He tapped her nose. "One. Two. Three."

She laughed, a lump lodged in her throat. "I love you."

"And I adore you. Your fiancé, too. That's saying a lot, considering we both recognize that no one, no matter how amazing, will ever be good enough for my little girl. Except maybe Monte Bowman."

"I'm glad you approve." Her joking tone didn't negate the truth in her words. As much as it meant that Monte's—and Martha's—people approved of her, she craved her father's blessing even more.

"All I've ever wanted is for you to be happy."

She kissed his cheek. "I know."

Whether it was her words or the moment, she wasn't sure,

but he looked as if his emotions were about ready to over-take him.

He took a deep breath and straightened, donning the tense expression she'd seen him wear countless times when trying to regain composure. "You know, your mother and I were concerned when you insisted on a Christmas wedding."

"I could tell."

"Your mom was quite relieved to discover you were right about hill country winters being so much warmer than our Grand Rapids ones." Clearing his throat, he glanced about. "Line up, everyone. The groomsmen are waiting outside."

Her mom fanned a hand in front of her face and stepped forward. "I almost forgot." In her palm, she held four satin roses attached to safety pins. "Something used." She fastened them to the embellished band of Evie's Juliet cap veil. "My mother-in-law gave these to me shortly before your father's and my wedding. Stitched by her mother."

"They're perfect." They fit so well with the design she'd chosen, one couldn't tell they were an addition. That felt like a God-thing, as had so many other unexpected blessings leading up to this day. She didn't doubt that Aunt Martha's steady prayers in the months before her death played a part in that.

Evie never would forget the depth of the woman's faith.

Her mom grabbed a wooden box from the window ledge and opened it. "And something blue."

Inside lay three envelopes. The first bore her name in Aunt Martha's beautiful cursive writing. She'd made the next two out for the twins.

Tears blurred her vision as she opened her handcrafted card to reveal dried, pressed bluebonnets and the words, "Today you and Monte will experience a taste of heaven, revealed in a love pure and sweet. Enjoy the ceremony, dear. Dance, laugh, sing and know I'll be waiting for the day you all join me for the party that'll never end."

Her mom handed her a tissue, and gave her a squeeze. "That Martha was some woman."

Evie nodded. "The best."

Her mom turned to her husband. "You ready for this, Mr. Bell?"

He looked at Evie, moisture pooling in his eyes once again. "Don't ask me that now, my dear. Otherwise, I may become a blubbering idiot on our daughter's special day."

"I'm sure your baby girl won't mind in the least." Her mom smiled, kissed his cheek, then exited the trailer to meet the groomsman escorting her.

Evie squeezed into the narrow space leading from the bed to the entrance to form a line behind her. The soft notes of a harp soon followed, and the women exited one by one, leaving Evie with her dad, her sister and maid of honor, and the twins.

Holding her train aside, she lowered to the girls' eye level. "Thank you both for agreeing to do this important job."

Clutching their baskets filled with the tops of red silk rose petals dusted with white glitter, they stood a bit taller and nodded, expressions solemn.

They were so precious!

"We drop one with every step, right?" Luna began marching lightly in place, as if practicing.

"Exactly." While she wasn't that concerned with frequency, she knew they'd feel most comfortable with clear instructions. Not to mention, everyone would find their careful precision adorable.

Her sister stepped around her, poked her head out the door, then held it open. "All right, kiddos, you're up."

Callie squealed. Luna blanched and seemed frozen in place.

Evie placed a hand on her shoulder. "Deep breath."

The child complied.

Evie smiled. "You've got this. And I'll be right behind you."

Although Luna didn't seem convinced, she followed her sister out of the trailer.

The music shifted to country. She didn't remember Monte mentioning anything about that, or discussing songs at all.

Brow furrowed, Evie looked at her sister.

She beamed back at her. "Ready to get blown away?"

A jittery sensation swept through her. "I am." This was really happening. "So long as my legs don't turn to jelly, I'll be fine."

Her father took her hand and placed it in the crook of his arm. "You can lean on me." He released her to descend the metal stairs before her, then helped her down.

She turned the corner and gasped, tears immediately blurring her vision. Monte and the girls had placed at least a hundred poinsettias around the base of the gazebo. Twinkle lights glimmered from within the gold tulle draped from the top and around its support beams.

Beyond this stood numerous glass cylinders—more than she could count—filled with small white, gold and silver balls that glimmered in the sun.

Oh, Monte.

She was certain this day couldn't get any better.

But then Monte began to sing, his voice low and smooth.

She wobbled, and the tears she'd been fighting to contain spilled out.

Her dad placed an arm around her waist and gave her a squeeze. "This is what assured me that I was placing my daughter in the best possible hands."

"You knew?"

He nodded.

She loved knowing Monte had confided in her dad. She expected they'd become great friends.

Father, You're giving me blessings upon blessings.

A man she couldn't wait to spend the rest of her life with. Two precious daughters she loved as if they were her own. A town full of people who had done so much to help them this past year, during Martha's last few months especially. And her parents—her entire family, really—unreservedly fond of her soon-to-be husband.

It was almost more than her heart could take in.

MONTE'S VOICE CAUGHT watching his bride walk toward him wearing that same sweet blush that had stolen his heart the first day she arrived—and every day after. That woman had no idea how beautiful she was, which made her so stunning. Her loveliness extended well beyond her soft smile, wavy hair and silver-blue eyes.

His throat felt scratchy as intense emotions swept over him, but he kept singing. He'd painstakingly wrestled out every line in an attempt to convey, through lyrics, a love deeper than words could explain.

By God's grace, coupled with his umpteen hours of practice, he timed the last line with her last step. He handed Travis his guitar and faced the woman he'd be thanking Jesus for until his dying breath.

"Monte, I—I don't know what to say."

"I think the words you're looking for are, 'I do.'" He smiled, knowing if he didn't lighten the mood, he might not make it through the rest of the ceremony.

She and their guests laughed.

"Um." Holding the Bible to his chest, Pastor Roger shifted. "Y'all mind if I lead you through your vows before you go traipsing off into the sunset?"

More snickers from the people.

Monte nodded. "I'd like that very much."

The man who'd baptized him as a teen, counseled him when his ex-wife left, comforted them all when Aunt Martha passed, and officiated over the funeral, read a short passage on a love that always hopes, always fights and never ends. Then, he led them through the traditional promises Monte intended to keep—and exceed.

Pastor Roger grinned. "Then, by the power vested in me, I

pronounce you husband and wife. Monte Bowman, you may kiss the bride."

He didn't need the prompt, because he'd already pulled her to him, knowing he would never let her go—figuratively. And in that moment, he wasn't sure he'd have the strength to release her physically, either.

He certainly wasn't in a hurry to do so.

Evie pulled away first. "I love you, Mr. Monte Bowman."

"And I love you, Mrs. Evie Bowman." He grinned. "Man, do I love the sound of that. Mrs. Bowman."

His girls, who'd been sitting *somewhat* patiently with his mom, ran up to him, pulling the bluebonnets from their hair. "Can we bring our flowers to Aunt Martha now?"

A lump lodged in Monte's throat as he surveyed the poinsettias, splashing the landscape with vibrant red. His aunt had planted their seeds the previous October, shortly before her death. Then, they'd housed the sprouting pots at Lucy's to keep Evie from discovering their plans.

The entire process had led to such joyful, anticipatory conversations between Aunt Martha, the girls and him. It had also allowed her to be a part of a special day that would never have come, if not for her.

They'd also created numerous priceless memories helping his aunt finish nearly half of her bucket list. When he expressed disappointment that they hadn't gotten to it all, she'd smiled and assured him they'd done more than she'd imagined, and that each excursion felt extra special because they'd all been together.

"Daddy?" Callie tugged on his arm. "Come *on*!"

He laughed. "Give us a minute to see to our guests."

Lucy stepped to his side. "You go. I'll direct everyone to the house for refreshments."

He smiled, grateful to retain yet another reminder of his aunt through his ongoing connection with her many friends. "I appreciate that."

He lifted Luna on his shoulders, twined his fingers with Evie as she reached for Callie, and walked toward his truck parked near the stables.

The mood felt hushed, sacred, on the drive into town, and even Callie spoke little as they made their way to his aunt's gravesite. But then, he handed them each an envelope. They were identical to the one his aunt had placed their cards in, only filled with dried bluebonnet petals.

Evie looked at him. "Did you know?"

"About what Aunt Martha made for you girls?" He nodded. "Decided to make the twins something similar, so they'd have something to give back to her." He knelt in front of his daughters and placed a hand on each of their shoulders, all of them encased in a solemn silence.

But then, as they deposited their flowers, one by one, on and around the gravestone, Luna began to sing softly. She was so quiet he almost didn't hear her, but then Callie joined in.

Tears pricked Monte's eyes as he thought back to that first spring, the despair he'd felt when his ex-wife had left him and the girls. His aunt had brought such joy when she arrived.

And with Evie by his side, he would experience joy for decades to come, much thanks to his aunt.

He'd probably never stop grieving the loss of someone so precious. But he also would be eternally grateful that God had brought something beautiful from it—a love so pure, so intense he still lost his breath whenever he held Evie Bowman in his arms.

* * * * *

WESTERN

Rugged men looking for love...

Available Next Month

The Maverick's Resolution Brenda Harlen
A Match For The Sheriff Lisa Childs

Fortune's Mystery Woman Allison Leigh
The Cowboy's Rodeo Redemption Susan Breeden

LOVE INSPIRED

The Texan's Journey Home Jolene Navarro
A Faithful Guardian Louise M. Gouge